WITHDRAWN

AVON PUBLIC LIBRARY
BOX 977 / 200 BENCHMARK RD.
AVON, CO 81620

the
QUEEN
of
HEARTS

the

QUEEN

of

HEARTS

Kimmery Martin

BERKLEY
NEW YORK

BERKLEY
An imprint of Penguin Random House LLC
375 Hudson Street, New York, New York 10014

Copyright © 2018 by Kimmery Martin
Penguin Random House supports copyright. Copyright fuels creativity, encourages diverse
voices, promotes free speech, and creates a vibrant culture. Thank you for buying an authorized
edition of this book and for complying with copyright laws by not reproducing, scanning, or
distributing any part of it in any form without permission. You are supporting writers and
allowing Penguin Random House to continue to publish books for every reader.

BERKLEY is a registered trademark and the B colophon is a trademark of
Penguin Random House LLC.

Library of Congress Cataloging-in-Publication Data

Names: Martin, Kimmery, author.
Title: The queen of hearts/Kimmery Martin.
Description: First edition. | New York: Berkley, 2018.
Identifiers: LCCN 2017009750 (print) | LCCN 2017027056 (ebook) |
ISBN 9780399585067 (ebook) | ISBN 9780399585050 (hardcover)
Subjects: LCSH: Female friendship—Fiction. | Life-change events—Fiction. |
Triangles (Interpersonal relations)—Fiction. | Domestic fiction. |
BISAC: FICTION/Contemporary Women. | FICTION/Family Life. |
FICTION/Medical. | GSAFD: Love stories.
Classification: LCC PS3613.A7822 (ebook) | LCC PS3613.A7822 Q44 2018 (print) |
DDC 813/.6—dc23
LC record available at https://lccn.loc.gov/2017009750

First Edition: February 2018

Printed in the United States of America
1   3   5   7   9   10   8   6   4   2

Jacket art: blue convolvulus by Pierre-Joseph Redoute/Fine Art; summer flowers by Florilegius;
scarlet and yellow flowered greater Indian cress by Florilegius; antique medical illustration of
heart by ilbusca; splint spike thorn by Florilegius; rose panachee by Florilegius; broad-bordered
bee and larva by Florilegius; red-throated bee-eater by Florilegius
Jacket design by Colleen Reinhart
Book design by Kelly Lipovich

This is a work of fiction. Names, characters, places, and incidents either are the product of the
author's imagination or are used fictitiously, and any resemblance to actual persons, living or
dead, business establishments, events, or locales is entirely coincidental.

For Judy Martin, who taught me to love books

the
QUEEN
of
HEARTS

PART
ONE

Summer

Chapter One

MEETINGS ARE THE
ENEMY OF PROGRESS

Zadie, Present Day, North Carolina

Almost a hundred years before I was born, a man named Samuel Langhorne Clemens—better known to most of us as Mark Twain—said this about the human heart: *You can't reason with your heart; it has its own laws, and thumps about things which the intellect scorns.* This is entirely true, as far as I'm concerned, and I should know: I've devoted my professional life to the study of hearts, to their intricate, indefatigable machinery, and to their endless propensity to go awry.

We thump for all sorts of reasons. Some are beautiful and life-affirming. Some are misguided, recognizable to everyone but you as catastrophically stupid. We thump for the unsuitable stoner in our college biochem class, with his easy, wicked grin. We thump when somebody we don't like gets their comeuppance. We thump at cruelty and danger.

I've never spent much time revisiting the past, having thought I'd reached a settled spot in life where most of my wildly inappropriate thumping was behind me. Even if I wanted to look backward, I'd slogged through the last two decades unglued by sleep deprivation—first by my medical training and then by an onslaught of babies—so my recall of some of those years has been washed as smooth as sand.

But there are some things I don't want to remember. Emma and I have an unspoken agreement regarding our third year of medical school: we don't bring it up. Maybe even more than me, Emma has good reason to avoid those topics, and if there's one characteristic you'd assign to my closest friend within a nanosecond of meeting her, it's self-discipline.

So I was completely dismantled when Emma texted me she wanted to talk about it.

———

I cast a sneaky glance at the phone screen in my lap, reading the text three times to be sure. It didn't change. The screen dimmed and I fumbled to keep it lit, somehow managing to dislodge the phone from my lap so it hit the wooden floor with a *clunk*. As I retrieved it and shoved it into my bag, ten pairs of judgmental eyeballs swiveled my way. Who would have the effrontery to read texts during an important meeting? At the head of the table, the speaker, Caroline Cooper (alma mater: Georgia, plus Vanderbilt Law School), gave me a frosty look.

"Zadie? You with us?" Clearly rhetorical. My friend Betsy Packard (Duke University) threw me a surreptitious wink as Caroline forged ahead without a pause for me to answer. "Okay . . . we need to evaluate the metrics so we're optimally positioned for next year. Let's leverage our assets." Caroline flipped her blond pageboy. She was wiry and lean, with the grizzled look of too much tennis. "Yes, Jennifer, did you have a question?"

Jennifer Grosset (B-school, UVA) cleared her throat. "I understand we need to incentivize, but it seems to me the mission-critical thing here is to bring the teachers online. I'm wondering if there's a good strategic alliance there."

Holy smoke. This was what happened when a bunch of highly educated bankers and lawyers took time off to raise their kids. You couldn't get five seconds into a preschool meeting without the need for a bizspeak translator. Same thing in my cardiology practice: the hospital execs and the docs who ran the office were all so deeply steeped in corporate culture that hours could go by without anyone clearly stating anything. Everything was "actionable" and "recontextualized" and "pursuant" to everything else.

In my opinion, meetings are the enemy of progress.

Everyone around the table was nodding about the alliance issue with the teachers. This was politically tricky, though, and a babble of heated voices sprang up. Caroline pitched her voice above the din: "Simmer down, y'all. Let's do a little crowdsourcing."

More nodding.

I shivered. Everyone looked cold, since they were all dressed skimpily and the AC was jacked up to arctic level in deference to the scorching temperature outdoors. Fashion-wise, the women fell into one of two camps. The first group looked like they'd just come from exercising, although they all had neat hair and no one smelled bad. It was considered socially acceptable to wear spandex workout gear around town to morning school meetings and whatnot, as long as you were under a size six, maximum, and had a nice ass.

The second group was beautifully pulled together. They sported gold-plated sandals, chiffon halters, Hermès bracelets, skintight jeggings, and metallic aviators pushed onto perfectly coiffed blond manes.

As the discussion veered toward teacher gifts, I felt my phone vibrating in my bag.

Unable to resist, I slid it out. Emma again. Can you stop by before work tmw? Need to talk about Nick.

My heart started to hammer, an anxious, involuntary little tachycardia. We all have a Nick in our pasts: a seemingly ordinary person who, through some mysterious subatomic combination of chemistry and personality, was capable of reaching inside you and exposing some luminescent core you didn't know you possessed. This kind of person could make you greater than you'd have been alone.

But he could also make you terrible.

If someone had told me when I was twenty-four that I'd be witness to many violent deaths that year, I would not have been surprised. I expected it, even desired it, with an anticipation that mirrored my general outlook on life: happy, heedless, and thirsty to learn. But if my omniscient adviser had gone on to tell me that I'd be the cause of one of the deaths, I'd have been dumbfounded. That kind of trauma was inconceivable to me.

I was thirty-six now. Although I was still happy and still possessed a wide-eyed, inquisitive nature, I was much more aware of how every moment had an infinitely complex number of options, and in turn, an infinitely complex number of outcomes. We think it's the big actions that shape us—the choice to pursue medical school over business school, turning down a date with one guy in favor of another, the regrettable decision to have an affair. But in reality, all of those things come about from the unconscious and barely considered actions that shape a life: blowing off studying one night to watch TV. Laughing at a lame joke to make someone feel better. Allowing more eye contact than necessary with a man you knew to be no good. It's the innumerable smaller choices that snowball into larger vectors, or, put another way: it's the choices we make when we ignore our scornful intellects and follow our thumping hearts.

———

Before I could text Emma back, there was a tap at the conference room door, which opened to reveal the gray head of Margery Blitstein, director of the Weekday Preschool. "Pardon me for the interruption, ladies," she said. "Could I steal you for a minute, Zadie?"

"Of course," I said pleasantly, feeling my stomach clench up. This could not be good. *Please, please, don't let Delaney have bitten anyone, please.*

"I'm afraid Delaney has bitten someone," Margery said as soon as the door had shut behind us. "Again. I'm terribly sorry, Zadie, but you know that our handbook specifies that if the biting is an ongoing problem unresolved by redirection and positive reinforcement, we have to ask the parents of the biter to remove the child. I sincerely hope you understand that we at the preschool feel tremendous love for Delaney, and for all of our children, but I think we've reached the point where we need to try something a little more actionable." (*Et tu*, Margery?)

"I . . . of course," I said weakly. "I am so sorry. I can't imagine why . . . Ah, who did she bite?"

"I regret to say that it was Sumner Cooper. Again."

Oh hell.

"Is there anything going on at home?" asked Margery kindly. "Any changes or potentially upsetting events for Delaney?"

"No! I mean, no, nothing. Everything's fine."

Margery Blitstein stopped walking and patted me on the shoulder. "Zadie," she said, "I've known you since Rowan, your oldest, was a baby—that's what, eight or nine years ago? Parenting four children isn't easy, but I know what a wonderful mother you are. And I know by reputation what a wonderful doctor you are. This is no reflection on you. Sometimes children bite. This will pass."

"Thank you, Margery," I mumbled. "Ah, when you say the child needs to be removed, what kind of time frame are we talking about?"

"Well, I am certainly not suggesting that Delaney has to stay out forever. Why don't you take a few days, a week maybe, and let's think outside the box here about ways to handle this?"

So Delaney was being suspended. From preschool. Wonderful. I mentally reviewed everything I had coming up in the next few days that was incompatible with having a three-year-old biter in tow, which of course was pretty much everything. I worked at my pediatric cardiology practice every Tuesday, Wednesday, and Thursday, and the rest of my time seemed to be spent juggling the schedules of my four children. In theory, that didn't sound difficult, but in reality, each child added an exponential level of complexity, so that we'd had to plaster an entire wall of the playroom at home with a whiteboard covered in Venn diagrams and annotations about the logistics of everyone's soccer, ballet, field hockey, and guitar lessons. I made a mental note to find help in the mornings: my college-age nanny, Nina, only worked early mornings and late afternoons.

We reached Margery's office. I could hear Delaney giggling inside, probably playing with Margery's assistant, Clare. Sure enough, as we entered, I could see that Delaney was utterly unfazed by her disgrace. "Hi, beloved dear!" she called out in delight as she caught sight of me.

I knelt down. "Delaney," I hissed quietly as Margery murmured something to Clare in the background, "why did you bite Sumner?"

Brightly: "I don't know, Mom."

"Delaney. This is not okay."

"Well . . . maybe I bited her because she is so bad."

I said, "Sumner is not bad. She is a nice little friend."

"She is bad. She breaked up my puzzle even though I telled her not to."

"Okay, we are going to have plenty of time to talk about this at home." *Plenty of time.* "Let's tell Mrs. Beaufort and Mrs. Blitstein thank you for taking care of you."

"Okay! Fank you, honey dears!"

After apologizing again, we headed for the parking lot. I checked my cell phone: shoot. Missed call from Emma. As I was contemplating returning it, the phone rang: Drew, my husband.

"Hello, beautiful wife," he said.

I was suspicious. "Are you working late tonight?"

A slight pause. "Um, yes," he said. "I'm flying to New York for the day. Can you hold down the fort?"

"I always hold down the fort," I pointed out. "I'm a fort-holding specialist."

He sighed. "I know," he said. "I'm sorry." Another silence, then: "I told the boys I'd hit balls with them after their lesson today."

The quietness of his tone strangled any irritation I might have felt. Drew was a frequent victim of his managing director's whims when it came to last-minute travel for their private equity business. He'd never complain to me about how much he minded canceling a promise to our little sons, but he didn't have to: I knew how to read all his inflections.

"You know what?" I said buoyantly. "I will distract them with my own fearsome tennis skills. Don't worry for a second about it."

His voice recovered. "That would be spectacular," he said, refraining from pointing out that I was more inept on the tennis court than a bi-lateral arm amputee. "Let's plan on me taking them out this weekend, okay?"

I told him I loved him and hung up. I glanced at my watch. I had an hour and a half, which was the perfect amount of time to knock out the shopping I had to do. I'd bring the vampire with me, and we would have a serious discussion about things.

For once Delaney did not fight as she was buckled into her car seat. She was uncharacteristically quiet as I lit into her, babbling about consequences and limits and privileges. I realized that much of this was over Delaney's head, but maybe venting would calm me down enough to come up with a plan. I raged all the way to the Target parking lot, finally winding down as I unbuckled Delaney.

"Mommy?"

"Yes. What?"

In a tiny voice: "Are we still in love?"

I looked at Delaney. Her fat cheeks were drooping with guilt and fear, and her great big eyes blinked, dislodging two perfect diamonds of tears. Her little shoulders shook as she fought not to cry. Finally unable to hold it back, she buried her face in her small hands and tried to stifle her sobs.

My irritation melted. A penitent toddler could conquer the hardest heart. I scooped Delaney up, letting my littlest child bury her wet face in my chest. Chubby arms and legs wound themselves around my torso.

"I'm sorry, darling honey. I'm sorry," cried Delaney. "I didn't meant to do it!"

"It's okay, baby," I said, stroking her heaving little back. "We are still in love."

———

Seven o'clock in the morning was a ridiculous hour to have a conversation with anyone, at least in my opinion, but it qualified as late morning for Emma. She arrived at work by six most days, but she had negotiated a late start on Tuesdays. She also received two days off every other week, which for her meant an unprecedented amount of leisure time. But then again, Emma has always been a workaholic, so I wasn't even sure she appreciated it.

I was an early riser too, but not by choice. A few years back, one of my female partners and I had managed to achieve a utopian ideal never before seen in my old-school, male-dominated cardiology practice: job sharing. During the three days a week I worked, I sometimes started early: at least once a week, I needed to be in the OR myself to perform echocardiograms on the little congenital heart patients. And of course, on my two days "off," I often awoke even earlier to find myself wedged to the edge of the bed by a highly energetic twenty-five-pound intruder who'd crept in during the night. Even though I was amped to find out what Emma had discovered about Nick, I couldn't suppress a yawn.

After my big kids—eight-year-old Rowan and six-year-old twins Eli and Finn—left for early care at school, I made my way to the car, Delaney hopping in sparky little circles around my feeble trudge. "Mom, is *this* a skipping?"

I assessed her exaggerated lurch. "Um, not quite."

"Now is it a skipping?"

"Well—"

"HOW ABOUT NOW?"

Sometimes you had to lie. "Yep. Looks like skipping to me."

It took forever to load Delaney into the SUV, since she pitched a full-blown fit if you didn't allow her to buckle her own car seat, despite fat little fingers that could barely manipulate the belt. Sometimes I gritted my teeth and overpowered Delaney in the interest of expediency, but what the hell? Everyone knew I was always late. I fanned myself as Delaney worked at the buckle.

We finally departed. "I'm all wet," Delaney announced from the backseat.

"What?" I asked, navigating around a slowing driver who apparently did not wish to tip his hand by using a turn signal. "Did you spill your drink?"

"No!" hollered Delaney. "I'm pouring wet!"

"Well, I mean . . . how did you get all wet, honey?"

"I don't know! Water is coming out of my head skin!"

I glanced in the rearview mirror to see Delaney pointing in alarm to her sweaty forehead.

After a brief discussion about perspiration, we arrived at Queens Road West, where Emma's home was one in a line of magnificent old trophy houses. I turned into the curved driveway, outlined with confluent rows of dwarf Korean boxwoods interrupted every fifteen feet by blooming crape myrtles. The ten-foot-high whitewashed fences on either side of the house were draped in luscious espaliered pear trees, leading to a half-acre backyard of Edenic splendor: dozens of lime green hydrangeas, pruned camellias grown into perfect small trees, and sculpted beds of cutting flowers in great swaths of bright colors.

Delaney and I traipsed down the driveway through a snowy cloud of floating crape myrtle petals, the oyster shells underfoot making a pleasant *critch-critch* noise that merged with the faint undertone of buzzing from bumblebees in the flower beds. Even though it was morning in September, it was hot as a waffle iron out here, but the trees in Myers Park—hundred-year-old oaks as tall as four-story buildings—reared up overhead to create a massive green tunnel over Queens Road West, which at least gave the illusion of cool.

Jerrie, Emma's Australian nanny, had agreed to watch Delaney this morning. She let us in and led me back to the massive kitchen, where Emma sat straight-backed at the breakfast table. She peered over a pair of tortoiseshell reading glasses and rose to greet us.

"Okay, hit me," I said, after Delaney had scampered off with Jerrie and Emma's son, Henry. "Maybe this will help startle me awake."

Emma handed me coffee and a spoon, clearly reluctant to start talking. "Okay, but I don't want you to get worked up. It . . . may be awkward, but we'll handle it. It's nothing to worry about."

"When people say it's nothing to worry about, it's generally the preamble to catastrophe," I pointed out. "Spill it."

Emma nodded, but got up to make another cappuccino. Her kitchen was immaculate. Even though I'd been here at least once a week since we'd both moved from Kentucky to North Carolina more than a decade ago, I never failed to appreciate the pristine room, especially compared to my own house. I was not a particularly piggish person, but I seemed to have lapsed into a life where every surface in my home was coated with kid paraphernalia and metastasized mail. Drew was tidy, but his finance career required slavish devotion—the sacrificing of one's firstborn, the swearing of blood oaths, and the total surrender of his balls. He was gone for sometimes as much as twenty hours a day even when he wasn't traveling, so any mitigating influence he might have had on the domestic disarray produced by four kids was wiped out. Not only could he not help with anything related to the household, but it was pointless to complain about your own fatigue to someone being slaughtered himself.

Emma, on the other hand, was one of those people who've achieved an aggressive level of organization. In the kitchen, the glass-fronted bisque cabinets revealed handmade pottery, lined up smirking at you like the valuable art it was. And if you opened a drawer, you were confronted by spice jars and oil dispensers of the same watercolor blues and greens, all facing the same direction, their labels in a complementary old-Americana font. The walls, painted a glowing pale gold, exploded in the daylight to look like an incandescent arm of the sun itself before an evening retreat into a gleaming fire-lit jewel.

"This is difficult," she called over the noise of the steamer. "I don't really know how to start."

"Could you be a little more cryptic? I'm already doomed to have a bad day. Delaney bit Sumner Cooper yesterday and is on some kind of double-secret preschool probation. And I'm behind on paperwork, which is going to murder my afternoon."

Emma rolled her eyes, grasping at the chance to stall. "I don't think you need to be concerned about the biting. It's a perfectly normal developmental stage, as you yourself would be the first to assure everyone. Of course no one wants their child to be bitten, but—"

"Oh, I'd love it if my child got bitten. I'd be able to comfort her and feel virtuous at the same time. It's humiliating to be the parent of the biter, especially when you are the biter's parent who is also trained in pediatrics," I groused. "People think I'm professionally incompetent."

"Biting is a rational approach to a threat when you're three," said Emma. "She'll learn. The real problem here is that Sumner's mother is a stone-cold shrew who is vindictive about everything. Plus she never wears anything except yoga pants."

"Hey," I said, since I was fond of yoga pants myself.

Emma returned to the banquette, fortified with caffeine, and faced me. "About Nick," she said, without preamble. "He might be moving to Charlotte."

For a moment her words hung in the air, scrambled and incomprehensible. Then they rearranged themselves into coherence and walloped me, stealing my breath.

"What?" I managed. "Please, tell me that's a sick joke."

Chapter Two

BLISSFULLY UNCONCERNED
WITH WRINKLES

Emma, Present Day

Zadie and I met two summers before college, when we were randomly assigned to be roommates at a camp for students interested in medicine. At the time, I had few female friends; in high school I associated with a loose confederacy of oddballs—a lank-haired D&D gamer, a pudgy fiddle player, and a sexually confused, eternally tormented Goth wannabe; all boys—so I was nervous about rooming with a strange girl. The camp had been designed by some crafty bureaucrat in hopes of stemming brain drain from the state of Kentucky, which needed more primary care doctors to practice in the eastern Appalachians. In theory, the plan held merit since they were offering combined scholarships to college and medical school. In actuality, it might have been a mistake to invite the prospective rural doctors to live for the summer in Louisville. I'd been in the city for thirty minutes, accompanied by Mrs. Varner, my science teacher, who'd volunteered to drive me, and already I was reeling from the urban, bohemian-flavored sights on display as we proceeded cautiously along the cacophonous Bardstown Road. I gaped at the juxtaposition of neon and hand-lettered signs, the warm, well-lit bars and shops, the dozens of restaurants of every ethnicity clustered along just this one road. It might as well have been a different planet.

When I arrived at the dorm, Zadie was already in the room, unpacking. I noticed her face first: bright, animated, inquisitive; the kind of expression you'd expect on a person who enjoys everything. She wore a T-shirt with an EKG tracing that had two normal beats followed by a flat line and then a third normal beat.

The caption read: FOR A MINUTE THERE, YOU BORED ME TO DEATH. This evidence of coolness, coupled with the tight jeans and the black eyeliner she also sported, rendered me silent with the pressing need not to say anything boring, like "Hello. I'm Emma." I settled for a firm, speechless nod. My roommate regarded me with interest and said, "Hello. I'm Zadie."

"Hi," I managed.

"You have beautiful hair," she said, eyeing its excessive length and uncut wispy ends. "Do you have a religious thing about not cutting it?"

"What? No. No, I just like it long."

"Whew!" she said. "I thought maybe you were in one of those fundamentalist groups that makes their women eschew modern conveniences, like pants and education."

Did she just say "eschew"? A dorky hope flared in me. "No, it's . . . more of a counterculture thing," I said, even though I was about as counterculture as Andy Griffith. "I am in favor of pants. And education."

"Oh good," she said. "I was worried about having to spend all summer with someone weird and unlikable."

Okay, I could do this. "Like a . . . kleptomaniac rich girl," I offered. "Or a bulimic hoarder."

"Or somebody with abhorrent musical taste."

"Or a boy-crazy flake."

Uh-oh. Wrong thing to say.

"Or how about one of those people who hisses 'Shhhh!' if you make a phone call while she's meditating?" she blurted.

"Um," I said, relieved that she'd overlooked my boy-crazy comment. "That last one sounds a little personal."

She giggled. "Yeah, that was my roommate at band camp one year. Oops. I think I revealed I went to band camp. Please don't move out."

"I'm a band geek too," I said. I realized I'd twirled a lock of hair around my finger into an irredeemable knot and began to try to extricate my finger without being too obvious. "Do you still play anything?"

"I was encouraged to find another interest. Turns out, I'm sort of tone-deaf."

"Sorry," I said. I felt a hard edge in my chest give way. I could tell she liked me.

The more I got to know Zadie, the more we connected: she was the first girlfriend I'd made because of—not despite—my intellect. More often than not, we stayed up all night, talking about books, current events, philosophy. As the summer wound on, I began to relax into a comfortable camaraderie around her, reveling in the opportunity to unleash my thoughts without watching the other person recoil. This sensation was so novel and so enjoyable, I became nostalgic for it before it even ended, hyperaware of the fleeting nature of happiness even as I was happy. I knew it couldn't last.

But somehow, it did. Zadie and I called each other often throughout the school year, and then we were roommates in college, and later, in med school. I knew her as well as I knew any human being.

And I'm sure she thought the same of me.

———

For a beat, Zadie didn't react to my statement about Nick. Then her eyes went wide as her hands fluttered up near her face, apparently trying to fan air into her flash-frozen lungs. "What?" she squeaked. "Please tell me that's a sick joke."

I regarded her carefully. "Are you going to faint?"

"No!" She yanked her hands down and sat on them. "How do you know he might be moving to Charlotte?" One of her arms escaped, flailing around and landing on her coffee mug. She took a giant slurp and then almost snorted it out her nose as my husband, Wyatt, came skidding around the counter in his underwear.

"Late!" he yelped, waving his coffee cup.

I'm aware of the uncharitable comparisons people make when they first meet me and Wyatt. They think we're Beauty and the Beast, evocative of those billionaire-supermodel combos you see in the tabloids. Or the racial aspect briefly trips them up: Wyatt's black. I'm white. One glance at Wyatt, a squatty endomorph, and me—all angular cheekbones and elbows—and people assume that Wyatt's loaded. He *is* loaded, but he's also both brilliant and mesmerizing. He can talk a herd of cats into a hot tub, and he's relentless when he wants something.

While us being an interracial couple rarely garners a second glance, the difference in our physical attractiveness sometimes does. My interior and exterior are an incongruous mismatch, seemingly designed to confuse. I've learned the hard way that people expect dull vapidity when they meet me: the pouty cast of my lips, my heavy-lidded blue eyes, my blond hair and emaciated height invoke a dim vibe no matter how I slouch or how I dress. People assume that Wyatt could not love me for my mind, or that I could not love him for his looks. Marrying each other might have seemed like an odd choice from a distance, but we complement each other well. He balances out my awkwardness, and I keep him reasonably reined in when his zest begins to overflow into the realm of mania. Once they get to know us, no one wonders why I love Wyatt.

"Tarnation!" he bellowed, having just spilled hot coffee on his feet. He began high-stepping around the room, trying to shake off the sizzling liquid from his bare toes, forgetting that he was still holding the sloshing cup. "Aah! Lord almighty. A little help here! Emma! This coffee is attacking me. And someone has stolen all my pants. Hey there, Zadie."

"Hey, Wyatt," Zadie said, trying not to smile.

"Your pants are hanging in your closet, Wy," I reminded him.

"No, they're not. It's like the world is clamoring for me to go out in my unders."

"I'll go look."

"No, no, no, no." Wyatt switched gears. "You ladies stay right here. I'll reassess."

I touched a drawer on the kitchen island, which sprang open, proffering baby wipes. I grabbed one, and after mopping up the coffee tsunami, I turned my attention back to Zadie. "I'm sorry. I should have figured out a better way to tell you. I just found out myself. I—"

From the adjacent first-floor master: "Muffin! Are we out of Product?"

Zadie and I glanced at each other, mutually agreeing not to continue in earshot of Wyatt.

"What's Product?" she whispered.

"His hairdresser suggested he try to manhandle the 'fro a little," I whispered back. "It's in your vanity shelf," I called.

"Thanks, beloved. By the way, I've located the pants. They were hidden in plastic stuff."

"That's how they come back from the dry cleaner's, Wy. How have you never noticed that before?"

"I'm sure I have, but in general I'm blissfully unconcerned with wrinkles," said Wyatt, emerging fully dressed from the bedroom, his hair now sporting an unnatural shine. "They're going to bunch up as soon as you put them on, so why bother? When you've got all this going on"—he motioned in an up-and-down gesture to himself—"people will let a few wrinkles slide—you know what I'm sayin'?"

"I think what you're saying is that before Emma, you always wore wrinkled pants?" Zadie asked. Wyatt and I had been married for three years, but he persisted in plenty of ingrained bachelor habits, which often required me to repress my reactions for the sake of our marriage.

"Wellll, I did have a little help from time to time. With laundry and such."

"Who helped you?" I asked.

"Really, that's irrelevant," Wyatt protested feebly.

"Who?"

"You're not going to let this drop, are you?"

Deadpan: "No."

"Fine. Sometimes Mama gave me a little hand with things," Wyatt muttered.

"I knew it!" I said. "Your mom did all your laundry. That explains a lot."

"Let's not go there, pumpkin. I'm late enough."

Zadie leapt to her feet. "Oh, shoot!" she yowled. "I'm going to be late for work."

I stood and kissed her on the cheek, thankful for this unexpected reprieve. "I'm off Friday. Let's get together then." I flicked a quick glance at Wyatt, who was incautiously pouring himself another coffee, and lowered my voice. "Listen. Zadie."

"Yeah?"

I felt my body language shift: a signaling of emotion I couldn't quite conceal. Over the years, Zadie'd learned to read the subtle telegraphs of my face: a raised eyebrow, a half smile, a quick blink were all you might get from me, whereas another person's visage would reflect open disgust or wild joy. But now I struggled to keep my expression impassive.

"I don't . . ." I began, but then stopped. I waited, but nothing happened. I was frozen.

"Em?" Zadie tried.

I blinked, feeling the corners of my mouth elevate in a parody of a smile.

"It's fine," I said. "See you Friday."

I could tell Zadie wanted to shake the details out of me, but she acquiesced with good grace, bounding out of the house and down the driveway in a tear. Although I couldn't prove it, I suspected Zadie's office staff actually scheduled her first patient fifteen minutes later than they told her they did, since she was late nearly one hundred percent of the time. I watched her peel out of the driveway, my mind churning. I had more than a decade of repression when it came to the subject of all the things that had gone wrong during our third year of medical school. There's an indescribable comfort in the telepathy that develops over many years of friendship; I knew exactly why Nick's reemergence would trigger embarrassment and anger for Zadie, and I could almost read her mind about how she'd approach him when she saw him again. Thinking of it, I lowered my face to my hands, squeezing my eyes shut, and settled into a familiar slumped-shoulder posture of defeat.

Chapter Three

MORE TUBES THAN
THE UNDERGROUND

Late Summer, 1999: Louisville, Kentucky
Zadie

"What are you waiting for? Stab him in the chest."

I was pretty certain this was the first time in my life I'd heard those precise words spoken in my vicinity. I didn't stab—mainly because I didn't think I was competent to stab anyone in the chest—but also because I wasn't certain the chief resident was talking to me. In case he was, I tried to banish the excitement I felt flitting across my face.

Clancy got it, however. He was our team's intern, and he was a notorious procedure hog, known for prematurely dashing in and inserting lines and tubes while everyone else was still fumbling to get their booties and gowns on. "She can't do the tube. She's a third-year med student," he protested, his words emerging behind his mask in a muffled whine.

"There are two more incoming," said our chief, as he ripped open a chest tube kit. He looked amused. "Get over to bay two and get ready for the next one. You can call it."

Clancy shot me a hostile look and huffed out.

"Go ahead, Sadie," said the chief. "Better hurry up. He's dying."

"Ah," I said, panicked. No time to correct him on my name. "When you say 'stab him in the chest . . .'"

"Well, it's a little more nuanced than that." He began squirting a brown antiseptic fluid over the patient's chest wall. "I'm assuming you've got more sense than Clancy. Can you locate his nipple? And his armpit?"

"Yes," I said, with complete confidence.

Dr. X, the chief, wheeled around to face a nurse standing behind us. "Eva," he commanded, "throw us two packs of sterile gloves." He grabbed one of my hands, which looked spindly and uncertain next to his. "Size six," he evaluated. To me, he said, "We'll do it together as soon as he's intubated. Then the next one's all you. Okay?"

I nodded, pleased. Insertion of a chest tube was a procedure I was anxious to learn.

Above me, a bank of monitors beeped hysterically. The room we were in—one of the emergency department trauma bays—had floor-to-ceiling shelves, which contained a slew of medieval-appearing implements: fat eight-inch needles to insert into the heart, instruments to slice open the chest and saw through ribs, IVs to thread into the central veins in the neck and chest and groin, and even horrifying giant needles designed to screw into the marrow of the bones. Hanging from the ceiling were swiveling cinema-quality spotlights. Who knew how many patients had regained consciousness with those blinding lights boring down on them, convinced they were facing the radiant blaze of the tunnel to heaven only to realize they were actually alive and naked in a roomful of strangers?

Only a few moments earlier, the EMTs had barreled in with a crushed, unconscious teenager. (". . . *Trauma code name is Silver*," one of them reported as he and his burly partner had heaved up the metal stretcher. "*Young male, unbelted driver of a T-bone MVC, no airbag deployment, GCS 3 on initial eval, decreased breath sounds on the right . . .*")

I'd learned earlier in the day the hospital assigned random nouns as code words for the trauma patients—in this case, Silver—since some were unconscious without ID, some were in need of protection from whatever sinister force had caused their plight, and some were high-profile enough to require privacy. None of us yet knew Silver's real name.

"Lidocaine, etomidate, succinylcholine," the ER resident called out. He was a skinny guy with a prominent Adam's apple, which bobbed up and down in nervous commiseration as he manipulated a breathing tube through Silver's vocal cords and into his trachea. A respiratory tech attached the tube to a bedside ventilator, which began pumping air into Silver's lungs, forcing his chest up and down at regular intervals.

Dr. Allison Kalena, our third-year surgery resident, held a stethoscope to Silver's chest. She was trim and self-contained, with symmetrical features and hair bundled into a crisp, precise bun. I found her inscrutability a little worrisome. I'd known her only one day, but I'd yet to see her have an actual expression. Her onyx eyes were smooth and alert over her mask as she instructed an XR tech to shoot a film, but she didn't bother to wait for the results to motion for Dr. X to set up the chest tube kit. I perked up. This confirmed his initial suspicion that something bad—maybe a big blood or air collection—was impeding Silver from expanding his lung on one side.

Reviewing my meager knowledge, I pulled the sterile gloves over my regular latex ones, being careful not to allow the outside of them to touch my skin. Trauma victims were evaluated according to the ABCs, starting with airway (A), breathing (B), and circulation (C). These were sequential actions taken to address life-threatening injuries, and the team had just handled the airway. Things were now hung up on B, because despite the breathing tube, he still wasn't getting enough air. All the alarms were blaring: Low oxygen! Low blood pressure! Fast heart rate!

Silver was dying.

Dr. X spoke up. "Sadie," he said to me. "Let's do this."

I nodded. He was directly behind me, guiding my hands as he talked me through the chest tube insertion. I watched, mesmerized, as my own hands performed the small operation: incising through Silver's skin, just over a rib, punching through the muscle to his chest cavity, releasing an angry crimson splash, which sprayed the front of my yellow plasticized gown and dripped down past my shoe covers. The cellular dimming of Silver's life reversed course as I piloted the tube in place through the gaping hole in his chest wall. An entirely new emotion surged through me: part exhilaration, part glorious relief, part absurd pride. I beamed at Dr. X, who stood assessing the action, his posture easy, arms folded loosely across his chest.

He gave me a thumbs-up. I was hooked.

From what I could see of him, Silver was young and slender. He'd been wearing jeans and a faded T-shirt with a picture of Stephen Hawking on the front, which puddled on the floor as the nurses finished clipping off his clothes with big shears. One of his shoes was missing, and the other was pointing almost backward, indicating a horrific fracture that seemed to have twisted his leg nearly off. I brought my gloved hand down gently to touch his broken face. A drop of fluid squeezed out of his left eye and ran down his cheek: a single bloody tear.

Practicing medicine had not been my lifelong goal, unlike for my roommate, Emma, who'd had a determination to be a surgeon since the age of three. Meanwhile, as a toddler, I'd aspired to be a bulldozer, a career plan that received the enthusiastic support of my older brother. There's something so appealing about the notion of achieving your aims by pulverizing obstacles into rubble, isn't there? Unfortunately, it soon became evident I did not have what it took to be an actual bulldozer, what with being human and all. I moved on, dreaming of jobs inspired by beloved literary influences: ballerina, wizard, authority on unicorn behavior. My interest in a more realistic career didn't manifest itself until my senior year of high school, when I was eating with a friend whose father was a family doctor in our small Kentucky town. I could still recall the reverence accorded to him from surrounding diners as he murmured into the restaurant's phone in response to a page, bolting midmeal for the hospital. The restaurant manager made a big show of comping our bill.

Doctors were beloved. This struck a nerve in my healthy imagination. They zipped around learning everyone's secrets, delivering babies, soothing the sick, showing up in the nick of time to save the day. When the shit really rains down, who needs a ballerina?

"Sadie."

I snapped to attention at the sound of my name. Or a name that was similar to mine, anyway. Apparently, I hadn't made a tremendous impression on my team yet, since none of them seemed to realize my name was Zadie.

But maybe I was wrong about making an impression, because I looked up to find the chief's eyes locked on me: a long, deliberate appraisal. I resisted the urge to squirm.

"Pay attention," he said finally, but his tone was mild. "This is Sandford Pelley." He gestured to a hulking Sasquatch with massive shoulders and animated chest hair spewing up from the V of his scrub top. "He's from ortho."

"Nice to meet you," I said.

"You too," rumbled the Sasquatch. "Have you ever reduced a fracture?"

"Not yet," I said hopefully.

"I'm sure Sadie can help you, Pelley, if you need some real muscle," Dr. X offered. "Send her to me when you're done; I'm going to check on whatever fresh hell just rolled in before Clancy manages to terminate somebody." He strode toward the curtain separating the trauma bay from the rest of the ER, but then swiveled around and directed his last comment to me.

"You were good," he said. "This kid owes you his life."

———

". . . excuse me, Doctor? Excuse me, Doctor?"

With a start, I realized the voice was addressing me. It belonged to a tiny, wizened man with a corona of wispy white hair. He was gimping along the hall, clutching a faded floral-print pillow, a Bible, and a leather strap attached to some kind of steamer trunk on wheels. "I can't find anybody," he told me plaintively. "Where did they go?"

"Oh," I began, but stopped as he turned to me, his withered hand suddenly clutching mine in a fierce grip.

It was after midnight. Silver had finally been stabilized and sent to the ICU, and I'd been slinking through the ER with my head down, hoping to sneak in a short sleep before someone recognized my white coat and handed me a laceration tray. I'd been blasted from an uneasy slumber at four o'clock yesterday morning by my roommate, who was also assigned to the trauma service this month on a different team. Emma is the kind of person who can effortlessly transition from sleep into a well-oiled machinelike functionality. By contrast, I have to be poured out of bed each morning like human syrup, and I lurch around, emitting miserable squeaks until I'm caffeinated. It was going to be a brutal month.

Patients were crammed into every thin-walled room of the ER, wheezing or bleeding or clutching their chests, spilling out into the halls, bellowing for somebody to bring some Dilaudid, or at least some fucking morphine. My new friend stared at me, ignoring the sideshow, his watery blue eyes locked on mine with the intensity of someone who has just discovered the key to cold fusion. Then his eyes clouded in a baffled fugue. "Where is Bertie?" he asked.

"I don't— Who is Bertie?" I tried.

My friend slowed his wobbly shuffle and began to cry. "Oh no," I said. His thin shoulders shuddered. I cast a desperate look around, but everyone seemed preoccupied with their own issues: stemming a torrential hemorrhage, or warding off asphyxiation, or whatever. The elderly man had now come to a complete halt, sobbing piteously in the middle of the hall.

"Oh no," I said again. I scooted his huge trunk over to the side, where it was less likely to cause a traffic jam, and then returned to him. Not knowing what else to do, I wrapped my arms around his frail torso and guided his weepy head onto my shoulder, patting the back of his neck ineffectually from time to time. A musty smell, like an old couch, wafted off him. He embraced me back, and I thought he might have felt some comfort by the hug, because after a while his cheek burrowed against my coat and the volume of his cries lessened a little. Still, there was no way to detach.

It's possible I might have stood there until I became petrified, but rescue arrived in the form of an amused but disembodied voice just out of my line of sight. I knew immediately who it was, though.

"Sadie? What are you doing?"

"He's lost," I explained.

"Bertie," howled my friend, wiping his nose on my sleeve with extravagant abandon.

"He can't find Bertie."

"Yes, I see," said Dr. X. "Well, let me help you out a bit." He disengaged my neck from the elderly gentleman's death grip and gently led him down the hall to an empty nurses' station, handing him a pack of crackers and a small generic lime soda before tucking him into a swivel chair. "There you are, sir," said Dr. X, extending his hand for a shake. He leaned in as the man said something, and laughed in delight.

"What was that about?" I asked as Dr. X returned.

"Can't tell you," he replied, smirking. "Male-bonding thing."

"Who's Bertie?" I asked.

Dr. X frowned. "Bertie was his wife," he said. He slowed and glanced at me, his attention apparently caught by the photo on my hospital-issued badge, which featured a goofy image of me smiling in midblink. Deftly, I turned the badge around.

Everyone—nurses, patients, hospital administrators—called him Dr. X. I wasn't sure if this was because he was mysterious, or if it was part of his unpronounceable name, or possibly a reference to the TV show *X-Files*. He had a reputation around the hospital for being a man's man: profane, cocky, decisive; but I decided I liked him. Just as you'd expect from a surgeon, he had authoritative hands and arms. And he was tall; he peered down at me now, trying to remind himself of the embroidered last name on my white coat.

"Sadie . . . Fletcher." He grinned. "Well, not much of a chance for us to chat today, so I'm glad we've got a little unexpected free time. Welcome to trauma call."

I smiled, running my fingers through my hair, which had responded to its release from the ER cap by springing out in all directions in a belligerent pale brown explosion. "Thanks for letting me do the chest tube."

"My pleasure, Sadie," he said.

Again, I considered correcting him on my name. But his pager chirped, and he glanced at it with a slight grimace. "I think you're going to be more useful than our intern this month, actually," he said, "not that there's a big hurdle there. Clancy is a pestilential twit. You're a better surgeon than him already"—his grin returned—"and you're definitely better looking."

Hmm. Although scrubs seem designed to render the wearer as rectangular as possible, I knew that my figure still came across as feminine. I was lucky: I was curvy but slender, even though I ate like a starving carnivorous beast.

Dr. X took a step toward me. He had dark blond eyebrows that reminded me of Jack Nicholson or the Grinch, perching with attractive malevolence above a face with deep linear dimples. "Let's grab a coffee and get acquainted," he offered. "The chance of sleeping is minimal. Trust me."

I was mildly surprised. Was this normal, or was this some kind of ambiguous flirtation? I mean, who wants to get acquainted in the middle of the night? Like every other industry, the hospital was awash in sexual harassment prohibitions crafted by committees who might look askance at a chief resident—who wielded considerable power in the training program—hitting on a lowly medical student. And we barely knew each other; how presumptuous of him to assume that I wouldn't be offended, whether it was, um, true or not.

Before I could answer, my pager went off. It had been only one day, but already I was beginning to loathe this device. Dr. X's pager blared too: something awry in the ICU. He'd been on the verge of saying something else, but now he bowed to the inevitable and stopped midword to silence the beeping at his hip. He brushed his hair back with his thumb and said, "Well, damn, Sadie."

———

The Trauma Intensive Care Unit was laid out in a rectangle, with a workstation full of nurses in the middle and robust orange walls probably deemed invigorating by some institutional decorator. Invigoration was sorely needed in here. The patients were, to a man, all unconscious. They lay, misshapen and inflated by edema, some swollen to three or four times their usual size from resuscitation fluid and overtaxed kidneys, hooked to ventilators and infusions. The current composition of my team's patients tilted toward the young: there were two teenage boys, both of whom were unbelted car crash victims with brain injuries; one drug-addled fool who had blundered onto an interstate; a fireworks-gone-wrong case; a guy in his thirties who had sawed down an oak tree, which promptly crushed him;

and my guy, Silver. Looking at his huge foamy hospital bed, I struggled to suppress an irrational, selfish burst of envy: yes, Silver was shattered and comatose, but at least he was resting on something soft.

Across the room, I could see Emma, her pale blond hair gleaming with nuclear intensity under the fluorescent lights of the TICU, filling in her chief on the status of Team B's patients. I returned my attention to the bed closest to us, which held the ill-fated lumberjack. This guy had more tubes than the London Underground. There were tubes in his bladder, his groin, his chest, his neck, his radial artery, his nose, his abdomen, and even one ghastly line going straight into his brain. There was a breathing tube in his trachea, which was connected to a scary bedside ventilator that had as many dials as a cockpit in a DC-10. I stared in horror.

"What's up?" Dr. X said to the charge nurse, a fit woman named Val. She adjusted a delicate pair of glasses on her nose and began spewing numbers on Lumberjack, none of which I understood. Dr. X nodded. "Book the OR," he said.

Before she could reply, Dr. X's gaze sharpened. Across the long room, a cluster of nurses surrounded Silver's bed, their raised voices competing with the jarring sounds of alarms. I followed Dr. X, edging my way into a space at the middle of the bed, uncertain of the cause of the commotion. I looked at the monitor: Silver's heart rate was thirty-two.

"What's happening to him?" I whispered.

Dr. X inspected Silver's eyes with a light. "Intracranial pressure's too high," he said shortly. "His brain stem is herniating."

"What does that m—"

Emma materialized at my side and took my hand. "His brain is swelling," she said softly. "See, his pupils are blown."

I looked. Silver's eyes were a featureless black, the green irises nearly eclipsed by the enlarged pupils.

"Can't they operate?"

Emma shook her head in the direction of Silver's chart, her usual incisive gaze blurred. "I don't think he has the kind of brain bleed that can be fixed by neurosurgery." She looked at his smooth young face, buried under tubes and tape.

"Wait, guys," I said, looking back and forth between Emma and Dr. X. "Wait. You mean he's going to die? Right now?"

The charge nurse, Val, glanced at the clock. "His mother isn't going to make it here in time," she said.

We watched Silver's heart rate fall. Val wrote down some numbers from one of Silver's drains; one of the other nurses did something to an IV; someone silenced the shrieking alarms. Without a word, Dr. X picked up Silver's hand and held it between his own. Silver's heart slowed further, ebbing down to a few last lonely beats. Then it stopped.

I thought about the geeky physics T-shirt he'd been wearing and his skinny broken leg and turned my head aside so no one would see me wrestling to control my expression.

One of the nurses left and returned with a small bag labeled PATIENT BELONGINGS. She took out a wallet and opened it.

"His name was Ryan," she said.

I felt a hand grip my shoulder. A low voice, in my ear: "Are you okay?"

I nodded, not wanting to be so self-absorbed that the focus of a tragedy would shift—even for a moment—to my reaction to it, but also I didn't trust myself to be able to speak. Dr. X leaned toward me, so close I could feel the warmth of his skin, and then gently, he reached past me to Silver's sightless green eyes and closed the lids, leaving his hand cupped for a moment against the boy's still face. Then, without looking at any of us, he turned and walked out of the room.

Chapter Four

BODY DYSMORPHIC DISORDER

Zadie, Present Day

I resented that I wasn't the kind of woman who felt sickened by the thought of food when I was upset, because that would have been easier than the realization that I'd scarfed down an entire container of leftover lasagna followed by a huge bag of chocolate chips, which is what happened last night when I was thinking about possibly seeing Nick again. A full-on binge was bad enough, but back-loading meals at midnight was stupid. And the night before going to the pool—well, words failed to describe how regrettable *that* was. Now I'd have bathing suit trauma on top of the rest of it. Something horrendous had happened to my metabolism in the last year or two so that one tiny food indiscretion would result in the sudden appearance of a five-months pregnant abdomen. The only way to atone was to forgo all appealing food in favor of vile green smoothies and then exercise as if I were afflicted with 'roid rage.

Despite this, I was looking forward to a day at the pool. One nice thing about living in the South: it was warm enough that the club didn't close the pool until the end of September, or sometimes later. Since Emma was bringing her nanny, in theory we could enjoy our Friday-morning-off work by stretching out on the comfy padded chaises by the big pool and sipping iced drinks and generally indulging in pampered sloth, which was something we'd talked about doing all summer. Since she was a trauma surgeon, Emma had a tough work schedule. Her days off rarely seemed to coordinate with my Mondays and Fridays off. Throw in a total of five kids, two husbands, one obese pet, various school and volunteering obligations, and a multitude of errands, and it was a testament to our friendship that we hung out as much as we did. We were due some fun, actually. The last couple of times we'd seen each other hadn't exactly been a barrel of laughs.

Three weeks ago, my household had gone viral, and not in any kind of positive marketing way. Every member of the Anson family was spewing vomit except Drew, who promptly claimed a work obligation requiring his presence in China. While the rational part of my brain understood he had zero control over his travel schedule, the vindictive part of my brain hoped he'd come down with E. coli on the plane as punishment for leaving me on my own with our four hurling offspring.

My immune system normally functioned like an impenetrable force field, bolstered by years of exposure to the germ factory of the hospital. But this time I went down hard. By the time the last of the kids got sick, a few days later, I was so feeble and demoralized I hadn't budged from the playroom—the most expendable room in the house—in almost twenty-four hours, except to retrieve Gatorade and broth. I'd dragged in a couple air mattresses and papered the room in wall-to-wall beach towels. I also established vomiting outposts at all four corners of the beds, consisting of plastic planters lined with grocery bags, in case the vomiter in question couldn't quite make it to the disgusting bathroom, which now resembled the seventh circle of hell. The kids and I languished on our beach-towel-covered air beds, moaning, occasionally raising our heads to check on the status of whatever was showing on Animal Planet.

When someone tapped on the playroom door, the kids looked at me quizzically, but I had no idea who it was. My part-time nanny had taken one look at us and bolted a few days earlier. Maybe one of the neighbors was checking to see why our house was emitting sewer fumes?

It was Emma. At least, I thought it was Emma; it was hard to say for sure, since the voice behind the door sounded weirdly muffled. "Can I come in?"

"Don't come in," I said valiantly. "We have the plague. It's like *The Exorcist* up in here."

"I'm coming in anyway," she said, and pushed the door open.

I took one look at her and burst out laughing. She was covered from head to toe in surgical bio-shield garments. Several layers of OR gloves covered her hands; her legs resembled blue sausages, encased to the knee in thick paper booties.

"What the hell is that?" I said, wheezing from the exertion of having laughed. "Are you wearing a level-four biohazard suit?"

"Don't be silly," she said briskly. "I snagged this stuff from the OR." She set down the bucket she carried, from which protruded the nozzles of a bunch of cleaning supplies. "I'm here to save you." She gave me a closer look, peering out from under her bizarre hat. "Dear God. Do you think you could possibly make it to the shower?"

You know you have a friendship more precious than rubies when the friend is willing to scrub your bathroom after the detonation of a gastrointestinal bomb. If I hadn't been so dehydrated, I'd have crawled into her lap and wept tears of gratitude.

So I owed Emma a relaxing day. But now, the anticipation of a lazy morning in the sunshine had evaporated in a flood of unease. *Nick.* I hadn't seen or talked to him in well over a decade.

The day started with the usual early-morning cluster. My second grader was an insomniac: something about her brain wiring prevented sleep, although she didn't need much and generally bounced around loudly and annoyingly when everyone else was still trying to snooze. The six-year-olds were groggy, incoherent slugs in the morning. They didn't want to be woken, and when forced to rise, they retaliated by acting as unpleasant and helpless as possible. They slumped over the back of the couch, their auburn heads and sturdy little frames motionless, whining because they didn't want to put on their school uniforms.

"I can't do it," Eli sniveled. "It's too hard."

"Eli, don't be ridiculous. Delaney can put on her shirt, and she's three."

"Yah," said Delaney in an uppity voice. "I can."

"Mom," Finn said limply. "Delaney is antagonizing us."

"Please do not think that I will be drawn into this. Put on your shirt, or, or . . . or you will have to go to school shirtless."

Rowan piped up. "Mom, don't say things unless you are prepared to follow through on them," she lectured in my voice. "And you can't follow through on that, because it will humiliate me to have half-naked brothers at school."

"That's not— Oh, shi . . . oot, the eggs are burning!"

A car horn sounded outside. "Mom, the carpool is here!"

"*What? What?* It can't be time for— Mother of God! Put on your shirts! Has anyone eaten?" A quick glance outside revealed Betsy Packard's idling black Suburban.

"I have! Me! I have eaten!"

"I meant, have any of the big kids eaten? Boys, where are your backpacks? Shi . . . oot!"

I stomped outside, slamming the door after me, and then forced a smile onto my face as I apologized to Betsy. "Looks like I'll have to drive them in late again," I said lamely. Betsy, who had two children and an army of minions to help her, nonetheless gave me a commiserating look. Everybody's been there.

Once Rowan, Eli, and Finn had been successfully deposited at the Oak Academy, I turned my attention to getting ready for the pool. This was labor-intensive. Unfortunately, shaving my legs required putting Delaney in the bath too; otherwise she'd be free to roam the bathroom and plunder approximately eight zillion dollars' worth of makeup, or plug up the toilet with scarves, or eat deodorant or something. Three-year-olds liked to imitate, investigate, and deconstruct, which led to all sorts of havoc when they were left to their own devices.

Then I had to try on all the bathing suits I owned in order to determine which one most successfully hid the results of last night's food debacle. (A downside to friendship with Emma: she was eight feet tall and weighed four ounces.) Delaney, of course, insisted on trying on multiple suits as well, and preened in admiration at her reflection. At least she hadn't picked up a case of crushing body dysmorphic disorder yet; she thought her convex toddler tummy and chubby thighs and fat bottom were extremely desirable, probably because everyone else in the family was always trying to squeeze her.

After the fashion show, the pool bag had to be located and packed. Delaney required ten pounds of gear for every pound of body weight in order to be able to leave the house. An hour later, we were finally ready to go. I had successfully avoided any troublesome thoughts during the hectic morning, but now, as I drove to meet Emma to continue yesterday's conversation, the memories assaulted me.

Nick had not been a nice guy. He was brilliant, he was gorgeous, he was never boring, but nobody would describe him as overly burdened with empathy, at least not most of the time. Even the worst tarantula on the planet has his moments—I could remember his kindness to the families of some of his patients, for instance—but overall Nick had been a black force of disorder and hurt, a swirling dark cloud raining volcanic ash onto a village of innocents. And there was another reason to avoid the thought of Nick, which still caused me to squirm with shame, even now, all these years later: the biggest professional error I'd ever made.

The entrance to the club reared up in my visual field, forcing me to make a sudden turn without braking. "Whoa there, lovely dear!" hollered Delaney, her head swaying.

You approached Emma's club via a serpentine lane lined with sculpted trees and a median teeming with snapdragons. The golf course was visible on the left side, with its green hills undulating gently into the distance. As you got closer, the bright snapdragons gave way to orderly beds of pansies flanking clipped yew bushes. Twin wisteria-draped pergolas stood at the corners of the drive, bordering a white bricked guardhouse in the widened median, covered with climbing ivy and roses.

I slowed to a crawl and rolled down the window. I did not belong to the club. As a part-time physician, I made less than your average plumber, once you factored in childcare and taxes and various work-related expenses. Drew's income, on the other hand, was growing nicely. You might think that he'd be willing to live it up a little, but no. Allocation of capital in the Anson household was tightly regulated. Drew was parsimonious, adhering to a strict budget that did not include dropping 100K on club initiation fees. He had all these spreadsheets and projections for our household expenses and had calculated basically down to the minute when we would reach a level of financial comfort sufficient for him to start blowing money on things like country clubs or luxury cars. Meanwhile, we went to the Y or mooched off friends when we wanted to swim.

The Colleys—Emma and Wyatt—were not subject to this degree of financial planning, or any degree of financial planning, as far as I could tell. Wyatt raked it in from his car dealerships and blew through it just as quickly. He was not one to overthink things, and he liked to roll large. Wyatt had joined the waiting list for the club even before he'd married Emma, and if he had any residual unease about having grown up as a dirt-poor kid in some blighted corner of Alabama, he hid it well. Hob-nobbing with a bunch of old-money Southerners didn't appear to faze him at all.

The guard knew me because I'd been the Colleys' guest frequently, and he waved us through with a big smile. The clubhouse, a rambling Georgian of the same white brick as the guardhouse, was visible directly ahead. The circular drive led to a porticoed entrance under thirty-foot white columns, but I veered off before reaching it, turning right toward the pool and tennis courts.

The pool was old-school: a sky blue rectangle with a diving board at the deep end and stairs into the shallow end. There was a separate round bubble of a baby pool with a little fence around it, and an expanse of flat white concrete surrounding the whole thing. But what the pool lacked in zero-entry areas and infinity edges and flagstone terraces, it more than made up for in the sheer beauty of the view. It was built into a hillside, with a one-hundred-eighty-degree vista of rolling green hills and cerulean sky and weeping willows swaying gracefully into ponds. The club had bowed to modernity by adding an outdoor thatched-roof bar with a dozen flat-screen TVs built into the ceiling joists and a breezy open-air dining pavilion with the same stunning view.

After dropping Delaney at the baby pool with Emma's nanny, I found Emma in a chaise near the bar. She was immobile, eyes closed behind gold sunglasses, her legs bent slightly at the knees so that the long taper of her calves into her delicate ankles was accentuated. She wore a broad-brimmed sun hat and a fuchsia bikini top with a wispy sarong.

She must have sensed me walking up, because she thrust off the sunglasses and sat up. "Zadie," she said. "I thought you weren't coming when you didn't text back."

"No, no," I said. "This morning was kind of a flail, and also I had a . . . a phone mishap." I held out my ruined cell phone, which I'd dropped in the morning's chaos.

"Ouch," Emma commiserated. "Did you text Marcus?"

Marcus, a seventeen-year-old nerd in my neighborhood, ran a thriving black-market business in iPhone repair. He could replace a damaged screen in ten minutes flat, and he charged half of the exorbitant Apple Store rate, with none of the hassle. With four device-addicted children, I had him on my favorites list.

"I did, but he hasn't replied yet. Probably wasting time in high school or something," I answered. I settled myself on the chaise next to Emma's and kicked off my sandals. "Okay, Em . . . how did you find out Nick might move here?"

"He applied for an opening with my surgery group," Emma said. She furled her limbs into a knot, lanky arms encircling lanky legs, resting her head gently on her knees.

"No way! When?"

"It happened while I was at that trauma conference—he interviewed with the hospital admin people last month apparently, and then with our practice manager and a couple of the partners while I was out of town. I almost vomited when I realized who he was."

"But he's not even a trauma surgeon. Is he?" I asked weakly, plucking at the untethered edge of my pool chair, where a plastic strap had worked its way loose from its binding.

"No, but the hospital wants to add reconstructive plastics and hepatobiliary and vascular to the group," Emma said. "Make us multidisciplinary, instead of all separate, and that way they can tell the Eastway Surgery guys to fuck off. They've been wrangling for years over call issues and reimbursement for uninsured patients and all kinds of stuff."

She paused and leaned back in her chair. Her once magnificent waist-length hair had been cut short into a stacked, sleek bob, but it flattered her, framing the planed bones of her face and her clear glowing eyes. She was lithe and smooth and perfectly maintained, every hair in place, not a single shaving nick or unsightly vein or blemish anywhere on her flawless skin. As long as I had known her, Emma had always managed to make everything look easy.

"Did he— Does he know you're in the group?" I asked.

"I don't—" Emma began.

"Well, *heyyy* there, babe!"

Emma and I both looked up, startled, as the chair next to me was suddenly occupied by a tiny blonde in a red one-piece. It was Mary Sarah Porcher, one of the pediatricians I worked with, who also had Fridays off. She grinned widely, curling her legs up under her and leaning in. "What the hell is going on?"

Mary Sarah was a walking contradiction. She had a shocking gravelly voice—I suspected she smoked—and her accent was pure Southern, so that *What the hell is going on?* came out as *Whut the hale is gowen own?* She loved to curse, an odd quality in a pediatrician, admittedly. But she was a legacy at the club and her husband was a blue-blooded Virginian whose family could trace their lineage back to the landed gentry in *Burke's Peerage.* She reminded me of my old med school friend Georgia, now a urologist.

Ordinarily, there was nothing I'd have enjoyed more than hanging out with Mary Sarah and Emma at the pool, but now I was desperate to hear what Emma had started to tell me, and there was no way to explain the background situation to a third party when Emma and I could barely articulate it ourselves. We'd have to wait until Mary Sarah left.

Mary Sarah was not showing any signs of movement, however. She was dug in like an Alabama tick, lounging on her chaise and lazily flicking through *Vogue* while commenting on the physical attributes of the men at the pool. Since it was Friday morning, there weren't many of these, but that didn't slow her down any.

"Hot diggity *dawg*, would you look at *those* swim trunks? Mmmm."

"Mary Sarah," I said, affecting a scandalized air. "That is a very young college person."

"I know, right? *Love* the view."

A server materialized. "Hi, Dr. Porcher, Dr. Colley, Dr. Anson. Can I get you ladies a beverage?"

"Oooh, yes. It's hot as balls out here. I'll have a sweet tea. Thanks, babe."

"Nonsweet tea," said Emma.

"Just ice water." I hated putting extras on Emma's tab, on top of the guest fee for the pool.

The morning sputtered along. After Mary Sarah had downed what seemed like five thousand sweet teas, each of which was the equivalent of drinking a pound of sugar laced with caffeine, she finally needed to use the bathroom. Evidently she had the metabolism of a newborn and a bladder the size of Canada. Emma and I watched as she somehow bounced away in her four-inch cork mules and then turned to each other.

"Quick," I hissed. "Fill me in. Did he get the job?"

Chapter Five

DRINK UP, HONEY

Emma, Present Day

I looked Zadie in the eye as I answered, "He did."

"Does he know you're in the group?"

"I don't honestly know," I said. This was true. "I assume he would've checked out our website at some point, and even though my last name has changed, he'd recognize my photo and bio. So surely he knows?" I shifted around in my chair. "He interviewed while I was out."

"So . . . so . . . where is he now? Do you know anything about him?" A band of worry lines crinkled Zadie's forehead.

"I got his CV. He's board certified in liver and gallbladder surgery, and he's been out west somewhere. Denver, I think. Sounds like he still does a lot of research; he had a lot of publications. He listed his interests as golfing, snowboarding, and running, but there was no mention of anything personal. I asked our manager why he's leaving, and she said—"

"Dr. Anson! Hiiii!"

Oh no. Not good. The mother of one of Zadie's patients stood in front of us. I knew her too, from the club. The kid appeared likable enough—for a kid—but I'd mentally diagnosed the mother as a hypochondriac veering toward full-on Munchausen by proxy, a psychiatric disorder in which people induce illness in their children because they enjoy the attention. Plus, I detest close talkers.

"Hi, Tillie," said Zadie, with baffling warmth.

"Hi," I said, striving for a pleasant but uninviting tone. "Zadie and I were just—"

Oblivious, Hypochondriac Mom interrupted me again. "What good luck to run into you, Dr. Anson! I was about to call," she said, plopping uninvited onto my chair, forcing me to shift over so that one buttock was dangling midair. I stared at her back. Was I invisible? "I hate to bother you"—clearly a lie—"but I've been noticing some potential issues with Newton's pulse ox, and—"

She prattled on. I sighed. This failed to gain attention, so I raised my eyebrows and cleared my throat, which neither woman noticed. Finally I broke in. "Oh," I said to Hypochondriac, gesturing across the pool to a clump of people standing near the bar. "Isn't that Dr. Porcher over there? Is she your pediatrician?"

Hypochondriac cut off midword and leapt up. The difficult moms tended to love Mary Sarah, whose effusive personality made everyone feel validated. "Great!" she shouted over her shoulder as she galloped off. "Thanks!"

"Two birds with one stone," I said, relieved. "I'll buy Mary Sarah a drink later."

"I think you'll have to buy her a whole pitcher." Zadie giggled, watching a little herd of men in golf shirts who'd been chatting with Mary Sarah disperse in all directions as soon as Hypochondriac descended on them.

We could faintly hear Mary Sarah's voice carry across the pool: "Well, *heyyy* there, sugar! What's wrong?"

"I don't understand," I said. "How do you tolerate those people?"

"Em, please," Zadie said. "Why is he leaving Denver? When does this become official?"

Unease percolated in my chest. Two million people live in the Charlotte metro area, but I would never be able to avoid Nick, even if he weren't joining my particular group. And actually, Zadie wouldn't either. There were lots of hospital functions and medical society events where doctors of various specialties ran into one another. Not to mention the social scene: if you had a house in one of the neighborhoods near the hospital, and your kids went to one of the schools nearby, and you or your spouse volunteered in the same philanthropic circles as everyone else (did Nick have a wife?), and you joined one of the main country clubs in town, then you were a de facto member of a group that knew everything about you. Could I dare hope that he'd be a confirmed bachelor who didn't mind commuting in from Lake Norman?

"Hey." Zadie snapped her fingers in front of my eyes. "Why is he coming here?"

"Nobody really said why he was leaving his current practice," I answered quickly. "Jack Inman"—this was one of my partners, the medical chair of the executive committee that managed my practice—"spoke with some of his current partners and didn't pick up on any glaring red flags. 'Technically gifted, innovative, strong presence in the American College of Surgeons'—that kind of thing. I asked him if anybody mentioned what he was *like* and Jack asked if I was looking to step out on Wyatt. You know what a pervert Jack is. Anyway, it's a done deal. They got him credentialed already. I found out today he's already here."

A rare moment of silence gripped Zadie.

"Well," she said, finally recovering, "I guess we will deal with this. But nothing gets said to Drew, okay?"

"He doesn't know?" I said with some surprise.

Despite her discomfort, her irrepressible good humor returned. She flashed me a mock-guilty grin. "I know this sounds weird," she said, "but we never really dissected our pasts with each other. Childhood, and families, and college angst—all that, yes. But the one time I tried to pry information out of him about old girlfriends, he got so embarrassed I had to terminate the conversation out of mercy." She stopped, apparently transfixed by a mental image of her blushing, grimacing husband. I pictured him too. Drew Anson was one of those guys who will always appear boyish; even when he's gray-haired and creaky, he'll probably look like he's fourteen.

"Zadie?" My turn to wave a hand in front of her face after a minute went by without the conversation resuming. She was staring at the horizon with the intent but sightless expression of a wax figure, her mouth hanging slightly ajar.

She blinked and said, "Oh, yeah."

Before I could steer us in a different direction, she relaunched the conversation right where we were. "And Drew doesn't want to hear a word about my, uh, romantic past with other guys, either. We never really had the 'how many people have you slept with' conversation. I tried one time, but he actually put his hands over his ears. Drew isn't the kind of guy who wants to delve into my every inner thought. He's, uh, fine with a little mystery here and there."

"Oh, that's like Wyatt too. Silent and mysterious," I said.

"It *is*?"

"I'm joking!" I always had to explain to people when I was joking, unfortunately. Even Zadie sometimes. "Of course not. He put me through a two-hour interrogation about my sexual past on our first date."

"What? He did? And it took you two hours to talk about it?" Zadie shrieked. I knew what she meant. One mysterious and wonderful thing about Wyatt: he never failed to behave exactly the opposite of what one might find appropriate, yet somehow he always got away with it. "How did you never tell me this before?"

"Well, you know Wy. At first I was shocked, but he was so straightforward, like this was normal, and also he conveyed such interest in me that after a few minutes of it, I actually felt charmed. He wasn't a bit judgmental, not that I was confessing any bizarre fetishes or anything— I was always shy with guys—but he asked me *everything.*"

Zadie mulled this over. "Did you tell him about . . . our third year of med school?"

"Yes. I did."

"All of it?"

"Yes, everything." Almost true. Wyatt knew more than Zadie did about what had happened that year. "On our first date."

It still astonished me, three years after marrying Wyatt, that he'd conjured up such a sense of ease in our relationship that I was capable of confiding in him. I was a fiercely private person. Before I met Wyatt, Zadie was my only close friend, and I loved her with a devotion born of shared history. Ours was a friendship forged when we were young, the kind that endures no matter what because losing it would be like losing an aspect of your own personality: your sense of humor or your ability to empathize. You wouldn't be the same person without your friend as your external hard drive. I know, because for quite a while I thought I would lose her.

But even so, there were things I'd never been able to articulate to Zadie. We didn't talk about certain topics, much the same way we didn't mention Nick: even now, more than a decade later, it was too threatening. I fixed my gaze on the far side of the pool and began silently counting chairs, trying to erase the memories crowding into my consciousness.

Zadie was clearly about to query further when I noticed some sort of commotion over by the bar. Two men were standing there, one hugging the other from behind, which was odd; the man in front began waving his hands around frantically. The hugger was shouting, but I couldn't quite make out the words. Behind the bar, a couple of servers were also gesticulating wildly, and there was an accumulating crowd of people. Were they fighting?

I craned my neck. As I did, Zadie jumped up, and in one fluid motion she was on her feet and running hard, yelling over her shoulder for me to follow her. As I rose, I saw the man who was getting hugged slump forward. Two women, one of them Mary Sarah, rushed forward and eased him to the ground.

Zadie was on her knees. The man on the ground was unconscious, his face a florid blue. I elbowed my way through the throng of horrified people and joined them.

Instantly, I assessed the situation: he was choking. I looked up at the bartender. "Get me a sharp knife, right away, and some napkins and straws. Also a couple forks." I looked back at Zadie. "Do you remember how to cric somebody? I need you to hold pressure if there's a lot of bleeding. Okay?"

"Okay," Zadie said, her eyes wide, but then she flashed me a resolute look. I was accustomed to cutting holes in people's tracheas—in this case, in the cricothyroid membrane of the trachea—but it wasn't a procedure that occurred in a cardiology office. It had been at least a dozen years since Zadie had seen this done, but in med school she'd been a competent assistant surgeon. I'd been surprised and then—almost—jealous when the class rankings for our surgery rotation had come out: I'd been ranked first, of course—no one was going to get a higher score than I was in my favorite subject—but when I realized Zadie was ranked second, I'd had to control an unattractive feeling of dismay.

I looked down at the unconscious man and realized I knew him. It was Buzzy Cooper, the owner of a local commercial real estate firm and the father of Sumner, who Zadie had informed me was Delaney's bitee. This needed to go well; imagine Caroline Cooper's wrath if Zadie was involved in both the repeated biting of her daughter and the grotesque mauling of her husband as he choked to death.

Buzzy was bluer by the second and twitching slightly, his face a dusky parody of itself. I nodded briskly when the bar server arrived with a tray of the items I'd requested, along with a bottle of gin and an entirely superfluous thermometer. Zadie upended the alcohol over Buzzy's outstretched neck and swiped it dry as I used the knife to cut a small bundle of the straws in half. I then palpated the thyroid and cricoid cartilage rings, which wasn't easy, given the blubber that ringed Buzzy's corpulent form, and made an unhesitating incision between them, cutting through the skin. Blood oozed out from some peripheral vessel, obscuring my view. Using the blunt end of the forks, I positioned them as makeshift retractors to hold the edges of the incision open, handing them to Zadie, while I used my finger to dissect down through the subcutaneous tissue. Meanwhile, there was no sign of any respiratory effort at all from Buzzy; were we too late? No, he was bleeding, and his heart was still pumping. We still had time. After making a horizontal incision through the cricothyroid membrane, I thrust my finger into the incision, widening it and holding it open. With my other hand, I positioned a few of the cut straws into the opening between the tracheal cartilage and blew gently into them.

There was an agonizing moment of nothing. Then I blew again, then waited . . . and waited . . . and then, with a lurch, Buzzy's chest rose a little and sank. There was an odd whistling sound from the straws as air moved through them. The color in Buzzy's hypoxic face improved slightly.

Now I became aware of the people around us; dozens of spectators were clustered in a vibrating hive, watching the impromptu surgery with wide eyes and still faces. A cry went up from the crowd when they realized Buzzy was alive.

Two EMTs appeared, toting a backboard. One was a smallish Asian man, the other a borderline obese white female, both of them moving swiftly. The crowd parted for them, and they knelt beside Buzzy, taking in the scene.

"Dr. Colley?" said the female, hitching at her pants. "I didn't recognize you!"

"Hey, Jen. I dress better at work," I said as casually as I could, despite having stabbed a man in the throat in front of half the club. While wearing a bikini, no less. "This here"—I motioned at the makeshift tube—"is not stable. Can you give me the smallest ET tube you've got, and something to use as a guide wire? And a suture, if you've got any. Meanwhile, let's get some blow-by oxygen going toward these . . . straws."

"Will do, Dr. C," said the man, turning and sprinting toward something behind them, while the chubby woman started fiddling with an oxygen mask.

Hurriedly, I managed to get a legitimate endotracheal tube in place, although it was not the correct size and was meant to be inserted through the mouth, so it looked completely wrong. I tried not to let this bother me; it did look better than a handful of straws. I threw a quick suture to stabilize the tube so we wouldn't lose the precarious airway on the way to the hospital.

The sun was beating down on us from directly overhead, and the pavement was scorching hot. A frozen margarita appeared, as if by magic, in my hand as I boarded the ambulance; I looked at it stupidly. "Drink up, honey," said Mary Sarah. "I think you need that."

Chapter Six

VERBAL EVISCERATION

Late Summer, 1999: Louisville, Kentucky
Zadie

An hour or so after Silver died, the TICU doors swung open and the rest of the team charged in for rounds. Dr. Hollister, the attending, looked remote and scary; Dr. Kalena looked remote and cool; Clancy wore a supercilious smirk; Ethan, the other med student on my team, looked tired; and Dr. X, who seemed restored to his usual hard-charging character, looked smoking hot, at least in my opinion. He noticed me and grinned, all traces of his earlier grimness gone. "Sadie. You ready to give us the lowdown on our unit players?"

"I think so," I replied, grabbing my list, now inexplicably covered in a dense array of hieroglyphics. Could this be my own handwriting?

"Excellent. Fire away."

I took a deep breath and looked around. Silver's mother had arrived, ashen and out of breath, ten minutes after the last beat of his heart.

A curtain pulled around his bed shielded them from view, but the sound of her weeping and the softer murmur of the hospital chaplain filtered out, blending with the babble from the people assembled for morning rounds. Bystanders had morphed from a few nurses into a crowd of about thirty people—surgeons, the other trauma teams, respiratory techs, physical therapists, social workers—who now all turned like a wheeling flock of birds, focused on me.

The chair of the Department of Surgery, Dr. Spencer Markham, cleared his throat. Trying to ignore everyone's stares, and the terrifying lidless gaze of Dr. Markham in particular, I stood in front of Bed 1. I glanced at the patient; he was perfectly still except for the forced rise and fall of his chest. My audience rustled.

"This is hospital day twenty for Mirror Trauma," I reported. "He's the nineteen-year-old unbelted driver of a high-speed MVA, resulting in splenic laceration, open left femur fracture, closed shear injury of the brain, and multiple skin lacerations and abrasions. He is day twenty status post exploratory laparotomy for splenectomy, day twenty for left femur rodding by the orthopedic service, and is being followed by neurosurgery for his head injury. Vital signs—"

"Stop there, please, and tell us what procedure of this patient's care you have forgotten."

I froze. Dr. Markham was legendary for the verbal evisceration he performed on anyone who did not straight-up know their shit. He fixed me in an unblinking reptilian stare. Phantom ice water surged up around my scalp as the weight of dozens of other eyeballs bored into me too. *What procedure is he talking about? I named all the procedures! Didn't I?*

"Let's try this another way. Please recount the injuries again."

Dr. Markham did nothing to disguise his disdain of yet another flailing student. Most of the audience kept their faces unrevealing, but I could discern an expression here and there: empathy mingled with fear (Ethan), pity (Emma), and undiluted schadenfreude (Clancy).

"Um. There was the splenic laceration, the femur fracture, and the closed head injury."

"And?"

There was a long-entrenched belief among the surgery residents: you never admitted that you didn't know. Even with Dr. Markham. Any answer, even a moronic one, was better than confirming that you were clueless. This position had filtered down to the medical students, resulting in many a ridiculous answer during various conferences and grand rounds. But try as I could, I could think of no other injury, and I couldn't just make one up. I'd singlehandedly brought trauma rounds to a screeching halt.

Salvation came from an unexpected source. "I'm afraid this is entirely my fault, sir," my benefactor said. "May I answer the question?"

———

Well, well, well. It seemed that someone should have instructed me that sutures needed to be removed somewhere between six and twelve days, depending on the body part in which they were located. Suture removal was definitely a third-year-student kind of job, so I was grateful that Dr. X had fallen on his sword for me during rounds.

I had no idea how Dr. Markham had been able to discern that the patient's sutures were still intact beneath his molting and scabbed exterior, but once Dr. X volunteered he'd forgotten them too, Dr. Markham lost interest. Mirror Trauma would likely have slightly more pronounced scarring from all his scattered lacerations than he would've had if we'd remembered to remove the sutures promptly, but everyone recognized that this was the least of his issues, and we'd moved on to the next battered guy. After rounds, I sought out Dr. X and said simply, "Thank you."

"Hey, it really was my fault," he answered, pleased that I'd acknowledged his protection. "I sometimes forget that you guys don't know your ass from your elbow in here."

"I'm stellar at ass recognition, actually," I said, which earned me a laugh from Dr. X and his counterpart, Dr. Ken Linker, the chief resident of Team B. They were conferring about issues likely to arise regarding the new patient admissions. The chiefs liked to touch base at a few points during the day, knowing that the afternoon sign-out to one another could be disrupted at any time by the thumping of the hospital's trauma copters.

"Keep it quiet in here, X-man," Ken said finally, and gave Dr. X a quick bro handshake. Ken's team included Emma, who regarded being on the trauma service the way a normal person might feel about spending a month at a luxury resort. Emma could be a little weird.

"Okay, guys." Dr. X clapped his hands and surveyed the rapidly wilting remains of Team A. "Another day dawns bright for us to rage against the motherfucking Grim Reaper. Let's go save lives and stamp out disease. Or . . . let's at least get breakfast. Bring your lists and we'll divvy this shit up."

The five of us—Dr. X, Dr. Kalena, Dr. Clancy, Ethan, and me—adjourned to the bustling cafeteria. Graced with floor-to-ceiling windows, the enormous room brightened my mood a little. If I couldn't be in nature, at least I could see nature. Well, at least I could see a parking lot ringed by a few trees.

We grabbed coffee and sat down in a corner to run the list. This produced a depressing amount of stuff to be done. I inhaled caffeine.

Dr. X assigned me the easiest but most repugnant of these tasks. As soon as we left the cafeteria, I met Emma, who had also been given a checklist for her team's patients. I considered telling her about the possible flirtation with Dr. X; unlike some of my friends, Emma had a filter and could be sworn to secrecy. But everyone knows evil genies will curse you if you actually state your most embarrassing hopes out loud. I decided to keep this one to myself.

Emma stood against the nurses' station, her long flaxen hair piled into a loose bun. She wore scrubs, but a hint of gray camisole and her bony clavicle peeked out at the top. The intensity of trauma surgery suited Emma, although she tended to be baffled by the patients themselves since so many of them had been injured because of their insistence on stupid behavior. "So this guy"—she motioned to one of the TICU beds behind us—"you remember what he did? He put a lit firecracker in his mouth."

"Remind me why?"

Emma riffled through the chart. "His friend said he was imitating Bugs Bunny."

Across the room, one of the respiratory techs—a red-faced, portly guy in his late twenties—leered in our direction. I frowned at him, and he blew me an exaggerated kiss. I made my frown meaner, but it didn't work: he pantomimed a dagger to the heart and cartwheeled dramatically out of sight behind the nurses' desk. I grinned in spite of myself.

"Well, I guess I'd better go drain some pus out of this guy's face," Emma announced with inappropriate relish.

"Right." I steeled myself. "I guess I gotta remove some scabbed-up sutures."

———

By afternoon, I was struggling through chin-deep murky water. I had gotten up at four o'clock in the morning—yesterday, not today—and had maybe an hour or two of sleep in the thirty-six hours since I'd been at the hospital. I began to sink into helpless micro-sleeps whenever I stopped moving. The rest of the team seemed more functional than I thought they should be, especially considering they'd been doing this every third day for years.

Dr. X was reviewing discharge instructions. "Return to the hospital for fever, bloody urine, severe pain, blah, blah, all the usual things; give him a scrip for some Vicodin for a couple days, tell him no sex for six weeks, and have him come back to the clinic in a week."

"Um, I can't actually write prescriptions," I reminded him.

"I'll cosign it. Do you know how to write it?"

I nodded. "Yes. Mostly. Well, sort of." I hesitated. "Okay, not really."

"Right, Zadie, I'll show you, then."

I had a quick little flush of pleasure that he'd noticed my actual name.

"Here we go." X handed me a prescription pad. Behind him, I noticed our coffeepot had a giant hole scorched in it. A resultant flood of foul coffee oozed across the counter and down to the cabinets below. So much for recaffeinating.

Clancy blearily raised his head. "Does anyone know when Hollister is showing up?"

With controlled emotion, Dr. Kalena said, "He's in a BMI 45 horrendoplasty over at Norton Hospital. His case got bumped, so he's just starting."

The rest of the team responded with uncontrolled emotion, namely dejection. Dr. Hollister was a general surgeon who agreed to act as trauma attending for a brief stint each year, but his primary concern involved patients at another hospital. Depending on what kind of case he was beginning, it could be hours before he arrived, and therefore, hours before we could leave. Tentatively I asked, "What's a BMI 45 horrendoplasty?"

Allison regarded me kindly. "He's starting a very long case on a very large patient," she said.

Miserable groaning from Clancy, on the couch. Mentally, I joined in, wondering if I could physically make it another couple hours.

"Okay, I'm going to page Ken and get the B Team over here for sign-outs so we can get that out of the way," Dr. X decided. "Then everybody can hit the deck until Hollister shows."

We met up with Team B as instructed and we filled them in on our new patients, in case intervention was needed during the night. Suddenly, I was incapable of speech. Knowing I had to return to the hospital in less than seven hours, I staggered over to the couch, wedging in between Clancy and Ethan. My vision blurred.

Someone shook me gently. I blinked and noticed Dr. X's face looming next to mine, wearing an indulgent smile. "Wake up, ray of sunshine," he said. "He's here." I looked at my watch.

It was nine p.m.

———

Limping out to the parking lot an hour later, I began to question my sanity. I drove a piece-of-crap Dodge Colt that might or might not survive the night, let alone another two years until I began to earn any money at all, and here I was, leaving the hospital at ten o'clock after a marathon forty-two hours since I'd last been home. And I had to return before five a.m. How had I become such a masochist?

Like many teaching institutions, Christ the Redeemer Hospital and the affiliated medical school campus were not located in a posh section of town. I was unnerved to hear clomping footsteps behind me in the creepy garage. The only illumination came from a dying streetlight located on the corner of the structure; the cars and pillars inside cast long shadows from its feeble tangerine glow. I glanced over my shoulder and made out a hulking shape moving toward me. I stifled a shriek. What ghastly irony it would be to survive an attack in the parking garage and wind up as a patient on the trauma service. An abhorrent visual image came to mind of my naked body on full display in the trauma room while a faux-somber Clancy topped off the assault with a chest tube. I was about to break into a panicked run when an arm reached out and gripped my shoulder.

I turned, and was barely able to make out the name on the white coat behind me: DR. XENOKOSTAS.

It was Dr. X.

Chapter Seven

EVERYONE THOUGHT
HE WAS DANCING

Late Summer, 1999: Louisville, Kentucky

"Are you okay?" asked Dr. X. Solicitously, he placed a hand on my shoulder, sending a thrill from the tip of my clavicle directly to that mysterious part of the abdomen that clenches up with sexual tension. The last little surge of energy I possessed eclipsed me. How could another person's touch do that to you?

"I'm fine," I said with fake perkiness, "aside from you scaring me witless. You're lucky I didn't scream and bash you on the head." I considered this. "Then you'd be the trauma patient."

Dr. X smiled. "You don't strike me as the murderous type, Zadie."

I started to protest, but was derailed by fatigue. "That's true," I acknowledged, slumping. "I'm actually kind of a pacifist."

Dr. X's grin widened. "Fortunately for me," he said.

I made my wavery way to my car. Dr. X opened the car door for me, but then appeared to reconsider. "You look like you're about to topple into a face-plant," he observed politely. "Can I drive you home?"

"Absolutely not," I said, waving my otoscope around for emphasis. "I'm great. I'll see you . . . in a few hours."

"Be careful, Zadie," he said, and closed the car door.

———

I was watching Graham watch Emma.

He sat in a booth at the Rooster. Kicked back, beer in hand, a languid half smile lighting his face, his sleepy doe eyes locked on her, he seemed oblivious to the escalating stupidity around him. In turn, Emma was equally oblivious to the smoldering gaze of her on-again, off-again boyfriend; she stared straight ahead at the spectacle of our other friends as Landley magnanimously distributed a round of 107-proof Old Forester.

Despite our near-constant exhaustion, my friends and I had survived the first weeks of our third year intact. Clearly, this required a depraved celebration. We'd packed ourselves into a decrepit Toyota Camry, referred to as the Caminator, and we'd tried to avoid the elderly bits of food festooning the floorboards. It was highly probable that the Caminator had never, even once, been cleaned by its owner, a shaggy-haired beast in our class called Rolfe. It reminded me of an archaeological dig: over here, one of Rolfe's term papers from college, era early 1990s; over there, registration items from the first year of medical school, circa 1996; near the top, a proximal layer of sediment containing pilfered items from the hospital.

We'd caromed down Bardstown Road, windows open to the night air, leaving in the Caminator's wake the carbonaceous odor of burned rubber and the sound of receding shrieking. We passed bar after bar after bar. Louisville was up there in terms of alcohol-serving establishments per capita, maybe even top five among US cities, with plenty of stylish places to choose from. Rolfe, however, had veered off toward a humbler destination: the Rooston Bar and Grille.

This was our fallback zone. "Unpretentious" would be a kind depiction of the Rooster, and if you were less charitable, it could be described as vile. Low-ceilinged and dim, the interior existed in everyone's mind as an amorphous hazy blob; whether because of its general nonnoteworthiness or because of the mind-erasing aspects of its beverages, or both, no one could really ever describe it later. You just retained an impression of dingy squalor.

In contrast, we were a good-looking lot. This wasn't lost on my loopy friend Georgia, who complained, "What the hell, Rolfe? The Rooster? Look at my clothes!" She bounced on her heels with a vigor usually reserved for meth addicts. Georgia was afflicted—or blessed—by a manic personality topped off with a bunch of oddball quirks, such as an insistence on dressing like a seventies-style pimp. Tonight she wore a vintage shirt with wide, frilly lapels in a screaming shade of orange, which fought with her shiny high-waisted purple pants.

"Take some off," offered the ever-lecherous Landley, setting Georgia's bourbon in front of her. He attempted a bra snap.

"Hands off me, bastard. I am too hot for you."

"How'm I going to pick up any chicks from this dump?" groused Landley, sweat dripping from his handsome blond head. "There's never anybody here except you asshats."

"Please. The last time you hit on a girl she looked like she would've slapped an infant to get away from you."

"Dude, no. You guys ruined it when you offered me a hundred bucks to fake a seizure, and—"

"That was bullshit. Everyone thought you were still dancing," interjected Rolfe, unbuttoning the top two buttons of his dress shirt and rolling up his sleeves.

"—and that was when she ran out. My moves were excelle—"

Landley shuddered to a dead stop, closing his eyes and flinging his hands in the air as if praising Jesus. At first I worried his brain had been entirely replaced by a sloshing fishbowl of bourbon, but then I realized the ancient jukebox was playing "Funkytown."

"Shut up!" screamed Georgia. She threw down her drink and began an exaggerated hip-grinding dirty dance toward Landley. Rolfe hooted approval and jumped in. He actually did have moves; he was a graceful but masculine guy, with dark eyes, black wavy hair, and a nicely squared jaw. He and Georgia made an attractive pair, with her fiery red locks bright against his shoulder. Our other friend Hannah joined them, her decorous sway providing some balance against the lurid debacle of whatever Landley was doing with his pelvis as he danced. I tried not to laugh.

Next to me, Emma put a hand in front of her eyes. "This is appalling."

"Close your eyes and think of England," I suggested. "It will all be over soon."

Graham leaned across the table toward Emma. "Dance with me," he said. I thought Emma would say no. But she extended her hand, and he took it, then folded her against his chest, his bearish build dwarfing even Emma's height.

"Well, I'm . . . sitting alone," I said to no one. But no matter. It was so good to be out of the hospital, to be having some drinks, to be dancing and flirting and carrying on like normal twenty-four-year-olds. Thank God for my friends. Thank God for this night off. Thank God, no one here had a Foley catheter or a ventricular drain or a subclavian line with which to contend. It was so nice to see people who were intact.

On the ersatz dance floor, both the song and the partners shifted. Landley and Georgia dangled their arms in a surprisingly coordinated side-by-side version of the Robot; Rolfe pulled Emma away from Graham into a low dip; Hannah retreated to the bathroom.

My booth creaked as Graham clunked back into it. He'd removed his blue flannel shirt and tied it around his waist, and his light brown hair was ruffled up on the sides, where he'd apparently run his hands through it. He twisted to keep Emma in view, finally turning to me as my body was hijacked by a massive yawn. "I might have to go," I said, embarrassed. "I'm turning into a social dud."

"You're the exact opposite of a dud, Zadie. I'm the boring one here."

"Graham," I said, offended on his behalf. "You might be shy, but you are not boring."

He smiled. "I am kind of boring, Zadie. I live ninety percent of my life in my own head."

I was intrigued. "What's going on in there?"

He shrugged, an easy, self-effacing grin transforming his face. "Are you up for a drunken existential conversation? Alcohol gives me log-orrhea."

"Absolutely," I said. "I like drunken existential conversations. It reminds me of college with Emma."

"Yes," he said, animation lighting his eyes. "That's the extraordinary thing about Emma. It's like she knows what I'm thinking before I say anything. And she does that by paying careful attention. Most people judge everything they see through a filter of how it affects them; they add their own bias and desire so that their perception of what's real is changed before they've even fully processed things. She doesn't do that. She notices things."

"Yep, she does," I agreed, as Landley and Rolfe crowded back into the booth. "And so do you, Graham." I felt a flush of vicarious pleasure for Emma, that she had someone who saw past her ice-queen facade, but I was also curious: Emma hadn't told me they were back together.

The door to the Rooston opened with unusual timidity, like it was having second thoughts already about this course of action, revealing a herd of fresh-faced girls: undergrads from the nearby University of Louisville. Despite the proximity to campus, attractive undergrads never wandered in here, apparently repelled by some subliminal warning signal. The girls blinked, caught in that moment where one realizes that this was the wrong sort of place, but as no graceful way out presented itself, they headed bravely to the bar.

"Sweet mother of God," breathed Landley. "What is this?"

"They must be lost."

Rolfe nodded sagely. "Follow me," he said.

Landley was already on the move. He lumbered over, materializing by the girls, his large damp head crooked hopefully toward them. He gestured, speaking quickly, making them laugh. Maybe the moves had some validity after all. Rolfe was helplessly drawn in, unable to resist even long enough to seem cool.

"Would you look at these fools?" grumbled Georgia.

"Hannah Banana!" I said. "How's it going on the hoo-ha service? Did you deliver any babies yet?"

"Oh my gosh! I love it! My first call night I delivered three, and it was as miraculous as everyone says," Hannah burbled, her big hazel eyes alight. We all loved Hannah. She never lowered herself to the level of the rest of humanity by saying derogatory things about others, unless the person in question was a full-on troll. Even then, she sounded about as menacing as a toddler armed with a wet noodle.

"Are you serious?" Georgia howled. "All we've done on pediatrics so far is listen to recordings of heart murmurs."

Graham, who had been assigned to the internal medicine service in the adjacent veterans hospital, weighed in. "The med students do everything at the VA," he said. "All the blood draws and EKGs. Whether we have any idea how to do them or not."

"So, it's one procedure after another all day?" Georgia asked.

"Well, no," Graham admitted. "I spend a lot of time in the smoking room with the old guys."

Emma looked alarmed. "You don't smoke," she said.

"I know," Graham said. He smiled at her: an easy, happy smile. "But I like listening to them tell their stories about the old days. They're great guys. Some of them were on the beach at Omaha, or they fought in the Mekong Delta. They know stuff we can't imagine."

"Well," Georgia said. "I'm bored. The good thing is that I can definitively rule out peds as a career. I need more action. Speaking of which, let's leave the Casanovas over there and head out. We can take the Cam."

We glanced at the guys. They seemed to be making progress; they had moved from the bar to an inexplicable grouping of club chairs clumped in a curvilinear arrangement facing the bathroom doors. The chairs had once been chenille-covered but now were so thread-worn and grubby that patches of stuffing had emerged, resembling scattered mold spores. This did not deter the guys at all. They were clearly misrepresenting themselves as clean-cut, functional doctors, judging by the rapt, admiring expressions on the undergrads' faces.

"That's going to end badly," I pointed out. "Let's go."

After we purloined the Cam's keys, there was a brief skirmish over who was most fit to drive. (Hands down, this was Emma, who rarely drank alcohol.) En route to a more glamorous locale, I found myself daydreaming about Dr. X. Since our interaction in the garage last week, I had watched him eagerly at the hospital, memorizing every curve and plane of his beautiful face, every intonation of his words, but we had not once been alone together and he did not seek me out. Still, when he looked at me, I could discern an extra layer of meaning in his glances; his face didn't convey the same interest when he spoke to Ethan, the other med student on our service.

It would have been splendid to be able to drop a little conversational bomb with the girls: *Did I mention that my chief asked me out?* They'd blow my eardrums out with their excitement. But it would have been foolish to bring it up now, after some generic flirtation. The entire hospital, down to the last comatose patient, would know every detail in about thirty seconds if I told my friends, and then thirty seconds after that, it would get back to him and he'd think I was a delusional blabbermouth.

———

"Good morning, ladies," intoned a male voice. Graham. He sounded unusually . . . upbeat. Graham was the stoic variety of guy, big and quiet, although sometimes he'd pipe up with a zinger that would leave the rest of us howling. His father was rumored to have a business empire worth gazillions from the manufacturing of some widget, but Graham dressed like a homeless guy and didn't display any overt signs of wealth, so it was hard to say whether this was accurate. I glanced up at him from my location on the living room carpet, where I was curled up against Georgia.

"Hope everybody slept well," Graham said.

"Why are you so chirpy, Graham?" Georgia groaned. "It's the crack of dawn!"

"It's eleven o'clock, George. I'm starving. I couldn't wait any longer to wake you guys."

"To make us breakfast?" Georgia mumbled hopefully, having fully returned to a prone position with her face smashed back into the hideous shag carpet.

"Uh, no," Graham said. "Let's go to Twig and Leaf."

"Graham, you don't even have a couch. How are you living like this?" I queried, looking around the desolate space.

"Oh, this isn't my place. It's Mack Wolfson's, but he already left. C'mon, princess," he said, nudging Georgia with his toe. She looked like she might bite him, so he hastily shifted to Hannah. "If we can find it, the Caminator is rolling out in five." He strolled out.

"What the . . . ? Has anybody ever seen Graham so peppy?"

Hannah abruptly leapt to her feet, startling everyone. "Wait, Graham!" she called. "Where's Emma?"

With a trace of envy, I noted the glow in Graham's voice as he answered.

"She's with me."

———

Twig and Leaf was, predictably, packed with bleary-eyed students. While waiting for a table, I sidled over to Emma and gave her a discreet but enthusiastic nudge. "What's going on with you and Graham?" I whispered. "I thought you said it was over?"

"Can't hear you," Emma shouted. "What's over?"

Graham looked at us. "Um," I said. Vivid morning sun streamed in through the restaurant's big windows, animating everyone's features and lighting up Graham's ugly, migraine-inducing striped shirt. He smiled at me.

After an eternity, a booth finally opened up and we dive-bombed in, not bothering to wait for it to be cleaned.

"Oh, Zadie," said Graham, draping an arm around me. "I heard something interesting about you and your chief resident yesterday."

"What?" I said, excited.

"He was talking to somebody in the cafeteria. I think the term he used was 'cerebral jailbait.'"

I beamed, and then bit my lip. "Wait. Is that good?"

Graham grinned at me. "I think it means he—"

I was beginning to inflate with wild, inappropriate hope when Graham was interrupted. Over the years, Georgia had earned the nickname "Princess Spills-a-Lot" by virtue of her perpetual clumsiness, and true to form, she managed to knock over a mug of somebody's used coffee before Graham could finish his sentence. A cascade of dark liquid went airborne and dumped itself onto my chest. I looked down. I was wearing a pale pink shirt made of fine cotton, which was now translucent and plastered to my breasts.

"Aw, HELL no!" hollered Georgia, aghast. "Dude! I'm sorry."

A table of raucous undergrad frat guys facing us pointed out the obvious. "Wet T-shirt!" chortled one dolt in delight. Whistling erupted.

I sat frozen. I had on a very thin bra that provided no cover in this spectacle, and since it was summer, no one had a jacket to offer me. I folded my arms across my chest. Across from me, Graham blinked. He fluttered his head violently like a dog shaking off water (Breasts! So mesmerizing!) and stood. The next thing I knew, he had pulled off his own shirt and draped it across me. "Thanks," I whispered, meeting his warm eyes. "Maybe I'll duck into the bathroom."

Graham nodded. "I don't need that shirt back," he offered.

Georgia agreed. "Please don't give it back to him," she said. "It's straight-up Flock of Seagulls."

"Georgia, you're wearing an orange tuxedo shirt," Graham pointed out.

Ignoring the banter, I slid out, creating a rustling rearrangement in the booth. Georgia followed me, disregarding the belated arrival of a waitress with some towels. We waded through the catcalling undergrads, not looking back at the table where Hannah was patting Graham on his magnificent bare chest and Emma was staring ahead, an empty look on her pretty face.

Chapter Eight

THE MENTAL FORTRESS

Emma, Present Day

Zadie followed Buzzy's ambulance so I'd have a way to get home after we turned him over to the surgical team at the hospital. She waited outside, apparently deterred by the thought of entering the ER in her bathing suit cover-up, a worry that also occurred to me. But I had no choice: Buzzy's makeshift airway was too precarious to leave in the otherwise very capable hands of the EMTs. He regained consciousness in the ambulance as his oxygenation improved, so I made the call to sedate him. God knew what he must have thought, awakening to a searing pain in his throat as I hovered over him, half-naked and bloody.

When we pulled up to the ambulance entrance, I hesitated: Mary Sarah had given me my cover-up, but it was sheer and hot pink, and I was still barefoot. Could I dare hope that no one would recognize me out of context?

Everyone recognized me. I jogged alongside the gurney as the EMTs hustled us into the ER, collecting a crowd of fascinated onlookers as we went. The ER expected us, of course, and they knew the basics, but EMTs don't give any identifying information when they call in over the radio. Therefore, no one was expecting to see me, one of their busiest trauma surgeons, arriving in a bikini with one of the city's most prominent citizens who'd just had his throat ripped open with a steak knife.

It takes a lot to break the concentration of ER doctors. But my attire seemed to be doing just that. Everyone's mouths fell open as they caught sight of me.

"Where's the trauma team?" I asked the ER attending, who was sponging Betadine over Buzzy's throat in a belated attempt to sterilize the area before replacing the tube with something more stable.

"Trauma's not taking him," she replied, ripping open a cric kit.

"They're not? Who is?"

"He is," she said, motioning to a guy who had just entered the room, his back to us as he donned a sterile gown.

"Who's that?"

"Well, we had quite the discussion about which service should wind up with this patient," she said. She nodded to a nurse, who began injecting medication into Buzzy's IV. "There was some disagreement over what kind of patient he is: Trauma? ENT? Internal medicine? We paged trauma, but they refused, on the grounds that an emergency surgical procedure doesn't constitute a trauma." She eyed the hole in Buzzy's throat. "Perhaps arguable, in this case. Then we tried internal medicine, but they declined because everyone always wants them to admit everything, and they're sick of it, yada, yada. ENT agreed to do the scope— they should be here in a sec—but they refuse to admit because specialty services always refuse to admit. So general surgery's gonna wind up with him in the SICU."

"Oh," I said, starting to add an apology on behalf of my trauma colleagues, when the guy in the yellow gown turned around.

"Have you met Dr. Xenokostas?" asked the ER doc. "He's new. Hepatobiliary surgeon, but he's taking general call today. Nick, this is Emma Colley, one of our trauma guys."

Nick and I stared at each other with identical expressions of shock.

I mumbled something lame about not being dressed for the occasion and bolted from the ER before Nick could say anything, my heart hammering a furious staccato beat. Zadie must've attributed my silence to distress about the emergency procedure, because she yammered on and on about my coolness under pressure during the ride home, thankfully sparing me from having to talk. Even though it was barely afternoon, I went to bed as soon as I got home, closing the blackout curtains in my room and pulling the covers over my head.

I loathed Nick. Not only because of what he had done to Zadie, but because he was an incarnate reminder of all my worst failings. It was one thing to know on an intellectual level that I'd have to see Nick again, and another to encounter him when I wasn't expecting it. I tossed, wide-eyed, to a silent slideshow of hazy, jumbled memories and pushy flashbacks, tormenting me every time I closed my eyes: me, holding a man's large, still, cold hand and feeling the weight of immeasurable shame descend upon me.

———

In the year 49 BC, Julius Caesar commanded his army to march across the shallow green waters of the Rubicon River in the north of Italy, committing himself to a treacherous course of action from which there would be no return. Caesar himself recognized the irrevocability of his decision, uttering the famous phrase *"alea iacta est"*—the die is cast—and in the process, he gifted the future with the well-known idiom "crossing the Rubicon." We've all heard it, even if we don't know its origin. I certainly didn't when I was twenty-four. Nonetheless, that is exactly what I did. One day, I made a fateful decision that cast my life neatly into two halves: Before and After. Unlike most people's Rubicons, my own personal point of no return was not subtle, or gradual, or something I didn't recognize until it was too late. It was an obvious demarcation, a clean line in the sand. I knew what I was doing when I stepped over it.

What I didn't know, and didn't see until it was too late, will haunt me forever. It has taken me an immense amount of mental discipline to get to the point where I can function without allowing these memories to surface. I've had to build a mental fortress, a no-fly zone where none of it can get in.

And now my wall was crumbling.

———

Everything seemed slightly better by Monday, as I fixed yet another cup of the world's most popular drug. This was already my second cup of coffee today, but that was fine. There was some good information about the health benefits of caffeine—decent research about decreases in the incidence of Parkinson's and some forms of cancer and heart disease, and even things like headache reduction. So having multiple doses in a day was okay. But I knew from experience that any more than four cups and my hands might shake. Too much adenosine antagonism.

My God. I was boring even inside my own head. When alighting on a particular subject, other people's minds did not fill with a torrent of evidence-based analysis of risks and benefits. Even if they were trying to avoid thinking of something else. Actually . . . what did other people think about?

"Wyatt?" I asked. "If I say the word 'coffee,' what comes to mind?"

Wyatt looked up. He had arisen unusually early and was searching for something in the kitchen junk drawer, probably his keys, which he refused to keep in a designated location. "Sex," he answered promptly. He flashed his gleaming symmetrical teeth at me and resumed his mauling of the tidy junk drawer.

"What? Why sex?" I asked. I knew his keys were not going to be in the junk drawer, but I restrained myself from going over to reorganize. Now I'd face having to choose between being late to the hospital or leaving the junk drawer in a state of violated disruption, both of which would cause me some anxiety.

"That's the male default mode," he answered, triumphantly holding aloft a small rectangle of purple plastic. "Looky here, muffin! I found that Zip drive you needed. It was in the junk drawer."

I sighed. "That's where I keep the old ones," I said. "Have you looked for the keys in the pants you were wearing yesterday?"

Wyatt tapped his forehead. "Brilliant!" he shouted, as if that wasn't where he always left his keys. As soon as he left the kitchen, I whirled around and quickly lined up the contents of the junk drawer in their bamboo divider. Whew.

I acknowledged to myself that my behavior was even more type A than usual. This was probably secondary to stress and poor sleep over the weekend. But you have to endure.

Usually, I responded to adversity by manning up: I stayed calm, I calculated the most advantageous response to a situation, and I carried it out with maximum efficiency. The only flaws in the system occurred when I was faced with the emotional vagaries and unpredictable behavior of other humans. People who respond irrationally throw me off. But in this case, things were further complicated by unusual circumstances.

This time, the irrational person was me.

Chapter Nine

TRAUMA SEASON

Late Summer, 1999: Louisville, Kentucky
Zadie

After the tantalizing burst of weekend bliss, I was back on call on Tuesday and again on Friday, trying to avoid staring at Dr. X every time we rounded together. It had only been a few days since breakfast at Twig and Leaf, but it seemed like a hundred years.

On the A Team, we established a rhythm. Ethan, the other student on the service, met me every morning at five o'clock to preround, give or take half an hour. Summer was trauma season, so this tended to be on the earlier side. Ethan was an ideal trauma partner; he didn't care about getting procedures, he had a keen wit once you got to know him, and he was blazingly honest. We covered for each other, each of us double-checking the other's work. In addition, Ethan showed up every morning with a delicious homemade vanilla cappuccino for me, and I'd given up on trying to get him to stop.

Clancy and Dr. Kalena and Dr. X met us at six o'clock to get an update on overnight events, although it seemed that most of the time Dr. X knew everything anyway. (Did he live here? Did he have spies?) Then we rounded again, for the third time, with Dr. Hollister, the attending surgeon, followed by formal trauma rounds in the TICU with Dr. Markham, the department chair.

On this particular morning, our OR day began with a laparoscopy—a surgery done via long slender instruments inserted through small incisions—on one of the patients who was suspected of having some complications related to his initial surgery. He'd had a steady and stubborn decline despite all indications that he should have been thriving, and Dr. X, who suspected Clancy of possibly having nicked the bowel during the first case, had scheduled a quick look with the scope. As Clancy finished writing orders, Dr. X got the ball rolling by prepping the patient, allowing me to make the initial laparoscopic incisions.

"Nice," he said, as I carefully incised through the skin near the patient's navel. "You have good hands. I've noticed that you're good at keeping your cool," he continued. "You're fun to have around this month."

"People don't usually accuse me of being calm," I answered honestly, although I was pleased. I *had* been doing a good job so far on trauma; the rhythms and technicalities of the procedures made an innate sense to me.

Dr. X's eyes crinkled behind his mask. "Maybe 'cool' was the wrong word," he acknowledged. "You do strike me as fairly . . . vivid. But it's good to have a med student so fired up about trauma."

The usual bright lights of the OR had been dimmed way down so we could all see the TV monitor, which featured a vast yellow sea bounded by pinkish blobby walls. The patient's abdomen had been insufflated with carbon dioxide, blowing it up like a balloon, which, from the outside, gave him the appearance of a late-stage pregnancy. The inside of the abdominal cavity had a bright, weird illumination from the fiber-optic light source. Dr. X demonstrated to me how to manipulate the instruments and pivot the camera so I could see. Clancy, holding his freshly scrubbed hands out in front of him, bumped open the OR doors with his ass and marched up to the circulating nurse for her to gown and glove him.

As things progressed, visualization of the intestine should have been good. Clancy, assuming control, repeatedly drove the camera in exactly the opposite direction as he intended. Consequently, all we had on the monitor screen was a super-close-up view of something that looked like half-squashed yellow grapes, which turned out to be a bunch of globular fat.

"Doh!" X said. "Clancy, get us out of this fucking fat forest. You're going left when you mean to go right and up when you mean to go down. Your instincts here are bass-ackward."

"Erpmpth," said Clancy helplessly, as the camera pivoted wildly and crashed into a glistening maroon structure.

"Attaboy," X said encouragingly. "You still completely suck, but that sucks a little less. Maybe."

On to the next case: a colostomy takedown and bowel reanastomosis for a perennial trauma patient named Clarence Higginbottom. Clarence, who had been shot on no fewer than five separate occasions, actually listed his profession as "street pharmacist" on hospital paperwork.

I was fascinated by Clarence's intestines. Seeing a disemboweled person up close was unnerving. The color, for one thing, was a bright, shiny pink, and the intestines were constantly in motion throughout the case, like a great snake hell-bent on escape. It was gross, but I found myself more mesmerized than repulsed. I was also acutely aware of Dr. X's presence across the OR table from me, his eyes intent windows into his thoughts, isolated from the rest of his face by his mask. We were doing the case together, just the two of us operating, alongside the scrub nurse, the circulator, and the nurse anesthetist. Clancy had been dispatched to handle some urgent pages emanating from the unit. It was a busy day in the OR, with trauma season kicked into high gear by the last gasp of miserable summer heat. We were on call today, so the circulator kept busy answering pages.

Dr. X showed me how to do the anastomosis. "Here," he offered. "You can take a couple of the sutures. No, use bigger bites. Yes, there. Angle the needle driver a little more. If Clarence develops an anastomotic leak, he will be your private patient for the rest of the year. I don't care what service you're on. I will hunt you down whenever he shows up to trauma clinic."

"I thought he was going to jail."

"Oh, the prison van has worn a groove in the road going back and forth to the clinic. It knows exactly how to find us. They all come to trauma clinic; it's a fun outing for them. There you go; that looks nice." His eyes scrunched up; he must have been smiling under his mask. He looked directly at me, then put his hand on mine, guiding my final suture with the needle driver. I could feel the warmth of his hand even through all our gloves (we were both double-gloved, on the theory that Clarence must have been a hepatitis factory by this point), and I felt a thrill. He left his hand on mine, kept his eyes on mine; we stared at each other and I knew, suddenly, that he wanted me too.

———

My pager was going off. I fumbled in the darkness to silence it, but it would not shut up. It dinged out its stupid little melody, which somehow transformed in my mind to an annoying ditty: *Someonespagingme, someonespagingme. Oh, someonespagingme.* Why would it not stop? Dimly, I realized that it was Ethan's pager, and thank the Lord, he had finally risen out of his coma to answer it. I could hear him murmuring obediently into the phone from his Spartan cot next to mine. I waited for my pager to start blaring too, while Ethan lumbered away, shutting the door behind him with a gentle nudge. Maybe I was safe for a while. My pager was strangely silent; I might as well catch another few winks while I could . . .

A hand covered my mouth, and I struggled up in terror. "Ethan!" I tried to scream, but I could only manage a garbled "Eeef."

"Shhh, it's okay. Don't yell," a whispered voice instructed, and the hand on my mouth moved away to my hair.

"Who—"

"It's me," Dr. X said quietly. "I'm so sorry I scared you."

"Oh, but Ethan—" I whispered.

"I took care of Ethan. He's going to be tied up for a long time. Zadie, I hope I'm not reading you wrong. Is it okay if I'm here?"

"Oh," I said. "Yes."

I had a fleeting—well, very fleeting—moment of remorse that Ethan's one pathetic hour of sleep had been stolen by his own chief for purposes so completely selfish, but then Dr. X kissed me, hyperextending my neck by pulling my hair, his other hand pinning my wrists back against the wall. I had never been so turned on in my life. The adrenaline surge from my fright and my sanity-stealing exhaustion were now fueling a monstrous lust. It was pitch-black in the room, and dead silent, and I barely recognized his whispered voice. I entertained the unpleasant idea that this could be someone else, anybody at all, even, but discarded it. Nobody else had the power to summon Ethan away without repercussion.

The proper thing to do here would have been to scream and slap him sideways, but I did not. Instead I wrenched a hand free and felt his face, realizing how much I had been longing to touch him. Not being able to see him intensified my other perceptions: surely, nothing had ever felt as good as this. I felt myself spinning in giant slow circles; my lips and fingers and toes were tingling. It was like falling in slow motion from a skyscraper: air whooshing past me, but gently, softly, currents of warm, sweet oxygen, somehow still roaring past my ears. There was this terrible urgency, too. Any second now our pagers could go off, Ethan could return, or we could make enough noise to rouse Allison Kalena or Clancy in their adjacent rooms. I grasped Dr. X's back, feeling the broad muscles that I'd memorized in anatomy class brought to spectacular life under my fingers. I raked my hands through his hair, something I'd wanted to do since I'd first seen him, and closed my eyes against the darkness.

———

When he turned on the light, I was motionless, sprawled on the bed, rendered docile. My hair and skin were both the color of honey in the yellow glow of the little bedside lamp, my lips just parted. I was still breathing quickly. He looked at me for a moment, his expression unreadable, and then bent and kissed my forehead.

"I wish you weren't so lovely," he said, and walked out.

Chapter Ten

THE CAPRICIOUS WHIM
OF THE TRAUMA GODS

Emma, Present Day

Another Monday on call, another day without Wyatt or Henry or sunshine. Even after years of this routine, I still enjoyed the adrenaline blast of a new case; it was missing my family and missing the outdoors I minded. It was scorching hot outside, but the hospital remained stubbornly climateless, with the same unnatural fluorescent light and the alien sensation of twenty-four-hour time, an endless clock rotating and rotating without the sweet opiate of sleep to break it up. I imagined a giant heart hidden in the mysterious center of the sprawling building, pumping away metronomically, a slave to exigency, with thousands of humans flowing through the corridors and staircases and ORs and ERs like little red blood cells circling through arteries and veins and organs. The same dramas and emergencies and life-altering catastrophes kept happening to new patients, and the same players inside kept working tirelessly to save them or patch them or at least figure out what in tarnation could be wrong with them.

I clipped my pager to my scrubs and headed for the doctors' lounge, hoping to scrounge a bit of food before I was summoned back to the OR. It was shaping up to be the kind of day where you get thumped from beginning to end; in other words, a fairly normal day on trauma call.

I'd thought there might have been a break after we finished our last case, but just as my team of residents and medical students was sitting down to a very delayed lunch of prepackaged sushi, our pagers went off. These days we carried cell phones in addition to pagers; they'd been converted to summoning devices, thus producing the stimulus-response effect of everyone lurching in dismay at the sound of our ringtones. Mine was standard-issue Apple Marimba, which was foolish because everyone else over the age of thirty had that ringtone too, resulting in all of us reaching for our hips in synchronization whenever anyone else's phone went off.

By contrast, all the younger doctors and medical students had overly personalized ringtones, so now a cacophony of disparate music blasted through the room, ranging from some narcissistic Kanye West song to that ominous Darth Vader riff. A glance at my screen revealed this one was a gunshot wound.

"Who's up for the pin?" I asked the team.

We kept a giant map of Charlotte fixed to the wall at the rear of the lounge, back by the dictation booths. Whenever anyone got shot, we stuck a red-topped pin in the map at the location of the shooting, assuming the victim was coherent enough to confirm the spot. If not, we had to rely on EMTs, or, occasionally, news reports. Since this map had been in place more than fifteen years, some areas of the city were so overrun with red pins that they looked like they were hemorrhaging, appropriately enough.

"I've got it, Dr. Colley," said Sanjay Patil, the fourth-year resident.

He was one of my favorites, because he was so self-possessed and polite. Many of the male surgery residents made me uneasy with their aggressive joking and their incessant urges to control everything. But Sanjay always kept it professional. I bestowed a small smile on him as we hustled down to the ER.

This code turned out to be a nonstarter. The patient was DOA, and by the time we got down there, the ER attending had already called it. A quick glance at the patient's body and it was evident why: he was riddled with entry and exit wounds from at least a dozen bullets, one of which had exploded his head and another of which had cratered his chest. Staring at the chest wound, I repressed a shudder of recognition. I hated GSWs to the chest.

My reaction aside, this was an unusual amount of violence for Charlotte. "What in the world?" I said to the ER attending. "Somebody wasn't concerned about overkill."

"He's MS-13," she answered, gesturing to one of his arms, which was so inked up it looked reptilian. I nodded, recognizing one of the tats: this boy belonged to Mara Salvatrucha, a notorious gang that had metastasized across the country to Charlotte from Los Angeles. MS-13 members weren't known for subtlety when it came to their hits. If they wanted you dead, going down in a haze of gun smoke was probably the best end you could hope for.

"Well," I said to no one in particular, realizing the futility of expressing concern for the multifaceted tragedy in front of me. "Maybe now we can grab something to—"

My pager went off, along with everyone else's pager. "Incoming," said the ER gal. Her round blue eyes blinked as she contemplated the bloody mess in front of her. She motioned to some techs. "Let's clear this guy out, since we're all already in here. Can we get the floor mopped real quick?"

"Dr. Colley," said Sanjay, my resident. He cast his eyes down at his pager. "It's a kid."

I nodded. I disliked pediatric trauma patients, especially the really young ones. Their little bodies were such a shock to behold after legions of high-mileage adults: smooth, unblemished skin; round little tummies; tiny pristine lungs and livers, as yet unmarred by lumpy adipose tissue and self-inflicted decay and the ravages of disease. They looked incredibly helpless on the OR table, with their lush eyelashes taped against fat cheeks, their small arms splayed out in surrender on IV boards.

They healed well, though. Their cells, accustomed to the vigorous demands of new people, went into ferocious overdrive when injured. A child could survive injuries that would send the average adult spiraling down in flames. Of course the stakes were higher when a child was hurt, but I could handle that kind of pressure. And the technical challenge of operating on miniature organs secretly pleased me; I liked demonstrating my competence in a difficult case.

It was dealing with the parents I didn't like.

All relatives of trauma victims were difficult, but none more so than the parents of a child. They wailed or stared sightlessly or collapsed in dramatic heaps. In any case, they never absorbed anything I said to them, which had led to multiple misunderstandings in the past. I understood why, of course. Some grief blots out the world.

But I was ill-equipped to deal with other people's incapacitating heartache. It wasn't that I'm too emotionally cool to relate to their pain; it was that I relate so much I choke. How can I, a stranger, presume to comfort anyone in their position? I become so awkward, so frozen, so unable to reach out, other than offering a dry, mechanical recitation of what was wrong and what I'd try to do to fix it. Everything I could possibly say to a devastated parent seems too inadequate, or sometimes, too blatantly false. I can't bring myself to tell them the only thing they want to hear.

The EMTs arrived, toting a gurney with a very small person strapped to it. I jumped aside to let the residents do their thing as the EMTs gave their report: *bike versus car, abdominal injuries*. This child, who looked to be three or four, was conscious and whimpering, managing a single half-strangled word ("Mommy!") before we drugged her.

Everyone performed their roles efficiently and tersely, all the usual intensity of a trauma code amplified into something almost superhuman. The ER people inserted a breathing tube, the residents obtained central IV lines and started fluid, and my intern ran the portable ultrasound probe over the child's distended little belly. No one spoke an extra word as we headed to the OR. I instructed Sanjay to call ahead to prepare them for an ex lap—an exploratory laparotomy—a surgery in which we'd open the little girl's abdomen to assess her internal injuries and try to fix them. I ran upstairs.

Steeling myself, I trotted down the empty corridor toward the family room, resolving to give the little girl's parents as encouraging a word as I could while the OR was being readied. Unusually, the parents had gotten here at the same time as the ambulance and had been moved upstairs, closer to the ORs.

To my dismay, I realized as soon as I entered the room that I knew them. Or not knew them, really, but recognized them: they were Betsy and Boyd Packard, one of Charlotte's most prominent couples. He was the scion of one of the banking overlords—his father had founded an investment bank that had merged with another behemoth financial institution, which he now ran. Betsy oversaw their philanthropic foundation and chaired all the important auxiliaries and charity boards in town. They belonged to our club, where I'd often seen Boyd ringed by a crew of powerful cronies, smoking cigars and throwing back scotches like a 1950s cliché returned to relevance. I hadn't known they had a daughter, although I did know they had a son—he was friends with Zadie's boys, and I remembered Zadie and Betsy were friends. Or maybe they shared a carpool. If their kids had any heart problems, Zadie was probably their doctor too. Unlike me, she has no problem commiserating with parents—she throws her arms open and people leap into them, unhesitating. It was impossible these days to get Zadie as your pediatric cardiologist—her schedule was clogged with Packards and the children of NASCAR drivers and other local luminaries. Somehow she'd become the specialist to the stars.

I told myself I was not intimidated. Reeling under the colossal weight of their fear, the Packards were ashen and gaspy. No amount of money can insulate you from the capricious whims of the trauma gods: they fling their lightning bolts at the rich and poor alike. You could bring trauma upon yourself, certainly, but you couldn't always protect yourself from it, a fact that was currently hammering Boyd Packard like an anvil to the head. He staggered toward me.

"Where did you train?" he demanded as soon as I'd introduced myself and explained the injuries I thought their daughter had suffered.

"I—I did my residency here," I said, wincing internally at the icy note that crept uninvited into my voice. "And I did a fellowship in trauma surgery at Vanderbilt."

"Vanderbilt, okay," said Boyd, as if he had the first clue which surgery programs were any good.

His wife, Betsy, placed a restraining hand on his arm. She turned to me, focusing her clear gray eyes on mine, her beauty stunning. She had jet-black hair and a sculpted, full-lipped face of such perfect symmetry it was hard to look away from her. She reminded me of Snow White.

"Will she be okay?" she asked, her voice distorted.

"I'll do my best," I said stiffly. "It depends on what we find. I need to go—they'll have the OR ready any second. I'll send one of the circulating nurses out with an update as soon as possible."

"Wait." Betsy Packard transferred her hand from her husband's arm to mine, causing me to involuntarily recoil. Her hand, white and smooth, capped with flawless pale nails, felt like an icicle. "Ten seconds," she said. "Please."

She dug around in her handbag, an autumn-hued buttery Birkin, and extracted a cell phone. She punched a button and thrust the phone into my hand. I accepted it automatically, realizing as I did that she had turned on a video.

The bass of a rap song, rendered tinny by the iPhone's speakers, filled the room. "Betsy, for Chrissake," said Boyd, but she turned her great gray eyes on him, and the power of her pain shut him up. I returned my attention to the screen, where a little girl was dancing. She had her mother's wispy black hair and perfect face, miniaturized and placed on an adorable toddler body. She wore a leotard and a look of fierce, utterly unself-conscious concentration as she wiggled her little booty in time to the music. "Eleanor," said a woman's musical voice, and the little girl startled and then burst into a peal of giggles as enchanting as a fairy chorus. The camera zoomed in on her face, capturing a look of such infectious joy it could have made the most hardened criminal melt. Despite the circumstances, I felt my face relax.

"See," said Betsy. She closed her eyes, swaying a little. She opened her mouth to speak again, but all that came out was a low, anguished rasp.

I took her hands in mine, and her eyes opened. For once I felt no hesitation at all about touching someone else. "I'll do everything," I said. "I understand. I do. She's the loveliest thing I've ever seen. I promise you, I will do everything as if she were mine. I promise."

"Thank you," Betsy Packard whispered. "Thank you."

Chapter Eleven

GAS, ASS, OR GRASS

Zadie, Present Day

Monday, ostensibly my day off work, always seemed to be occupied with catching up on work at my practice. I'd just spent the last four hours on electronic charting—none of which was reimbursable time—trying to avoid excommunication from the hospital. I sighed as I finished the last one.

Nina, my nanny, would be taking Rowan to acting class at our city's vibrant downtown library this afternoon, so I had to collect Delaney from her before I hit the grocery store and fetched the boys. Panting as I raced to the parking lot, I calculated I'd make it in time if I hit every light perfectly and didn't get stuck behind any plodding Southern drivers.

The traffic gods were smiling; I made it to the store and then to Nina's and school with time to spare. There was a strict no-cell-phones policy for the carpool lanes of the Oak Academy, and this included texting, but I really could not see the harm in sneaking out a little message to Emma while idling in place. I threw this tiny guilt on top of the guilt that came from idling in a large SUV spewing Freon and hydrocarbons into the air next to a playground where my asthma-prone boys were currently rolling around in a heap of other boys. They looked like a wriggling mass of puppies. Six-year-old arms and legs were flying everywhere.

Yo! I typed. Are you at the hospital? How's Buzzy?

No reply. Evidently Emma prioritized saving someone's life over communication with her best friend. I *harrumph*ed to myself.

Thinking of Emma led to thinking of Nick, despite my resolve to banish the memories of the calamitous black whirlwind that had accompanied Nick's presence in my life. Until Emma's announcement, he hadn't crossed my mind in a while, although I'd be lying if I said I'd never Googled him. Of course I had. But it had been a long time, back in the days when Facebook was competing with Myspace for fledgling social media dominance. I knew next to nothing about Nick now. I glanced ahead of me; still no movement in the line of cars. I clicked the Facebook icon on my phone.

I was relatively certain that Nick wouldn't be on it, and I was right; typing in his name produced no results. Well, he wasn't the sort of guy who would tolerate a daily blast of other people's dinner photos or endless memes featuring sarcastic kittens. But you have to start somewhere. Almost absentmindedly, I closed Facebook and opened Twitter.

I was surprised. Nick had a Twitter account.

I opened his page. Even on the small screen of my phone, the photo was recognizably of him. He was skiing, or possibly snowboarding—some outdoor winter sport, in any case. Goggles were pushed up against his forehead, partly obscuring his hair, and behind him, the powdery white of some snowcapped mountain was just visible. He must have been laughing at whoever had taken the photo; his head was thrown back, exposing the bright, even row of his teeth, and his eyes were crinkled up, an unfamiliar but attractive row of laugh wrinkles at their outer corners. I stared at his face.

Finally I wrenched my eyes from his photo to read his tweets. He wasn't exactly prolific. In the last two years, he'd posted ten tweets, all of them related to a game between the Denver Broncos and Baltimore Ravens. Even the self-description underneath his picture gave nothing away, since all it said was Billionaire Philanthropist.

Right.

I closed Twitter and opened the browser on my phone. Even though the only other occupant of the car was illiterate and strapped into a re-straining car seat, I hunched over furtively as I typed Nick's name into the Google search bar. Immediately, I was rewarded with a flood of entries, most of them stupid health-care-rating sites offering every troll on the planet free rein to bash his doctor. All my colleagues loathed these sites, since privacy laws prevent physicians from responding, no matter how slanderous and untrue the comments. I scrolled past a page or two of these things, finally arriving at Nick's legitimate Internet entries. The first couple were research-related: papers he'd authored, conferences at which he'd presented. Then I came to the website for his last practice.

From Emma's comments at the pool the other day, as well as his Bronco-obsessed tweets, I was reasonably sure he'd been living in Den-ver. His medical practice there, a big surgery group, had not yet removed him from their website. I clicked on his name, near the bottom of the alphabetized list.

Quickly—any second now the carpool line would begin moving—I scanned the academic stuff. Medical school, Johns Hopkins; general sur-gery residency; fellowship in hepatobiliary surgery; Alpha Omega Alpha Medical Honor Society; Fellow, American College of Surgeons, on and on. There was no mention of a wife or a family. Where was the good stuff?

Finally, there it was: a paragraph at the bottom of Nick's CV.

In addition to his surgical practice, Dr. Xenokostas is an ardent skier, golfer, and macramé artist. (Wait. What? Macramé artist? Although— that last one did sound like Nick, not because he actually was a macramé artist, but because it was the kind of bullshit he'd slip into his CV to check for signs of consciousness in the HR department.) Ignoring a contrary little *zing* in my chest, I read on.

He also enjoys hiking with Zadie, his beloved black Lab.

Whaaat?

With a jolt, I realized that the massive SUV in front of me had already pulled ahead and was picking up cute ponytailed kindergartners. The mother in the massive SUV behind me politely refrained from honking, but she was drumming her long fingernails on the steering wheel. I thrust the car into drive and lurched forward.

Now I could see Eli and Finn. They were standing with their friends along the wall of the building adjacent to the curb, all twitching violently as if they'd been Tasered. One of the teachers had probably told them to stop running around, which forced them to emit pent-up energy by flailing in place. How these teachers managed to instill order in a group of six-year-old boys was a mystery on par with the creation of the universe. I hit the unlock button on the driver's-side-door control panel, and a teacher beckoned Eli, Finn, and the two other boys in their afternoon carpool forward. They charged like bulls.

"Hey, der's my brothers," Delaney hollered. "Hello! Hello, big kids!"

The boys were tangled in a logjam at the SUV's door. "Hustle up, buttercups!" I called.

"Hurry up, pigs!" added Delaney, who had not quite mastered the art of the idiom.

Finn's teacher, Mrs. Rhodes, trotted over to assist. The carpool line was a finely tuned machine, which managed to deposit scores of meandering kindergartners into their vehicles in less than eight minutes, in order to allow room for the next grade's mothers to begin rolling in. We were holding up progress.

"There you go," said Mrs. Rhodes, patting Finn on the shoulder as he climbed in. She gave me an odd look, the kind you'd reserve for an enthusiastic nose picker. "Hmm. Have a nice afternoon," she said dryly.

Well, really. It had been only about thirty seconds since the car door had opened. That wasn't that ba—

"Hey, Mom!" Eli said brightly. "Turn it more up!"

My arm reached out automatically to adjust the volume and then recoiled as I realized what was blaring on the car's speakers:

"—gotta roll, gotta bounce,
but first she say let's burn an ounce—"

Now Eli was singing along enthusiastically.

Herbal Life's "Bitch Ain't Sharing." That explained the acerbic look from Mrs. Rhodes. My car and my iPhone had some mysterious relationship where the Bluetooth was always activating random inappropriate stoner music without my consent. I hastily punched the button to forward to the next song.

"—Yeah, 4 big blunts 4 my J-town playaz—"

Mother of God. This was even worse. Where was all my normal music? Actually . . . this was a hilarious bluegrass version of Down with the Man's "Sippin' Sizzurp"—aside from the profane, misogynistic lyrics, of course—but still. I turned off the stereo.

"Hey!" said Eli. "I liked that song."

"Hey, Lainie!" said Finn, patting her benevolently as he climbed in. Although the boys considered their older sister, Rowan, to be a mortal enemy, they were fond of Delaney and frequently allowed her to tag after them. As a result, she had acquired some less-than-desirable characteristics, including a disturbing preoccupation with the NFL and an extensive bathroom vocabulary. She greeted her brothers by making some arm-fart noises. This was received with enthusiasm. The other two boys, Will Grainger and Will Packard, appeared impressed. Who knew that very small girls could be so cool?

Trying not to think about the fact that Nick had apparently named his dog after me—his dog!—I turned into the Eastover section of the city. If anything, it was even posher than Myers Park, with enormous green lawns rolling uphill toward the stately homes. Charlotte was somewhat unusual in that some of its nicest neighborhoods bordered downtown, which was handy for the hordes of converging bankers every morning, but it also meant that these enclaves were in close proximity to some of the city's less affluent areas.

As if to reinforce this line of thought, a pimped-out Honda turned onto the street ahead of us. Someone had gone to the expense of modifying its tailpipe, which was now enormous and bright silver and quite noisy; it made a tremendously loud *rern-rern* sound every time the driver hit the gas pedal. As if this weren't classy enough, there was also a bumper sticker reading GAS, ASS, OR GRASS: NOBODY RIDES FOR FREE. Well, those were some poor options, really, if you were in desperate need of a lift. Suppose you didn't have any money or weed on you?

I wrenched my mind back to more pertinent issues. I tended to miss the driveway to Will Packard's house and then would have to pull into the wrong mansion's driveway to turn around. Ah, there it was. Will's father or grandfather or someone had done something financially important, like founding a bank or a major hedge fund. This meant that Will's family was one of the wealthiest in Charlotte. Wealthy, as in private planes, vacation houses in Sea Island and Vail, and their own charitable foundation. Will himself gave absolutely no clue to his family's prominence. He was a shaggy-haired, freckled kid, wearing the same currently fashionable getup as all the other little boys, namely, a hoodie emblazoned with the name of a sports manufacturer and tall, garish neon socks. There was some discernible irony in all these private-school kids desperately trying to look like sports figures, but I couldn't quite articulate it. Maybe I could flag down GAS, ASS OR GRASS and ask him what the fascination was with those stupid hoodies.

The Packards' driveway wound between an iron-and-brick gate mighty enough to front a castle and then meandered up a hill in large, graceful arcs. I eased the car to a stop at the bottom of the driveway, narrowly avoiding a child's bicycle lying half on the pavement and half on the grass. I stopped the car. The back wheel was bent nearly in two, doubling back on itself like a folded tortilla, a training wheel dangling by a thread. Apparently being rich did not insulate you from the maddening inability of children to put away their expensive possessions.

Finn, in a rare moment of lucid observation, was more charitable than me. "Gosh, I hope nobody was riding that bike when the dad ran over it," he said. Finn had lost plenty of his own toys by leaving them inexplicably positioned underneath the back wheels of Drew's car, so he spoke from experience.

My phone buzzed as I tried to navigate around the abandoned bicycle. Text! I stopped again and peered down. It was from Will P's mom, Betsy: Can you drop Will off at Ryder's house?

Blast. I was short on time, because I still had to drop the other Will off (he lived in a normal rich-person house down the street from us), get the kids to tennis lessons at Emma's club, get Rowan from Nina, get home, unload grocery bags, supervise homework, make dinner, clean up, get everyone bathed, brushed, and pajamaed, read to Delaney and the boys, and get everyone into bed. Driving an extra fifteen minutes to Ryder's house threw a wrench into the entire system. Still, I could not bring myself to attempt to explain all this to Betsy Packard via text.

Sure, I typed. Before I could hit send, she called me.

"Zadie," she said, "is Will in the car?"

"I got him!" I said brightly. There had been an embarrassing flail last year when I'd left him behind at the Oak Academy, but I thought we'd moved past that.

Betsy made a rusty, half-sobbing noise. "Is your phone on speaker?"

I blinked and switched off the Bluetooth. "Not anymore," I said. "Are you okay?"

I had to strain to hear her. "No," she said. "No, no. No— I." She stopped and tried again. "Eleanor," she said.

"Betsy," I said, staring at the small shredded bicycle on the grass beside the monstrous bulk of my SUV. "What happened to Eleanor?"

Chapter Twelve

WHAMMIFIED

Zadie, Present Day

"I ran into her," said Betsy. Her voice was alien, awful: a corroded gate croaking out human language.

"Oh, Betsy," I said, a hot flood of tears immediately escaping my eyes and nose in an undignified gush. I put my head on the steering wheel to hide my face from the children. Eleanor was three, and a bubbly, pink-cheeked sprite who'd been at our house just last week. She and Delaney had commandeered the space under the dining room table, industriously filling it with rocks, dirt, and the uprooted remains of all my basil plants. "Please tell me she's going to be okay."

"I didn't know she was outside." After every few words, she sucked in her breath with a sickening audible creak. "The surgeon—Dr. Colley; do you know Dr. Colley?—says they don't think she has a head injury, but she's in the OR for, uh, abdominal injuries." She caught her breath again. "They don't know how bad it is yet."

"Listen, Betsy," I said. "I know Emma Colley—you couldn't have a better surgeon. I'll take Will to Ryder's house right now." I glanced in the rearview mirror at the blissfully oblivious occupants of the backseat, roiling like an octopus convention as they crowed and guffawed and invaded one another's personal space.

"Sometimes, at night, I actually used to think about them getting hurt in a car wreck," Betsy said, and then she gave in to the urge to cry—helpless, frightened sobbing that rang in my ears. My chest heaved in commiseration. *There but for the grace of God* . . . Betsy had just run smack up against one of those fallacious universal parenting beliefs: the idea that if you envision some terrible thing happening to your child, then it would not, in fact, actually happen. We make these implicit bargains with fate all the time, lulling ourselves into a false comfort, thinking we can ward off the worst just by acknowledging that it exists. A close corollary to this belief is the notion that if something ghastly happens to the child of someone you know, then your child is somehow mysteriously protected from that same thing.

But my job exposed me far too often to the truth; unspeakable fears do lunge out of our imaginations into reality, and it doesn't matter who has gone down before you. Childhood cancers happen. Abuse from trusted adults happens.

And trauma happens.

———

Five o'clock p.m. Absolute worst hour of the day. Still reeling from the news of Eleanor Packard's accident, I checked my phone for the thousandth time, hoping for an update. Nothing.

The children, post-school, post-tennis, were tired and cranky and had just expended the last of their brainpower on homework. I could not bring myself to tell them about Eleanor. Delaney, who'd been carted around in the car seat all afternoon, had finally fallen asleep just before we pulled into the driveway and had undergone a terrible transformation from her normal perky self to wordless screeching demon. One side of her face shone bright red from where she'd been lying on it, and she howled to be held. I had made the horrific mistake of waking her before bringing in all the grocery stuff, so I was forced to carry her to and from the car multiple times as I brought in all the bags.

Now, attempting to cook dinner, I staggered around the kitchen with the wailing Delaney clamped to my leg, while everyone pleaded for junk food. With the tip of my outstretched left pinkie finger, I managed to hit the home screen button on my phone in case Emma had tried to reach me. I'd been dying to tell her about Nick's dog's name, but now all I wanted to do was hear about Eleanor's prognosis.

No missed texts.

"Rowan!" I snapped. "Get over here and assist me with your sister."

"I can't, Mom," said Rowan coolly. "I have to text Isabelle." Rowan seemed to be developing into the sort of girl whose presence caused other girls to go into paroxysms of insecurity. She was confident and cheeky, with a finely wrought face dominated by huge sea glass eyes and a great swathe of inky hair.

"You most certainly do not have to text Isabelle. What you have to do is get your sister off my leg. Now."

"I'm sorry, but this is urgent."

"It is not urgent. What is urgent is responding to your mother before she flies off the handle," I yelled.

The whimpering coming from my ankle suddenly stopped. I looked down. Delaney was staring at me, mouth wide open. "Mom," she said, awestruck. "You can fly?"

There was a pause, and then Rowan and I both started to laugh. I turned off my induction cooktop and leaned over to pick up Delaney, who smiled faintly, unsure of what she'd done to break the tension but pleased that she had gained undivided attention.

"Lainie," I said. I stroked her corn silk curls and breathed in her baby fragrance, guiltily availing myself of the comfort of her perfect, unbroken body. "I can't fly. I meant that I was getting mad. I'm going to finish this cooking and Sissy will read to you for a few minutes, and then we can cuddle on the couch."

"Mom!" Rowan fumed. "I do not have time to read baby books! Why can't the boys do it? In my opinion—"

"Your opinion is immaterial," I interrupted. "Only my opinion matters here."

"Well, *that's* offensive."

"Rowan, do it."

Rowan grumbled, but she moved over to the comfortable couch in the sitting area off the kitchen and grabbed a book—our much-loved copy of *Bink and Gollie*—off the bookshelf. Delaney followed her and climbed up into Rowan's lap, settling with her head resting sleepily on her big sister's shoulder. Rowan tucked an arm around her and began to read.

The evening slogged along. No call from Emma, no call from Betsy. These sun-filled late-summer days tended to go forever, making it especially hard to convince the children that it was bedtime. They fought the good fight, complaining loudly of thirst, hunger, feeling unloved and lonely, hearing strange noises, and my personal favorite, suffering from "itchy teeth." In response, I had begun barking, "Stall! Stall! Stall!" every time a small head poked out of its room, which made me sound like a plane going down. It was effective, though: it so annoyed the children that eventually they surrendered. I was a noodle by this point: droopy limbs, half-mast eyes, and garbled thoughts swirling around in my tired head. But the quiet peace of the house was way too precious to waste on sleep. I poured myself a glass of wine and ran a bath. I put in a few drops of rosemary-infused massage oil, which turned the water into warm liquid silk while giving the bathroom a seductive clean smell. I caught a glimpse of myself in the mirror. My hair, which has a tendency to go haywire by the end of the day, sprang out from my head in uncontrolled coils so that I resembled a demented lion. I gathered it up into a hasty topknot.

After sinking into the water, I closed my eyes and exhaled into a luxurious cloud of rosemary steam. Total bliss. On the ledge, my phone began to buzz like an angry wasp, but it was an out-of-state number so I ignored it.

I felt my body unwind, muscles unclenching and relaxing into my curves, as I submerged myself up to my ears. My body was not exactly perfect, especially given that I was in my late thirties and had had three pregnancies, one of them twins. I'd even considered a breast augmentation, which my friends referred to as a "refill." That a refill was aesthetically desirable was incontestable: after the pregnancies and a total of four-plus years of breastfeeding, my breasts looked like they belonged on a four-hundred-year-old Yoda. But in the end I decided my babe status was still intact, despite having all those babies. And Drew wasn't complaining either, not that he'd had much contact with me lately.

The thought of Drew and his absentee status from our home life was a touchy one. When we'd first met—on one random evening at Selwyn Pub—I had been in the beginning of my residency in Charlotte. My nonmedical girlfriends gape when they first learn the breakdown of my education: four years of college, four years of medical school, three years of pediatrics residency, and—because that clearly wasn't enough—another three years of fellowship in pediatric cardiology, with a year of research worked in. Every now and then during that first year of peds residency, I'd escape the hospital, desperate to interact with humans who didn't wear blue pajamas and white coats all the time.

Charlotte was chock-full of men like Drew, since the local economy was fueled by the financial industry. Uptown crawled with them: handsome, jet-lagged guys in button-downs. But Drew stood out in the horde of i-bankers and private equity guys.

I'd been sitting at the bar the night I met him, trying to simultaneously project aloof unavailability to the guy to my left (an opinionated tool) and cautious interest to the guy to my right (cute, good hair), when a beer came sliding down the length of the bar and planted itself in my cupped hand. I stared at it in delight and turned with the entire rest of the bar to see where it had come from. A guy at the end of the bar lifted his hand in a wave and mouthed, *Hi.*

I waved back. The guy smiled—he had a nice face, open and affable— and motioned to the stool next to him with a hopeful look. I hopped up, ignoring the crude leer from Mr. Tool, and joined Drew at the end of the bar.

The first thing he said: "I can't believe I did that."

He looked so shocked at his success I had to laugh. "It'll make a good story to tell our kids," I said cheerfully, and then clamped my hands over my mouth in horror. Oh God, no. Unrecoverable.

But he didn't run out screaming: he laughed. And we talked until the bar closed. Everything happened in a whirlwind after that: our marriage, the kids, the blistering insanity of trying to parent very young children while one of us was working hundred-hour weeks, mostly at the hospital, and the other was working hundred-hour weeks, mostly on last-minute flights to Abu Dhabi or Hong Kong. Somehow we survived it.

Thinking of how we met reminded me I'd barely seen Drew this week. Maybe this weekend, we could—

The bathroom door flew open. Delaney staggered in, blinking against the sudden light. "Oh, hi, Mom!" she chirped.

"Lainie," I began, resigned, standing and reaching for a towel to wrap around my wet hair. "Why, why, WHY are you up?"

"I missted you, beloved dear!"

"Well, you need to get back in your bed. Right now. It's very late."

Alarm crossed Delaney's features, replaced quickly by cunning. "So, darling," she began, clearly casting around for a conversational topic to distract me. Her huge owlish eyes lit on my wrapped head. "Is that . . . is that the same towel you wore in your wedding?"

It was an effort to keep my stern look in place. "Mommy wore a veil in the wedding, darling girl. No stalling. You are going back to bed."

An epic battle ensued, which I won by virtue of superior strength and the fact that Drew had doctored up the children's doors so that the locking mechanism was now on the outside. Padding back down the hall, I felt naked. I *was* more or less naked, but I realized the sensation of something missing was coming from my absent iPhone, which had gained the status of an extracorporeal appendage since I was never without it. Suppose Emma was texting me right now! Everyone agreed that these smartphones had rewired all the neural circuitry in the brain, setting up a feedback loop where you required more and more and more screen time, or else you suffered from a depletion of neurotransmitters and became all twitchy. This was problematic enough at my age, but just imagine what it was doing to the plastic little minds of preschoolers. Well, best not to think about that, or I'd be guilt-stricken at my failure to parent like my own parents. Of course, they had not even had cable TV to contend with, let alone fiendish mobile computers.

Ah! I spied the phone still resting on the bathtub ledge. Just as I reached for it, the bathroom door opened again. I whirled around, flailing for a towel, mentally cursing the children and their insistence on hopping out of bed seven thousand times a night, and nearly screamed as I collided with someone much larger.

"Oh my God, Drew," I breathed. "How about a warning knock? I almost peed on the floor!"

Drew, who had been enthusiastically reaching toward me, pulled back. "That's not a good visual," he mumbled.

"What are you doing home so early?" I smiled. "It's not even midnight."

"Ha-ha," he said, pushing his glasses up and rubbing the bridge of his nose. Drew had deeply etched symmetrical laugh lines bordering a strong chin, thick dark hair, and agreeable green eyes, which crinkled into half-moons when he smiled. In college, he had been vaguely embarrassed by his myopic vision, but someone had gotten him a pair of those dark-rimmed rectangular nerd glasses that really suited him; they brought to mind an intellectual but still sexy male model, perhaps reading the *New York Times* while smoldering postcoitally amid rumpled silk sheets in some trendy loft.

"I would have been home hours ago"—he grimaced—"but I got McGuired on the way out." Reginald McGuire was one of the upper-echelon partners at Elwood Capital, and his propensity to corner colleagues and underlings and talk until their ears bled was much feared around Drew's division. Reginald adored meetings and would produce elaborate multipage agendas with various subheadings about the most trivial issues, which absolutely tortured the shit out of everyone else. Resistance was useless though, because any attempt to tone him down resulted in him taking such miserable offense that the fallout was worse than just gritting your teeth and enduring the original McGuiring.

"I'm sorry, darling," I said, coming over and rubbing his neck. "Was it very terrible?"

"It was," Drew said happily. He loved a good rub. "He's all over me about the securitization of the French thing, which, frankly, looks a little sketch." Sometimes Drew lapsed into gangsta speak, which I found hilarious, given that he had been born in some lily-white suburb of DC. I reflected that I lived in a world where suburban moms were trying to sound like bankers, bankers were trying to sound like rappers, and the privileged offspring of the moms and the bankers were trying to look like gangsta-rapper football players.

"Anyway, I said how about we run this by Edgar? And Edgar said— Oh, that's good, Zadie. I'm forgetting all about Edgar, actually. I can't believe I even brought this up while I'm getting a massage from my hot, naked wife."

I smiled. "But *you* aren't naked."

"I can fix that. Prepare to get lucky."

Really, men were very impressive in the biological-urge department. If I got as little sleep as Drew did at this age, sex would disappear right off the radar screen. But he managed to rally, taking advantage of the rare night where he was home and I was awake and the kids were asleep all at the same time.

Afterward, Drew immediately lapsed into a postcoital semicomatose state that we referred to as being whammified. Since he was whammified—drooling, fetal-positioned, unable to respond—there was no point in babbling to him about Delaney's biting, or Rowan's girl drama, or the fact that Finn had appeared at school today without shoes. And there was certainly no point in waking him up to tell him the awful news about Eleanor Packard. I patted his face—in whammified mode it had relaxed into an expression of unfiltered peace—and with tremendous effort he grasped my hand and kissed it.

Now thoroughly awake, I wandered back into the bathroom. The iPhone still waited, lurking innocently in its little pink case. I pushed the home screen button and saw the call from the unknown number.

I punched the button to listen to the message and immediately dropped the phone onto the marble floor, shattering what remained of the already-cracked screen into a spiderweb of shards. But even so, I could still hear the inflection in that voice: the piercing intelligence, the razor-edged note of humor. I knew who it was as soon as he said my name.

Zadie, it's Nick. Any chance you would have lunch with me tomorrow? I really need to see you.

Chapter Thirteen

A LATE SIGN OF DOOM

Emma, Present Day

Our unnatural quiet from the ER carried over to the OR. The worst trauma cases are often desperate affairs, but rarely were they this solemn and silent. Just before the case started, Eleanor's blood pressure finally dropped—a late sign of doom in children; they tended to maintain their pressure until just before the end—and we all held our breaths as she was positioned on the table. I had a great scrub nurse, with experience in both trauma surgery and pediatric surgery, and she handed the correct instruments to me and Sanjay even before we could ask for them.

Despite the urgency, a sense of calm engulfed me. The only sounds I could hear were the *whoosh-hush* of the ventilator and the nasally breathing of the medical student peering over my shoulder. The subdued sounds, along with the sea green color of the tiled walls, combined to create an underwater, otherworldly ambience, and I felt my breath slowing as my focus narrowed. Ever since I was a resident, I've had a ritual in the seconds before a case starts: I close my eyes and visualize the anatomy I'm about to see.

I opened my eyes. In front of me, Eleanor Packard's vulnerable little form gleamed in the brilliance of the OR lights: a shining fish caught in a shaft of sunlight. She was swathed in blue OR towels, framing a yellowish sheet of sticky film clinging to her abdomen.

Sanjay, his hand steady, made a deft incision down the length of Eleanor's tummy, curving around her little outie belly button. I followed with the cautery. Without needing to confer, we manipulated our instruments with balletic intricacy, elevating and snipping through the lining of her abdomen. Even though I expected it, I exhaled behind my mask as a torrent of blood gushed out at us. The anesthesiologist, peering over the sterile blue curtain dividing Eleanor's face from her body, took one look at the red lake we'd uncovered and called to the circulator for another unit of blood to hang. Sanjay and I rapidly packed OR sponges into the little girl's abdominal cavity, trying to stem the hemorrhage long enough to get her stabilized.

It worked. With the blood loss slowed and the anesthesiologist transfusing her, Eleanor's vital signs began to rebound. Still, we didn't know where the bleeding was coming from. I suspected the spleen, but it could also have been the liver. Or both.

Or maybe it was something else. I felt the first little flurries of panic trying to worm their way into my consciousness as I removed some of the packing; the lake of blood immediately repooled. I shut off my mind, silently chanting to myself. *No bad thoughts, no bad thoughts, no bad thoughts.* The panic receded. "It's the spleen," I said.

Sanjay and I worked quickly but carefully, first identifying and then clamping the blood supply to Eleanor's macerated spleen. This improved matters, but the hemorrhaging didn't fully stop. An hour went by, and then another one, as we painstakingly identified the little bleeders scattered around Eleanor's belly. Thank goodness for the anesthesiologist, who was fighting as hard as we were to keep her alive.

"Send word to the Packards that we're closing," I said finally. "I think we got them all."

For the first time, the atmosphere in the room relaxed. "Bless you, Dr. Colley," said the circulator, clasping her hands prayerfully toward the heavens. "That was a hard one." Behind his curtain, Bart Fisk, the anesthesiologist, started whistling as he clicked at his computer.

The medical student behind me shifted his weight from foot to foot, probably sick to death of just standing there. "Can I help close?" he asked.

"Absolutely not," I said. "We are going to make this scar so pretty they'll think plastics did it. But you can have the next drunk that comes in."

Only Sanjay seemed unaffected by the good cheer suffusing the OR. He studied the little body in front of him. "Maybe we should leave her open," he said.

I frowned, considering this. What Sanjay suggested—not closing the surgical incision, in favor of leaving the packing in place and the huge gaping wound covered only by skin or surgical dressings—had some considerable disadvantages. The risk of infection was higher, and we'd have to keep the child fully sedated, among other things. And it felt barbaric: the image of a tiny girl with her belly split open is not one anyone wants to contemplate, especially the child's parents. But it offered the advantage of easy access if we'd missed anything, and we could even leave the packing in place temporarily to try to get the bleeding to stop on its own if it started again. It was a drastic effort, but it also offered protection after a catastrophic injury.

I made my decision. "We're not going to do that," I said. "We got this. And I don't want to put this family through any more."

Sanjay studied the area where we'd ligated—tied off—the biggest blood vessels. I knew what he was thinking.

"We didn't hit the pancreas," I said. "I'm sure."

"Okay," said Sanjay. I could not read his expression.

"Have a little faith in us," I said, starting to close the first layer. "Her abdominal pressures will be fine."

"Of course," said Sanjay.

"You finish up," I said. Sanjay's closures were meticulous and beautiful, maybe even better than mine. I turned to the med student, reconsidering. "Come up here," I offered. "You can cut sutures for Dr. Patil. You might as well get something out of standing there sterile all this time."

"Thank you!" yelped the student.

"Don't do anything stupid," I told him. "Cut them exactly the length Dr. Patil tells you."

"Yes, ma'am," said the student, eyeing his hands warily. I made a mental note to look up his name as soon as I left the OR; for some reason, I kept forgetting it.

"Great job, everyone. Thank you," I said to the room as I broke scrub. "Now I'm going to find the Packards to tell them their little one should be fine."

Chapter Fourteen

NO SEX FOR SIX WEEKS

Late Summer, 1999: Louisville, Kentucky
Zadie

Some fourteen hours after my call room encounter with Dr. X, I let myself into the old house I shared with Emma, who was out. Both of us had a flair for design, and although we were impoverished medical students, we'd managed to cobble together a stylish abode, with metallic green and purple and yellow throw pillows, brightly hued quilts, framed posters of the obscure hippie sixties bands we loved, photographs of our friends scattered about, and many recently deceased plants.

It was the first time I'd been alone in almost forty hours. I wanted a moment to savor the astonishing events of the preceding long day. I'd done some actual surgery, I had survived a volley of questioning by Dr. Markham at TICU rounds—not just survived, even, but distinguished myself with coherent answers miraculously pulled out of the ether—and finally, I'd had the dizzying encounter with Dr. X.

Men in general were difficult to interpret, as every woman since the dawn of time will attest, but it was hard to know what to make of this. There was quite an unequal footing. Dr. X was a fifth-year resident, a chief; at the end of this year he would be in private practice or, more likely, in a fellowship somewhere, tacking on an extra year or more of subspecialty training. I actually knew very little about him. He was from somewhere in the Northeast, he drove a sports car of some sort, he lived in Louisville's Highlands neighborhood, and he liked Rage Against the Machine. I had gleaned these things from casual conversation with the team, but now, with a mixture of dawning shame and curiosity, I realized he might as well have been Dr. Markham for all I knew about him.

My pager vibrated. It was an unfamiliar number; not the hospital's prefix, so it was probably one of my girlfriends trying to lure me out.

"What's up, Zadie?" It was Dr. X, apparently summoned by the power of my musings. His voice was low and smooth; suddenly, I couldn't remember what he looked like.

"Hi," I said, for lack of anything witty to say.

"How are you?" he asked.

"I'm . . . whirling around in confusion," I admitted. "And I'm wiped."

"Why are you confused?" He sounded concerned.

"I don't make a habit of hurtling into bed with strange surgeons. Or anybody at work. Or anybody, actually."

"Yeah." There was a short silence, then: "Just so you know, I generally don't hurtle into bed with medical students either."

"Good." I smiled to myself.

"Usually they're nurses."

"What?"

"Kidding! This is an unusual feeling, though." I recalled his face after he'd turned on the light in my call room: What had that look been? Interest? Calculation? Attraction?

"What feeling is that?"

"Well . . . you're an intriguing girl—you know that? You are hard to intimidate, and you're funny." He lowered his voice even more. "And you're very sexy."

"You're not hideous yourself."

In a smooth growl: "Why don't you come over?"

"What, now?" I would have sworn I'd have been unconscious within two seconds of getting home, but now I felt a perverse spike of energy.

"Yes, now."

"I . . . Aren't you tired?"

"I don't get tired. And I kind of miss having a med student around; there's nobody here to cater to my whims."

"Wow, this conversation has really taken a turn for the worse," I said, smiling in spite of—or maybe because of—the absolute wrongness of this. I paused. "That was revolting. I'm contacting an attorney."

"Are you?" he asked, after the tiniest hesitation.

I smiled again. "No," I said. "I'm coming over."

———

I awoke late the next morning, feeling excited, although it took me a moment to remember why. The light was streaming in through my bedroom window, matching the ridiculous, sunny grin that I could feel plastered to my face.

Last night had been dreamy, otherworldly; my memory of it came back in wispy, wordless fragments. I'd knocked on his door and he'd opened it and pulled me inside without a sound. The feel of his slightly rough cheek pressed to mine, his hands in my hair. A pulsing, engulfing, crazy longing. Darkness and sweetness.

I'd seen nothing of his apartment beyond the foyer, where we'd fallen to the floor. Afterward, he had insisted on driving me home, apparently worried that I'd plow into a building as soon as I was out of sight. Despite the minimal sleep I'd gotten, I felt exuberant. I'd been telling the truth when I told him it wasn't a habit for me to do this; I'd been celibate, and somewhat lonely, since the end of my relationship with my longtime college boyfriend more than a year ago. In Dr. X's presence I felt that weird, supercharged *zing* that you get only a few times in life, when you are perfectly compatible with someone else. With him, I was a more vivid version of myself.

———

Morning trauma rounds commenced. Dr. Markham was grilling the unlucky intern on Emma's team with some incomprehensible questions about the ventilation-perfusion curve. I was consumed with impatience: Dr. X had leaned into me at the start of prerounds, his breath warm on my ear, and whispered, "What are you doing later?"

"Depends on what my chief has planned," I whispered back.

With an insouciant grin: "Postrounds evaluation in my call room, Z."

My month on trauma was almost finished; tonight would be the last night of in-house call. As much as I liked the service, I was happy that it was nearly over. The thrill of sneaking around with Dr. X had waned. I wanted a real date.

We ran the list after trauma rounds concluded, Dr. X assigning us our workload for the morning. We were instructed to be finished before the day's new carnage began rolling in.

"Last but not least: Garage Trauma. Sixty-two-year-old Abdominal Catastrophe, first day of graduation from the unit. Still some fallout from the last FUBAR, when good Dr. Clancy here nicked the bowel. Obviously, that one is for you, Ellington, since you now specialize in bowel disasters; schedule a washout for today. Speedy here can assist you." Dr. X motioned toward Ethan.

Val, the charge nurse, cut a quick glance at Clancy, who was unabashedly ogling a nursing assistant's butt. Val turned back to Dr. X.

"You're going to supervise the washout, right?" she asked.

"Yes, ma'am," Dr. X said hastily, saluting. "Zadie, did you write discharge instructions for the floor patients for me to sign?"

"I did. Mostly. I have a question," I said, scribbling away on the last set of papers for the patients going home that day.

"Proceed."

"Why do we tell them no sex for six weeks?"

A flash of deep dimples. The rest of the team began to giggle. I blinked; I'd been industriously writing this on every patient's discharge for the last several weeks. I looked up as they broke into full-on laughter.

"We are controlling future trauma populations," Dr. X said firmly. "But, ah, no need to mention this to Dr. Hollister. Okay, everybody disperse."

I waited a beat for the dispersal to take place and then stuck out my tongue. He cocked an eyebrow at me and smirked. "Yes, Z?"

I decided not to give him the satisfaction of admitting he'd gotten me. Again. He delighted in coming up with the most preposterous things solely for the fun of messing with me. "Nothing," I cooed. "I have a ton of work to do."

"Zadie."

I turned back, unable to suppress a smile tinged with triumph.

He craned his head toward me, growling directly in my ear. "I'll help you."

"Oooh! How nice. In exchange for what?"

"Meet me in my call room in five minutes, you little witch." He walked off, his long white coat flapping with each lengthy stride. Even looking at the back of his head made me weak with desire. This was likely not the way the medical school had envisioned the student experience, to be sure, but it was a good . . . education.

I gave him the requested five minutes and headed for the stairs. When I opened the door to the stairwell, the hall looked empty. I bolted out and ducked into Dr. X's room.

Inside, a desk lamp offered a pale circle of light in the windowless space. X was seated at the veneered desk, and rose at my entrance. I took a single step inside and we fell into each other, brutally kissing, tearing at our scrubs, knocking over the lamp and the books piled on his desk. He plunged his hands into my hair, roughly twisting it. My lips parted and I let my head fall back, exposing my throat. I was unaware that I was crying out until he shoved something into my mouth—a sock? an OR mask?—and murmured "Shhh" into my ear. I struggled to breathe through my nose. He turned me away from him, still holding the cloth in my mouth. His other hand was savagely gripping the curve of my hip bone. Our pagers both sounded, and I registered the sound dimly. I struggled and spat the cloth out, but Dr. X, still standing behind me, stifled me by wrapping his arm around my neck so that I could not move my head. With his other hand, he reached up to my face and, with startling gentleness, caressed my cheekbones and eyelids and lips. A drumming noise filled my ears and my head and my chest, the dominating pulse of my blood churning through my carotid arteries. I closed my eyes, my arousal nearly unbearable.

He was motionless behind me except for the fine, soft exploration of his fingers on my immobilized face. The rushing in my ears faded but— oh, no—the drumming noise continued. Grudgingly, I accepted that this must have been the blades of the hospital helicopter, pulsing some ten floors above us, but just audible enough through the ventilation system so that there was never really an escape from the sound of some incoming disaster. Our pagers beeped again.

We stood still for a moment longer, trying to regain our breath, fighting the longing to ignore the summons and give in to what was now a maddening desire. Dr. X swore. The code was doubtless starting by now. He released me and said, "You first. Run."

I ran. My lips were chapped and swollen, my skin was flushed to an alarming pink, my hair was bunched up in a comb-proof combination of tangles and dreadlocks, and I was hyperventilating in uncontrolled gasps. There was no doubt I'd be of little use to anyone during the trauma code; I'd be lucky not to actively impede it by bursting in and passing out.

When I reached the ER, I slowed to a trot and tried to slip behind the curtain to Trauma Bay 2 as unobtrusively as possible.

This actually proved to be easy. The patient on the table had some sort of ghastly neck injury; he was spraying bright red arterial blood in staccato spurts, which had doused the ceiling, walls, and floors with the force of a fire hose. Everyone in the abattoir appeared to have sustained a direct hit, as they were all bloody to the point of being nearly unrecognizable.

"Continue CPR," said Allison Kalena to the ER nurse, who was most directly in the line of fire.

"What are you doing?" screamed Clancy at another nurse who was holding a syringe. "Don't give him any more fucking epinephrine!"

"His heart's stopping," the nurse said to Dr. Kalena, ignoring Clancy. "What do you want me to do?"

"He's going to bleed out faster with the pressors, so hold the epi until we get some more fluid in him," said Allison. "Where's our O neg?"

"On the way."

"Okay, get another quad lumen kit; I'll add a femoral line, and you guys keep pumping it in. Ah, Zadie," she said, catching sight of me. "Get up here."

I obeyed. Dr. Kalena handed me a wad of sterile dressings and instructed, "Hold pressure right here. We might keep him alive long enough to get to the OR."

"Allison, he's toast," Clancy argued. "He must have ripped off every branch of the external carotid. He's stroked out by now."

"We can ligate what we have to—he should have good posterior circulation," she replied, deftly threading a wire through a large needle jutting out of the patient's groin.

I couldn't resist. "What happened?"

"Meet Lima Trauma," Clancy answered. "Piñata mishap at his kid's birthday party—he got gouged through the neck with the splintered end of a stick."

"Hold CPR," a voice from the back of the room called. Dr. X appeared. He surveyed the havoc briefly, and noting that the patient did have a heartbeat again—someone had hung the blood and I was still holding on, literally, for dear life—he called out, "Call the OR. We're going in."

We scrubbed quickly, watching through the OR window as the nurses flew around the room opening various instrument kits. Just as we were about to start, the trauma pagers blared again. Dr. Kalena, Clancy, and Ethan departed.

I braced for a long and uncomfortable slog. For the first hour, I held a delicate retractor while the two men grafted and ligated, my arms locked in an increasingly uncomfortable position until I could no longer control their shaking. The vascular surgeon, a genial British fellow named Markey, peered out over his loupes as my tired forearm muscles started vibrating enough to shake the entire surgical field, and said, "Have a little stretch, dear. I remember those days of endless retractor holding. Dr. X will have to make this up to you later." Even in the midst of this hushed life-or-death drama, I could tell X was grinning under his mask.

"Yes, sir, he will," I replied. "I'm so sorry to distract you."

"Not at all. Dr. X can take your place for a moment."

I had not yet released my hand when the anesthesiologist let out a muffled curse from behind the patient's head. "Sorry, boys. We've got some rhythm issues," he said.

"What's going on?" Dr. Markey asked.

"Runs of V-tach. We're waiting on repeat electrolytes— Oh shit." A nonstop beeping sound began. "He's in V-fib," the anesthesiologist called. "Shock him."

The nurses sprang into action, ordering everyone to stand clear. Dr. Markey said sharply to the anesthesiologist, "What's the last hemoglobin?"

"Waiting on it now. How much have we lost in the last ten minutes?"

"Third shock delivered," said the circulator, as the patient's body jerked on the table.

"Five hundred CCs," Markey replied, backing away from the table with his hands up as if surrendering.

"Resuming CPR," announced the scrub nurse. The surgeons jumped back up to the table, everyone craning their heads to see the monitor, which demonstrated an ominous series of jagged green peaks and valleys. The anesthesiologist called out, "Giving epi now, one milligram," at the exact moment that the monitor changed back into a recognizable sinus rhythm. With no one holding pressure on the myriad little open arteries in the neck, the vasoconstriction of the epinephrine caused a Vesuvius of blood to erupt, a high-force hail of magma pulsing out in all directions. Dr. X and Dr. Markey were instantly drenched, even behind their eye shields. The circulator bounded over to sponge off their faces.

"Motherfuckingshitsonofabitch," swore Dr. X. Then, to Dr. Markey: "Can you ligate anything?"

"I'm afraid I can't see shit," replied Dr. Markey in his posh British voice. "Suction! Here!"

"Aaaah!" cried the scrub nurse, who was blasted in the face while leaning over with a Yankauer tip. Dr. Markey snatched the tube from her and attempted to suction as much blood as possible from the field. Inspired, I rolled up a small surgical cloth and carefully placed it at the inferior aspect of the open wound, compressing as firmly as possible everything beneath it. This slowed the battalion of geysers in Lima's neck, dulling them down to burbling red fountains. "Oh, well-done," breathed Dr. Markey. We peered into the bloodbath. There were oozing little vessels everywhere, and one or two larger ones, on which Dr. Markey and X immediately set to work.

"Dr. Markey?" I asked timidly, looking at the white face of the young father. "Will he make it?"

X's pager chirped, a reminder beep for a message we'd all missed during the explosion.

"It's from Dr. Kalena," the circulator read. "She says they've got the new one—Edict Trauma. Twenty-six-year-old pregnant female, gunshot wound to the head."

———

"Last but not least, this is hospital day two for Edict Trauma, a twenty-six-year-old female at eighteen weeks gestation, status post-GSW to the left temporal lobe," Ethan droned the next morning, by now immune to sentiment even though he was talking about a pregnant person who'd been shot in the head. We'd just finished rounding on Lima Trauma, who had somehow survived surgery and hung on through the night. "She's day-one status post craniotomy with clot evacuation."

"You can skip the rest of the history, Speedy, since we just spent all night with her," X allowed. He hadn't shaved, and he sported blond stubble that lent him a rakish look. "Vitals?"

Ethan vomited a cascade of numbers. "Pulse of 84, BP 105/65, temperature 98.2. She remains on the vent, with 96 percent O_2 saturation on AC 10, PEEP of 5, FiO_2 50 percent."

"We need to replace her line," said X, reading something on his sign-off sheet and frowning. "A femoral line from the ER is not the most sterile access."

"Yes, sir, you did mention that yesterday," Ethan mumbled.

"Val?" X was still looking at his notes. "Page me when the family gets back so I can discuss her prognosis. We'll do it first thing after rounds. Respiratory was concerned that her endotracheal tube might be developing a cuff leak, so we'll change that out. Ethan, you have a case with Hollister, so, Zadie, you stay with me and we'll get it done. Let's try to get out at a decent time today, team; I have important plans tonight."

"Yes, Dr. X," Val said.

I smiled to myself. X had finally bowed to the inevitable and agreed to do "something romantic" with me tonight. This was good. It was doubtless unhealthy to conduct nearly one hundred percent of a relationship at work. I made him solemnly vow to forgo our usual lustful frenzy—um, physical contact—and have a sit-down dinner, complete with intellectual conversation, candles, and music of some non-Rage genre. X had complained briefly about this last request ("What am I supposed to play, Enya?") but capitulated, although he did insist on takeout instead of a restaurant.

"Ethan? What are the OB guys saying? Any changes?"

"Um . . . they are . . . continuing tocolysis?"

"For Chrissake, Speedy, wake the fuck up. You might be a future flea, but you still have a day left on this service. Now is not the time to drop the ball. Did you read their note?"

Ethan, an orderly and methodical guy who would indeed be well suited to the cerebral world of internal medicine, fidgeted. X had nicknamed him Speedy because of his deliberate, thoughtful speech patterns and his habit of producing beautifully written, meticulous H&Ps. Despite the fodder he provided for the action-oriented surgeons in their highly macho environment, and his total lack of interest in pursuing surgery as a career, he was well regarded on the rotation; it was impossible not to like him.

"I'm sorry, Dr. X," he apologized now, rubbing his little round wire-rimmed glasses. "I'm sort of fuzzy-headed today."

"Okay. Read their note and get back to me immediately, if not sooner. I'm going to meet with Edict's family, and we need to know what the endgame is here. Does OB want us to keep her in the trauma unit until they can deliver, or move her there once she's stable? The last I heard from neurology, Edict's brain scan looked unfavorable yesterday, but it's early."

"Yes, sir, thank you," Ethan said.

X continued. "On to the floor patients. We'll run the list and then you guys can go with Allison into the rooms. Clancy, you've got room 1016. How's she doing?"

"LGFD," Clancy answered. Ethan and I dutifully wrote this down.

"Clancy," X said, irritated, "did you actually examine her?"

"What's LGFD?" Ethan asked.

"Looks Good from Door," Clancy said, abashed. "Uh, I'll check again during rounds. Or," he added hastily, registering a lethal glare from X, "maybe I'll go right now." He darted off.

"Don't emulate Dr. Ellington, young doctors-in-training," Dr. Kalena advised us. "He's got issues."

"We won't, Dr. Kalena," said Ethan.

"You can call me Allison. It's fine," she told us.

We looked at Dr. X.

"You can call me Dr. X," he said. I waited until no one was looking and stuck my tongue out at him.

"Right," he continued. "Moving on. Ethan, you're up again. Did you get the drain pulled from room 1018?"

Room 1018, Mrs. Andreozzi, was an old lady who'd been beaten by a couple of trolls she surprised in the act of burgling her apartment. Rather than attempting to flee like any sensible senior citizen, she had leapt out at them with a Tarzan yell, striking one of them square in the face with a teakettle. Every time I looked at her, with her swollen eyes and her casted arms and her vivid purplish yellow bruised abdomen, I felt a strong urge to find those guys and take up the teakettle myself.

Ethan hung his head and groaned a little. "I'm sorry—again—but she won't let me do anything. Every time I go in there, she tries to order breakfast from me. She refuses to believe I'm not from the cafeteria."

"Speedy, that's ridiculous. Just tell her you are the medical student. Or hell, say 'doctor' if that makes her feel better."

Ethan looked even more miserable. "I've tried, Dr. X. I brought her some coffee the first day she was on the floor, and now she recognizes my voice and refuses to accept that I'm not food services. I don't think she can see anything."

"Ethan, Ethan. You have officially crashed and burned this morning," X groused. "All right. We'll all march in there and reassure Mrs. A that you're legit."

We plodded en masse down the brightly lit hallway connecting the TICU to the regular hospital floor, picking up speed as we passed the nurses' station. The floor was laid out in an open-ended loop anchored by the family waiting room so that if you didn't project a harried and intimidating air as you went by, you were likely to be besieged by hordes of anxious relatives.

It was true that Mrs. Andreozzi might have limited vision, as her eyelids were gargantuan, swollen to probably ten times their normal size. Still, she perked up at the sounds of footsteps, casting a delighted smile in our general direction.

"Hello, Mrs. A. It's Ethan," said Ethan cheerfully. "I've brought some doctors in to see you."

"Well, hello yourself, sonny boy," she chirped back. "Did you get those scrambled eggs done yet?"

"No, ma'am, I didn't get those for you, because I am the medical student. This is Dr. Xenokostas," he said, gesturing. "He's going to talk to you about removing your drain."

"Why, it is so nice to meet you, Dr. Xenokostas," said Mrs. Andreozzi, turning and addressing the floor nurse, who had wandered in behind us.

"I'm actually over here, ma'am," said Dr. X. "Would it be all right if Ethan took this pesky drain out of your belly?"

"My goodness, I don't know," said Mrs. Andreozzi, flustered. "Do you think he should be doing a thing like that?"

"Oh, yes, Mrs. Andreozzi, he is very, um, qualified. He does this a lot."

"Well, to be perfectly honest, I think I'd feel a *teeny* bit better if one of the medical folks could do it." She lowered her voice and said in a confiding tone, "He's not even a very good *cook*."

Bemused, X sent Ethan an apologetic look. "Well, how about one of our other students, then, Mrs. A? Zadie Fletcher is here too. She can take care of it for you."

"Oh my dear. That would be wonderful." Mrs. Andreozzi beamed, swiveling this time to address her IV pole.

Val, the charge nurse from the TICU, poked her head in the door.

"Excuse me, Dr. X," she said. "Edict's family is back."

"Right. I'll come talk with him, but see if you can get Lara Danielson from OB here too, and one of the neurosurgery guys. Zadie, get this drain removed for Mrs. Andreozzi. And, Speedy?"

"Yes, Dr. X?" said Ethan, smirking slightly.

"Order Mrs. A an ophthalmology consult."

———

We split up, X heading back toward the TICU to talk with Edict's father.

After the removal of Mrs. Andreozzi's drain, I wrote a note in the chart and waited for X.

"Jesus, last night was a bloodbath," X said, appearing at the nurses' station. We walked back down the hall toward the TICU. "Those are two cases I'll definitely remember—a pregnant gunshot victim and a near beheading by a piñata."

"How did her dad take it?" I asked.

"Not well," he said. His face rearranged itself into a blank mask. "I gave him my call room, actually, so he could try to get it together without twenty strangers watching."

"Oh no," I replied, casting about for something to distract him from the pain of relaying so much grief. "Well, Dr. Markey was right. You were brilliant in the OR yesterday." After Lima's case had ended, Dr. Markey had praised Dr. X for his tenacity and skill.

"Are you thinking of going into vascular surgery?" I continued.

"No. I'm doing an HPB fellowship next year. I thought you knew that," said X, jerking out of his reverie. "At Duke." At my befuddled expression, he added, "Hepatopancreatobiliary. That's liver, gallbladder and pancreatic surgery."

"I know what hepatopanc— I know what that means," I squeaked. "I didn't know you were leaving though. Will I . . . see you next year?"

"Next year is a long time away, Z," he replied carelessly, but then, noticing my crestfallen face, added, "But I hope so."

There was an awkward pause.

I stole a glance at him. His eyes closed briefly and his jaw twitched. He was clearly exhibiting symptoms of a universal male malady, namely, the panic that occurs when confronted with the prospect of *discussing the relationship*. Nevertheless, this was overdue; we had been dating for nearly a month. I took a deep breath and plunged in.

"I don't want you to be acting under the misimpression that there is some sort of serflike *droit du seigneur* situation going on here."

"Some . . . serf du what?"

"I'm not a . . . hospital booty call," I said.

"Oh. Certainly not."

"I mean, it's not like I'm some fawning nurse's assistant or something."

A trace of a smile had emerged on his face. "Well, I *am* Chief X. It wouldn't kill you to fawn a little."

"I did say you were brilliant in the OR," I reminded him.

"Correct. I am brilliant in many situations. As you well know."

"Yes, yes, your brilliance is acknowledged."

His smile widened; then a slightly rueful look passed over his handsome face. "Every time I think I'm going to— Well, never mind."

"What?"

"Nothing. You are adorable. Do you know that?"

"Thank you. So are you. I just want us to be clear that this is going somewhere."

The wistful look was replaced by seriousness. He stopped walking and leaned up against the wall outside the TICU. "Zadie, you know we have to keep this on the down low. Dr. Markham would have my balls removed and donated to the cadaver lab if there was even a rumor that I was fu—involved with a student on the service. I like living dangerously as much as the next guy, but. Well. You shouldn't even bring it up with your merry band of girlfriends. You understand, right?"

"I'm off the service tomorrow."

"And trauma surgery's loss is internal medicine's gain. I mean it, Z." He chucked me under the chin, then glanced around and gave me a light kiss, followed by a wicked grin. "You've been an outstanding student, and I'd say that even if you hadn't seduced and attacked me. Let's get Edict taken care of. I'll let you do the line and reintubation all by yourself, okay? Then I'll help you with your intern chores, as promised. We can talk about the rest of this tonight."

"Great!" My weariness fell away at the thought of two procedures, one of them brand-new. I'd been angling to get an intubation in before I rotated off the service.

"Let's hit it." He smacked the button on the wall to open the TICU doors. "Oh, and, Zadie . . . ?"

"Yes?"

"I recommend you wash up a bit. You have blood on your nose."

Chapter Fifteen

THE ASS PHOTO

Zadie, Present Day

Another hot day. It was hard to dress professionally when you were melting. I had settled on a sleeveless pale pink rayon shirt that I dressed up with an enormous gold-and-tourmaline necklace. I didn't wear a white coat since some children found them alarming, so my arms were on display. But that was okay because I'd been working out with Aaron, Emma's trainer, once a week. He was a sadistic demon straight from hell. My arms were looking good, though. I'd never have achieved that on my own.

I dropped off Delaney at the early-birds room at preschool—they'd finally let her back in—and headed to the office. Parking was a bit tricky in this part of town. Dilworth was one of those boho districts where the zoning laws allowed businesses right next to a residence so that what looked like a homey arts-and-crafts family bungalow nestled among the trees was actually a tax attorney or an architect, or, in this case, a pediatric cardiology office. But the parking lot was tiny, so employees, including the doctors, were encouraged to park on the street, which didn't exactly improve the chances of striding into work looking crisp and refreshed. I was already sweaty by the time I dragged myself in through the employee entrance in the back.

The door opened into a staff workroom, which had once been the kitchen of the dwelling. There were still a refrigerator, a microwave, and an immense old oak table in place. Everyone congregated in here before the official opening of the day, and as I stepped in, I found myself greeted by whoops and hollers from the staff. Today was Tuesday. I hadn't been to work since last Thursday, and in the interim, the story of Buzzy's poolside rescue had gone viral.

"All hail the conquering hero!" shouted Della Rae, the receptionist. "You done good, girl!"

Scattered applause. "Look here, Dr. Anson!" said one of the office girls excitedly, waving Sunday's edition of the *Charlotte Observer* in the air. "You're in the newspaper!"

"I cannot believe," I said, snatching the paper, "that *this* is the picture they chose. For the front page."

We all regarded it. The headline read, Local Doctors Save Choking Real Estate Magnate, with a subheading stating, Emergency Surgery Performed with Fork at Country Club. The large photo underneath it, which had undoubtedly been captured with a cell phone, had been taken from the vantage point of someone kneeling a few feet behind me. It showed Emma's face, a bit fuzzily, frowning in beautiful concentration as she leaned over the unconscious man; in the foreground was a spectacular close-up of my bikinied bottom. I must have been hunched over Buzzy, with my shoulders lower than my hindquarters, because aside from my giant posterior, the only other parts of me you could make out were my forearm and hand jutting menacingly off to the side, clenching a fork.

"You were on the news too, Dr. Anson," enthused Carolyn, one of the echo techs. "And all over the Internet!"

"I know," I said. I'd been deluged with e-mails from well-intentioned people sending copies of the Ass Photo from various Internet sites. The news stories accompanying the picture varied from the lurid (BuzzFeed: BATHING SUIT BEAUTIES DRENCHED IN BLOOD!) to the factual (NPR: EMERGENCY CRICOTHYROTOMY PERFORMED POOLSIDE).

"Did you really poke a hole in him with a fork?" wondered one of the younger office girls.

"No, no," I said, resigned. I'd been getting this question, or some variant of it, a lot over the weekend. "We had a kitchen knife. And Emma, my friend, did the actual cric. I just assisted."

"Looks like a fork *there*," pointed out Della Rae, gesturing toward the newspaper.

"Well, I did *have* a fork. For retracting purposes only."

"I bet he's sooo grateful. Maybe he'll give you a huge reward." This from Abigail, my loyal nurse. "Have you heard from him?"

I had not, in fact, heard from any of the Coopers. This worried me a little, although I knew from Emma that during his revision procedure, Buzzy had undergone a laryngoscopy to retrieve what turned out to be a hunk of steak that had been obstructing his windpipe. He'd tolerated this well, and was recovering in the hospital.

While the rest of the world fixated on Buzzy, I fixated on Eleanor Packard. Since I hadn't yet heard from Emma, I'd called an anesthesiologist friend at the hospital this morning in hope of an update, learning only that she remained on the ventilator.

My first patient of the day only wanted to talk about the cric (or rather, his mother did). It was an effort to redirect her to her son's murmur evaluation. It seemed that there was no escaping this discussion; everyone, from the most remote cave-dwelling hermit on down to my ninety-eight-year-old next-door neighbor, had heard about it and wanted all the grisly details. I began to get a glimpse of how unpleasant it must be to be a celebrity.

At noon I took a break while the office closed for lunch. I'd been planning to walk down East Boulevard to grab a bite, since making the children's lunches every morning incapacitated me to the point where I couldn't stand the thought of making one more, even for my noon meal. This was expensive, but a luxury I allowed myself. But today my cell phone rang right as I was gearing up to head out into the swampy midday heat.

It was an unfamiliar number. I hesitated a moment; sometimes parents of patients got ahold of my number—it was published in my kids' school directories, so a zillion people had access to it—and I really didn't feel like answering any unsolicited medical questions. Or any more fork questions.

But it was Emma, calling from work.

"Oh, Emma," I said. "I'm dying to talk to you. How is Eleanor?"

"Sorry," she said. "It was too late for me to call you last night by the time things finally calmed down, but her mother asked me to let you know. She's in the pediatric ICU, and she's doing well." I listened intently as Emma ran through the specifics of the case, but my mind inevitably branched off toward Betsy. She must have been in agony. I made a note to try calling her again.

"Listen, Zadie, I should have told you Friday: he saw me."

"Who saw you?" I asked, confused. She must have meant Buzzy Cooper. Had he been floating over us in one of those disembodied hovering-soul death experiences? Yikes.

"Nick," said Emma. "Nick Xenokostas. He's already started at the hospital. In fact, he was on call when Buzzy came in."

"*What?*"

"Yes! And today I had a message. It says he wants to congratulate me on the . . . incident . . . and asks if we could meet."

126

"Oh my gosh! He asked me the same thing. He called me and asked me to lunch. I haven't had the chance to tell you about—"

"Did you answer him?"

"I texted him. My answer was: 'No.'"

"That's it?" Emma sounded amused. "You told him no. A one-word response. You?"

I arched a haughty eyebrow, even though Emma couldn't see me, and responded with quiet one-word dignity: "Yes."

She waited.

"Fine," I snapped. "I texted he had a lot of nerve asking me to lunch, and I said I'd rather gnaw off my arm and eat it than ever have another meal with him. I said he shouldn't bother contacting me ever ag—"

Emma snorted. "I get the drift."

"Well, did you answer him when he asked you?"

"No. I ignored him." Emma sounded hesitant.

"Well, are you going to?"

"No! I mean, no? Should I?"

"Oh gosh." I was conflicted. Did I want Emma meeting with Nick? "I don't know. I would have said no—I just want to ignore him—but there is something I'm curious about."

"What's that?"

I was embarrassed. "Well, I googled him the other day, and I read that . . . he namedhisdogZadie."

"What did you say? He named something Zadie?"

"His . . . dog. A black Lab."

"What does that mean?"

"I don't know! Is it a compliment, or . . . does he think of me as a dog?"

Emma was apparently trying to reason this out. "Hmm. Black Labs are notoriously berserk."

"Are you saying his dog reminds him of me because it's such a spaz? Thanks a lot."

"That came out wrong."

I decided to take the high road. "Listen. Emma. My preference would probably be to repress all thought of him, but you do whatever you think is best, I guess; he's your partner. Meanwhile, I am going to hibernate until everyone gets over this . . . event. My bottom is famous, by the way."

"Yeah, someone posted a blown-up picture of it in the hospital lounge." I sent up a quick prayer that this was a joke as Emma went on. "Listen, Z, we keep getting interrupted when we try to talk about this, so I don't want to assume anything about how you want me to act with him."

"Okaay . . ."

"Why don't we have dinner? It will have to be in a couple weeks; I'm on this week and then I'm traveling to Finland for a conference. Is that okay?" More quietly: "I know I've never really talked with you about what happened that year."

This was extraordinary. I had long ago made peace with Emma's reticent nature.

"Well, yes," I said hesitantly. "All these years . . . I have wondered what happened with you and Graham . . ."

"I know, Zadie." Emma's voice was uncharacteristically soft. "I never tell you how grateful I am to still have you as my friend. I'll text you about a date and we'll talk."

"Okay. Try not to stab anyone in the neck in the meantime."

"How can I promise that?" asked Emma, and hung up.

Chapter Sixteen

FILTERLESS FRONTAL-LOBE DISASTER

Emma, Present Day

I hung up with Zadie, tenderness engulfing me. I'd teased her, but in truth I admired her endearing ability to simultaneously project both sunniness and anger. I don't know how to do that. Example: in the middle of my last case, the circulator had given me the message from Dr. Zeenacost. At first it didn't even register. Dr. Zeenacost? Who? Then it dawned on me who that must be. "Is he here?" I'd snapped. Everyone looked at me.

"Now, how you reckon I'm gon' know something like that, Dr. Colley?" the circulator answered, unfazed. "He just say he got something he need to discuss with you." She was an older African-American woman named Meeka, whom I secretly appreciated for her ability to come right out and say whatever she thought without the slightest concern that someone might take offense. It wasn't like she was one of those filterless frontal-lobe disasters who blurt out things without thinking; rather, she simply said what needed to be said without tolerating any nonsense from highfalutin surgeons. They could take it or leave it. I respected this kind of person mightily, especially since I had always been a little too aware of how socially awkward I was to be able to say what I really thought.

I made a conscious effort to clear my mind of the conversation I'd just had with Zadie and all the dissonant memories it triggered. Usually I was good at this. The mind was an entity subject to control just like everything else in the world, and I was a firm believer that you could skew your environment toward a desired result if you were thoughtful and disciplined enough. Most people seemed to slog through life with perpetual bewilderment at their fates, no matter how self-inflicted those were. They were quick to denounce anyone else's carelessness, but never seemed to acknowledge that whatever idiotic thing they themselves had done had contributed to their circumstances. Sometimes you're the victim of random bad luck, but sometimes—and the trauma service was the prime example of this—you brought it on yourself.

The other thing that I loathed was the complete inability of most people to think critically. They accepted as gospel all kinds of things without ever objectively examining for themselves why they so fervently believed them. Take childhood vaccinations, for example. There was such tremendous bias against them among some groups that people are willing to seize on one or two dubious bits of pseudo-research that someone parroted to them, completely disregarding the thousands of well-designed studies analyzing the issue, oblivious to how many of their children would have died from infectious diseases in another era. I couldn't fathom it. All you need to do to believe anything is surround yourself with a herd of like-minded reinforcers, and there's no need for objective reality at all. My favorite quotation ever, from some senator from New York, went something like this: *You are entitled to your own opinion, but you are not entitled to your own facts.*

All of this made it even more astonishing that I, Emma, had been the one to bring about a chain of events that ultimately tsunamied into tragedy, all because I had done something without thinking. I'd acted impulsively, based on my feelings, and ignored all the clanging warning bells. And I was forever enduring the shame of this, which was going to be even harder to forget now that Nick had joined my group.

Dwelling on this was unacceptable. I had to pull it together and get ready for my next case, an abdominal washout, right now. Where was all my self-control? What in the hell was wrong with me?

Trying not to break out into a flat-out sprint, I hurried to the women's locker room off the lounge, flung myself into a toilet stall, and sat, burying my face in my hands, counting and recounting backward from one hundred.

Maybe this lasted a minute, or maybe five, but I jolted back to reality when I heard myself paged overhead by the OR front desk. I quickly splashed some water on my face, dabbed a slight mascara smear away, and hustled over to OR 4, where my next case was scheduled, rapping on the glass to let them know I was there.

Outside each OR was a steel, troughlike sink with foot pedals to control the water. I set up to scrub at mine. This was no half-assed swipe under some running water. Scrubbing up for surgery is an involved process. You start by using scrub brushes under the nails and alongside each finger, really working up a good lather, and then proceed up the arms to the elbows, carefully holding your hands aloft so that no con-tamination would run down onto your clean fingers, and then you rinse just as carefully, hands to elbows, with no extra pass-throughs under the water. The whole process ideally takes about five minutes, but this ritual gave me another respite to collect myself. It was unlike me to get carried away with emotion. Time to man up.

I bumped my way into the OR, holding out my hands in front of me like Frankenstein's monster, and got gowned and gloved. I had to admit that my mind was not fully on the patient in front of me, but luckily, I could handle this kind of case in my sleep. It was Nick that had me tied in knots.

At first I figured that I'd ignore the message. Screw Nick. There was no need to be overly communicative with the bastard. I would engage in whatever discourse was needed from a work-related standpoint, when and if it came to that; I'd be cordial but frosty, so that he got the message that we weren't going to be pals. Bygones were not bygones.

But then I had second thoughts. Curiosity was killing me; I wondered what he thought about my presence in the group and how he intended to handle it. He might not have known initially that Zadie lived in Charlotte too, but now he certainly did. Her last name might have been different, but there weren't too many Zadies around, especially ones who were friends of mine. Knowing Nick, he probably thought she'd be thrilled to reunite with him. So maybe I should have called him back and discussed the situation under circumstances that I controlled, rather than waiting until I randomly bumped into him in the hospital.

All this musing proved to be academic, however, because when I finished the latest case and went back to the surgeons' lounge to rest for a minute, the man sitting on the leather couch next to me turned out to be him. It was Nick.

———

"Emma!" he said, the corners of his mouth lifting in an ostensible smile. "It's Nick, Nick Xenokostas. We obviously couldn't chat last week."

"I know who you are, Nick," I said, feeling like my tongue had gained a massive amount of weight. "I got a message from you."

"Yeah, sorry. I wanted to let you know our mutual patient is doing well—I hadn't realized that you were in the group at first. What are the odds?" He shifted on the sofa to face me.

So that answered one question. He hadn't known I was here at first.

(But . . . really? "Dr. Emma Colley" was listed first under Meet Our Physicians on the practice website. But he sounded so believable.)

". . . and before I moved, I didn't even know you were a surgeon, let alone practicing in Charlotte. How do you like it here?"

"Fine," I growled, looking around. So much for a controlled situation. The surgeons' lounge, which was deserted half of the time, was all of a sudden chock-full. Sitting right next to us was old Dr. Dinsmore, who had been practicing since the dawn of time and who didn't approve of women doctors, and on his left was an egomaniacal orthopedic surgeon named Chas Dunworthy, and across from him were two residents and my eager-beaver medical student. (Hopefully I had not been such a shameless kiss-ass as a student.) They all looked intrigued by the conversation.

"Yeah? It's a good group? How do you—"

"Excuse me, Nick," I said, abruptly standing. "I need to stretch my legs for a minute. Nice to see you." I headed toward the door.

"Actually, I could use a walk too," said Nick, following me. "Been in the OR all day. You know how—"

I spun around as soon as the door had shut behind us, looking right at him for the first time. Naturally, he'd aged well. He was what, six, seven years older than me? But he looked as vital and commanding as ever at six foot two, with strong, broad shoulders, a head of thick dark blond hair, and a chiseled jaw like he was made to order from a catalog of TV surgeons. His handsome face reflected some concern, probably because I was glowering at him like he'd whipped out his penis and waggled it at me.

"What are you doing here, Nick? This is not exactly welcome news," I exploded.

His expression progressed to full-blown alarm.

"Oh, hell, I'm sorry, Emma. I didn't . . . I thought . . . I mean, I didn't know this would happen. I'm getting a divorce. I needed a fresh start, and there was a job opening up here, and it's hard—harder than you would think—to find a job in a decent city right now." He raised his eyebrows but then quickly lowered them, chastened by my stony look. "Emma, this can work out. We have to work together."

This didn't merit a response. "Are you definitely staying in Charlotte?"

He grinned a little, a return to the Nick I recognized. "Well, your group gave me a very attractive package. So, yes. I want to move past . . . the past. I know you think I'm an ogre, and maybe that's true."

I tried not to snarl.

"Emma," he said, his expression shifting into something harder. "You should give it some thought."

I ignored this too. "I heard you know Zadie's here."

"I do, yes. I saw her name on TV that night."

"And?"

"I take it the two of you repaired your friendship?"

My lips parted, but nothing came out.

Nick stiffened. I could almost hear the cerebral cogs start churning as he realized what I wasn't saying. An undefinable expression crossed his face.

"She still doesn't know what you did," he said. He began blinking, hard and fast. "Oh my God."

Fury filled me. "How about what you did?" I spun around and started away from him, but his voice stopped me dead.

"What I did," he said, "didn't kill anyone."

A drumbeat of poisonous air filled the hall. I tried to inhale but began to choke, the crystallized cruelty of his words shredding my lungs. I turned my head aside and forced myself to breathe anyway, until a cold rage accumulated in my brain. I whirled back around.

"If you stay here," I said, "I will find a way to ruin you."

"Emma," he said.

"I swear it. I swear it. I will find a way, so help me God."

"I only—"

"Get away from me."

There was a throat-clearing sound next to us, and a familiar voice said, "Ahem."

I pivoted. Wyatt stood a bit forlornly, holding a box of Krispy Kreme doughnuts. "I bought a treat for your call night," he said. "Have I blundered into something?"

"Not at all," I said. I strode away, forcing a calm tone into my voice as I walked. "I'm heading back to the lounge in a second," I told Wyatt, careful not to look behind me. "Let me walk you out."

As soon as we were a suitable distance down the corridor, Wyatt said, "Darling. Why were you having a heated discussion in the hall with that man?"

I sighed. "Wyatt. Why are you bringing me doughnuts? You know I don't eat those."

"A little sugar won't kill you, beloved. I happened to find myself near the hospital and had to come up with an excuse to barge in on you, which turned out to be quite interesting. I ask again: why were you and that man so intense?"

Wyatt said this without the slightest trace of jealousy. It never seemed to occur to him that other men might be a threat, even though the hospital was fully stocked with alpha-male surgeons. But Wyatt blazed confidence.

I sighed again, giving my husband a look of fond exasperation. "I've got another case, Wy. I'll call you this evening if there's a lull. I really can't get into it right now, but you're right—it is interesting, in a grim sort of way. Okay?"

"All right," Wyatt said, thrusting the box of doughnuts at me. "But eat the damn sugar bombs. Otherwise I'm going to."

I accepted the box reluctantly, gave Wyatt a quick kiss, and headed back toward the OR.

———

The lull didn't present itself until after evening rounds.

I decided to get in TICU afternoon rounds while we could, offering my beleaguered team of residents a doughnut in return for a day's hard work. Evening rounds were informal. The team that had been on last night with me was long gone, since the Graduate Medical Education Council had limited the hours of the resident work week back in 2003. This meant that a lot of the information on the day's events was coming from the nurses, so afternoon rounds were something I took seriously. I didn't want to miss something vital on my watch.

Finally, around four o'clock, I was free. Who to call first, Zadie or Wyatt? I owed Zadie a call. But even though I hadn't shown it, I felt grateful to Wyatt for visiting me. He generally had a predictable schedule: he went in to the office every morning at eight; worked there until noon; had a nice, tax-deductible business lunch at a downtown restaurant, which he enjoyed mightily and refused to give up despite some cholesterol issues; and then spent the afternoon at one of his five dealerships, bestowing his presence on favored salesmen and an occasional flattered customer. He rarely deviated from this schedule; he was a creature of habit. In fact, I could not recall him ever having shown up at my work before, at least not unannounced. Wyatt sometimes seemed to possess a supernatural awareness of when things were going badly for me.

Still, he would want to talk my ear off, and Zadie would likely be getting clobbered by the demands of afternoon in the Anson house, so she was a better bet for a brief call. I texted her.

Have time to chat?

I got an instant reply.

Filled up car with diesel instead of regular gas on way home
today—v. bad. 10K damage to engine and stranded all kids and D.
barfed on neighbor who was helping. Gonna have Xanax or nice
glass wine, but . . . sure. For you.

I had to smile. For someone so intelligent, Zadie was always managing to shoot first and ask questions later. She was a loving mother, a doting wife, an ethical, thoughtful cardiologist, a loyal friend, a concerned and energetic citizen, and an all-around stellar representative of the human race, but she was also kind of a lovable dingbat.

"That's horrible about the car," I said when she answered. "Does Drew know?"

"Oh yes," said Zadie. "Yes, he does. He figured it out when he had to leave some vitally important conference call and pick up our vomiting three-year-old preschool dropout from Jean Anne's."

"What do you mean, 'preschool dropout'?" I asked. "I thought she was back in."

"Ohhh, that's a story for later." Zadie sounded a little unhinged. Probably she wasn't kidding about the Xanax and wine. "I can only relate one disaster at a time. It wasn't exactly a voluntary dropout, though. Let me just say it's a mistake in a preschool classroom to allow easy access to a bag containing twenty-two birthday cupcakes."

"Oh dear."

"Drew actually took it well. The car, I mean. He could have gotten really pissed, but when I finally saw him, he took one look at me and then held me. I've never been so grateful in my life."

"Well, at least that's good. You could be married to a pig who would hold things like that against you," I said, assailed for the thousandth time by the thought of how much men loved Zadie.

"Right," she said, a little uncertainly. "So—what's up?"

"Oh." I briefly debated with myself. Maybe now was not the best time for this.

"Go ahead, Em," Zadie broke in. "Out with it. My day is not going to get worse."

"I talked to Nick. He said he wants to tell you he's sorry."

". . ."

"Zadie? Are you there?"

"My day is getting worse. You called him back? Did he say anything about the dog?"

"I didn't call him," I replied. I paused, choosing my words carefully. "He showed up at the hospital. Said he's getting a divorce, plans to stay here, and he saw us both on the news and he wants us to be friends. I'm sorry. I forgot to ask about the dog's name."

Silence, then a faint crashing sound.

"Zadie?"

More silence, then some background rustling. Finally: "Sorry! Going to have to get some more wine here!"

Maybe I should have called Wyatt first after all.

Chapter Seventeen

NONNEGOTIABLE RULES

Emma, Present Day

In contrast to the rules for the residents I trained, there were no limits on how many hours I could work in a week. There were no limits on the number of hours I could work in a row. There were only so many trauma surgeons, and one of us had to be at the hospital at all times. Thus I found myself back on in-house call again on Wednesday night, covering for a colleague whose mother had died, only two days after the marathon call beginning Monday morning that brought me the Packard child.

It was the middle of the night and I was tired. Being tired wasn't unusual though; I've been working this kind of schedule for many years. But yesterday's interaction with Nick had left me uneasy and unsettled in a way I couldn't seem to shake. He held the power to upend my life, and I had no idea what to do about it.

But I also lacked the luxury of time to fret about it. If there's any consistency to trauma call, it's the likelihood that all hell will break loose at the darkest, most forlorn hour of the night. While most of America sleeps, the ER docs, the anesthesiologists, and the surgeons (among others) are toiling away, trying to stem a tide of catastrophes that can't wait until morning. (I'm not including the OBs in this list, although they get hammered more than anyone else at night. But at least their nocturnal work is more likely to be happy.)

Three o'clock in the morning: my least favorite time of day. There's a lull sometime around this point every night, lasting just long enough to bring on an internal debate about whether or not it's worth it to try to sleep. I used to be able to catnap and get some benefit from it, but after I had Henry, I couldn't rally like I used to. It was better not to sleep at all than to be forced into action forty-five minutes after you lay down. On the other hand, if I could get a few solid hours in a row, I'd feel much better.

So I eased myself onto the uncomfortably firm bed in my call room, and of course my pager went off a few minutes after I finally fell into a desperate, hard-edged sleep. A dull heaviness encased me as I awoke, as if my metabolism had slowed to a tenth of its normal speed. I jumped up and was forced to bend forward at the waist as a wave of nauseating dizziness pulsed through me.

I panted for a moment, head between my knees. Was I sick? Or was this some physical manifestation of stress? Maybe I was too old for this. I'd always prided myself on my toughness, especially since I work in a field so completely dominated by men. My phone beeped a reminder, and I forced myself upright. Another level-one trauma en route. I started down the hall, staring at the maroon carpet under my feet.

From years of painstakingly patching up people who'd been squashed, shot, stabbed, and mangled, I'd developed a healthy degree of safety consciousness. Everyone who knew me also knew my nonnegotiable rules: no alcohol or cell phone usage if driving, no guns, no climbing on roofs, and of course, you didn't set foot in my car without a seat belt.

(Although my safety measures didn't quite approach the level of paranoia manifested by one of my med school professors, a guy named Cyril Herring, who insisted on wearing a ridiculously conspicuous NASCAR-type helmet everywhere he drove.) I also privately believed alcohol should be off-limits for anyone who exhibited poor impulse control, although I hadn't quite worked out how to implement that one.

As I regarded the scene in the ER, I reflected that maybe Dr. Herring had been onto something. Head injuries are the bane of trauma surgeons: most often these patients aren't fixable. Our brains contain one hundred billion neurons, but exactly how they function is still something of a mystery. Especially when they've been flung into a dashboard at forty-five miles per hour.

The other injury I detest in trauma patients is a bunch of broken bones. I couldn't do anything for broken bones, and the people who could—orthopedic surgeons —intimidated me. A race of overgrown, jocular, self-appointed surgical overlords, they lumber around the hospital confident in the belief that nothing trumps a fracture. As an illustration of this, the orthopedic surgeon standing in the ER right now had once stormed up to me in the TICU, commanding me to book an operating room for him stat so he could fix our mutual patient's femur fracture. I declined to call the OR for him, which prompted a condescending lecture about the time-critical nature of restoring a pulseless extremity. I listened without interrupting and then politely informed him (a) I was the trauma surgeon, not the nurse, and (b) perhaps the patient's leg was pulseless because he had died several hours ago, a fact that had escaped this doctor but not the family of the patient, who were watching this exchange with open mouths. I was right, of course, but despite this, none of the ortho guys here seemed to like me.

So this patient had a nonoperable head injury and a broken leg and some spine fractures and was going to be absolutely uninteresting from a management standpoint, but he was my responsibility because he had multiple body systems involved. Neurosurgeons and orthopedists don't manage patients who have other injuries. I nodded to our midlevel resident and intern to take over the workup, and I headed for the door.

Before I could get ten feet outside the ER, my pager informed me the EMTs were five minutes out with another one. I resigned myself to yet another night without sleep.

This one was more palatable: another guy, another drunken car crash, but at least he had chest and abdominal injuries instead of a head injury. I wasn't particularly fired up about going back to the OR, but it would have the benefit of keeping me awake. And it would make the time pass quickly until morning. Sanjay, along with our med student, barreled off to scrub; I limped along behind them, battling another surge of nausea and fatigue. I straightened my shoulders and told myself not to be a wimp.

But I felt even worse when I got to the OR. One of the scrub techs, a vapid, tattooed woman named Darla, cut off her droning chatter mid-word as I entered the room. She might as well have worn a sign around her neck: I WAS COMPLAINING ABOUT YOU, DR. COLLEY. I waved a tired hand at her.

The circulating nurse mistook this for permission to resume their conversation. Ignoring them both, I buttressed my leaden body against the solidity of the OR table, trying to breathe deeply enough to stave off the urge to crumple up in the fetal position.

Some of Darla's giggly words filtered out to me: ". . . foxy *and* nice . . . Sherry says . . . just divorced . . ."

"Can we get it quiet in here?" I said, my tone harsher than I intended. All conversation ceased.

Trembling, I considered my options. I could let Sanjay and the medical student do the case, but it was too early in the year for that: the medical student, eager though he was, was only one step up from the average fool on the street when it came to surgical ability. I trusted Sanjay as much as I trusted anyone who wasn't me, but that wasn't saying a lot: it's widely acknowledged that I have control issues.

But I should have. I should have. I should have let Sanjay take over. Something was wrong with me—fatigue, or sickness, or stress—and only a few minutes into the case, I made a mistake. A big mistake, a stupid, completely avoidable mistake: I wasn't careful enough as we cut open the lining of the abdomen, and I sliced a hole, a very big one, in the patient's small intestine. At this hour of the night, one might hope for a relatively empty GI tract, but unfortunately this was not the case here. Not only had this man gotten all liquored up before wrecking his car, but at some point in the evening, he'd apparently ingested a meal gigantic enough to power an entire NFL team, which was now enthusiastically coursing its way out of the unexpected opening in the bowel. I stared, horrified, for a second before Sanjay grabbed the loop of bowel and elevated it, calling for the scrub nurse to give him some irrigation.

"Ah," I stuttered. What had been a relatively straightforward case had suddenly veered off into unexpected territory, placing the patient at much greater risk of complications. He might even have to have an ileostomy, or an artificial opening made along his abdomen to allow waste to exit his body.

"Dr. Colley," said the circulating nurse on the other side of the room, oblivious to what I'd just done. "It's Dr. Garber." She gestured behind her, where the cord of the phone looped down from the wall onto a long counter. Dr. Garber was Melinda Garber, our team's intern. "She says she keeps getting paged about one of the patients—something about a falling urine output—and she wants to know if somebody can go evaluate."

"Why can't she do it?" I snapped, aggravation momentarily eclipsing my distress. Melinda had a reputation for trying to pawn off her work onto other people. "How long have they been paging her?"

"She says she's with the other trauma patient you guys got tonight. A head injury."

"I know that," I said. "So?"

I returned my attention to the unfolding disaster in front of me as the circulator murmured into the phone. Caustic bowel contents were flooding everywhere, along with what appeared to be several dozen kernels of intact corn. I shuddered, close to vomiting.

"She says he's not stable," the circulator said, as the medical student reared up behind me for a better look.

"Wow," he said.

"Not stable? What does that mean?"

More murmuring. "She says she has to go," the circulator announced, hanging up the phone. "She said she and Dr. Schreiber"—Dr. Schreiber was the midlevel resident—"are going to work on him."

"What? Work on him? What does that mean?" I said. "Call her back." The only part of Sanjay's face I could see behind his mask was his eyes, but I could tell he was grimacing, although whether from Melinda's uselessness or the fiasco in front of us, I couldn't tell. We worked in grim silence.

"She's not answering," the circulator said several minutes later, at the same time as Sanjay announced, "I think we need to divert him, Dr. A." Silently I concurred with the need to place an ostomy; without an artificial opening from the intestine to the outside of his abdomen, the patient was now at risk of a giant, festering infection if this leak continued. Shame crept up my body in a wave of heat.

The anesthesiologist popped his head over the blue curtain. "We're having trouble ventilating here," he said. "We sure there was no pneumo?"

He wanted to know if the lung could be collapsing. "No, there—"

"One of the ICUs is calling you, Dr. Colley," interrupted the circulator.

"Because we're getting a really high airway pressure here." An alarm began to sound behind the anesthesiologist.

"Dr. Colley, look out," said Sanjay suddenly, ignoring the anesthesiologist. "We've got a bleeder somewhere."

"Suction," I ordered, reeling. I turned to the medical student. "Break scrub and call the radiologist; ask him to review for a small pneumothorax that we might have missed when we read the films originally." At his look of befuddlement, I added, "Pneumothorax. It's an air leak that's compressing the lung so it can't expand. Every time we blow a breath into him with the ventilator, we're making the pneumo bigger and collapsing the lung further. We think." To the circulator, I barked, "Get a chest tube kit."

"What do you want me to tell the ICU?"

"Tell them to handle it, or to page Melinda if it's urgent."

"Oh my, where is this coming from?" said Sanjay, suctioning furiously. Blood burbled up at us in a hostile spew. "We need to pack this."

"They can't reach Melinda, Dr. Colley. They say they need you to come now."

"Emma." The anesthesiologist again. "We're starting to deoxygenate here. I'm pretty sure he's got a tension pneumothorax."

"Put them on speaker," I yelled at the circulator. To Sanjay, I said, "Forget the bowel injury for now. You pack. I'm going to decompress his chest."

The circulator held up the phone, which crackled anticlimactically for a moment. Then we could hear a panicked voice. "Dr. Colley?"

"Yes, what?" I said. I moved laterally along the patient's body, preparing to stick a large needle in his chest wall, as the scrub nurse tore open the chest tube kit.

More crackles. ". . . the little girl. Packard."

I stopped, my hand arrested just above the middle of my patient's chest wall. "Hurry," said the anesthesiologist. The loud beeping behind him began to accelerate, followed by a second, continuous alarm sound.

"What about the Packard girl?" I yelled. I plunged the needle into the left side of the chest, a few inches below the clavicle. Nothing.

"Shit! It's not this side. Where's the tube kit?"

"She's coding," said the voice on the phone.

I was reaching across my patient's body, ready to decompress the other side of the chest as soon as the scrub nurse handed me another catheter. I froze again. "What did you say?" I said, the burning in my cheeks so extreme I thought I'd be consumed by their fire. I plunged the second needle into my patient's chest, my hand shaking.

"I said, Eleanor Packard is coding," the nurse on the other end cried. Dimly, we could all hear shouting and the tiny, plucky sound of alarms through the phone's speakers, adding to the nerve-jangling shriek of our own alarms. "Please come. She's coding."

Chapter Eighteen

COMBAT WITH THE MAXIMUM BAD GUY

Late Summer, 1999: Louisville, Kentucky
Zadie

I was holding the phone between my chin and shoulder, lying with my head propped up on a pile of Emma's pillows, which she'd transposed to the foot of the bed. Graham, who was omnipresent these days, was lounging outside the open bedroom door, watching some stupid movie. I could hear a steady drone of racing car engines, which were no doubt engaged in a superfluous violent cross-city car chase. Emma faced me, reclining against the headboard, watching the call transpire with undisguised interest. Her entire body had perked up; even her hair seemed to be magnetized with concentrated attention. I felt too weary to hide anything. I wanted comfort, and the best place to be for that right now was curled up with my beloved roommate, wearing my oldest, softest, and least flattering pajamas, trying to distract myself with some bad TV. Well, some bad TV other than whatever ridiculous testosterone-fest

Graham was watching. The last thing I felt like doing was romancing it up outside the hospital, even though I'd been clamoring for this for weeks.

"Ah, c'mon, Z. You got me all excited about the date night, and I want to celebrate your last day on the rotation. I had lots of flowery things to say," X offered.

"Ooh," I blurted, momentarily intrigued in spite of myself. "Give me a little illustration."

"Not happening, unless you get your hot little ass over here."

"We-ell . . ." I said, torn. Maybe I should have rallied. Maybe the best way to erase my blues would have been distraction.

Sensing weakness, X pounced. "I got you something, Zadie," he said, his voice softening. "You've been on my mind all day, and I know I should be more courtly to you, especially when it was such a rough day. I know you're upset"—he hesitated—"and I really want to comfort you."

Yes, that sealed it. For all his many virtues—brilliance, wit, dedication, scorching talent in bed—X was a man most comfortable in a world of other men; he didn't normally seem given to expressing emotion or producing spontaneous gestures of thoughtfulness. *I know I should be more courtly* was, in X parlance, akin to saying *I feel a passionate connection of our souls.* Or something like that. High drama on a normal day for him might have consisted of a creative cursing streak if a scrub tech dropped his hemostats.

But I knew he was capable of caring deeply about things; I had seen his face go white late this morning when Lima Trauma, the young father with the neck injury, suddenly had a massive stroke and died. X had summoned Lima's wife, a woman in her early twenties with that kind of pale English skin that is more pink than white. Her hair had been reduced to the consistency of pillow stuffing from repeated bleaching and she was built like a dumpling. Nevertheless, she was a pretty thing, and friendly, even despite the ordeal of her husband's injury. I could hear her anguished sobbing through the thick family room door as Dr. X broke the news. Lima's body was gone by the time we finished afternoon sign-out. Dr. X had stood silently by the empty unit bed, expressionless, until the charge nurse Val had walked up behind him and slipped something into his pocket.

I snuck back in and asked Val about it. I suspected Val might be the one person at the hospital who knew about our affair. She was always perceptive, and her glance had gone straight to me a few times during rounds when Dr. X had thrown out some subtle double entendres. But then, charge nurses generally knew everything. When I asked about the item Val had given Dr. X after Lima's death, I'd been surprised to hear the answer. "Lima's wife's name and address," Val told me. "He always writes to their families. And they almost always write him back; some of them have been corresponding with him for years. He rarely ever talks about it."

So, should I get out of bed and activate my hot little ass into mobility while the night was still young and X was still in an unusually gushy mood? After this week, we could date openly, since I'd no longer be on the trauma service, and I felt eager to see how that was going to play out. I murmured a capitulation into the phone and hung up, turning to find Emma staring at me with laserlike intensity.

"Spill it," said Emma.

"Ah . . ."

"It's X, that fifth-year general-surgery resident," called Graham from the other room, without tearing his eyes away from what now sounded like a decapitation by chain saw.

Both of us turned to him in astonishment.

"How did you know—" I began.

"Why didn't you tell—" burst out Emma at the same time, both of us bolting toward him.

Graham tore his attention away from the television gore and held his hands up in surrender. "Whoa, ladies," he said. "I just know things. How'd it happen, Fletch?"

"Dr. *X*?" Emma said. "Dr. *Xenokostas*, your chief resident? That's who you've been sneaking around with?"

"Well, I wouldn't exactly say sneaking around—"

Emma, sporting two bright pink patches on her cheeks, had a gift for getting right to the point. She was having none of this bullshit. "Have you gone out anywhere outside the hospital? Have you told anyone you were dating? Did you tell *me* you were dating? I bet he told you not to, didn't he?"

Huffily: "Em, you know we couldn't—"

"Zadie, he *grades* you."

"Oh, he told me he's having Allison do the evaluation," I retorted after a weak attempt at a joke about it. Actually, this was the first time this had occurred to me, and X had in fact told me nothing of the sort. It was a good idea though; I'd better mention it to him immediately. "Don't be all judgmental, Em. I grant you that it's somewhat awkward at the moment, what with the whole chief/med student thing, which means we have to keep it secret. But think about it: he's leaving next year; there is only a short time we *could* be together to know if it has long-term potential. You know I've always been a jackass magnet. I think this is different. I can hardly stop thinking about him."

Emma softened. "You don't look all that happy," she said uncertainly.

"I had a brutal day. Something went wrong at work, but I don't want to talk about it. I promise, Em, we'll have a big talk after the exams, and I'll fill you in on everything."

"But do you think he's good for you? There's a reason why the medical school frowns on this," Emma said, eyebrows scrunched.

"Well, obviously, things will be a little less weird once I'm off the service in a few days, and we can spend more, ah, appropriate time together."

"But when did this happen?"

I tried to look dignified. "It was gradual . . . Sometime early in my trauma rotation. I know I should've told you."

"Yes, but— Okay. Okay, I know I have to let you make your own decisions," Emma said, smiling too brightly at me.

"They grow up so fast, dear," bellowed Graham, riveted once more by the screen, now featuring two men attacking each other with karate moves.

Emma rolled her eyes. "Excuse me, G," she said. "How could you not mention that you knew about this?"

"Zadie would've told us if she wanted us to know," he said. "Besides, it was a guess."

"How did you think to guess him, though?" I asked, wondering how indiscreet we'd been. Maybe everyone—except Emma—knew.

Graham was quiet for a minute, apparently mulling this over. "You looked a little different whenever you mentioned him," he said finally.

"Ugh," Emma groused. "Not only does my own boyfriend keep extremely vital information to himself, but he's also more perceptive than me."

"Well," he said, his attention returning to the movie, where the martial arts combat had been usurped by a full-blown gun battle in which everyone was blown to pieces except the hero, who was, of course, able to dodge bullets. "Right now I am keenly observing this badass shoot-out."

I studied the TV. "What, no bulletectomy?" I asked, as the bloody sidekick lay writhing in the hero's arms. "Isn't there usually a pointless bullet extraction in these movies?"

"Bulletectomies are cool, Zadie," said Graham seriously. "All you need is some whiskey and rusty toenail clippers or something and the victim will spring right up. But mainly it's important that there be a car chase and some mano a mano combat with the maximum bad guy."

He grinned and turned off the TV, then padded over and enveloped both Emma and me in a big bear hug. "You know, Zadie," he said, ruffling my hair, "I love you, but you *are* a jackass magnet. Be careful, okay?"

———

You had to give him credit. X had clearly spent more than a few minutes trying to fathom the unfathomable emotional needs of the fairer sex and had then taken the time to systematically implement an array of romantic clichés in the bachelor pad. This began with sultry music (Cowboy Junkies, good choice), flowers (wilted daisies and carnations, which were not my preference—or any woman's preference really—but it was the thought that counted), candles (this was definitely the weak link because one of them was a half-melted Santa shape, and the other, even more bizarrely, was emblazoned with the face of Ray Lewis of the Baltimore Ravens—but again: the thought), and a table set with actual plates and cutlery and a bottle of cabernet. There was even a smallish gift-wrapped box at one of the places. I could appreciate why X had not wanted to cancel.

"If you blew me off, I was going to have to go outside and drag some chick in off the street, caveman style, so all this would not go to waste," he said, gesturing proudly. As a romantic statement this was something of a failure, but nonetheless, I was touched. His face, which could be uncharitably described as haughty, was now beaming with what appeared to be tenderness.

"It's all lovely," I said. "Thank you."

"Yes. Er, well. Now what? I suppose we should eat?"

"X, did you seriously get to the age of"—I paused, calculating—"thirty without knowing how to proceed on a date if you can't immediately commence some action? Have you not ever had a proper girlfriend?"

"Of course I have," he huffed. "It's not me. I can't help it if I radiate sex appeal. Normally, I'd be having to beat you off me if I wanted to eat first."

There was some truth to this, so I let it slide. We were insanely sexually compatible, to the point where it was hard to be productive at work while constantly fighting the urge to rip each other's clothes off and go at it right there in the surgeons' lounge, or on the operating room table, or wherever. How often in life did you meet someone whose presence caused you to blaze into an immediate erotic meltdown every single time you saw them? Every glance between us was charged; every utterance, every physical contact, no matter how slight, seemed to rearrange the very molecules of the air around us into incandescent conductors of longing. No wonder people used heat metaphors to describe passion.

However. We were adults, and in general, adults who considered themselves to be intelligent, decent human beings often had standards for ongoing relationships that involved more than enthusiastically screwing each other's brains out. We stared at each other politely over a meal of green chili wontons and salads from the Bristol restaurant down the street.

"Are you upset about what happened with the pregnant lady?" X asked.

"Yes," I said. "But I don't want to think about it. Besides, I'm pretty familiar with Dr. X, genius surgeon. Let's discuss something non-work-related."

"Please," said X. "Say Nick."

"Nick," I tried. It sounded really strange. "I wish I knew more about your life outside medicine."

"Uh-oh. Here we go," said Nick. "Next you'll be wanting to know what I'm thinking and feeling."

"It's a slippery slope," I agreed.

"Okay. I'm from Maryland, went to med school there, then landed here because my aunt lives here and I'd heard how great the surgery program is. I've always wanted to be a surgeon—my dad's a surgeon—and I have two brothers who are my best friends. What else? I love poetry, moonlight, and long walks on the beach."

"That started off well," I said encouragingly. "I feel like I know you so much better now."

He laughed. "Honestly, Zadie, it was definitely not my plan to seduce a twenty-four-year-old medical student, beautiful though you are. But do you know why I can't stay away from you?"

"Yep," I said, guiltily flushing with pleasure at being described as beautiful.

"No, you don't," he said. "It's not the sex, even though that's fucking unbelievable. It's that I love the quirky way you think. You are never boring."

"Oh my God," I said, dropping my fork in delight. "Jackpot!"

"What?" he asked.

"You just said—sincerely—that you love me for my mind. That completely legitimizes all the hot sex!"

For a second he just looked at me. Then he lost the battle and lunged up, and in one fluid motion he knocked his chair back and lifted me out of mine. I flung myself into him. He kissed me, hoisting me up so that my legs wrapped around his waist. Then somehow we were rolling on the ground where we'd been standing, tearing off our clothes. I was reeling from a familiar wave as an exquisite storm of dopamine flooded my brain. *So good, so good, so good* . . . This feeling was why people got addicted to heroin, why people risked everything for affairs, why people jumped from airplanes . . . this rush of being as completely alive as it is possible to be, a honey-thick ecstasy coursing through your veins. I gasped as I felt him wrench my legs apart, his mouth still on mine. His jaw was recognizably male in shape just by feeling it against my cheek, with its flawless right angle and its golden sandpapery roughness. I felt nearly liquid, a butter girl left in the sun.

He closed his eyes, lost in whatever ecstatic grip had command of him; but then he paused for an interminable second, still except for a slight heaving of his chest. He lifted his face so he could see mine and said hoarsely, "I think I love you, Zadie."

"I think I love you too," I whispered.

———

Later, after we replaced our clothes and ate the cold wontons and drank the wine, we wrapped up in an ugly camel-colored fuzzy blanket and entwined ourselves on Nick's fat sofa, drowsing in the extinguishing light of Santa and Ray Lewis.

"I think we did pretty well tonight on the date, Z," Nick said. "We made it at least five minutes before we knocked boots."

I sniffed. "I know there's a lot of satisfied machismo going on here, but could you phrase that more delicately?"

"Sorry, my little dumpling," he said. "We held off as long as possible before we became intimate."

"Thank you. That's much sweeter."

Nick blinked and sat up. "Oh hell, I never gave you the present," he said. "Want me to go get it?"

"No worries," I assured him. "You don't need to get up. I already know what it is."

"No, you don't," he protested, arching his back to see if the flat box still appeared to be fully wrapped.

"I hate to break this to you, Rico Suave," I said, "but based on the rest of your setup in here, I'd say it is one hundred percent obvious that that box contains naughty lingerie."

"Huh," he mumbled. Then, hopefully: "Well, maybe you can wear it tomorrow?"

"I'd love to," I said happily, burying my face in his chest.

In the wash of contentment that swept over me as I lay in his arms, it was easier to banish the *bad thought*. It retreated to the periphery of my conscience, trying to creep back into the daylight of my mind. I shut it down.

But it was still back there: earlier in the day, I had made a mistake that would kill someone.

Chapter Nineteen

THE SOBER KITCHEN

Early Autumn, 1999: Louisville, Kentucky
Zadie

"Do you know," asked Rolfe, waving his glass around, "what Louisville was originally called?"

"No, but I have a bad feeling you're about to tell us," said Landley.

"Corn Island," announced Rolfe, ignoring Landley. "Louisville started out as a forty-three-acre outpost by the falls of the Ohio River, where early settlers planted crops, presumably corn. Then in 1778, George Rogers Clark, a famous leader of the Revolutionary War, departed from the island with his militia to whup up on the English, leaving behind a band of hardy farmers. Over time, these predecessors of present-day Kentuckians relocated to the main banks of the Ohio, and the thriving metropolis of Louisville was born."

"Please, God, make it stop," mumbled Landley. He slumped forward with his hands over his ears.

Rolfe was undeterred. "Corn Island—the original Louisville—didn't actually fare so well. It eroded and sank in 1895, after the Louisville Cement Company removed most of its trees."

I was intrigued in spite of my bleak mood. "Really?" I asked. "That can happen?"

"Oh yes. And the history of corn itself is fascinating. It isn't natural; it was genetically engineered by early humans from an inedible wild plant called teosinte. But that's not the most interesting thing about corn."

Rolfe paused dramatically.

"Without corn, there would be no bourbon."

Landley perked up. "Oh, sweet nectar of the Gods!" he roared, holding up a small glass. "Skål!"

We couldn't usually afford the really good bourbons. Landley was something of an aficionado, however, and following an excellent day at Churchill Downs, he had sprung for a 120-proof bottle of Woodford Reserve. He'd hit a trifecta on the fifth race of the day, which paid out more than a thousand dollars, all of which he vowed to spend that evening. (*"Mi dinero, su dinero, amigos!"*) We started with dinner for six. My friends—Rolfe, Landley, Graham, Emma, and Georgia—were in a rousing mood; I was more subdued than usual. As delighted as I'd been by X telling me he loved me, I'd suffered a return of the blues as soon as I'd gotten home. I couldn't stop thinking about what had happened to Edict Trauma, the pregnant patient who had come in on my last call day.

I forced myself to listen to my ridiculous friends, who were engaged in a heated debate on the relative merits of Knob Creek versus Buffalo Trace. If anything could cheer me up, it was these turkeys. Despite my mood, I felt a fond smile cross my face.

". . . and a smoother finish," Landley puffed, his hair standing straight up in odd peaks. "I concede there is initially a slight burn. But it segues into a robust silkiness, a hint of tobacco and orange and possibly even mint."

"My dear fellow," bawled Rolfe. "You are so wrecked, your palate couldn't distinguish a tobacco-orange-mint shot of bourbon from a bowl of horseshit."

Emma turned to me. "Z," she said. "I've been thinking. What do you suppose would happen to X if the hospital knew about you two?"

"Shh," I hissed, but the bourbon debate had escalated and no one was listening. "He'd get his ass kicked. I'm not sure about the specifics. He did mention castration . . ."

"Hmm. How are things going with him?"

"Stellar," I said.

Graham perked up on the other side of us. "How's my harem holding up tonight?" he asked.

"Graham, I think you have misunderstood the nature of our recent cohabitation," I said. "I tolerate you because you sing so well in the shower, and I've got this strange fondness for the smell of sweaty athletic clothes draped everywhere. But you're really only shacking up with Emma."

Graham smiled at my banter, but he reached across Emma to clasp my shoulder. "You're a good friend, Zadie," he said, his voice soft and serious. "Thanks for putting up with me."

———

Outside, we conferred about transportation, abandoning the Caminator and walking to the corner of Bardstown and Cherokee, where the street traffic and the revelers coasted by in the last of the day's light. Restaurants, bars, boutiques, galleries, head shops, music stores, every possible nonchain enterprise crammed both sides of Bardstown Road. This section of town, known as the Highlands, wanted you to get your freak on.

Hannah rolled up in the White Hog, her roommate's retro Thunderbird, her round Muppet face smiley and pink. My friends crammed in, still arguing bourbons.

"If you say the word 'palate' one more time, Rolfe, I'm gonna kick you in the *huevos*," Georgia threatened.

"Speaking of palates, mine is a bit dry," Rolfe said.

"Yo, li'l dawg," drawled Landley, contorting in the backseat to somehow produce a bottle of Woodford from his pants. "Who's your daddy?"

"Oh dear," Hannah murmured. "Is it really bad tonight?"

"Is *what* really bad? Who wants a wee dram?"

"Me! Me!"

"Oh, why does James live in this really confusing neighborhood?" wailed Hannah. "Is this where I turn?"

"Hannah! Watch out!"

We all shrieked as the Hog abruptly wheeled down a side alley, narrowly avoiding a head-on collision with a truck, which screeched to a stop next to us. The window creaked down and an angry man stuck his head out.

"What in the Sam Hill is wrong with you, missy?" he barked. "You nearly hit me!"

"I'm so sorry. I didn't see—" Hannah started. She was interrupted by Rolfe from the front seat, who was raising and lowering both arms in a *Settle down. I've got this* gesture.

"Sorry about that, Bald Truck Dude," he began.

"Say what?" sputtered Bald Truck Dude, who did not appear to appreciate his new moniker.

"Perhaps if your farm vehicle were a brighter color. Oh my. Are those overalls?"

The man was now opening the truck door, gripping something in his right hand.

"Go, go, go, Hannah," Georgia screamed. In one fluid motion, Hannah threw the car into first and gunned it, burning rubber down the alley behind James's apartment in Cherokee Park.

"Roffff. Were you trying to get us killed? That guy weigh two-fiddy and had tire iron," Landley slurred.

"Whew," Hannah said shakily. "Has anybody ever wondered who Sam Hill was, anyway?"

Rolfe: "There were several famous Sam Hills. An early-nineteenth-century businessman whose establishments carried a wide array of odd inventory; a road builder in the Pacific Northwest who was thought to represent impossible projects; and my fav, Samuel Ewing Hill, an emissary of the governor of Kentucky, who was sent to intervene with the Hatfields and McCoys in 1887."

Dead silence.

Then, from Georgia: "What the hell, Rolfe? Did you just eat an encyclopedia?"

"My IQ is stratospheric. Please try to keep up."

"Your IQ is about the same as your penis circumference, jackass."

"Exactly." Rolfe smirked. "Thank you for acknowledging that, Georgia. Oh, here it is, Hannah."

We wandered in. The party appeared to be full-blast, which is to say the guests ran the gamut from sweet and well-dressed wives who would fit in nicely at a Wednesday evening Bible study, to a bunch of barbaric drunks. The med student wives were clustered in the Sober Kitchen, having an occasional sip of white wine, blond coifs gleaming. The drunks were scattered, but we located a conglomeration of them outside near the keg.

The party took place in a rambling old townhome from the early part of the nineteenth century, with soaring ceilings and ornate crown moldings, along with unusable, drafty fireplaces and Stone Age plumbing. With extensive renovation it could have been spectacular, but as it was, it languished in a row of ghettoized student housing. Nearly every house on the street sported crumbling trim and rickety back fire escapes, along with the requisite bedsheets in the windows—the universal denotation of student decorating budgets.

Ignoring the revelry, I plunked myself down on a hideous purple futon just off the kitchen, wrapping my arms around my knees. Suddenly my head felt unbearably heavy, the gargantuan weight of my thoughts squashing my neck straight down into my chest. I moaned a little and toppled onto my side.

"Whoa, Zadie! How wasted are *you*?" I felt the impact of a large body crashing down next to mine.

"I'm not drunk," I protested feebly.

"Yeah, well, you look like you're trying to cling to that couch to keep from falling off the earth."

Blearily, I opened one eye: Graham. He wore a flannel button-down and cargo shorts, and his wavy brown hair was rumpled endearingly. His cheeks were flushed.

"I am very drunk," he said happily.

"Yes," I agreed. "You are."

"Yes."

I waited, but nothing more came. Since the conversation appeared to have stalled, I closed my eyes and returned to my pit of misery. All the endorphins generated at Nick's apartment a couple days ago had fled, leaving me stuck in an endless feedback loop of *the bad thought*. I kept replaying it in my mind: I'd messed up. I'd done something very bad, something catastrophic, and I couldn't undo it. I moaned again.

"Zadie? Zadie? You okay?"

This time I opened both eyes, to find Graham's face an inch or two from mine, his brow furrowed in alarm. Gently, he hooked his arms under my armpits and heaved me into a sitting position. One of his hands wiggled out from my armpit and began patting my back in a rhythmic thump. The thumping was a little too vigorous, but also nice, like I was a baby or something. I hiccupped.

"Is it bad?" His voice was soft. "Whatever's bothering you?"

"Oh," I said. I hiccupped again, which then turned into a full-blown sob. I covered my face.

"It's okay. It's okay," he said. "Shhh, Zadie, it's going to be okay. Do you want to talk about it?"

It came flooding back: the knifelike awareness that had struck me as Edict's intubation had changed from exciting to terrible. One minute, I was blithe and confident; the next minute, a rush of shame and fear engulfed me in a clanging drumbeat. *Don't keep trying for longer than you can hold your own breath,* Nick told me. Without the tube to breathe for her, she would suffocate to death in a matter of moments. I'd felt my lungs screaming for air and still all I could see was a featureless landscape of homogenous pink in her airway; there was no sign of the vertically slanted whitish vocal cords, which were the structures I had to locate in order to get the tube into her trachea. Nick had taken over as soon as it was clear that disaster loomed, and we bagged her, but her oxygen levels had not risen. After an eternal agony of time, Nick had managed to get her reintubated. But by then crucial minutes had passed without oxygen.

She was twenty-seven. She was pregnant.

Again, I felt the nausea rise as I thought of my carelessness in preparing for the intubation. "I do and I don't," I said to Graham in a tiny voice.

"It's okay if you want to tell somebody," he said. "I think it's making you sick."

My tears surged up, little balloons of shame against my closed lids. An indeterminate choking noise escaped me.

I felt Graham slide over, and then his big arms were around me. "What I did, it's unforgivable," I told him, my tears wetting the front of his soft flannel shirt. He was quiet, patting my hair gently from time to time until I got ahold of myself. I could hear his heartbeat, a steady, distant, reassuring thud.

"Nothing's unforgivable, Zadie," he whispered.

I shuddered and closed my eyes. We sat like that, lost in our separate reflections, until my voice was steady enough to talk. Graham listened silently to my account, his face hardening as I talked.

"How could Dr. X—" he began.

"What's wrong with Zadie?"

We both looked up, startled. I scooted out of Graham's arms. Emma peered down at us, undoing her pinned-up knot of hair, releasing a buttery flow of silk. With her pink cheeks and swimming-pool-clear blue eyes, she looked like an arctic beauty queen.

Graham gestured to the futon. Emma sat down beside me, primly perched at the edge, her head half-cocked. "Are you okay?" she asked.

I shook my head, knowing if I tried to speak, I'd start wailing again. I glanced helplessly at Graham.

He leaned around me toward Emma and, in a low tone I could barely hear, filled her in. She listened, quietly at first, and then with increasing incredulousness.

"Zadie, none of that is your fault!" Emma sounded appalled. "Where were the respiratory therapists when this happened?"

"He asked me if I had everything ready, and I said yes." I shut my eyes, remembering. "It was just the two of us; there weren't any RTs there. Ni— Dr. X knows all about ventilators; he gave us the lecture on ventilator management, remember? We paged them, but he got tired of waiting and told me to go ahead. So I did."

Emma jumped up. "Dr. X holds one hundred percent of the responsibility there. He never should have attempted a complicated intubation in a pregnant trauma patient without the respiratory techs present, let alone tell an absolutely ignorant third-year medical student to 'get everything set up.' And the truth is, that girl was never going to survive anyway."

"You don't know that," I said miserably. "I kept pestering him to let me do it. I thought I knew what I was doing, and I didn't. And he probably only let me do it because . . ." My voice trailed off. I didn't have to say what we were all thinking. Nick had let me do the procedure without adequate preparation because I was sleeping with him.

"Anyway, the short version is, I messed it up. I failed that patient." I spoke quietly. I thought of the suction I hadn't hooked up, the disconnected oxygen. "It turned out her airway was swollen. I couldn't see anything at all when I looked with the laryngoscope. Her lungs were already trashed, so she didn't have any reserve. He finally did it somehow, but . . . she died a few hours later, when her family decided to pull the plug."

I hesitated and then gave voice to the thought I'd been trying to suppress:

"I don't think I can be a doctor now."

Graham and Emma began speaking at once; Graham's voice was steady and quiet, Emma's higher-pitched and insistent. Graham deferred to her and went silent, both of us absorbed by her vehemence. She swung in my direction.

"Listen to me, Zadie." Her eyes bored into mine. "I could go on and on about how none of us are perfect, how everyone makes mistakes, and all of that shit. It's trite, but it's true. And in your case, she was going to die anyway, and I don't think the responsibility lies with you. But regardless, there's good that will come from this terrible thing. And it's not you giving up a career you're going to be great at."

I dropped my eyes.

Emma twisted until I looked at her again. "Maybe none of us can be truly gifted at medicine until we've grasped the consequences of what we do. In most jobs, most of the time, you can put in a half-assed effort and the world isn't going to stop spinning. But in this case, the world did stop spinning, at least for one person—two people, actually. It's not enough to understand intellectually that lives depend on you. You have to feel it; and maybe you have to experience the crushing weight of responsibility that comes with all the accolades and respect and financial comfort accompanying medicine. You'd be a brilliant physician and a caring one no matter what. Now you'll be the most conscientious doctor you can be, because you know what it's like to fall into the depths. Maybe it seems easier to quit at this point, but, Zadie, you owe it to her to keep going."

I tried not to cry again—all this crying was getting really old—but there was no stopping it. I recognized some truth in what Emma said. But even if there was a silver lining, the thought of benefiting from the grotesquerie of someone's death in any way seemed monstrous. I thought of the way she'd looked—her delicate jaw, her dark hair fashioned in a pixie cut—and misery swamped me so thoroughly I wondered if it was possible to die from it. I cried, feeling as cut off and alone as it was possible to feel, spinning away in my own little joyless universe.

Then, from somewhere in the void, I felt a hand clasp mine and squeeze briefly before letting go. "Oh, Zadie," Emma murmured in a voice I'd never heard before. She hesitated and then drew me against her. She and Graham linked their hands behind my back and around my front, hugging me in the middle until I wasn't sure where I ended and they began. To my surprise, Emma pressed her cheek against mine, letting my tears wet her face as the three of us clung to one another, rocking slightly back and forth, oblivious to the party raging all around us.

Chapter Twenty

A FORCE FIELD OF PAIN

Emma, Present Day

There were 147 steps between the pediatric ICU and the Family Conference Room. I knew because I counted as I walked, and when I reached the conference room, I turned and retraced my steps. This time the count was off by two: 149. I'd have to redo it, both ways.

It took five minutes to confirm the total—147, correct the first time—but I added a third retracing to be sure. It didn't help: no march to the gallows had ever been heralded by such dread. I reached the door of the family room for the third time, but I could not raise my hand to knock.

After they'd finally dragged me from the Packard child's bedside, I'd hurled the contents of my stomach into the nearest trash can. I could feel my mewling stomach now, acid eating away at the lining, consuming me from within. I tipped my head backward and began to count the rectangular ceiling tiles.

Something no one knew: in med school, I began to have panic attacks. I didn't know that's what they were; I thought I suffered a form of hereditary insanity, my mind turning inward on itself in a cannibalistic fury. Black formless dread would seep over me like an unexpected immersion in a cave; I couldn't catch my breath and sometimes I couldn't feel my body. Gripped by sharp talons of terror, I'd have to hold on to the nearest object to keep from being swept away into the void.

Eventually, I learned what was happening, and the doctor at the student clinic, an early practitioner of Eastern meditative medicine, taught me techniques to soothe myself back from the brink. What worked for her didn't necessarily work for me, but I figured out I could calm myself by counting, or by physically arranging items into a logical progression by size, or sometimes by repeating a phrase in my mind until it became meaningless. And if I could, I'd run. Sometimes I ran for ten miles or more, the thudding repetition of my steps one more thing I could count.

So there I stood: thirty-six years old, number one in my medical school class, the top choice of my acclaimed surgical residency, the recipient of a perfect score on Part 3 of the USMLE, a surgeon, a wife, a mother; there I stood, outside this bland beige door, my head tilted so far back it hurt, frantically counting and recounting the dingy speckled tiles of the hospital's ceiling, the numbers churning and blurring in my mind, as I waited for a relief that I knew would never come.

Chapter Twenty-one

NONE OF THEM HAS
EVER BEEN HUNGRY

Emma, Present Day

"What did you just say?" I could hear other voices behind Zadie's: a low-level buzzing, phones ringing, an outraged baby yelling. Of course: she worked on Thursday mornings. I should have called her before she got to work, but I'd spent the last few hours rocking back and forth in my call room, leaving Sanjay to mop up the other patients from last night. "Emma, what did you say?"

"I need to see you," I whispered. My throat felt broken.

"I'm at w— Okay. Okay," she repeated. Her voice changed. "I'll see if Melanie can cover my morning patients. Are you at the hospital?"

I forced myself to speak audibly. "Yes," I said. "Call room."

"I'm on the way."

I hung up, glancing around dumbly as if seeing my surroundings for the first time: gray-beige walls, a twin bed fashioned from a chemical-emitting laminate, industrial maroon carpet. The call rooms were awful, but they were palatial compared to the rooms in which I'd been raised. Usually, I tried not to let myself dwell on the subject of my humble origins, but in my present circumstances, any topic would have been an improvement.

It was one of the many ways I separated myself from others. The women who surrounded me now were urbane and sophisticated; they thought nothing of dropping two grand on a handbag; this was true even of many doctors where I worked. They bought art. They lived in beautiful homes. They were cerebral, including the stay-at-home moms. They read Man Booker winners and science journals; or at least they read the clever, intricate wordsmiths of *Vanity Fair* and the *New Yorker*. At dinner parties, they could discuss foreign policy and the corporate world, casting their polished voices with assurance. Their parents were doctors or CEOs; the older ones had shiny, beautiful children at Carolina or Duke or one of the Ivies; the younger ones had fair-haired cherubs in smocked clothing. They owned heirloom china and silver. They knew how to write a proper thank-you. They understood how to manage nannies and housekeepers. None of them has ever been hungry.

On the exterior, I blended with them perfectly.

I did now, anyway. When I first got to college, I thought I'd outgrown my childhood: I read voraciously. I spoke correctly. I was careful not to betray my upbringing. But the things I didn't know about a fine life were legion.

Charlotte isn't New York, but it's glamorous enough. Every time I drove home from work, there was still enough of the rube in me to marvel at the life I had somehow landed. I pictured my childhood self, a blond, skinny, shy waif, sitting on the cinder-block steps of our three-room home drawing shapes in the dust, and I knew how she would gape if she could see through her future eyes. She'd glance down and note the luxury car logo emblazoned on the steering wheel, and although she might not give it conscious thought, the sound quality of the music coming through the top-notch speakers and the softness of the leather seats would register. She'd recognize the white coat she wore, and then she'd run her hands along the fine fabrics of her clothing: the slippery silk, the kitteny cashmere, the fine, soft flare of breathable cotton.

And outside her car windows: Oh! Skyscrapers, silver sculptures the size of houses, streets like living creatures, awash with women in suits pulling wheeled cases and trim bankers waiting for the light-rail. A hospital complex so large it qualified as its own city. An alien world.

Even Zadie, the child of vaguely hippieish college professors, had a childhood exponentially more cultured than mine. She might not have been rich, but her family prized literacy and craft, two qualities not exactly abundant in my upbringing. If you took a bird's-eye view of the home where Zadie was raised—lofting yourself high above the line-drying quilts and the neat rows of butter beans and tomatoes—and you flew due east into the Appalachians, you'd eventually come to a county near the West Virginia border with only one stoplight. One stoplight and a scant row of crumbling two-story 1940s-era buildings lining the main drag, giving way within a few hundred yards to the likes of concrete-block gas stations and one-room churches. When some urban decadent from New York or LA needed a smug reference to a provincial glob of ignorance, this was the Kentucky they invoked (assuming for some reason Mississippi was unavailable, of course). From every vantage point, you could see the mountains: looming, dark monsters blocking the light, forcing the road to curve back on itself like a snake trying to eat its tail. The mountains of my childhood had once possessed a wild kind of beauty, but by the time I was born, this was gone. Now they resembled cancer survivors, their tops hacked off, trailing grime and silt, denuded of trees.

If you followed the road from the town for a mile or two, you'd come to the entrance of the coal mines. In my granddaddy's day, they mined underground in shafts and tunnels, and while the company made it terrible for the men, it left the mountaintops intact. If you mined in those days, the company owned you: the only homes you could live in were rented out by the company, and the only food you could buy came from the company store, which gave you "credit" against a payday that never quite arrived. My granddaddy worked all his life to pay back the company for the cost of living.

My dad was a miner too, but by the 1970s, the company had figured out it was cheaper and easier to blow the tops off the mountains rather than tunnel through them. Nobody made them replant the trees back then: they just disintegrated all the green and moved on when the only thing remaining was a sky-sized heap of dirt. My dad moved on too, in a manner of speaking: he died from lung cancer when I was five. We lived two hours from the nearest hospital.

Logically, I should not be ashamed that once I was poor. I knew this, and I detested myself for my own snobbery toward the naïve little ghost-girl of my past. She could not help it if she'd grown up without an indoor bathroom, but I resented her for embodying this ridiculous cliché of the Appalachians. She could not help it if it had been difficult to be clean. She could not help it if her mother had accepted government assistance in a town virtually without well-paying jobs.

It left me so vulnerable, this perception of myself as an impostor. I was brittle and rude sometimes, trying to overcome the ache of pretending. The only people who knew were Wyatt, who had his own hard-earned knowledge of the need to blend, and Zadie, the only friend who had visited my childhood home.

As if on cue, the door to my call room banged open and Zadie burst in. She'd always been prone to noisy entrances, but I could tell she'd been running hard: her cheeks glowed and her breath sounded like it was coming from a small steam engine. I blinked at the vitality of her movements as she crossed the small room in one bound, landing on the bed next to me.

"Em, what's wrong?" she wailed. "Are you okay?"

"All I said was I needed to see you."

"Which you would never say in the middle of a workday. Is— Do you have cancer?"

"No!"

"Does Wyatt? Oh!" She sucked in her breath. "Is it Henry?"

"My family is okay, Zadie. I'm okay. I'm not sick. But." I stopped, unable to find words. Or—that's inaccurate—I knew the words. I could hear them pulsing in my mind, but I could not say them out loud.

Zadie nodded, recognizing the problem. She cocked her head, thinking, and then nodded again. "You lost a patient, and it was bad," she said.

I nodded back, staring at the rough weave of the white blanket on the bed.

All her vitality suddenly dimmed down. "Is— Was it Eleanor?" she asked.

"Yes," I croaked. A bubble rose in my chest.

"Oh, Em," said Zadie. To my surprise, she didn't start crying. "I am so, so sorry. I know you must have fought like crazy to save her. You can't blame yourself—you know that."

"I—" I tried. I stopped and shook my head. All at once I was furious with myself for wallowing in speechless grief. I steeled myself and I said it.

"It shouldn't have happened."

Zadie didn't say anything.

I waited a beat, and then I started talking. I told her the story, and I didn't spare any of it. I couldn't know for sure at this point, but it was easy enough to surmise: I must have hit the tail of the child's pancreas, causing an enzymatic leak that ate her from the inside out, its corrosive fluid burning a hole in her stomach, sending bacteria through her bloodstream. Or maybe it was something else, given the short time frame. The pressure in her abdomen could have grown after the surgery, straining against the incision I'd insisted on closing, until her organs began to fail.

Then a series of miscues and mistakes ensued during the chaos of call, when everything blew up at once. I didn't get to her in time.

I could have saved her. I should have saved her. The realization that I hadn't saved her kept hitting me with a gale-force punch: first, disbelief—this could not be happening—and then a cataclysmic rush of horror.

Zadie listened with intense absorption, not flinching at the worst parts, which surprised me again. In general, Zadie could be described as a sappy, tenderhearted mess, especially when it came to anyone she cared about. But I recognized now a facet of her I didn't often see: her game face. This was her professional side kicking in, the part that allowed her to function when she had to tell parents their son needed a heart transplant, or had to explain to them their newborn daughter would not be likely to live past the age of one.

"You will endure this, and you'll be better for it," she said.

Shame upon shame. I said, "No, I won't." Adding: "The Packards."

She shook her head. "I'll help with Boyd and Betsy," she said. "Give them time. Boyd can be vindictive, but Betsy will listen. And she's a kind person—she'll understand that only lawyers would benefit from a lawsuit. The Packards don't need money from you, and piling hatred on top of heartbreak would only consume the strength they'll need to heal."

A flicker of something stirred in my memory. "Resentment is like drinking poison and then hoping it will kill your enemies."

"Yes!" she said. "Who said that?"

"I think it was Nelson Mandela."

"That's perfect."

I shrugged listlessly. "Somehow, I don't think Boyd Packard is a scholar of South African antiapartheid revolutionaries. And if I were him, I wouldn't forgive me either."

"Okay, then how about this one: how often shall my sister cause me harm, and I forgive her? As many as seven times?"

"Is that Mandela too?"

"That one," she said, "was Jesus Christ. I'm paraphrasing, but you get the drift. And his answer, in case you're wondering, was not seven times, but seventy times seven." She placed her hands on my shoulders. "You're allowed forgiveness for one mistake."

If there was anything in the world I longed for more than forgiveness, I couldn't have named it, but wishing for it was useless. The enormity of my error racked me; I couldn't respond any longer to Zadie's loyal efforts to bolster my spirits.

She picked up my hand and gripped it between hers. In an affectless, almost dreamy tone, she said, "Look at me."

I looked.

Her eyes, round and clear and lovely, bored into mine. "You are not alone," she said. "You carried me when it happened to me, and I'll carry you too."

I blinked hard, certain that if I let myself cry, I'd never stop.

PART
TWO

Autumn

Chapter Twenty-two

THE EXPLOSIVE METHOD OF INTERMITTENT CONTROL

Zadie, Present Day

It had been a hard few months. Not a day went by that I didn't ache for Betsy and ache for Emma, who had both withdrawn into shellacked cocoons of misery, albeit for very different reasons. It made me feel guilty to admit, but I was longing to think of something happy.

The Arts Ball, the biggest social event of the year, was coming up this October, and Drew and I were invited for the first time. We'd made it onto the list because of Drew; the cochair of the ball this year was Hattie McGuire. Hattie was married to Reginald, Drew's managing partner, and she was presumably well equipped to deal with the complexities of organizing an intimate dinner-dance for five hundred couples, since she had endured a twenty-year barrage of ol' Reg. Everything else probably seemed like a walk in the park.

Drew was heading out this morning for another overseas work trip, so if I wanted to discuss a shopping spree for a new dress, now was the time. I could hear him in the shower, warbling along to something on the bathroom TV. The home's AV system was one of the very few things on which Drew had been willing to splurge. We'd bought the house from a builder who'd been in the process of renovating it a few years back, and he customized it for us. I'd presented a wish list consisting of a few nice items: upgraded tiles (vetoed by Drew after a silent, incredulous trip to a posh tile distributor), a fantastic vintage chandelier for the foyer (also vetoed), and myriad smaller-ticket items, a few of which were grudgingly agreed upon. But when we met with the AV guys, he suddenly started throwing money around like the Sun King. As a result, we now had six televisions scattered throughout the house, including a smallish plasma screen in the playroom (very bad parenting) and this one here in the master bathroom, which was embedded into the huge vanity mirror, invisible unless it was turned on, and which Drew claimed to need so he could watch the ticker on CNBC while shaving. All of these TVs had basically become obsolete at the moment of their purchase, since now you could view downloaded and live-streaming content at any moment on your tablet, or implanted brain chip, or whatever.

"Hello, handsome," I said to Drew as he exited the shower. I glanced quickly at the mirror TV, which was set not to CNBC, but to something featuring small primary-colored singing pigs. He winked at me and said, "Brace yourself." Sure enough, the shower door swung open again, and out popped Delaney, butt-naked and sopping.

"Hi, honey dear. I getted in the shower! With Daddy! Now I'm all wet." She beamed, strutting around. Drew raised his hands above his head, bear-like, and pretended to chase Delaney around the bathroom as she shrieked in delight. "Aaah! Daddy-Bear! Daddy-Bear! Hiii-yah!" This last exclamation was accompanied by an enthusiastic flail of Delaney's elbow, which struck Drew squarely in the groin. He yelped in pain and doubled over.

I rushed over to check on him. "I'm fine," he said weakly, waving me off. "I just hope she remembers that move when she starts dating."

Delaney considered this. "What's dating?"

"It's when two people like each other, and they, ah, talk a lot."

"Am I dating Henry?"

I took this one. "No. You and Henry are just friends. Dating is a kind of love."

"Was I dating Eleanor?"

Drew and I met each other's eyes in the mirror. It had been several months since Eleanor's death, and Delaney had stopped asking to play with her some time ago. We'd thought she had forgotten.

"Eleanor died," Delaney announced. "And now she is very dead."

"Honey," I said, kneeling down and gathering Delaney in my arms, acutely aware of her warmth and her firm, wiggly little body. "Do you miss Eleanor?"

"Not really, Mom."

I blinked, surprised. "Why not, baby?"

"Because I am going to see her tomorrow, when she comes back alive."

Drew knelt down too. He'd started to apply shaving cream, and a strip of foamy white ran down one side of his face. Delaney poked her finger into it, delighted. "Ellie's not coming back alive, lovebug," he said. "It's okay to miss her."

"Daddy! She is." Delaney wriggled out of our grasp. "We are going to play mermaids."

Drew and I rose together. "You're the child expert." His eyes were sad. "What do we say?"

"I think we don't push it," I whispered. "Children this age view death through a filter of magical thinking; they can't process that kind of finality. Let her process it however it comforts her."

"Whisper secrets are not nice," Delaney said, popping back up between us.

"That's true, Lainie," I acknowledged, attempting to corner her to wrap her in a towel. "Why don't we put some clothes on before you get too cold?"

Delaney clamped her hands over her eyes and sank to the floor.

"Lainiebug." I smiled. "I can still see you."

Delaney removed her hands from her eyes but kept them squeezed shut. "No, I'm hiding!"

"Clothes on," I commanded.

"Nope," said Delaney, opening her eyes and wiggling her tiny, perfect bottom at us. "I love me like this." I lunged at her, but she shrieked, "Scatter!" and ran off.

I looked in the mirror. For a brief moment my face looked completely foreign, before it rearranged itself back into its familiar countenance: small, rounded nose; wide, rounded greenish eyes under arched eyebrows; slightly parted full lips. My resting expression was one of mild surprise, which, over the years, had led to a lot of people overexplaining things to me. But for a moment I hadn't recognized myself, as, for the thousandth time, I'd wondered what it must be like to lose a child.

I looked at the small heap of Delaney's pajamas puddled in front of the shower. Best not to dwell on this. "I need to buy something," I said.

Leaping on the chance to lighten the mood, Drew dropped his towel and swatted me with it. "I'm sensing some defensiveness here," he said.

Defensively: "What makes you think I'm defensive?"

"Because," said Drew, replacing his towel and fumbling around the counter for his razor, "you just got that stubborn, sort-of-sly look that you always get when you're about to say something outrageous." He assessed me. "There, that one."

I started to protest, but unfortunately I was still facing the mirror. Hastily, I rearranged my face to simpering sweetness. "Is this better?"

"Much," he said, grinning at me. "Out with it."

"It's a dress crisis. Dire. I was thinking I might get another one, right away, for the Arts Ball."

"What happens if you don't?" he asked pleasantly over the hum of his electric shaver.

"Social doom."

Drew finished with the shaver and reached for his toothbrush. "Well, you'd better do it, then. I can't have a socially crippled wife. Do I have to get a new monkey suit?"

"No, darling, you're fine," I said, pleased that he hadn't whipped out his laptop on the spot and recalculated the monthly budget. Maybe he was loosening up a little.

I met his eyes in the mirror. His face transformed from blandly handsome into fully gorgeous when he smiled, despite a mouthful of toothpaste. "You know whazeben more essciting thandisippy soshellebent?" he asked.

"Can you try that again, maybe without the toothpaste?"

He spat into the sink and grinned again. "I said, do you know what's even more exciting than your dippy social event?"

"Um, no. I didn't think there was anything you like more than formal wear."

"Very funny. I was referring to the weekend after the Arts Ball. You know what it is?"

I racked my brain, which had not yet been activated by morning coffee. Nothing came to mind, except the virtual certainty that at least one of our offspring would have an early Saturday morning sports event. That didn't seem worth mentioning as a special thing, though.

"I give up. What is it?"

He gave me a superior look. "Well, I don't mean to brag, but at least *one* of us remembers what happened ten years ago on November seventh. Ring any bells?"

Our ten-year anniversary! "Right, of course. I knew that," I said lamely.

Drew winked at me, then turned around and rustled through his top bathroom drawer. He handed me a large envelope.

"Here you go," he said. "I heart you."

Ever since my cardiology fellowship, Drew has adorned every gift to me with a quotation about the heart. You'd think he'd have run out of them by now, but no. Is there any anatomical entity subject to more literary devotion than the human heart? This one was short but instantly recognizable, from Bob Marley: "One Love, One Heart."

I opened it. There were two smaller envelopes inside. I unsealed the first one, which contained two tickets to the Panthers-Falcons game and a gift certificate to the Ritz-Carlton downtown. I smiled and started to thank Drew, but he interrupted me.

"That brings back happy memories, yeah?" He crossed the few feet between us and wrapped me up in his arms, whispering in my ear, "That's for the eighth. My mom will keep the kids, and we'll sneak downtown for the weekend. You like?"

"Of course. I love—"

He let me go and held up a hand. "Open the other one," he said.

I did. Inside were two first-class tickets to Paris and a handwritten confirmation for a reservation at the Four Seasons Hotel George V. I looked at Drew.

"I'm finally taking you on one of my business trips," he said. "Only this time, it'll be a lot more classy than usual. And I'll take a few days off. It will be like a second honeymoon."

"Oh my gosh!" I yelled. *"Je suis très excitée!"*

I hadn't spoken a lick of French since college, unlike Drew, who traveled to France at least five or six weeks a year. He started laughing.

"Zadie," he said, "I think you just told me that you're feeling lustful."

"Oh," I said, chagrined. Then I brightened and pulled off his towel. "Well, hell yeah!" I said. "I definitely am."

———

After Drew left, I thudded back to earth. Time to wake up the hellions. I bundled my hair up into a messy bun, selected an outfit for work, and did a quick visual assessment of my appearance before beginning the morning ritual of preparing breakfast. Ugh, there was an enormous disfiguring wrinkle in the squint spot next to my left eye. Why hadn't I gone into dermatology? Well, never mind; character wrinkle. I was just a very smiley person.

Downstairs, I set out bowls, grabbed the milk, and examined the pantry for options with a decided lack of enthusiasm. I normally enjoyed being in the kitchen; it was a pleasant, light-filled room with a rectangular nook enclosing a huge old farm table where we ate and a massive marble-topped island. The children, who were sitting dispiritedly at the table, voiced their utter disdain for all proposed breakfast items. I pulled rank and served scrambled eggs, along with Cheerios and milk.

"I hope you can do better than this for lunch," groused Finn, staring at his egg like it was a pile of vomit.

"Yeah," seconded Eli, although he was eating his eggs.

Calm parenting. You were supposed to acknowledge their feelings, thus communicating that you accept their personhood. At the same time, you should allow zero tolerance for rudeness, while exhibiting an authoritative but calm demeanor so as not to escalate the battle. No raised voices, no passive-aggressive muttering. Calm.

"I hear you that this is not your favorite breakfast," I said quietly but firmly. "However, this is what I am serving, and there will be no other food given."

Finn was investigating his lunch box. His mouth dropped open in abject horror. "Mom! What *is* this? You know I don't dig on pretzels!"

Eli backed him up again. "Me neither."

Now Rowan was butting in. "Mom, we *told* you that we were sick of turkey sandwiches! You never care what we want."

In a low, pleasant voice: "May I remind everyone that you asked for turkey and pretzels yesterday?"

"No, we didn't! We hate turkey and pretzels!"

Delaney, whose head was ping-ponging back and forth between her sister and brothers, suddenly threw her plate on the floor and burst into shrieking tears. "I don't like it! I telled you already I don't like it!"

Ed, the golden retriever, trotted in smartly, alerted by the siren call of a plastic toddler bowl hitting the ground, and gobbled the egg and Cheerios before I could stop him. I grabbed a paper towel to wipe up the milk dripping off the table and all over the floor. Calm. A raised voice would only escalate. Calm.

"Delaney, we do not throw food," I said. "Ever. You need to help wipe this up, and then you will get a new bowl from the drawer."

"No! I won't!" Delaney screamed.

Zero tolerance.

Still pleasantly, "Then I'm afraid you will have to stand in the corner."

"I will not! I will not stand in the corner!"

With a desperately pleasant smile plastered on my face, I wrestled the shrieking, spitting Delaney into the corner and tried to hold her in place. Zero tolerance; you had to train them *the first time it happened* that intolerable behavior would be addressed promptly and without negative emotion. For a person three feet tall, Delaney was shockingly strong. I felt a stream of sweat snake its way down my temple.

Delaney got an arm free and smacked me in the face, still screaming. It actually hurt quite a bit. I was still processing this, fighting the overwhelming temptation to smack back, when Rowan said snippily, "You bring this on yourself, Mom. I bet she'd be better if you fed her something more good."

I let go of Delaney. "WHAT IS WRONG WITH YOU UN-GRATEFUL, HORRIBLE CHILDREN?" I screamed, loud enough to hurt my throat. "I HAVE SPENT THE LAST HOUR TENDING TO YOUR EVERY NEED, AND ALL YOU DO IS ENDLESSLY COM-PLAIN."

The children stared at me, shocked. It felt good to yell, but I really was hurting my throat, so I continued at slightly lower volume: "You have no idea what it is like to be hungry; you think everything you have appears magically and your slave of a mother will get you more and more and more. Well, I'm done! I'm done! I can't take it anymore. I'm done!"

The children's eyes were so wide they looked like they were in the grip of a hyperthyroid storm. There was silence.

Finally: "I'm so sorry, Mommy. I love turkey and pretzels in my lunch. I won't complain anymore."

I looked at Rowan with gratitude. Eli and Finn were still silent, but they were nodding metronomically, their eyes locked on me. Delaney, her big eyes still dripping tears, padded over and began stroking my leg, repeating, "It's okay. It's okay, sweetie babe," over and over.

Hmmm. So much for calm parenting. Maybe I could write a book called *Volcanic Parenting: The Explosive Method of Intermittent Control.* It would probably be a best seller.

"Hello." Betsy Packard walked into the kitchen, followed by her son, Will. "Everybody ready to go?"

Horrified, I glanced at the clock. "Betsy!" I said, rushing out from behind the counter. "Yes! Give us five minutes." I motioned to the children with a furtive, frantic hand wave behind Betsy's back. "Rowan, please help the boys tie their shoes."

"But we haven't had—"

"Thank you, honey!" I trilled. "Don't forget your backpacks!" I pulled Betsy aside and gave her a hug, trying to strike a balance between the kind of welcome that dwells too much on someone's bereavement and one that ignores it altogether. This was Betsy's first day back driving the carpool. Naturally, I'd told her not to worry about it, even though I'd been twisting my schedule into hellish knots and calling in every favor from every person I knew in order to make it work over the last few months. But she insisted she was ready to return, saying she couldn't stand another morning alone in bed after everyone left the house.

"How are you?" I asked after a moment's awkward pause. I'd expected her to look wraithlike and frail—she'd had the ropy thinness common to wealthy women even before Eleanor's death—but the only change in her appearance was her expression, which seemed vague.

"I'm functioning," she said, her gaze landing on the boys after sweeping past Delaney. "I guess it's good to be out of the house."

"Okay, but don't push it," I said. "I'm happy to keep driving."

"Zadie," she said, gripping my wrist. Now I noticed her nails were ragged and yellowish. "I came in because I need to tell you something."

Chapter Twenty-three

EMERGENCY CHOCOLATE

Zadie, Present Day

I tensed, certain I would not want to hear whatever Betsy was about to say. "Of course," I said.

"I'm not in favor of it, but he's . . . latched onto the idea that it will bring him some kind of relief. I know you're close to her, but he thinks he's protecting other people from the same kind of tragedy, or he's forcing a closer look at hospital policies, or something like that. He thinks it's the only thing to do."

"Are you . . . talking about Boyd?"

Her neck jerked in a small, tight nod. "He's going to sue your friend, and he's leaning on Nestor"—she meant Nestor Connolly, the CEO of Charlotte's immense hospital complex—"to take some action against her."

Most physicians dread lawsuits, and it's not because they think they'll lose. Every doctor has a colleague who's been sued. Or maybe they've been sued themselves. It lurks over everyone like a ten-foot-tall grizzly, waiting for you to stumble, poised to sink its fangs into your helplessly exposed neck.

Or maybe that's not an accurate metaphor. One of my partners, a bright-eyed, white-bearded older guy named Charles Frank, known for his consistently terrible jokes and his unflagging enthusiasm for getting to know his little patients, had been sued after one of his teenage patients died. The kid, who had structural problems in his heart, had bled profusely during his last surgery, nearly dying on the OR table. He needed a defibrillator but couldn't have another immediate surgery. In the meantime, he had taken off the external defibrillator he was supposed to be wearing and gone to a friend's house to lift weights, defying both his parents and his doctors. Watching Charles negotiate the lawsuit was more like watching the slow agony of someone with an intestinal parasite than like watching someone get his head chomped by a bear. Every month he bled a little more. I began to dread the hangdog look he wore to the office, especially each time he had to ask the rest of us to cover his patients because of a court date or disposition, which were held according to the schedules of the lawyers. People who knew nothing of the details of his defense rushed to censure him on social media. Patients left the practice. To save money, his insurer forced him to settle, even though, like the overwhelming majority of doctors who are sued, he'd have likely won his case.

Charles Frank took an early retirement.

"Is Boyd suing the hospital too?"

"No." In the background, I could see the boys, who had apparently tied all their shoelaces together, thudding en masse across the living room. They lurched drunkenly and fell over, shrieking with laughter. Betsy stood like a stone. "He says he'll indemnify the hospital if they fire her. Our lawyer is screaming about it, but Boyd will get his way. He's going to bring Nestor down on her like a ton of bricks. He wants her fired."

I let out an involuntary squeak.

She broke from her lethargy enough to swivel toward me, still expressionless. Her lack of animation struck me—depending on how you looked at her, she could be mistaken for serene, or possibly lobotomized. I reached toward her, but she pivoted again and stared past me. "How is she?" she asked.

"Emma?" I said, surprised at the question. "She's . . . she's awful, actually. I've barely seen her."

Betsy nodded. "Well," she said. "I'm late getting the kids to school."

We looked toward the front door, where a knotted pile of shoes sat heaped. Out of nowhere, Delaney appeared and clamped onto my pants leg. "Mom," she puffed, "I am done with being human. I need you to buy me a tail."

Betsy closed her eyes.

I dislodged Delaney and said quietly, "Delaney, go wait in my room. Okay?"

"Can I have a tail?"

"It's possible," I hissed. "Go."

Betsy zombie-walked toward a torrent of sunshine pouring through the front doorframe. I followed her, scooping up the shoes as I went, hoping the boys hadn't migrated to a mud puddle in the two minutes we'd stood talking. Just before we reached her new car—a Volvo station wagon, quite unlike the massive black Suburban she'd had before— Betsy turned to me. She whispered into the cuff of my shirt, so faint I could hardly hear her, "Will you talk to Boyd?"

"Of course. Of course I will. But what do you want me to say?"

She blinked, haggard-faced, the skin beneath her eyes so pale it was almost pearlescent, shot through with the faintest of violet undertones. "I don't know," she said. "I was hoping you could help me figure out the right thing to do. Should I ask him not to sue her?"

———

First patient of the day: referred for fainting. Second patient: referred for murmur. The third patient broke up the monotony only slightly—valve surgery follow-up—but the fourth one was interesting: a fourteen-year-old who had collapsed while playing soccer.

Shortly after he was born, Christian Kajowski's delivery room nurses noticed a loud murmur when they auscultated his chest. They called the pediatrician, who ordered an echocardiogram—an ultrasound of the heart—which confirmed a problem: aortic stenosis. The vessel carrying blood from Chris's heart was too small. A few weeks after birth, he had a temporary procedure to widen the stricture, followed by an aortic graft last year as we waited for him to reach his adult size so he could finally have a valve replacement. Meanwhile, he'd been an active, healthy kid.

But unbeknownst to anyone, a minor infection after Chris's last surgery had created a small area of scarring in his heart. One afternoon in September, after a warm-up lap around his school's track, he jogged to the soccer field, waved to his coach, and slow-motion crumpled to the ground.

I knocked on the exam room door, lugging my cumbersome COW (Computer on Wheels) behind me. "Hello there, Chris!" I said, smiling. "I'm happy to see you!"

Chris looked reasonably happy to see me too. He was an amiable kid with broad shoulders, wide gray eyes, and the kind of lush, curving eyelashes often unfairly bestowed on boys. "Hey, Dr. Anson," he said, lounging in a slumped, knees-wide-apart posture reminiscent of a professional athlete. His mother elbowed him and he politely sat up. If he was feeling any angst related to the possibility that he could die at any moment, he hid it well.

Chris's mother, Deborah, was not as successful in hiding her angst. Her eyes darted around the room in rabbity assessment, finally locking on me with unsettling intensity. But her voice, when she spoke, held a note of forced calm. "No shocks," she said, motioning to her son's chest.

"I know," I said gently. "That's good." Chris had an implantable defibrillator in his chest, which meant he lived with the unsettling knowledge that if his heart rhythm deteriorated again, the device inside his chest would suddenly shock him. This paled in comparison, however, to what he faced next: tomorrow, the surgeons would slice out part of his heart and replace it with a hunk of manufactured pyrolytic carbon.

One of the reasons I love the heart so much is its immense complexity. On the surface, it's a simple mechanical pump, taking in depleted blood and whooshing out rich, oxygenated red cells to all the nooks and crannies of the human form. But the physics underlying the pump are truly majestic. Every beat is precipitated by an electrical cascade, a sub-cellular chain of dominoes, alighting like fire along the fibers and muscles that bear the brunt of our bodies' unceasing demand for fuel. When it works as it should, it's spectacular.

After Chris collapsed on the soccer field, his heart spasming arrhythmically and uselessly, his cells screaming for oxygen that wasn't coming, his teammates and his coaches reacted fast. They reached him in seconds, and his coach began CPR as his friend Billy took off in a desperate, all-out sprint to the football field, where the school kept a portable defibrillator. They shocked him three times before the paramedics arrived, and the paramedics shocked him twice more en route to the hospital. Had he been alone, or had he been somewhere without a defibrillator and people who knew CPR, he'd have stayed dead. But his schoolmates brought him back.

I looked over his latest EKG and echo, then placed my stethoscope on his chest. My ears, long attuned to the subtle gradations of the heart's gray noise, registered no changes from last week. "You're doing great, Chris," I said. "Tell me what questions you have."

He nodded seriously, his eyes a little cloudy. "I just want it to be over with."

Deborah stirred. "Go change clothes, honey," she said, waving toward the door of the exam room. I realized she was trembling.

After Chris left, she raised her head and looked at me. I abandoned my professional remove and gathered her into my arms, where she began to weep. "I can't. I can't . . ." She sobbed quietly, clutching my back.

"Oh, Deborah," I said. "I know."

There was a knock on the door. One of the front desk girls sidled in and whispered to me that I had a phone call, to which I naturally responded that phone calls were not my most pressing priority at the moment. The desk girl nodded but persisted: "I think it's a doctor from Finland."

This was perplexing. "See if he can call me back," I said.

"She says it's urgent."

I sighed. "Okay. I'll be there in one minute."

On the way to my desk to answer the call, I suddenly realized who it must be. Emma was attending a conference in Helsinki; it had to be her, or possibly someone calling on her behalf. I sped up.

I pressed the blinking button on my office phone. "Hello?" I said.

Emma's voice, imbued with the same flat melancholy I'd heard in Betsy's this morning: "Hi. Sorry to bother you at work."

"Oh, that's fine!" I chirped. I could count on one hand the number of times I'd seen Emma since Eleanor's death a few months ago. She avoided our morning coffees with one lame excuse after another, responding to most texts with the digital equivalent of monosyllabic grunting. I wanted desperately to comfort her.

"Do you have a second to talk?"

"Yes, yes, yes," I said. I would give Deborah a few minutes alone and would return soon. "What's going on?"

Emma exhaled a long, stiff sigh. "I got off the plane in Finland and checked my phone. And I have all these e-mails from my lawyer."

"I guess that's not good."

"No. No, it's bad. Boyd Packard's attorneys are revving up. Tons of subpoenas, discovery materials—they're interviewing people I work with." Her voice dropped another notch. "They filed an affidavit called 'intent to sue.'"

I waited. If she didn't know that Boyd was also gunning to have her fired, I certainly wasn't going to tell her. Suing an individual physician is one thing, but most lawsuits also name the hospital system, which has considerably deeper pockets. But the potential of a bigger payout comes at a cost; hospitals are prepared to defend themselves. They have in-house legal counsel and the resources to dig in and ride it out. Aligning oneself with a hospital in a suit isn't always in a doctor's best interest—sometimes they force you to settle, even if you're in the right—but it adds protection. If Nestor Connolly decided to throw Emma under the bus, it could make things exponentially worse for her: it's hard to win a case if your own employer won't stand behind you.

This was premature, but I couldn't stand the despair in her tone. "Emma, I . . . I talked to Betsy this morning about it."

"You did?" An unmistakable note of hope.

"Yes. She's about how you'd expect her to be: depressed. Grieving. But there was one positive thing. Em, I probably shouldn't tell you this, but you deserve to hear something hopeful."

Cautiously: "What is it?"

"She asked me to talk to Boyd. Despite her grief, I don't think she wants to go after you; maybe I can persuade them to drop the suit."

I could hear the sharp intake of her breath over a hum of many voices. She must have been calling on a break at her conference. "Are you . . . ? Will you do it?"

"Emma! Of course I will. Of course. I would do anything to help you. And I hope you can find some comfort in the fact that Betsy asked me about it. She doesn't hate you, Emma."

This was a stretch. Betsy's feelings regarding Emma were unknown to me; owing to time constraints, her whispered request this morning led to minimal discussion. But surely she wouldn't have talked about interceding with Boyd if she wanted retribution.

Emma made a noise. "Thank you."

"Well, don't thank me ye—"

Emma cleared her throat. "There will never be a way for me to thank you enough, Zadie. I just— This isn't even why I called, actually. It was something else."

"Okay. What?"

When she spoke, her voice struck a different note of caution. "When I checked my phone, I also had a bunch of texts from Nick."

I made a noise registering somewhere between disgust and alarm. I knew Nick had assimilated into Emma's large surgical group with ease. Through the grapevine, I'd heard he lavished the office girls with good-natured teasing, so they were hopelessly charmed within minutes of meeting him. He was particularly attentive to the scheduler, who adored him; she'd begun giving him better call days and OR times than he probably deserved.

"You know, he's always willing to switch one of his call days with the other guys, right?" Emma asked, sounding peevish but more lively. "They think he's the best partner. He golfs with Jack Inman, and Jack's introduced him to Buzzy Cooper and that crowd, so now we'll probably have to endure him leering at us at the pool next summer too. Why can't he leave us alone?"

"Emma?" I asked. "What did the texts say?"

"That's why I called. He keeps asking for your address."

"Which under no circumstances you would share with him," I said.

"Of course not. But this last message I got—it's from hours ago now—said that he's stopping by your office. Today. It said he's stopping by today."

"What?" I shrieked. This was a really bad time to get attacked by the past. I glanced at my schedule, which stared back at me reproachfully. I was already two patients behind, and there was no way I could insert a wholly undesirable encounter with a detested ex-boyfriend into the middle of my work day.

"Hang on, hang on," said Emma. "I called him. We had a brief but emphatic discussion of why that would be the stupidest idea ever, and he relented. But he says he sent you something."

Perfectly on cue, there was a knock on my door. I hung up with Emma and swung the door open to reveal Della Rae, our receptionist. Or at least the person looked like Della Rae from the bottom half. Her torso and head were obscured by a gigantic tower of gold foil boxes of various sizes, topped off with an enormous blobby thing in the shape of a bow.

"What *is* that?" I asked weakly.

"Chocolate!" She beamed, lowering the monstrosity onto my desk. "Somebody knows you pretty well, Dr. Anson. Even the bow is made of candy."

"I don't like candy!" I protested, hastily shoving closed the top drawer of my desk, which was full of emergency chocolate bars. "Give it to the girls out front."

"Ooh, okay," said Della Rae, scooping it back up. "But here's the card." She grinned and flipped a white envelope at me. A strange mix of repulsion and intrigue gripped me as I caught sight of the spiky handwriting inside. I opened it.

Zadie,

I promise I am not stalking you. I want to say I am sorry for what I did to you, and I miss you. And I am still so sorry about what happened to your friend Graham.

    I hope we can be friends.

All my best,
Nick

Chapter Twenty-four

GET IN THERE WITH
YOUR ELBOWS

Emma, Present Day

Because Zadie is my closest friend—my only close friend, really—I find myself willing to overlook traits that would ordinarily disturb me. Like a certain lack of punctuality and a tendency to believe that obligations mysteriously pop up on her calendar without her placing them there.

So I wasn't surprised when, on my first Saturday back from Finland, Zadie failed to appear for a run we'd scheduled for eight a.m. in order to discuss the situation with the Packards. A quick call to her cell revealed the reason: she had forgotten which day it was and was at her twins' basketball game.

"I'm so sorry, Em!" she wailed. "They have three games and the first one is almost over. . . . Why don't you meet me here? Drew can stay at the game and we can still run."

I agreed. I knew that Zadie had reached out to Boyd Packard in an attempt to save my career and hadn't heard back yet. Over the last few months, I'd tried to soothe myself by running or reading or organizing, but it was like trying to relax before you were beheaded. I struggled to present a normal facade to the world. Depression had wormed its way into my core, each sonorous beat of my heart sending out a wash of dread. I walked around in a fugue of resignation, certain I'd never again feel the absence of worry.

Still, I held on to one hope: that Zadie would save me.

When I reached the Presbyterian church where the games were played, a sea of people churned in the lobby outside the gymnasium, all squawking and chattering with the bright, mindless intensity of birds. Moms in tight, sweat-wicking performance athletic pants, clutching to-go cups from Starbucks; clumps of dads in golf shirts; shrieking children weaving through everyone's legs. I hugged my arms in at my sides. I didn't see Zadie anywhere.

I kept to the periphery of the room, my eyes darting through the crowd for a friendly face. No one spoke to me as I edged closer to the indoor basketball courts. Finally, I spotted Delaney by the vending machine, which she was attempting to manipulate by shoving crinkled-up paper towels into the coin slots. Because I was distracted by the hapless vending machine—which was making a grinding noise as it tried to reject the onslaught of counterfeit funds—it took me a second to realize something was off in Delaney's appearance. Closer inspection revealed she had lodged a wad of scrunched-up paper towels under her headband. That, and her outfit was odd: she was decked out in a pair of tight-fitting camo shorts and a T-shirt emblazoned with a photo of a deranged-looking older gentleman with a full beard. The caption read, Y'ALL OUGHTA GO BY WALMART AND PICK YOU UP A PERSONALITY.

Zadie appeared out of the crowd and stared at Delaney. "Honey," she said in a calm but ominous tone. "What are you wearing?"

Delaney looked down. "This?" she asked pertly.

"Yes."

"I look very attractive, sweetie dear." She twirled.

"Where did you get those clothes, Lainie?"

"I traded."

"With who?"

"I don't know. Do you love it?"

Rowan was dispatched to help Delaney hunt for her clothes as Zadie and I tried to find Drew. The girls eventually returned with a bewildered two-year-old boy, who had been unable to articulate to his alarmed parents why he was now clad only in pink smocked overalls. Apologies were issued and suspiciously accepted; a clothing exchange was conducted. The Ansons and I slunk away.

"Thank you, baby," Zadie called to Drew as he strode away from us with Delaney tucked like a football under one arm, her legs furiously churning in the air behind him. With his other arm, he was gesticulating at the twins, who appeared to be zooming in different directions. There was no sign of Rowan.

"Have a good jog," he replied cheerfully over his shoulder, blowing her a kiss. I looked away.

We hit the sidewalk outside the church at a fast clip. The streets surrounding the church were a riotous blaze of fall colors: the gusty wind blew gold- and flame-colored leaves into our faces as we flew along. I concentrated on the rhythmic pounding of our shoes on the pavement, enjoying the absence of thought, until Zadie finally spoke.

"How are you?" she panted.

I answered the question honestly. "I'm depressed."

She slowed to a trot and looked at me. "I know that's normal, but it still sucks. I'm sorry."

I nodded. "Right," I said briskly. "Tell me what you're thinking about how to approach the Packards."

This seemed like a straightforward question to me—what exactly to say to them and how to phrase it—but Zadie launched into an analysis of first Boyd's and then Betsy's personalities, complete with anecdotes from her friendship with them, and how they'd reacted to various social occurrences, and how she'd reacted in turn to them, until my head was reeling with emotional overload. By the time she wrapped up, I decided just to trust her on the subject of the Packards.

"Tell me about the note from Nick."

Her face, which had been cast in an expression of empathetic concern, became instantly animated. "The note!" she squawked. "Can you believe that? He's still trying to make contact. Why would he care if we were friends?"

"He said that to me too," I offered warily. This conversational path was strewn with potential pitfalls, but I couldn't see a way to avoid it.

Zadie's jog turned into an agitated hop. "I think he can't relax unless he's messing with somebody," she said. "And he didn't just send a note. There was an obscene pile of chocolate, too."

"Did you keep it?" I asked.

"I did not," she said piously. "I gave it to the front office people."

"All of it? You didn't have one bite?"

"Oh, shut up," she growled. "It was too busy for me to get lunch that day."

I smiled at her, but then I felt a flash of disquiet. I stopped jogging.

"I hate working with him," I said to her quietly. "I hope you know that."

Zadie stopped too. "Oh, Emma, I know you do," she said, her big golden eyes glistening. "You are so good to me." We were quiet for a moment, and then she grinned at me, her humor restored. "If you were thinking of having him murdered, you can proceed."

"I'll consider that carefully," I said. I hadn't followed through on my futile threat to ruin him after he'd joined my practice. At first I'd tried the noble route by simply ignoring him. This became more and more difficult, as he seemingly went out of his way to annoy me: he befriended the scheduler and sucked up all the best OR block time; he befriended Nestor Connolly, the hospital's CEO, and somehow convinced him hepatobiliary surgeons should be excused from taking overflow trauma call; he befriended all the clerical girls on our shared surgical office floor, who now tittered and grimaced when I walked by. He turned my favorite scrub nurse against me. I endured it, because what else could I do? He possessed the ability to destroy what was left of my life.

Zadie started walking, but then stopped and gave me a big hug. "Nick can go to hell, Em," she said. "I don't care what he does. And it's fine with me if you work with him; you do whatever you need to do to make that okay."

"Thank you," I said, marveling for the millionth time at her ability to love me, but she was already walking again. She looked back over her shoulder, reading something in my face.

"But, Emma," she said cheerfully. "I was kidding. Don't actually kill him."

––––––

We returned to the gym in time for the boys' last game. It was kind of cute, actually. I found myself watching intently, wondering if there was any way Henry would ever become this coordinated. I was graced with height, but I'm klutzy and dysfunctional when it comes to sports, and sadly, Wyatt wasn't any better. Henry would have to figure out a way to socially compensate. Zadie's son Finn was the opposite. I watched him as he strutted around the basketball court, blissfully ignorant of the fact that he was a tiny forty-six-pound white person. In his mind, apparently, he was Stephen Curry. He flicked a lock of sweaty hair out of his eyes and hollered, "Hey, guys! Guys! I'm open!"

The church gymnasium roared. Finn got the ball and passed to Eli, Zadie's other son, who, although the more timid of the two, was actually the better shot. His ball sailed up and hovered tantalizingly on the rim of the basket before finally plunging through, which left Finn and Eli's team down by one with thirty-four seconds left in the game. The other coach promptly called a time-out.

Beside me, I could feel Zadie and Drew beaming; Drew had an arm draped around Zadie's neck, and she leaned into him. I watched as he picked up her free hand in his larger one and squeezed it. He whispered something into her ear and she smiled.

Ignoring the game, Mickie Blanchard leaned out across me to talk to Zadie. "Are y'all going to the thing at the Mint next week?" she asked, blinking her pale eyelashes.

Before I had time to fully register the social sting of not having been invited to the thing at the Mint—really, I had donated to Mickie's committee for funding guest speakers at the Mint Museum! So why wouldn't—

A *thud* of shock belted me in the stomach. Instantly, I felt my physiology change: my heartbeat sped up, my hands went cold, and my breathing accelerated. I tried to make myself look small as the intense, consuming terror of cornered prey swept over me.

Hovering alongside the first row of bleachers, Boyd Packard leaned in the direction of the coach's huddle, dispensing loud and doubtless unwanted advice to his son some twenty feet away.

"Get in there with your elbows, Willard," he bellowed. "You're running like you're locked in a damn straitjacket." He wiped a streak of perspiration from the overworked sweat glands at his temple and advanced closer to the court. Even before I let his daughter die, I'd recognized Boyd was one of those people who generally got what he wanted. Had he not been born into spectacular wealth, he would have been successful by virtue of sheer cussedness. He was not handsome or intelligent or pleasant, but he was indefatigable.

Keeping my movements slow and nonchalant, I stood and eased myself behind the bleachers, where I gripped one of the rickety metal legs. But this offered scant protection; there were only five rows of seats, so my head and torso stuck up like a scarecrow behind the people seated in the top row. This was worse than if I'd stayed seated. A wordless bubble of dismay escaped my lips as I risked a glance in Boyd's direction.

He was now ten feet in front of me, practically frothing at the mouth in his urgency to communicate to the coach and players that they needed to get the ball back in order to win. Tension gripped the gymnasium as the final seconds of the game ticked away. Will Packard made a desperate lunge toward the hoop, hurling the ball into the air with both hands.

It missed.

The defeated Myers Park Pres boys lined up for the postgame handshake. Most of them appeared to be handling the loss with good grace, but both Finn's and Will's shoulders heaved as they fought off tears. As a stream of parents, including Boyd, headed into the lobby, I saw Drew kneel down, pulling a sobbing Finn in for a hug.

"There you are," someone said, causing me to leap backward like a startled gazelle and actually knock my head—hard—against the painted cinder-block wall. I winced.

"Ouch," said Zadie. "You okay?"

"Boyd Packard is here."

"Yeah," she said calmly. "I saw him." She gave me a speculative look. "C'mon, let's talk to him."

"No," I gasped, but Zadie was already boinging away from me, her characteristic springy gait almost lost in the swell of people at the gym's doors. I slumped back against the wall and then started after her.

Battling against a tide of incoming parents as the whistle blew for the next game, I momentarily lost sight of her. The doors of the gym opened up to the massive lobby, where we'd met before our run; apparently it served as a daylong repository for families to socialize before and after games. I dodged a conversational clump of women I recognized from Henry's preschool, not bothering to speak to them as I barreled past. Where had Zadie gone?

Then through the large windows at the front of the room, I caught a glimpse of her outside. She and Boyd were standing in the parking lot. I assessed his body language: cocked head, torso turned, leaning slightly toward her; he seemed receptive enough. No smile, but no overt hostility either. I opened the door and walked outside.

I came from Zadie's blind side, so Boyd saw me first.

He stiffened, his chest expanding. For a ridiculous moment, he reminded me of an angry peacock, puffing out its feathers, but the illusion shattered when he spoke.

"Get this bitch away from me," he said.

I stopped in my tracks.

"Boyd," said Zadie, "accord me one minute. Please. I've been thinking of nothing besides you and Betsy, and I know we all want the same thing here."

"What?"

Who knows why the physical arrangement of some faces invokes trust? Zadie's was one of those, all shining earnestness and sincerity, with her lilting, lovely eyes and the childish sweep of her snub nose and her little chin. You wanted to look at her and you liked her on sight. Boyd softened.

"We want to ease your sorrow, Boyd. And, especially, we want to make things more bearable for Betsy."

"And how would you do that, Zadie?" Boyd asked, ignoring me.

She stayed upbeat. "Well, I know you are fond of Macon Bradford"—I recognized the name instantly: another country club pal, and Boyd's family attorney—"but call off the dogs, at least temporarily. Give Emma a chance to sit down with you and Betsy, alone, and allow yourself the chance to hear her out." I startled a little—my lawyer would never agree to this—but Zadie forged ahead. "Nobody except Macon stands to gain anything from going to court, Boyd. You know that. You owe it to yourself to have all the information first, and you owe it to yourself—and Betsy—to see if this is something you can understand, or even forgive."

He stared past Zadie, eyes fixed on the horizon.

She stood her ground. "It might even bring you some comfort, Boyd."

His posture grew uncertain. "I don't think so."

"I want to hear what she has to say."

My head jerked together with Zadie's and Boyd's toward the speaker, who had silently come up behind me. Betsy Packard took an elegant step past me, not stopping, and alighted beside Zadie. She reached for her husband's arm.

"For me," she said. "Please, Boyd. I'd like to try this."

His head shook in jowly disbelief. "Why?"

Betsy's lips trembled, belying her straight-backed poise. "I can't go on," she said. "I can't go on like this, Boyd." She paused and squeezed her eyes shut. When she spoke again, it was to address Zadie. "I trust you," she said simply.

Zadie reached for Betsy's hand.

Boyd withered under the unified female assault, raising his arms in surrender. "Okay," he said heavily. "Okay, if you want this, Bets."

"I do."

For the first time, he aimed his glance toward me. "How about tonight?"

"Tonight's the Arts Ball," Zadie and Betsy said in unison.

"Hell," growled Boyd. "Twenty K for 'performance' art and a bunch of fa—men in tights, you'd think I'd remember."

Betsy addressed me. "We aren't attending this year, but I'm sure you and Zadie are," she said, her cultured voice warming me. "How about tomorrow after church?"

I was not a church attender, but in the South this registered as a bizarre personal failing akin to owning four hundred cats or having an unusual sexual fetish. You didn't bring it up in public. "Thank you," I rasped.

Boyd pointed a finger at Zadie. "Let's do next Saturday evening instead," he decided. "A week from today. You'll come too?"

"Of course," she said without hesitation, even though I knew she was spending next weekend downtown on a mini getaway with Drew. She clasped his hand. "Thank you, Boyd."

He offered a small smile to Zadie, then eyed me again. "Okay. Guess we'll be hearing what you've got to say."

Chapter Twenty-five

TRY NOT TO WORRY

Autumn, 1999: Louisville, Kentucky
Zadie

Abdominal pain.

All charts in the ER had a chief complaint written across the top, and this was one I felt eager to tackle, having recently attended a lengthy lecture on the topic. People who had completed medical school and a three- or four-year residency in emergency medicine, followed by the successful completion of two rigorous and lengthy exams, one oral, one written—actual board-certified ER doctors—tended to approach the chief complaint of abdominal pain with something less-than-keen excitement. There were plenty of chances for things to go awry.

The chair of the Department of Emergency Medicine was the polar opposite of the fearsome Dr. Markham. Dr. Bernard Elsdon was an energetic, possibly manic beanpole with an odd poof of Einsteinesque hair and a flair for teaching. He resembled an agitated Q-tip, often becoming so overwrought during medical student lectures that he required a change of shirts. He was not exactly a fashion plate—it appeared he owned several identical pairs of shirts and pants—and so when he worked himself into a clothes-changing froth, he could quickly substitute one boring button-down for another. He avoided sport coats, probably because another layer of clothing was not helpful when one was prone to torrential sweating, and simply threw a battered, long white doctor's coat over his ensemble if he needed to look more polished. Like every other medical student who had not yet had the pleasure of being graded by him, I was enchanted. As with all good teachers, his zeal for his topic was infectious; everyone saw themselves as potential ER doctors during this rotation.

I mentally reviewed the differential diagnosis for abdominal pain as I walked toward this, my very first ER patient of my own. I liked the structure of this rotation: daily seven a.m. lectures with Dr. Elsdon, followed by either a twelve-hour day shift or, if I was finishing the overnight shift, heading home to crash into bed. Each student had two days off each week, which meant despite the mental confusion of switching back and forth between working days and nights, the total number of hours worked in a week was going to be significantly less than on the trauma rotation. I also loved the concept of seeing patients on my own before presenting them to an attending or upper-level resident to review together. The key, I thought smugly, was not to get overwhelmed with the dizzying array of possibilities for what could be wrong, and also to remain calm if all hell was breaking loose. After trauma surgery, how hard could that be?

Concentrating intently, I almost collided with some people flying down the hall, carrying a limp figure. I caught a quick glimpse of a dangling corpse white arm—a man's arm—as they skidded into one of the trauma rooms, a vivid trail of blood in their wake. Curious, I stood for a moment—where were the EMTs? Were they coming from somewhere else in the hospital?—but then I shook it off. I was here to tackle abdominal pain, not trauma.

I knocked on the door of room 22 and entered. Occupying a metal chair in the corner was a stringy woman of about fifty-five, sitting ramrod straight with her arms crossed in hostile fashion. Perched next to the chair on the exam table sat a massive lady with a face squinched up into a thunderous scowl. Before I could extend a hand and introduce myself, the lady—Mrs. Goodhouse, according to the chart—shifted her ponderous bulk and emitted a room-shaking blast of wrath.

"One hour and forty-five minutes! One hour and forty-five minutes! Like I ain't got nowhere more important to be. Like I don't have things I need to get *done*. And what happens if I up and *die* in here? How's anybody gonna know? What kind of hospital just lets you *die* on them?"

"I'm so sorry, Mrs. Goodhouse. My name is—"

"Sorry! Don't be thinking 'so sorry' gone make anything okay," interrupted Mrs. Goodhouse. "What happens if I just go ahead and *die* on you? You gone just keep saying 'so sorry'?"

"No, I—"

"Well, I'll tell you about 'so sorry.' 'So sorry' gone be the fool who did this to me. I am *sick*. I need something for this *now*. You best get to stopping this *sick* and doing something to fix my weave."

The woman on the chair, still seated with militaristic rigidity, nodded knowingly and fixed me with a stone-cold stare. "Mmmm-hmmm!" she said, her voice rising significantly on the second syllable.

This was not going according to my mental image of my first patient encounter, but I gamely plowed ahead.

"Can you tell me about your abdominal pain?" I asked.

"Abdominal pain? Woo Lord. What in the world you talkin' about, ab-dom-i-nal pain? Can't you read? I never said nothing about no abdominal pain."

"Ah, well, it says here, 'Patient states she is sick to her stomach.'"

"Why, yes, I am sick to my stomach. Who's not gonna be sick, they have their hair *burned off* their head? That not gonna bother you? Uh-huh. I am *sick*."

The other woman backed her up again. "Mmm-hmm. That's right."

Now thoroughly bewildered, I asked, "You're here for something about your hair?"

"Are you blind too?" screeched Mrs. Goodhouse. "Look at my *head*!"

I looked. There was indeed something wrong with Mrs. Goodhouse's hair. The scalp appeared normal but the hair itself was radiating out from her head in teeny shriveled corkscrews, like the corona on an angry dandelion. There was also a . . . scorched appearance, an impression bolstered by a distinctly unpleasant odor.

"What happened?" I wondered.

"What does it look like happened?" barked Mrs. G. "This damn fool working on my weave put some *chemical* on there and done burned it near off! What I want to know is how you aim to *fix* it. I ain't waiting no one hour and forty-five minutes to hear 'so sorry.'"

I was literally speechless. Chemical damage to one's weave had not yet been covered in any lecture I'd attended. Was there even a diagnosis for this? And what kind of shoddy triage had led to this being described as "abdominal pain"? It seemed sharing this sentiment with the unhinged Mrs. Goodhouse would be unlikely to result in commiseration.

"I'm just going to consult with a . . . hair doctor," I blurted. "Be right back."

The ER was abuzz. People scurried every which way, and several ambulance gurneys tied up traffic in the hall. I wanted to locate the third-year ER resident, a blustery guy by the name of Micah Abbott, although it seemed unlikely he'd be much help in soothing the aggrieved Mrs. Goodhouse. He was even less likely to be fruitful regarding a solution to the hair crisis, since he was blindingly white and bald as a snake. But presumably he'd seen chemical burns to the scalp before and would know how to write a quick note while effecting an expedient, if unsatisfactory, dismissal. After searching every part of our assigned hallway, I finally caught sight of him standing in a crowd outside the closed curtain to one of the trauma bays across the ER, where the noise from some tremendous ruckus was emanating out.

"Hey, Dr. Abbott," I said, waving at him across the hall as I hustled in his direction. "I have a lady who—"

"Ah, there you are!" someone said, interrupting me. I found myself grasped by the elbow so I was pivoted in the opposite direction. A little rustle went through the crowd outside the trauma bay, many of whom appeared to be staring at me. I opened my mouth to protest but shut it abruptly as I realized the elbow grabber was none other than Dr. Elsdon himself. "Let's head into my office for a second," he said.

"But I . . . Shouldn't I tell Micah about room twenty-two?" I asked, bewildered. Had I screwed up somehow? Surely they didn't have video cameras in the exam rooms.

"We'll let him handle that one," said Dr. Elsdon, walking quickly. We turned down the long corridor outside the emergency department entrance. I remembered Dr. Elsdon's office was actually located in a separate building connected to the hospital by an underground pedway. This was probably a ten-minute walk. What had I done to warrant such an intervention, and from the chair of the emergency department, no less?

Dr. Elsdon had only one speed: snappy. We hurtled around a corner, where a grim-faced blond woman dressed chest to toe in a startling shade of purple was waiting. I recognized her as Dr. Elsdon's administrative assistant. Oddly, she was standing next to Emma, who had also been placed on the ED rotation this month—this meant she and I would have alternating shifts—along with James DeMarco, our class president, who was one of the other third-year students on the rotation. James was a tenderhearted guy who carried out his responsibilities as class president in an avuncular fashion, being a few years older than most of his peers. He was the only bearded dude in our grade, and he was gawky and earnest and people absolutely loved him. Our classmates went to him with a litany of troubles: financial, romantic, academic, even, in a couple of disturbing instances, sexual. But he was that kind of guy: people knew they could trust him.

Neither Emma nor James was currently working; Emma had just finished the first night shift, and James was off today. So whatever was going down was not Zadie-specific, then.

"Ah, Mrs. Lukeson," said Dr. Elsdon. "Excellent. I will turn our third years over to you for the time being. Kids, I'll see you in a few. Hang tight and try not to worry." With that admonishment, which was of course the most worrying thing yet, he spun around and strode back toward the emergency department.

"What the heck's going on?" I whispered to Emma and James as they timidly trailed Mrs. Lukeson. Unlike her boss, she was not endowed with hypersonic energy; her pace was glacial. She glanced backward and gave us a poker-faced appraisal before she said, "Dr. Elsdon said you can wait in the conference room. He wants you to go through some of those old papers in there."

We waited until she deposited us, along with the threatened stack of journals and xeroxed papers, in a rectangular carpeted room containing a medium-sized table before we began conferring again in heated whispers.

"What exactly are we supposed to do with these?" Emma muttered, flicking aside something entitled *A Decision Rule for the Use of the D-dimer Assay in Suspected Pulmonary Thromboembolism*.

"Right," I said. "We can't read all these. And how did you guys wind up in here? Did anybody say what was wrong?"

"No. We finished the lecture with you, and then we went back into the ED because I had to finish some charting," Emma contributed.

"James went with me because he wanted to observe before his shift tonight. So we were sitting at the doctors' area behind the main ED desk, and *she*"—she motioned toward the open conference room door, through which Mrs. Lukeson could be seen at her desk presiding over the entrance to the department's offices—"came up to us and said we had to follow her. No explanation at all."

James looked pensive. "There was a lot of commotion over by the trauma room. Even for the ER, I mean."

"Oh yeah," I remembered. Micah had been standing there, looking up—guiltily?—when I beckoned to him, a faint impression, which I'd attributed to him being so hard to find. But why was he lurking outside a trauma room?

"Well, why in the world would they want to hide a trauma from us?" wondered Emma. "Zadie and I were on the trauma service a couple months ago. We were in and out of those rooms constantly."

An answer to that question—an unpleasant answer—was pushing itself into the margins of my consciousness, but I shoved the thought away, reluctant to give voice to it. Emma must have been thinking along the same lines, though, because she said, "Unless it was someone we know."

"Well, how would they even know who we know?" I asked, realizing a split second too late the answer was obvious. One thing bound the three of us together; since this was our first day on the rotation, Dr. Elsdon and the rest of the ED staff had very little knowledge of us personally.

But of course he knew we were all third-year medical students.

We thought about this silently for a moment, and then James said, in an inappropriately positive tone, "It might be somebody on the faculty. Or somebody famous, even."

Of course it was *possible* some celebrity had been cruising around Louisville unheralded and managed to get bashed up in some fashion.

But why would such an event require the hasty removal of only the third-year students, leaving everyone else to gawk away? This seemed unlikely.

We amused ourselves for the next hour as best we could, largely ignoring the option of reading the elderly emergency medicine journals, although we did thumb through some of them to look for gruesome photos. At last we heard the phone ring in the outer chamber of the ED offices, and unlike with previous phone calls, Mrs. Lukeson gave this one away by flicking a quick glance in our direction as she lowered her voice to answer. We could not discern much.

". . . yes, yes, fine, still sitting . . . How did . . . ? Oh no. Oh, poor . . . Yes, I'll . . . Oh dear. Okay. Yes. Yes, of course."

She hung up the receiver and stood, smoothing her purple skirt, and then ambled in her poky fashion down the hall toward us. For once, she did not look fussy. She looked . . . sad.

"Dr. Elsdon is on his way to get you," she said, not meeting our eyes. "He'll be here in five minutes."

Chapter Twenty-six

NO EASY WAY TO SAY THIS

Autumn, 1999: Louisville, Kentucky

There were two ways to reach the academic offices of the Department of Emergency Medicine. Most people—employees, civilians, visitors, mailmen—used the front entrance, a set of glass doors facing a large foyer with elevators and fake ficuses and directories to all the various other medical departments in this building. Mrs. Lukeson reigned at her desk in an open space with several carpeted hallways branching off behind her, one of them leading to the conference room in which the three of us waited. The less conventional means of approach to the department involved the subterranean tunnel coming from the main building of the hospital. It was ancient, with a concrete floor and tenuous fluorescent lighting, and seemed to narrow imperceptibly as you traveled it, so by the time you neared the end, you were somewhat panicked even if you'd not previously considered yourself claustrophobic. In the million years or so in which it had been in existence, no one had ever thought to attack it with a duster, so the ceilings were festooned with creepy swaths of cobwebs. It was one of a series of tunnels referred to as the "Catacombs."

The entrance to the Catacombs from the academic building was right next to the conference room in which we sat, so we could hear Dr. Elsdon approaching well before he pushed open the door to the reception area. He had a characteristic canter that did not seem to be diminished by today's events, whatever they might have been. And since he generally barreled around with an entourage, it was impossible for him to sneak up on anyone. It sounded like they might have been charging in on horseback. As the footsteps got closer, it was plain he was in fact not alone; judging by the noise level, there were at least a couple of people trying to keep up.

When he finally did appear, he was quiet, pausing at Mrs. Lukeson's desk to murmur something to her and to introduce his companions. Emma, who had a better view through the open conference room doorway than I did, stiffened in surprise. "It's Dr. X," she hissed.

I craned my neck. It was indeed Nick. Unlike us, he was still on the trauma service, since the chiefs did their rotations in three-month blocks. He must have caught sight of my movement, because he turned and looked directly at me. His face was unreadable. There was also a woman with them whom I did not recognize. She had frizzy gray hair and was evidently unconcerned with fashion; she was wearing a dress resembling a bathrobe made from some bluish pilled material. Dr. Elsdon turned and saw the three of us staring in his direction, and he at once made for the conference room, sweeping in with Nick and the bathrobe woman behind him. Nick closed the door.

"I must apologize to you for the long wait," Dr. Elsdon said, his alert face scanning us. "Of course we did not intend for your first day of emergency medicine to begin this way. I'd like to introduce you to Dr. X—one of the fifth-year surgery residents and our current trauma chief—and this is Reverend Ania, our hospital chaplain. I apologize again because I haven't learned your names yet. Normally, I take care to get to know you all well during my month with you."

"Of course, it's fine," said James. "I'm James DeMarco."

"Zadie Fletcher," I said.

"Then you must be Emma Bingham," said Dr. Elsdon, addressing her. She nodded.

"James, Zadie, Emma. Thank you for your patience. This is difficult. Ah. I don't think we've ever before . . . Well, anyway. There is no easy way to say this so I'll just come out with it: one of your classmates has died."

Why Dr. Elsdon felt it necessary to insert a dramatic pause here was beyond me. We waited in agony for him to get on with it. He looked at Nick, but Nick threw the ball back to him, gazing at him impassively. A fleeting expression of something—distaste? resignation? sadness?—crossed his face. Dr. Elsdon cleared his throat and said:

"Graham O'Kane."

Chapter Twenty-seven

THE FAMILY BED

Emma, Present Day

Although I should have been rehearsing what in the world I'd say to Boyd and Betsy Packard to explain the death of their child on my watch, it wasn't them on my mind as I crunched through the golden leaves on my way home from the basketball game. It was Graham.

This time of year was always bittersweet. In the Carolinas, nature gifts us with perfect fall weather: the languid, sticky days of summer give way to bright, invigorating air, showered with crimson and orange and gold, doused in crisp sunshine. Ordinarily, it's hard not to feel happy.

But all the beauty also accentuates the imperviousness of nature, because to me, the heralds of autumn are also searing reminders of shame. Graham, the first man who ever loved me, died in the fall, on a perfect day like this one.

I often thought about what would have happened if he had lived.

Would he have forgiven me? Would we still be together? By the time I met Wyatt, most of my fertile years were behind me. Of course, I can't imagine life without Wyatt and my son. But would I have had other children, more children, if I had married Graham?

"Do you want kids?" I'd asked him once, leaning against him on a bench in the quad, where we were taking a break from a marathon cram for some examination or other.

"Of course," he answered promptly, his face relaxing into unguarded happiness. "I love kids. I want a little girl like you and a little boy like . . . you."

"Me?"

He laughed. "Yeah. Like their mom. You're perfect."

I sat up in alarm. "I don't even want kids, Graham. How can you see me as a mother? I'm clearly not mother material."

"I have a perfect visual image of you as a mom, Em." He turned to me, serious. "I can see you kneeling by some little girl, showing her the stars, or holding her on your lap as you explain how gravity works, and I can see the wonder on her face. You'll just . . . re-create your genius in a smaller form. Another tiny, brilliant, beautiful Emma. Or two."

I almost choked, thinking back on it now. That conversation had taken place a few months before a gunshot blast to the chest ended his life, and I could hardly stand to think of the juxtaposition between his happy confidence that someday he'd have kids and the immutable reality of his death. He'd been so comfortable, so sure he'd one day be a father. While he had envisioned his children as clones of me, I hadn't envisioned children at all. I didn't know any small children at that point in my life, and I didn't feel any strong pull toward acquiring one. But if you'd forced me to picture it, I guess I'd have described someone like him. Sturdy. Contemplative. Quietly sunny.

What would Graham have thought of me as a mother if he'd lived?

The reality of motherhood had been a huge shock to me. I got pregnant almost as soon as Wyatt and I were married. Someone told me about a popular advice book for the parents of infants, which advocated tidy blocks of scheduled sleeping and feeding. This appealed to me immediately. Despite the chaos of my profession, I love schedules, love order and predictability, and have an inverse dislike of entropy. My baby, I felt sure, would thrive with a set routine. Naturally, I would have to be somewhat flexible; sometimes there would be small shifts in the feeding start time, or naps, or cuddle time, or whatever, because babies are . . . babies. I would adjust.

Yet right from the moment of his birth, Henry was hell-bent on avoiding a schedule. Under his thatch of wispy hair, his tiny face was permanently red from the strain of yelling so much. He did not sleep more than an hour at a time, and he seemed angry every time he nursed, as if he were being simultaneously starved and choked. This dragged out the process of feeding him because as soon as he finished, it was time to feed him again.

If you'd asked me before Henry was born, I'd have sworn I'd be the last person on earth ever to allow a child to sleep in my bed. Cosleeping was a good example of the mushy, lenient, laissez-faire-type parenting springing up among a certain subset of Gen X parents, the kind who didn't believe in negative reinforcement and stopped breastfeeding only when their kids were old enough to drive. You'd think most of these people would be kind of crunchy, but attachment parenting has infiltrated all ideologies: conservative, liberal, hippies, tea-partiers, everybody.

Everyone said the first three months would be rough. In fact, they were brutal beyond anything I had imagined. It was worse than my residency. I became a drooling, irritable zombie with zero regard for hygiene. In desperation, I read all the baby sleep books: *Secrets of the Baby Whisperer; The Girlfriends' Guide to Surviving the First Year of Motherhood; What to Expect the First Year; Healthy Sleep Habits, Happy Child.* They didn't help. Henry was completely resistant to sleep.

At four months, the pediatrician gave me the okay to let Henry "cry it out." I was warned it would be heartrending, that I should resist the urge to rush in and comfort him, in the interest of teaching him he could, in fact, fall asleep on his own. It might take a half hour or more, but no baby can cry forever. Right?

Henry didn't get the memo. He bellowed in outrage for five solid hours before he succumbed for forty-five minutes. Then he woke up and commenced his usual roaring. Wyatt resisted the urge to comfort Henry during the marathon screaming session, but only because he comforted himself by downing a bottle of Maker's Mark while staring in horror at the blaring red lights on the baby monitor.

"The hell with this, muffin," he said finally. "Can we see if he'll sleep in our bed?"

Babies are helpless but brilliant parasites who have survived the millennia by enslaving adults. They accomplish this by (a) making people think they're cute and (b) producing a noxious noise until you do their bidding. Henry was excellent at both. He didn't sleep long stretches in our bed either, but any attempt to remove him resulted in torrential screeching. If allowed to remain, he would drift off more pleasantly and could be silenced upon reawakening by nursing, all without anyone having to pace the floor.

Now that Henry was nearly three, he was finally weaned. I had taken to breastfeeding with less-than-total enthusiasm, unable to shake an unpleasant bovine sensation. Everybody breastfed, though. It was better for babies, and people who didn't want to do it were regarded with politely masked disdain. It was not even enough just to do it. You were supposed to love it. Most mothers—like Zadie, for example—waxed poetic about the bonding, the sweetness, the comfort of holding a milk-scented lump of warmth, the flood of endorphins when a baby locked its little gaze on theirs. I mainly felt a raging impatience as I was trapped in a chair, and frustration with Henry, who cried so much he would intermittently stop drinking in order to look up and holler at me. I knew better than to bring this up with Zadie, though. Every time Zadie held a baby, her own or not, she began to emit authentic waves of maternal warmth and love.

But I kept on breastfeeding at night, even after I went back to work, because at least that way we all got a little sleep. On the nights I was at the hospital, Wyatt had to resort to pacifiers and bottles, which Henry would tolerate only in my absence.

He was finally cut off now, though. That was a tremendous ordeal, but nothing compared to our attempts to get him into his own bed. He systemically destroyed us every time we tried. It was genius, really. He'd even managed to ensure there was no sibling competition for his parents' affection, since our sex life was decimated.

Thank goodness his personality improved. He was not very verbal, but he was clearly smart; he could efficiently disassemble any electronic device to its component parts in less than three minutes, and he had learned how to operate the complicated TV remote without instruction. And now that he'd escaped whatever demons had possessed his baby phase, he was fun. He adored Wyatt and erupted into helpless, snorty giggles whenever they played. With me, he was calmer; he loved burrowing into my lap and rubbing his soft little cheeks against me. And now I felt it: the helpless, searing wash of love for my baby that meant I'd do anything for him. I was relieved to finally have the sense that I must have been a normal mother.

I turned up the sidewalk in front of our huge house, surveying its gables and its beautiful old slate roof. Following a pebbled path along the side of the house, I arrived at the back door, calling "I'm back!" as I tucked my running shoes away in their cubby. From overhead a pattering sound struck my ears, which gave way to the steady thump of small feet on the stairs. Henry came into view, making the excited grunting sounds he always reserved for welcoming me home. I knelt down and opened my arms, and he careened into me, his solid little body wriggling with wordless joy.

I drank it in: his baby softness, the invisible tether between us, the undeserved adoration he always showered on me. I thought about whether I'd give him up if I could bring back Eleanor Packard, and the thought of losing him was so terrible tears came to my eyes. This is what I'd say to Boyd and Betsy, if I could: *I understand what you lost.*

I understand what I took from you.

And somewhere, somehow, in the vast universe above me, I felt Graham's presence. And for the first time since he died, I was able to set aside my self-loathing long enough to remember him with more clarity. He'd have been the most wonderful father.

I'd like to think if he could have seen me and Henry, he'd be smiling.

Chapter Twenty-eight

A LITERAL WINDOW TO
A BROKEN HEART

Autumn, 1999: Louisville, Kentucky
Zadie

James and I froze, but there was not even a second's reprieve for Emma. She clapped her hands over her mouth, a high, thin sound escaping around the edges of her fingers. She stood, then stumbled over to the corner of the room, her cheeks glazed with two crimson patches, as she still tried to hold in sound with her hands.

I started to rise, but the chaplain was already there. She was saying something to Emma in a low voice. "What happened? What happened?" James was asking, but my vision went swimmy for a moment, and by the time I could focus again, Emma and the chaplain were gone.

Dr. Elsdon wordlessly conferred with Nick, one emotive eyebrow locked in question mode. Nick nodded. "Her friend," he confirmed. Dr. Elsdon manually pushed his inquisitive eyebrow down with one abstracted finger and surveyed me and James.

We were crying. We both stared out straight in front of us, bewildered by our tears, especially in the presence of the powerful and unfamiliar chair of the ER department, but we were as helpless as babies to control ourselves. James ineffectually swiped at his streaming face with one gangly arm, which prompted Dr. Elsdon into action; he sprang out of the room on a mission to find tissues.

As soon as he was gone, Nick sank to his knees in front of us, his handsome face anguished. He bowed his golden head and took my hand, saying, "We did everything, Z. We tried for more than an hour. He was still alive when he came in, but barely. I swear they had to force me to stop. Please tell her I'm sorry."

I cried some more.

Graham. Last week: the last time I'd seen him. Mingled sounds drifting down the hallway of our apartment: a booming baritone, with an exaggerated crescendoing gargle at the end of each line, mixed with the splattering noise of water. Elvis, he was singing Elvis in our shower. The water cut off, and I'd listened, amused, as Elvis forgot for the twentieth time that he was too tall to exit through the flimsy shower door without banging his head on the horizontal support bar.

"Ow! Motherf—" The twinging sound of the support bar vibrating from the impact. Muffled curses, then more singing, softer now that he was no longer competing with the shower.

I cried more. I could see him clearly, emerging from the bathroom clad in a too-small towel. He'd startled as he caught sight of me, his warbling Elvis cutting off midword, but then he recovered. His face changed to that patient, focused expression he often had. He looked happy.

"What happened?" James asked again, his voice thick.

I realized I knew what Nick was going to say a beat before he said it, but I couldn't imagine why.

"He took his own life," said Nick gently. "Shot himself in the chest."

"In the *chest*?" said James through a barrage of tears. Even a third-year med student knew that if you wanted to die immediately and painlessly, you had to take out the brain stem. Shooting yourself in the chest was in every way bad: messy, not always fatal, and there was no guarantee of instant loss of consciousness. To be sure, shooting yourself in the head had its chance of horrendous unintended consequence—perhaps it was this that had influenced Graham, since every trauma surgeon had gruesome stories of some would-be suicide who had only managed to blow off his face. They often failed to aim properly (or, even likelier, they flinched at the last second). But a bullet to the chest! It wasn't a common means of suicide. Both James and I were stricken with the image of Graham surviving long enough to suffer agonizing regret.

"Are you sure he did it to himself?" I said through my sobs. "Couldn't it have been someone else?"

"He was in the quad, Zadie. A dozen people saw it," Nick said grimly.

"Oh God," said James. "Oh no."

Watching him now, it dawned on me that, next to Emma, he was probably Graham's closest friend in our class. Along with sadness and horror, his honest face was emblazoned with guilt. I reached out to him and pulled him to me; we grasped each other in a weepy, shattered embrace. "James," I choked. "James. It's not your fault."

James pulled away. He seemed unaware he was making a weird, high keening sound. Even through my own pain—oh God, I had to get to Emma—it was wrenching to see a man trying so hard to stop crying, especially James, with his bearded face now resting on his skinny arms. Nick was blinking rapidly, his beautiful jaw set, turning away so as not to have to look at him.

Dr. Elsdon skidded back into the room, laden with enough Kleenex to manage an army of flu victims. He took immediate measure of us and beckoned to Nick. "Help her find her friend," he ordered.

Although I had no memory of leaving the room, or entering the

Catacombs, somehow we emerged into the lobby of Christ the Redeemer, where the light seemed insanely bright and the people were scurrying around with offensive normality. Nick, who had been babbling—wondering if Graham would have left a note, wondering if I had thought he'd seemed depressed—badged our way into the ED, in the hope we'd find Emma there, because I refused to do anything or even say anything else until we'd located her. Graham's body was still in the trauma room. Nick steered me away from it, but after we checked the family room and the waiting room and even the chapel without success, I knew Emma had to be there. As I got closer, I thought I heard Emma's voice inside—distorted and raspy, but still recognizably Emma's—and I flung aside the curtain and ran in.

She held Graham's hand. There was no sheet covering his face and no one had closed his eyes, so he gazed up sightlessly at her, his face a dusky blue. An endotracheal tube lilted up from his mouth. His chest was exposed and it had been opened on the left, with a rib spreader still in place: a literal window to his broken heart. Then, at some point in the frenzy to save him, someone, probably Nick, had decided to extend the incision to the right, so his sternum had been sawed in half. Emma was not looking at his mangled chest, however; she was focused on his hand.

"Did you feed Baxter this morning?" she asked in a toneless voice without looking up at me. "I promised him we'd take care of Baxter."

"Emma," I said, helpless.

"I didn't know. I didn't know why he was asking me to take care of Baxter."

"Emma. Can I hold you?"

"I didn't know this would happen. I didn't know. I didn't know. We have to keep the dog, Zadie. He wants us to keep the dog."

She began stroking Graham's large bloodless hand with her own pink ones, rocking back and forth. I was paralyzed. I stood rooted to the middle of the room, watching Emma rocking next to the ravaged immobile thing that was Graham.

The curtain swished aside and Nick came in. Emma looked up at him, almost with a look of hatred. He went to her and, without hesitation, pulled her up and into him, burying her face in his big shoulder, one hand gently bolstering the back of her wobbly head. With the other, he reached into his pocket and threw me a set of keys. "Take these to Ken. He's in the ER. He's going to pull my car around and take you two home. I'll bring Emma out front in ten minutes."

I nodded and mutely started for the exit.

"Zadie," Nick said softly. I turned back.

He met my eyes above Emma's heaving form. *I love you*, he mouthed.

———

Ken Linker, one of the fifth-year surgery residents, marched me through the ER. People looked at us and occasionally called out, the drama of Graham's death either unknown to them or already receding. Again I was stricken with the reality of a world proceeding along with or without you. How could everything seem so normal to other people?

We reached the quad. It was a lovely autumn day, with brilliant sun showering the large square brick-rimmed beds of late-fall flowers. Cascading orange and yellow leaves were caught in swirling currents of sweet, crisp air, dancing and pirouetting merrily before bowing themselves out on the flagstone of the quad's surface. Nature was, as always, indifferent, but the humans present were another story. Unlike at the vast hospital, things were not normal here at all, since this was the site where Graham had chosen to end his life. The precise spot where it happened was evident, as there was still a police presence, complete with crime scene tape and misshapen black bloodstains, along with a slowly gathering crowd of medical students. They milled around in shocked little huddles, gazing in disbelief at the sticky pools of congealed blood, which were as discordant on the sunshiny courtyard as an assault rifle at a preschool. I saw Rolfe and Landley at a distance, facing away from the crime scene tape; both of their faces dropped into their hands, Rolfe's dark head and Landley's fair one hanging parallel to the ground.

I took a step backward as something loomed up in front of me. A small distraught tornado—Hannah—blew into me, almost knocking me over in a teary hug. She was, predictably, incoherent. Her face was swollen to unrecognizable proportions, an anguished balloon at its bursting point.

"Maybe I should take her home too," Ken offered uneasily, as Hannah attempted unsuccessfully to speak. "What service is she on?"

I answered slowly, ". . . Trauma."

Oh no. Oh no. Hannah was on Nick's service. She would have been paged and gone to the trauma room; it was probably her first-ever trauma code. She would have been there as Graham was brought in, and she would have realized who he was, and she would have been watching as they cracked his chest and fought to save him. She would have seen him die.

Although I'd been too stricken to comfort my best friend, I had no hesitation with Hannah. I gathered her up, rubbing her shoulders as Hannah clutched me. I managed a nod to Ken, who said, "I'll let X know I've got her too. She can take the day off. If you guys can wait for a few minutes, I'll swing by with the car right over there." He gestured to a roundabout at one end of the quad and hastily retreated toward the garage.

"Oh God, Hannahbear," I murmured into Hannah's soft hair. "I'm so sorry. Did you go in to the code?"

Hannah, who was nearly four inches shorter than me, nodded into my chest, hiccupping a little as her sobs quieted down, giving me the oddly maternal comfort of being able to soothe someone else. We kept holding each other, ignoring the sad, hushed chatter vibrating through the courtyard and the bloodstains and the police and the muted city sounds, until finally I became aware Ken was patiently idling nearby.

We were almost to the car when I caught sight of a bright iridescent flash in my peripheral vision: Georgia. She was charging toward us, wearing a lime green rhinestoned pantsuit under her white coat, her flaming hair in a fat bun secured by metal chopsticks, her forehead and eyebrows creased by confusion. Across the quad, Rolfe and Landley took notice of Georgia's presence and began shuffling toward us too.

Georgia reached out uncertainly. "Dudes," she said. "Why is everybody crying?"

Chapter Twenty-nine

A GOOD WAKE NEEDS
HARD LIQUOR

Autumn, 1999: Louisville, Kentucky

For a moment nobody could answer. Georgia's eyes traced across the yellow police tape down to the oily dark patches on the stone, then over to Rolfe, who had almost reached us. "Who—" she began. She stopped. "What is all this? What happened?"

Rolfe looked wrecked. For the first time I could ever remember, there was not a trace of his insouciant light; he was lifeless and dull. Landley gestured toward him and mouthed to me, *Can't talk about it.*

"Can't talk about what?" Georgia cried. "Will somebody tell me what the hell is going on?"

"Graham is dead," Landley said. "He shot himself."

We waited while Georgia cycled through the facial gymnastics of shock: incomprehension, disbelief, pain, and finally openmouthed horror. Her vivid features crumpled on themselves in dismay as Landley, in a low voice, filled her in.

After a terse consultation, everyone agreed to reconvene at my apartment that evening, with a backup plan in place—Rolfe's—if Emma objected.

Ken swung the growly sports car back into the street, alighting a short time later under the porticoed ambulance entrance to the ER. At first it looked as though only Nick was there, inexplicably re-dressed in a white cape, but as we drew up, it became apparent he was wrapped in a coarse blanket from one of the ER's warmers. Emma huddled underneath it, her face mashed against his chest, her hair in its two long French braids giving her the appearance of a young child. She did not open her eyes as they tucked her into the backseat next to me.

Nick and Ken had a hushed conversation at the driver's-side window, their deep, low voices indecipherable but soothing, somehow, like the barely heard sound of protective grown-up voices murmuring outside your room when you are small. I saw Nick hand Ken a slip of paper (a prescription?), which he folded and tucked in his pocket. Beside me, Emma was a frozen lump, her harsh breathing the only sign she was alive.

———

By seven o'clock my friends were convened in our apartment. The rooms glowed with candlelight, warm air suffusing through the tidied open kitchen-living space, which I had hastily purged of random Graham paraphernalia: *Sports Illustrated*s, which had accumulated in the bathroom, providing Emma and me with a source of long-running mockery— what *did* guys do in there that took so long?—enormous stinky shoes and socks, which tended to fester under the grubby plaid reclining chair Graham favored; on the kitchen counter bottles of creatine, which Graham took for some dubious workout-related benefit; baseball caps clinging to doorknobs; faded, soft Graham-smelling T-shirts; a few nasty tins of snuff, which many of the guys took at the hospital when required to stay awake for obscene periods of time; and, sadly, Graham's white coat, embroidered with his name, hanging with forlorn droopiness in the tiny foyer, waiting in vain for his large form to fill it again.

All of this and more I scooped up and placed in a plastic storage bin under my bed, giving each little everyday object a bittersweet caress, not wanting Emma to be confronted with Graham detritus at every glance. But I didn't have the audacity to enter Emma's room, where, of course, most of Graham's things resided.

"A good wake needs hard liquor," Landley said, morosely draped over the edge of the sofa. "Whaddaya got, Fletch?"

"I think there's some Four Roses above the fridge," I remembered. I fetched it along with some shot glasses and handed them to Landley, who distributed them. "To Graham," he intoned, and we raised our glasses, holding them in the air for a great deal longer than the usual toast, as if waiting for Graham to materialize and join us.

Instead, the door to Emma's room opened and she drifted out, bumping slightly against the doorframe on the way. Her braids were down and her beautiful hair waved around her, floating halfway down her back. Nick had indeed given her a prescription for Xanax, which went a long way in Emma's virgin system; she drooped over to the couch and plopped down, half onto me and half onto Landley, the back of her head frizzed up and a tiny bit of dried drool crusting the corner of her lower lip. But the medicine had its intended effect: she was very calm.

"I love you guysh," she mumbled, and closed her eyes.

"We love you too, Em," said Georgia, stroking Emma's foot from her spot on the floor. "Anything you need . . ."

"Emma." Rolfe stood up and began meandering around the room, picking things up and setting them down, as restless as Emma was blunted. "Should we not talk about it?"

"S'okay," said Emma without opening her eyes. She leaned back into the couch, her face a smooth mask.

"How could he do this?" blurted Rolfe. "I mean, why? Why?"

"He went to see James this morning," said Landley. "Some kind of money troubles."

I couldn't fathom it. This made no sense.

". . . and I think that his dad used to be an orthopod or something," Landley was saying, with a sideways glance at Emma, who had fallen asleep; her mouth was open and her head thrown back. "But he retired after he signed with one of those medical device companies. He invented something that made him a fortune, and apparently he had a lot to begin with."

"So what?" Rolfe said.

"So, I heard he donated *mucho dinero* to the med school, that's what. Graham would never talk about him, but his name's on some plaque of high rollers outside Wormer's office. Maybe this was some family fight?"

"He didn't give jack shit to his son—that's for sure," said Rolfe. "Graham was always broke."

"Hard to imagine Graham ever doing anything to warrant getting frozen out by his own dad, though, right?" said Landley, chugging another generous pour of the bourbon. He blinked hard and abruptly turned his head to look at a poster behind the sofa, but not before I saw the tears on his cheeks.

"Were you in the ER?" Rolfe asked, nodding at me.

"I was, but they realized what was happening and Dr. Elsdon hustled me out. Me and Em and James, too. They tucked us in the ED offices so we had no idea what was going on. Where were you?"

"I was in the quad," said Rolfe.

It was the first time he'd confirmed this. We all looked again at Emma, who was snoring lightly, now shifted so her head was resting in Landley's lap. His small gray eyes flashed a fleeting but fiercely tender expression, and he moved a little so Emma's ear on one side was firmly pressed against his abdomen; he covered her other with a couch pillow. He looked up a little sheepishly: "Just in case."

We looked back at Rolfe. He was transfixed by the searing memory replaying itself in the empty air in front of him. Rolfe was handsome, beautiful even, his unkempt black hair flipping at the ends ever so slightly into curls, all angelic curved eyelashes and very white teeth. It was difficult to reconcile his beauty with the story he was telling, his words flying out like shards of broken glass.

"I saw him," he said. "He was across the quad from me, closer to the street, and I was coming out of the library. I think I meant to wave him over—but then the door to the side of me opened, and it was Breath of Freshness."

We all nodded meaningfully. Rolfe had just finished his rotation on the general surgery service and he had fared poorly. It had been a brutal stint: the service was slammed, all the beds filling up and overflowing onto some of the internal medicine floors, much to the consternation of the nurses. There was never any sleep. Rolfe had become perpetually unkempt, staggering around with two-day stubble and reeking of tired perspiration. Grayish creases formed under his eyes, and he occasionally was spotted wearing a blob of drool-covered foam around his neck; he fell asleep with such prompt regularity during the seductive dimness of morning Morbidity and Mortality conferences that the surgeons had taken to slipping a neck brace on him to support his sagging cervical spine as soon as he crashed.

In the midst of all this grim deprivation, he'd become obsessed with an ethereal creature who worked as a unit secretary in the ER. He'd dubbed her Breath of Freshness because she was as wholesome and gorgeous as a gust of spring mountain wind roaring through a scorching slum; she had flawless white skin with blooming cheeks, pale red-gold Rapunzel hair, abundant breasts, straight pearly teeth, and clear eyes the color of heather. When looking at her, you almost had to shield your eyes from the luminous backlit shaft of celestial light in which she seemed to dwell. Nobody knew her name, and Rolfe was too downtrodden by the erosion of his own attractive countenance to approach her. Despoiling her blinding beauty by getting too close would have been like admiring a delicate, perfect monarch butterfly and then crushing it under a muddy boot.

So all of us knew spotting Breath of Freshness outside the ER, when he was clean-shaven and restored, would instantly distract Rolfe from anything else. He'd babbled about her the entire month of his rotation.

"I turned away the second I saw her," he said hoarsely. "I don't know how long I stood there talking to her—a minute or two, maybe. I can't even remember what she said her name was."

Silence. No one, save Emma, seemed to be breathing. We waited for him to go on.

"It was loud. I knew right away it was a gunshot. But it was so out of context, and there was only one shot. I looked around, and I didn't see what had happened at first. I was entertaining the idea of throwing Breath of Freshness down and rolling on top of her—um, in case there were more shots—but then I heard people screaming at the other end of the quad. None of them were dropping or running, though. They were just screaming.

"I could see a pool of blood dripping out on the rocks, then a hand. A big hand, a guy's hand. There were people crouched all around him, so I couldn't see his face. Most of the people seemed stunned, but one guy was trying to tamponade the bleeding—he had taken off his shirt and had stuffed it into this crater in the other guy's chest. I still couldn't see who was shot, but the guy on the ground with him was Mack Wolfson—you know, Graham's friend in the class below us. He saw me and he yelled for me to help him. I took my shirt off too, and I knelt down beside Mack, and then I saw it was Graham."

He paused again and then resumed.

"He was alive. His eyes were kind of glazed, but they were open and he was looking at me. He didn't say anything. I don't think he could speak; he was making a rattling sound when he breathed, and he was a chalky color. Mack was screaming for help, and he was doing everything he could to keep Graham's blood in him. I don't know how many minutes went by. Then Graham moved his hand toward me, and I picked it up and I held his hand until somebody official got there. He kept looking at me—he knew I was there and that I had his hand and I think he wanted to say something, but he couldn't. He looked at me and looked at me and then he seemed not to see me anymore."

Chapter Thirty

BUCKETS OF MONEY

Zadie, Present Day

I kept an eye on Emma as I gathered my voluminous skirts aloft, trying to cross the street without tripping on the fabric and face-planting onto the asphalt. Part of me had been certain she'd bail on the Arts Ball tonight, given her social isolation in recent months; even in the best of spirits, she tended to dislike parties. But her demeanor in the car on the way here had surprised me. Her voice, leaden and dull since Eleanor's death, held a note of vibrancy, and she laughed—a real, unforced laugh—when Wyatt accidentally but gallantly presented his arm to help Drew out of the car. I realized how much I had missed seeing a happy expression on her face.

It was unseasonably warm for the Saturday before Halloween, which was fortunate, because a significant percentage of the people walking around the streets of uptown Charlotte appeared to be nude. The sidewalks and plazas were bright, with ambient light from the skyscraper lobbies mingling with the shine of the streetlamps, casting a warm glow over the revelers. Soft puffs of warm air wafted around the corners of the side streets onto Tryon Street, as if being exhaled from some hidden lounging giant, capriciously ruffling hair and thrusting stray scraps of paper aloft, whirling them around like fall leaves. Where Drew, Emma, Wyatt, and I stood, the most eye-catching thing nearby was a conga line of attractive women in their twenties wearing nothing but skillfully applied body paint. Next to this vision was a group clad in firefighting gear, with hoses draped in strategic locations but sans actual pants. They were a merry bunch, calling out bons mots to one another and trilling laughter in their wake. In front of them, cars inched down Tryon, windows open, the occupants ogling the throngs on the sidewalks: superheroes, naughty nurses, giant food items, aliens, leering political figures, enormous zoo mammals, football players, adults in diapers clutching pacifiers, and a whole host of young hipsters in bizarre dress we could not identify.

"I am *so* tired of the same old scene every time we go uptown," remarked Wyatt as the light changed, and he nearly collided with a brigade of dudes who were naked except for inexplicable thatches of wispy purple troll hair covering their unmentionables.

"Sorry!" I breathed to an irritated kangaroo upon whose tail I'd just trod. The kangaroo sniffed and exaggeratedly stepped over the small train on the back of my gown, wiggling its bottom as it *boing*ed away.

We made our way down Tryon, passing Trade Street with three of its corners crowned by glorious statues of Transportation, Commerce, and Industry, all of them looking toward the fourth corner, where a bronzed mother stood holding a baby aloft. We stopped in silence. On a more typical day, while whizzing by in a stream of disgruntled commuters, one didn't really appreciate the subtleties expressed here: the foundations of the city's past gazing solemnly and hopefully at its future.

"Ah," said Wyatt finally. "I think we're having a moment."

"I never really noticed they're all facing toward the moth—" I began, then stopped. "Wait. Where's Emma?"

A search ensued. It really was very crowded here; we'd had no idea when we left the house for the Arts Ball that uptown would be overrun by costumed millennials. Drew, in an effort to avoid valeting at the Ritz, had insisted on parking in his personal space at Elwood Capital, but the garage turned out to be crammed with illicit vehicles, thereby necessitating a long slog from another parking structure farther away. I was fairly certain the Halloween frolickers must have come as a surprise to Hattie McGuire, too, since she and Reg were about as hip as dentures. But some advance warning would have been helpful, since strolling multiple city blocks in four-inch Jimmy Choos was a serious commitment.

We located Emma. She'd been waylaid a block back by some LGBT-ers who were convinced, probably because of her staggering height, that she was a man in drag. ". . . and I couldn't look that *fantastically dewy* if I had a *hyperbaric chamber* in my boudoir," one was gushing in admiration.

"Darling," Wyatt said, bestowing a fabulous air kiss on Emma, who looked petrified, "I hate to tear you away from your people, but we really must scoot."

"What's he got that I haven't?" the person muttered as we strode (limped) away.

"Buckets of money," Wyatt called back over his shoulder. "Obviously."

The Arts Ball, when we finally reached it, was worth the walk. Outside the hotel the tuxedoed and gowned couples formed a sinuous line snaking from the covered entrance all the way down the block. The theme this year was "Pompeii and Herculaneum," so all along the line there were servants in tunics waving gigantic palm-frond fans over the partygoers as they inched toward a fantastic fifteen-foot-high volcano at the entrance. Roman aqueducts defined the borders of the line, with running water gushing into two lush pools representing the famed Roman bathhouses.

The line slowly advanced. A photographer dressed as Pliny the Elder stopped each couple as they neared the volcano to snap a photo for the local society magazine. "Friends, Romans, countrymen, give me a smile," called Pliny, his camera flashing well before we had a chance to rearrange our startled faces.

We reached the volcanic entrance. The twenty-eight members of the Arts Council board clustered around the doors, clad in togas—not a universally flattering look, especially on hairy older businessmen— handing out small gold bags stuffed with gift certificates to upscale restaurants, boutiques, and sports venues. Wyatt peered into his. "Acceptable," he pronounced.

We stepped into the hotel lobby, where more togas materialized with glasses of champagne and wordlessly ushered us to a tucked-away set of elevators. There was a backlog here, naturally, so we trudged up the stairs to the fourth floor—Emma and I grimacing with every step—until we reached a vast glass atrium sandwiched between buildings. The interior had been transformed by rows of roofless columned buildings representing the ruins of Pompeii, and an even larger volcano jutted out from the elevated stage on the loftlike area at the rear of the space, this one spewing some kind of red bubbles. We gaped.

"Who has the time to build this stuff?" wondered Drew, accepting a miniature crab cake from a passing tray.

Next to Drew, who had femurs of NBA quality, Wyatt looked like a chubby fifth grader. He waved off a group of elegant beauties from the club who were beckoning him to the dance floor.

"Because I'm African-American," he commented, "everyone makes two assumptions, only one of which is correct: that I can boogie and that I'm hung like a forty-ounce beer can."

I fell for it. "I don't think I've ever seen you dance," I mused.

Wyatt lowered his chin and made meaningful eye contact. "That's because I'm an appalling dancer," he said.

Emma rolled her eyes and dragged him off, both of them returning a moment later with glasses of champagne. She handed one to me and clinked hers against it. "Thank you for talking to Boyd," she whispered. "For the first time in months, I think I might survive this."

Optimism suffused me along with the alcohol as I downed my glass. "It's going to get better," I said. "I feel good about next week. This could be over."

A tiny cloud passed over Emma's face at my injudicious words. I could read her mind: *It will never be over.* Before I could speak, she took a decorous sip of her drink, but then abruptly upended her glass, guzzling the champagne in one swoop. "Wow," she said, reeling a little. "Wow, wow." I burst into laughter.

Along the far wall of the atrium there was a table with place cards and, next to that, a bar. We meandered in that direction, but progress was slow, since all four of us were stopped repeatedly by effusive greetings from other partygoers. All the women looked lovely. I had managed to score in the dress department: I'd found a spectacular vintage Chanel at Design to Consign, and even though there was a nearly one hundred percent chance somebody here was going to recognize me as a dress consignee, I didn't care. I wasn't likely to rewear this one, and I wasn't going to spend a fortune on something I'd only don once. It was a champagne strapless gown blending almost perfectly with my leonine hair. At home, getting ready, I'd had that elusive sense of pleasure that comes with feeling beautiful: the dress complemented my curves, somehow managing to make me feel both light as air and voluptuous; aside from my tortured feet, I was ready to dance all night.

Emma wore a skintight rose-colored dress. She looked stunning, but she didn't appear to know or care. Her sleek blond hair was pinned back, showing off her lovely cheekbones and her aqua eyes, and her full lips were a glistening pale pink. Her heels lofted her to well over six feet tall, dwarfing Wyatt, who declared he didn't mind: "It is hard," he observed to Drew, "to object to finding oneself smack-dab at breast height."

"Yep," agreed Drew, grabbing another appetizer.

I reviewed our table card with interest. The hostesses at these things generally alternated males and females, so you never knew what kind of random conversation would result. So: Blake Porcher; Emma; Buzzy Cooper; me; Jack Inman, who was Emma's lecherous partner; Caroline Cooper, who had finally mailed me a dry card of thanks for my role in Buzzy's resuscitation; Wyatt; Tricia Inman, Jack's beleaguered wife; Drew; and my partner, Mary Sarah. Hattie must have found it amusing to seat the Coopers at a table with Buzzy's erstwhile surgeons, probably figuring it would generate some lively discussion.

I looked around. Ancient Rome sprang to life in the elaborate table decor. The chargers were golden coins, expanded to plate size, graced by profiles of some gent with an aggressive nose. The candles rested on Doric, Ionic, and Corinthian pillars made of real plaster. Each place setting offered another beautifully wrapped freebie: gold-plated bracelets made of interlocking Roman numerals for the ladies and similar cuff links for the men. The whole thing reeked of decadent expenditure. Clearly Reginald, who was even more parsimonious than Drew, had not been consulted.

The party roared around us. Alcohol flowed in rivers out of the open bar, everyone chugging down premium labels with abandon. I wandered outside to a pleasant flower-filled balcony and found myself knocking back bourbon as if I were back in my Louisville school days, which brought on a sudden memory of my friends: fiery Georgia, intemperate and gregarious, now living in Charleston, with a thriving urology practice (of all things!); Hannah, an ob-gyn in California, sweet and maternal, ironically cursed with infertility; and the guys, Rolfe and Landley. Rolfe was a cardiologist, still living in Louisville, but to everyone's shock,

Landley had barged out of the closet after residency and was a nationally renowned ophthalmologist whose husband was a B-list Hollywood actor currently playing the role of a serial killer. Their Christmas card this year featured a bloodshot eye gazing upon a partially opened door with some lacerated limbs hanging out, which stuck out like a humungous pimple on a cover model when I'd hung it alongside the wholesome happy family cards from everyone else.

Lost in this reverie—it was somehow sad thinking of my friends as serious adults when they'd once been so cheerfully stupid—I realized I must have missed the call to be seated for dinner; the people around me had all dispersed. Okay: nothing awkward at all about standing by yourself pounding a bourbon and looking wistful.

I pivoted toward my table and smacked into someone, knocking my drink and spilling the remainder onto the front of my dress. I stifled a curse, and started to apologize.

"I cannot believe it," the someone said, his voice instantly, achingly familiar. "You are still—literally—running into men?"

I looked first at his shoes—black, Italian, very nice—my eyes traveling reluctantly up; long legs, trim waist, NFL-quality shoulders encased in a crisp tuxedo, chalky white predatory smile set in a square jaw that made me want to touch it. Even the skin on his face—faintly golden, faintly stubbled, rent with laugh lines—was at once dear and also repellent, sweeping me up in a vortex of incompatible emotions. Maybe I could satisfy both desires by smacking him.

"Nick," I said, feeling heat zoom into my face.

"Damn," he said in a low voice. "Zadie. I got your e-mail."

"Huh?" I said, and then realized what he meant: he had my e-mail address. He'd sent me a couple of e-mails after I'd ignored his ridiculous chocolate delivery, but I had marked these messages as junk mail, unread.

"I've been hoping you'd change your mind about meeting me," he said, keeping his gaze steady on mine. "Did you enjoy the chocolate?"

"Yes," I said evenly. This had to happen eventually, I told myself. Be polite. Be brief.

The way he looked at me was unsettling: a rapacious gaze, too familiar, still somehow electrifying after the passage of years. Some people seem to rearrange the air around them when they enter a room, subtly altering the atmosphere until it bends to their will; it was hard to resist having the focus of such a person beamed onto you. Call them charismatic, or compelling, but the end result was these people had the ability to draw you in.

Despite all that, and despite the undeniable, indefinable sexual pull toward him I'd always felt, I told myself to sprint for the nearest exit. I was older; my life had irrevocably changed. My younger self had thrived on intensity, but now I knew the bottomless, elementary pull of love for my husband and children. I should no longer want to be consumed by the sun when I could bask safely in the glow of the moon.

Nick was talking, probably sensing this conversation was going to be short-lived. He walked as he spoke, and I followed him. "It's hard to believe," he said, "that you are a married mother."

"Well, believe it," I said. "I have a million kids."

"You're still very beautiful," he said, in a careful, benign tone.

Best to ignore this. "Do you?" I asked.

"Do I what?"

"Do you have children?"

He looked rueful. "I had a stepchild," he said. "I didn't see him much, though."

"Did you want children of your own?" Why had I asked that?

"I didn't think so," he said, answering with surprising slowness. "I don't know; maybe that was a mistake. Never thought I'd be a good father. But now that I'm alone . . ." He shrugged. "Look, Zadie, I don't know how many chances I'll have to say this, so I'd better seize the moment. I've thought about you a lot over the years. A lot more than you'd believe. From the perspective of someone who's in his forties, I look back and wonder why I treated you the way I did. I was narcissistic. I was greedy; there are a lot of bad adjectives for me in that phase of life, and I seem to remember"—he smiled—"you applying most of them very creatively toward me there at the end. But"—serious again—"Zadie, I failed to realize how unusual it was, what we had."

This was coming more than a decade too late. And it was inappropriate. Impossible not to listen to, however.

"So," he said, bowing his gilded head, "for what it's worth: I'm sorry."

"Oh," I breathed, flummoxed. But whatever response I would have given would forever remain a mystery, because at that moment, over the ringing of some kind of a dinner gong, a voice said, "There you are."

I turned. It was Emma.

Chapter Thirty-one

CROSSING THE RUBICON

Emma, Present Day

The Arts Ball was off to a reasonable start, considering I hadn't wanted to come. But an unfamiliar feeling had been sweeping through me since the conversation with the Packards this morning at the gym, and since my reverie about Graham after that. It took me a while to recognize it, since it had been such a long time since I'd felt anything positive.

It was exhilaration.

Long-dormant endorphins swirled in my brain, flooding me with an alertness I could hardly believe. I shouldn't have allowed myself to hope, but I couldn't help it; even a tiny relief from worry felt so enjoyable I surpassed hope and proceeded to actual pleasure.

I was having fun.

Maybe Boyd and Betsy would hear my side of things and reject me after all. Maybe the technical explanation of how this could happen, coupled with my vast and sincere contrition, would not be enough. Maybe even Zadie would not be able to persuade them. But even so, I was somewhat freed from the self-loathing and fear that had buried me for months. Just the idea that they'd listen to me—the idea that I could say I was sorry—was a relief.

I threw back my drink. I was normally very careful about what I ate and drank. I had no background in oncology, or even internal medicine, beyond what we had all learned in medical school, but I believed modern processed diets were chock-full of poorly understood carcinogens, in addition to all the usual artery-clogging fat-bombs. And alcohol: half the interpersonal problems in the world could be attributed to alcohol. Besides, it was in my nature to be disciplined.

But tonight I was scarfing down everything they handed to me.

I glanced across the table at Wyatt. I could hear his voice over the din. Flushed and animated, eyebrows raised and both palms extended, he was telling some story from his workweek. He was seated between Caroline Cooper and Tricia Inman, who both tended to be humorless dullards, but even they were unable to resist Wyatt's charm. He was slaying them. Both of them had thrown their heads back in full-on helpless laughter.

It was miserable to think of a Wyatt-less world. Right away I would regress back into an uptight iCalendar slave, responding to its pings like a well-programmed fembot. There would be no one to force me to unwind with a glass of wine and a dinner full of bright, charming witticisms having nothing to do with the medical world. There would be no one to stroke my head and listen when things were bad, no one to break into my narrative of woe with outraged denunciations of my enemies. And Henry! The thought of never again seeing his urgent, ecstatic waddle to the mudroom every afternoon at the sound of his father's car was heartbreaking. How long would it be until he forgot he ever had a parent who changed his voice for every character in a book, who pretended every morning that he'd forgotten how to get dressed without Henry's help? How long would it be before he forgot a parent could be fun?

I helped myself to another drink, watching the women at the table as they watched Wyatt.

The servers were clearing the salad plates. On my other side, the men were leaning toward one another, embroiled in a heated discussion about somebody's golf score.

"Drew," I interrupted, leaning in his direction. "Do you know where Zadie is?"

"I think I saw her talking to some guy outside," he said.

"Oh?" I asked, forcing a casual note into my voice. "What does he look like?"

Drew shrugged. "He's tall?" he offered. "Light hair. Kind of intense." He returned his attention to Buzzy's booming, boorish voice.

I pushed back my chair without a word and hurried to the atrium, trying not to feel Wyatt's perceptive gaze at my back. She wasn't there. Ditto for the coat check area, the bar, and the hotel lobby. I finally found them outside, standing near a bench in an enclosed and deserted court-yard beyond the atrium.

———

"Zadie," I said, and nearly lost my balance as I shuddered to a stop.

"Oho," said Nick, his handsome face rendered almost ugly as he caught sight of me. "It's the trauma queen." He'd abandoned his initial attempts at reconciliation in the face of my hostility; this was an expression I'd grown used to, as he'd evidently begun to wonder why my enmity toward him had not lessened.

My self-possession kicked in. "Hello, Nick," I said coolly. I turned my back to him, and lied. "Zadie, Drew was wondering where you are."

"I'm comin—"

"She's going to be busy for a few minutes more, Emma. Can you make an excuse for her?" Nick smiled at me, but his eyes were furious. It took me a minute to remember how hard I'd had to work to stop him from going to Zadie's office last week. I'd ultimately had to pull a weapon from my arsenal of the past: e-mail. I hated impersonating her. But Nick was mistaken if he thought he'd coast into my world and threaten my most treasured friendship without me fighting back. I had to separate them.

"I'm not making excuses for Zadie, as she's coming with me. Nice seeing you, Nick."

"You really don't want to get into a pissing contest with me here, Emma," Nick growled, abandoning his fake smile. "Once you've crossed the Rubicon, you can't ever turn back."

I faltered, taken aback by Nick's use of the esoteric metaphor I often reserved in my mind for our initial encounter in med school. But then I forged ahead. I'd already crossed that river, more than a decade ago.

"Fuck you, Nick," I said. "We're leaving."

"Fuck me? Fuck me? Why don't—"

"What is going on?" exclaimed Zadie, startling us both. She placed a restraining hand on my arm. "It's okay, Em. This is ancient history. Why are you cursing at each other?"

"Because we are standing here talking to fucking Lucifer," I hissed, "and I'm trying to protect you."

"Well, there's an interesting concept, you protecting Zadie," Nick drawled.

Maybe it was the alcohol; maybe it was the unaccustomed release I'd felt by hurling the f-bomb at this man I hated, but every molecule of my being was consumed by a sudden incandescent fury. "Stay the hell away from her, Nick," I said, when I could form words again. I forced myself to speak slowly. "Stay away from me, too. You are a despicable human being." I turned to Zadie. "Come on, let's go."

I extended my hand to her, and like a bewildered child, she took it. We started for the door.

"Zadie," called Nick. He held something out to her. To my dismay, she looked back over her shoulder, her eyes widening at the flat object in his hand. She reached for it.

The physicists have a term: "gravitational time delay." It's derived from Einstein's theory of general relativity, referring to the fact that speeding objects seem to slow down as they near the gravitational pull of a massive physical object—thus effectively producing the slowing of time. With dim amazement, I observed with my own eyes as time slowed to a crawl, hobbled by the enormity of the betrayal Zadie was about to discover. I spun helplessly in a suspended animation of my own creation, as Zadie's hand inched ever closer to Nick's.

She took the photograph from him. She looked at it.

She began to cry.

Chapter Thirty-two

A COLLECTION OF
MARBLE ANGELS

Late Autumn, 1999: Louisville, Kentucky
Zadie

Graham's funeral took place on a day so sunny I sweated through my one good black dress. As I scanned the crowd filing in to the hushed marble interior of the Cathedral of the Assumption, the wash of grim solemnity on every face struck me. It looked as if body snatchers had replaced my friends with black-clad cheerless automatons.

Conspicuously missing was Emma. A couple days after Graham's death, she'd managed to contact his father, Dr. O'Kane. He had retired from his active medical practice at this point, but he kept busy working as some sort of consultant to the orthopedic device companies that manufactured his widget. In addition to that, he and his current wife ran a foundation supporting reactionary political causes; because of this he owned a private jet from which he was evidently deplaning as they spoke.

I could faintly hear Dr. O'Kane's side of the conversation. Emma and I were huddled together in a cubicle at the back corner of the residents' lounge where there were telephones for dictating encased in little glass partitions. Though sound was rendered tinny and distant by the gap between me and the telephone and by the machine hum of the plane in the background, it was still possible to hear the barely controlled annoyance in Dr. O'Kane's voice as Emma held out the receiver. "You say you met him at the hospital? Are you a nurse?" he inquired, after Emma had finished her plea for him to contribute to Graham's memorial service.

"I'm a classmate of Graham's. We've been friends for years and dating for—"

"Classmate." Dr. O'Kane sighed with faint scorn. "Well, listen, Emily—"

"Emma."

"Emma, then. Do you have any idea what a tremendous embarrassment it is to have to speak to the bishop about planning a funeral mass for someone who died in this manner?"

"Would it be all right if I read something?"

Another disdainful sigh. "I know you mean well. And it is touching he had anyone willing to stand up for him. But I think it would be best if you left this to the family."

"I am also going to contact his mother," Emma said in a small voice.

A sharp, almost barking laugh: "Graham's mother made the decision to leave us close to ten years ago. I doubt very much she'll be attending since she's had no contact with him, and she certainly will not be making any decisions regarding the arrangements. Marilyn and I will handle that. Now, if you don't mind—"

The line buzzed with an angry dial tone. Emma replaced the receiver in its cradle with an incongruous gentleness.

"Whoa. No wonder Graham was . . ." I trailed off, unable to complete the sentence both inoffensively and accurately. "Sad," I finished lamely. "What a jackass."

"Was it something I said?"

I looked up. Nick peered around the partition at me. In open defiance of Dr. Markham's sartorial policy, he wore a white coat over scrubs and again had dissolute stubble blurring his face, but his expression was unfiltered: alert, amused, slightly sardonic.

"If there is simultaneous crying and cursing in here, it's a given that you're going to be in the vicinity," he said. "I don't know how I survived the boredom before." He started to say something else, then stopped abruptly as he caught sight of Emma.

Emma's face was unreadable. "I need to freshen up," she said. "I'll take my theatrics elsewhere."

"Well . . . bye," I called to her retreating back. She did not look up.

So Emma did not attend Graham's funeral. After the conversation with Dr. O'Kane, she refused to go, mumbling to me that she would rather mourn him in private.

It wasn't a bad service. As Dr. O'Kane had promised, it seemed impersonal; but despite that, it was lovely. The ceremony conjured a mournful grace, an ancient sense of the sweeping and adversarial nature of death: *Do not rejoice over me, my enemy! Though I have fallen, I will arise; though I sit in darkness, the LORD is my light.*

The light in the church filtered in through windows so high and celestial that the rays of sun, shot through with lazily dancing golden dust motes, seemed to be tendrils reaching from heaven, an impression reinforced by the majestic blue starry-night ceiling. Everything was luminous marble and lustrous gilt; all the opulence was as un-Graham-like as it was possible to be, but a place of such somber, magnificent glory somehow seemed right for grieving my friend. The beautiful unearthly voices of the choir washed over me with almost palpable grace, soaring and swooping and hanging in the air above the congregation as if they were the very soul for whom they mourned, finally twisting up with the shafts of light from the upper windows until they vanished into the eternal sky. For moments afterward, I observed the mourners sitting perfectly still, seemingly not even breathing, a collection of marble angels watching one of their own depart.

After the last note from the last song died away and the priest finished, and the rest of my classmates had clambered past me, I finally stood. The sanctuary was empty as at last I walked out.

When I arrived back at the apartment, Emma was gone. I found myself in an unfamiliar situation: a block of time with nothing to do. Feeling hollow, I wandered into Emma's room, wondering again how much she had known or suspected prior to his suicide. I'd barely seen her: unlike surgery, our ER rotation lacked thirty- or forty-hour periods of enforced wakefulness, but the constant switching between day and night disoriented me. I hadn't seen Emma for days.

I looked around. Emma was irritatingly organized. Her clothes hung with precision on identical hangers; her bed was crisply made; her makeup was neatly arranged in clear Lucite dividers: an obedient little regiment of lipstick soldiers. I reached for one, an unassuming pink shade, and absently twirled it up and down. An image of Emma and Graham sitting on the bed rose in my mind: Emma, wearing little granny glasses, her long hair caught up in a golden bun, her cheekbones appleing up as she laughed, leaning into Graham. His face had been partly hidden—he was turned to the side and looking down—but even from the partial glimpse of one eye and half of his mouth, it was obvious he was gazing at Emma, looking both fierce and fond, his contentment visible. He was whole and young, his skin warm, his heartbeat thrumming steadily, his eyes quick and aware. The trillions of cells in his body were vibrant, industrious little factories; electrolytes moving, ion channels opening, neurons firing. *Alive.* There was nothing, no hint, that all of this could just cease to be. One moment someone you know was whole, and the next he could be stilled and buried. The thought of Graham's beautiful body alone under the ground suddenly doubled me over; despite the deaths I'd seen this year, my thoughts had not extended to what came after.

I tried to catch my breath, but all I could manage was a shuddering gasp; it took a second to realize I was on my knees, tears caught in my throat. I bowed my head and howled.

When my grief storm finally dimmed, I got to my feet, my mind blank. I paced around the generously sized room. My bedroom had an attached bathroom, but Emma had opted for the prettier space; it had high white-washed wood ceilings and two big dormer windows, and the floor was padded by a lovely old oval braided rag rug. She had a fat red reading chair and a huge painted oak bookcase, which was filled with hardbacks, alpha-betized and grouped by category, their dust jackets removed to reveal muted jewel-toned spines. I ran my finger along them: here, the history books, there, the biographies, then the fiction: *Sophie's Choice, The Bonfire of the Vanities, Bridget Jones's Diary, The Secret History, A Prayer for Owen Meany.* Among the many things causing me to envy Emma, her book collection was foremost. She had hundreds of well-loved volumes, most of them hard-backs, which had value not only for the inherent pleasure of reading them, but also for their beauty. More classifications: poetry, beloved children's books, science texts, and finally a sizable selection of popular psychology and spirituality, a little surprising for Emma. Although she respected my at-tempts to attend church, she believed the only rational position on religios-ity was agnosticism; she also considered clinical psychology to be a load of bunk. Something about this last group of books drew my eye. What was it? I regarded them again and realized one slender volume had broken ranks, sticking out an inch or so from the others. I pulled it free from the shelf.

It was *The Screwtape Letters* by C. S. Lewis. I'd been a huge fan of the Narnia series as a child but hadn't read much of Lewis's overtly reli-gious writing. I knew vaguely of the theme: the demons plotting for the damnation of a human life, hoping to enmesh their victim in his own failings and temptations, the final betrayal. But I had never heard Emma mention it as a favorite.

I opened it, and a folded sheet of paper fell out. It was a poem, to Emma from Graham, dated October 18, the day he had died.

I walked all night
through clouds and mist
My blurry tears concealed the stars
and melted the air around me.
I called your name
but there was no answer
My voice echoed through the darkness
reaching every corner of the sky
but you were gone and did not hear me.
I found a painting in shades of blue
My hungry eyes saw your image
walking in the rain
I reached out to pull you through
and hold you in my arms
I grasped and clawed throughout the dampness
searching for your hands
but you were gone and did not feel me.
I had a dream
of dark content
My sleepless soul felt your body
looming over me
I struggled upward
to kiss your face and touch your hair
and hold you close once more
But I awoke and you were gone.

I read the words again. A swirl of new confusion enveloped me; had Emma and Graham broken up before he died? The paper on which the poem was printed held an unexpected heft; I turned it over, figuring something was stuck to the back.

A photograph: taped neatly on all four sides with the picture side facedown. I fingered the tape-blunted edges, burning with curiosity. It appeared Emma had not untaped it to see what it was.

Hesitantly, I picked at one edge of the tape, beginning to elevate the edge of the picture when I heard a rustling noise behind me. Shrieking, I whirled around with my hands up, only to realize the air-conditioning had activated, rustling the crackly dead leaves of Emma's houseplant. My heart pittering in relief and embarrassment, I retrieved the piece of paper, which had gone flying under a chair as I'd surrendered to the plant. Hastily refolding the paper, I placed it back in the book and fled from the room.

Our old house, usually so cheerful on sunny days like this one, felt oppressive. The bright pillows and posters, and the dozens of framed photographs, were a silent rebuke: *where are the people who belong here?* It was creepy, like an empty home in an apocalyptic film, the now-useless possessions outlasting the human occupants. Suddenly I could not bear to be alone another second. I grabbed my handbag and ran out.

I had seen Graham every day for months. He was more than a friend to me; he was like a benevolent brother. Shouldn't I have noticed something terrible was happening to him? How much pain did it take to decide ending your life was the better option? And now that he was gone, Emma must have been feeling everything I was, only on a magnified scale. People should not have to deal with the horror of death when they are in their twenties, a sentiment I knew all too well. Death should be reserved for the very old.

By the time I neared Bardstown Road, I was regretting the decision to walk, since I was still in my funeral dress and a pair of seldom-worn heels. I limped along, forlorn. The sunshine faded: the molting trees loomed with bereft spikiness along the side roads, their branches rattling a little in a blast of cooler wind. My earlier agony had subsided, now superseded by more banal concerns—chiefly, an intense hunger and an absolutely killer blister on my left big toe. I decided to go to Wick's.

Inside, I slid into a seat and ordered, slipping off my stupid shoes. Ahhh. Better. I was going to have to rustle up a ride, because there was no way my battered feet were trudging all the way back home. It was an Immutable Law of the Universe that I could not go out to eat without running into at least one person I knew, generally a disgruntled former boyfriend on a hot date, or someone to whom I owed money. Still. As long as they owned a car.

My food arrived—yes!—and I dove in with piggish abandon. It was certainly possible I looked like a total loser, ensconced solo at a large table eating as fast and as much as possible, but this was kind of liberating in a way. I did not require social validation for every little thing, and furthermore I was able to comfort myself on a horrific day without going to pieces again just because I was unexpectedly alone. I was self-reliant! The sort of person who could find solace in her own company when things were bad! The sort of person who— Oh, thank heavens, there was Rolfe.

He slid into the booth next to me and gave me a hug. "How you holding up?" he asked.

"I don't know," I said. Rolfe nodded. I seemed to be having little respites, where I would forget for a moment or two, and then I'd remember, like a sucker punch to the gut. Through waves of disbelief, I'd feel myself adjusting, again: *Graham is gone.* Then I would forget for a moment or so, and the cycle would repeat.

"Have you seen Emma?" I asked.

Rolfe nodded. "She's in Cherokee Park," he said. "With Baxter, Graham's dog."

"She's in the park?" I was surprised. "How do you know?"

"Landley saw her there, early this morning. She's sitting on a blanket, on Dog Hill. He and I went by again, before I dropped him off, and she was still there. We tried to get her to leave with us, but she wouldn't budge. She wouldn't talk, either, except for saying it was because of her."

"What do you mean?" I asked, feeling my stomach tighten.

Rolfe met my eyes. "What Graham did. She said it was her fault."

Chapter Thirty-three

AVOID THE PATIENTS AS
MUCH AS POSSIBLE

Late Autumn, 1999: Louisville, Kentucky

I glanced across the room at Emma, who was staring straight ahead, her features expressionless. Even at a casual glance, it was apparent she did not look good. She'd lost at least ten pounds in the three weeks since Graham's death, and though both of us were slender, I was also curvaceous; Emma's angular form did not have ten pounds to spare. She'd always liked to run, but now she ran obsessively, sometimes for hours. Her face was gaunt, with shadowy hollows beneath her sharp cheekbones; her look had edged from modelesque to heroin chic to cancerous. She steadfastly refused to talk with me about what had happened between her and Graham, and since she was working nights and I was working days, I hardly ever saw her.

The topic of this morning's ER lecture was acid-base disorders, a subject that might not enthrall the average listener, but it aroused great ardor in Dr. Elsdon, who raged with evangelical zeal around the room.

"Henderson-Hasselbalch equation! Go!" he shouted, whirling around and pointing at James, who gaped helplessly.

"Aaah . . ."

"Nothing? You've got nothing? Let's back up a little." He spun around again with his index finger outstretched, this time landing on Cameron Dooley, a full-on dud who was known for remaining virtually mute during the first two years of school. Perhaps he suffered from a debilitating social phobia. In any case, he was now cowering in a seat in the back, Dr. Elsdon clearly representing his absolute worst nightmare.

"Give me five causes of normal gap acidosis!"

". . ."

"What? What? Has nobody had their coffee this morning? HARDUP? MUDPILES? Ring any bells?"

Tonelessly, Emma came to the rescue. "HARDUP. Hyperventilation, Addison's disease, renal tubular acidosis, diarrhea, ureteral diversion/ ureterosigmoidostomy, pancreatic fistula."

"Excellent!" roared Dr. Elsdon, his wild hair electrified. "Now give me the causes of elevated gap acidosis."

I let my mind drift as Emma dutifully began reciting the mnemonic MUDPILES, resolving the next chance I got, I'd confront her to get some help. Nobody could endure such a loss without support.

Dr. Elsdon was winding down with no noticeable dimming of his fervor, despite his having given this particular lecture dozens of times before. Well, obviously some things just stir the human heart. The students might have been slow to realize the inherent beauty of acid-base disorders in the beginning, but now everyone was swept away with passion. Toxic alcohols! Respiratory alkalosis! This *was* exciting stuff!

At eight o'clock, Emma nodded at me and headed home to sleep for the day. I waited until she was gone and waylaid Dr. Elsdon as he packed up his lecture materials.

"Zadie," I began, pointing at myself in case he didn't remember my name.

"Bernard," he said, pointing at himself. "Glad we got that straightened out."

"Sorry to bother you, ah, Dr. Elsdon, but I was wondering something." I collected my thoughts. "If you thought a person might need medicine for, ah, sadness, would you bring them to the ER?"

His expression changed. "Do we think this person might be having a reaction to a recent tragedy?"

"Yes! A grief reaction."

"Are you— Does this person have any thoughts of harming themselves?"

"Oh! It's not me," I said. "I'm asking for a friend."

He waited, his face kind. Then he nodded, extracting a small piece of paper from his pocket. He scribbled something on it. "Okay," he said. "Take her to Dr. Butler today. She's our best staff psychiatrist, and she sees students through the clinic. She'll help your friend."

———

I trotted out to the ED main desk and signed myself in, then grabbed the first chart in my section. Today I was paired with a third-year resident I didn't know named Dr. Alanna Tamara, who went by the nickname *Sensei*. Apparently she was really good at martial arts of some kind. I looked around but didn't see anyone who could possibly be Dr. Tamara, so I scooted toward room 35, reading the triage sheet as I went.

The patient's name was Jack Dmitriy-Rau and he had ankle pain. This sounded boring, but easy enough. Today I was going to be a model of efficiency; I was not going to allow myself to be bogged down in inane conversation. Starting right now, with Mr. Dmitriy-Rau.

I tapped on the door and entered. Mr. Dmitriy-Rau, a portly gentleman sporting a relaxed expression, was sitting fully dressed in a business suit. The patients were all given a gown and asked to disrobe when they were brought back to the exam rooms, but many of them misunderstood or ignored these instructions, leading to a bottleneck as the day progressed. In Mr. Dmitriy-Rau's case, however, fully undressing in the chilly exam room did seem superfluous for an ankle injury.

After introductions, he stood and extended a lavish hand to me, launching unbidden into a thorough account of his day.

"... And then after the breakfast, which was a bit heavy, to be true—I am the early riser, yes, but I do not often care for the full breakfast. But my wife, she like to cook, so sometimes I have quite more than I mean. So. I must be more careful in future with my figure, you can see"—here he rubbed his ample belly—"but is done with love, so how can I refuse?"

I politely attempted to bring the train back to the station. "It sounds delicious. How did you hurt your ankle?"

"Well. I take my time with the breakfast, proper compliment to the chef, so, and then we have the full tea. Also I watch the early-morning newscast. To see the weather, the traffic, you know. But this often lead to the argument. My wife, she does not like news, until *Today Show*. She like the man newscaster there." He chuckled. "Maybe she like him little too much."

"Is that when you sprained your—"

"No, no. That come later. First, she make me stay until the *Today Show* start. So. Also have more of the tea." He gestured expansively. "Why not? By now is too late for the moderation, so may as well enjoy. Right?"

"Right, but—"

"Yes, so, and then dog start to bark. We have little dog, 'yap, yap, yap' all the time, yap-yap, is enough to drive you crazy. *Yap, yap.* I say if you are going to have the dog, why not have the more man dog? This dog, it sound like the little bird."

"Did you—"

"*Yap-yap-yap-yap*. I cannot stand it. Finally, I say I must go to work. And my wife say, 'Wait. You must walk dog.' I do not wish to walk dog. I do not even like dog, now the yap-yap is going to make me late for work? Intolerable. But she is very strong personality, my wife."

I abandoned politeness. "Mr. Dmitriy-Rau, where are you hurt?"

"This I am getting to. *Yap, yap*. The leash we have misplaced. Everywhere we look; all the while, *yap, yap*. Enough to make you tear out the hair. Or maybe you give the very small nudge."

"Nudge?"

"With the foot. Certainly not a . . . injury nudge."

"You have no injury?"

"Certainly I have the injury. I am telling you it now."

Desperately: "Yes, but what is the injury?"

"Well, so. The dog, he is fine. I do not harm him. Smallest nudge only, with little bit of the foot." Mr. Dmitriy-Rau nodded in agreement with himself.

"You kicked the dog?"

"'Kick' is too strong. I nudge him. With the foot."

"Can I see?"

"Certainly you must see; this is why I come to the hospital."

I rolled up Mr. Dmitriy-Rau's pant leg, discovering the imprint of a tiny row of teeth.

"Ah! The dog bit you!"

"Yes. It was unprovoked bite. Very painful. Perhaps you will have to do stitching?"

I peered at the bite. It looked as if Mr. Dmitriy-Rau had been lightly drilled at regular intervals with a toothpick. There was no tearing of the skin.

"I don't think so. Let me grab the other doctor, but I think we will be able to get you out of here quickly, assuming your dog has had all his shots."

"Yes, yes, he go to the vet quite often. All the time, really. Perhaps some issues there. So I will wait for you and then we will do the ass rape. Then I will go home."

"I'm sorry?"

"Soon we will do the ass rape. Then I may go."

"The ass . . . what?"

"Ass rape. No?"

"No, I . . ." Cautiously: "Can you describe it?"

"Well, so. You are the doctor here, no? But I will try. It is the very tight rape, for the pain, the swelling. It goes like so"—he motioned in a circular fashion—"and then you may apply metal bits for completion." He regarded me, adding kindly, "Well, perhaps you do not do this here."

"I don't—"

"Is okay. The brown fabric? No?"

"Ace wrap!" I shouted triumphantly. "Yes! Yes, I will get you an Ace wrap."

"Thank you, dear. You are the very nice student doctor. Keep up with studies."

I stood in the D hallway, watching the bustle of the ER. The layout was essentially a large square; there were four long hallways at perpendicular angles, which contained the patient rooms, with a huge blocky desk in the center comprising the departmental workstation. There were unit secretaries seated at computers, armed with telephones and intercoms, and radiating out next to them were areas for the doctors to chart. In the central square of the department there was a closed cube manned by radiology residents, which contained lighted screens to view X-ray films. I felt a tad anxious. I had yet to present my first patient to my upper-level resident, and truth be told, that was going to be one very sparse presentation. I had spent nearly twenty minutes in the room and yet completely failed to obtain most of the required elements: no past medical history, no allergies, no medication list, no review of systems, and no exam of any body parts other than the bitten ankle. Well, so, perhaps I could write "yap-yap-yap" on the chart. No, no, no: focus. I'd better get Dr. Tamara located posthaste, and see how to fill in the details without (a) completely fabricating them or (b) getting sucked back into Mr. Dmitriy-Rau's flood of extraneous information.

I found Dr. Tamara yukking it up with some nurses at the main desk. She turned out to be an enormous brunette in her mid-thirties who was embarking on a second, or possibly third, career, which explained the odd nickname. Having just met her, I found it awkward to refer to her as "Sensei," even though Dr. Tamara explained she preferred it. "No need to be formal," she blared, unself-consciously tugging at her bottom in an effort to dislodge some migrating underwear.

I couldn't resist. "Yes, Sensei," I said, bowing deeply, which caused Dr. Tamara to howl and offer up a stout hand for a high five.

"Atta girl!"

"Yes, er, thank you," I said. The ER certainly seemed to have its share of eccentric characters. "What do the patients call you?"

"Oh, I try to avoid the patients as much as possible. That's what you're for. Now tell what you've got in twenty-five there."

I filled Dr. Tamara in on the yapping and the nudging and the ass rape. This resulted in such mirth I was forgiven for my otherwise shoddy history and physical exam; Sensei said she would handle it. "Laurie, get the man in twenty-five an ass rape, stat!" she bellowed at a passing nurse, who glanced quizzically at us but did not break stride. "Huh," said Dr. Tamara, undeterred. "Guess we'll have to do the ass rape ourselves."

Just then my pager sounded. I gave it a quick glance: it was my home number. I excused myself and trotted to a phone in the doctors' charting area.

It was Emma, and she sounded strained. I resolved to try to put her at ease.

"Well, hello there," I boomed.

There was a brief hesitation. "Zadie?" asked Emma. "Are you drinking?"

"What? No. Actually, I'm seeing patients. I was . . . trying to sound cheery. How are you?"

"I've been better," Emma said.

Breakthrough! I decided to let her take the lead on this one. "Yeah," I agreed.

"I think," Emma said in a small voice. "I think I want to tell you why Graham died."

I was stunned. "Right now?" I asked.

"No, no, not on the phone. I have to work overnight, but I'll call you if it gets slow. You can come in. Uh, if you will."

"Of course. Of course I will, Emma. I'm so sorry I'm not home right now. Do you want me to try to get out of here?"

"No," said Emma, her voice stronger. "No. You can't leave the hospital in the middle of a shift. We'll talk tonight, one way or another. It's important that I commit to this, before anything else happens. I'm sorry to call. I just . . . I wanted to hear your voice for a second."

Tenderness engulfed me. Emma was finally reaching out! Whatever had happened with Graham, at least she'd get it off her chest, and I would be there for her.

"Okay," I told her. "I'll be there tonight, late, once it calms down. And I got the name of a doctor who can help you too. Everything's gonna be okay, Emma. I'm with you, no matter what."

Emma sounded sad. "Don't say that," she said, "until you've heard what I have to say."

Chapter Thirty-four

AN ETERNAL GASP

Zadie, Present Day

A shining disk of moon hung suspended above Nick, Emma, and me, emerging in the little window of night sky visible between the spiky tops of the skyscrapers. The three of us stood voiceless in the courtyard of the Ritz as I looked at the object Nick had handed me.

It was a photograph.

After thrusting it into my hand, Nick took a small step backward, breathing like an angry elephant. I ignored him and stared at the picture in my hand, my disbelief so profound it seemed possible the image would rearrange itself into something else. But the people in the photograph remained immutable, even though I stared until they blurred into fuzzy blobs.

The picture was old; it curled at the corners. Years of someone's fingerprints rubbing across it had dulled the glossy sheen of the photographic paper, but the image was still visible. Taken from the vantage point of someone standing in a doorway, it showed a cheap, utilitarian twin bed, with a twist of dingy sheets. The subjects of the photo—standing in front of the bed—had clearly been photographed against their will; both of them faced the camera, the slight blurring of their torsos indicating motion as if they'd just heaved themselves upright. The woman looked disheveled: her hair blowsy and askew, her face red, her hands clutched defensively just above her unbuttoned shirt. Mascara was beginning to pool underneath her eyes, giving her a trampy, intoxicated look. Additional moisture leaked out of her nose; her mouth was frozen in an eternal gasp.

Emma.

Nick fared better; his face blended surprise with a little hostility, but I knew him well enough to recognize a calculating appraisal too. I'd be willing to bet if another picture had been snapped a moment later, his expression would have morphed to a grinning, sheepish okay-dude-you-caught-me look.

Emma's skin shone with the kind of dewy radiance you never see in people over thirty, no matter how good they look. Her hair tumbled down her back in a luxuriant gold waterfall, errant wisps dive-bombing across her horror-struck face. I cast my mind back, rewinding through memories like an unspooling reel of film, until I reached our third year of medical school: she'd cut her hair just after Graham died, and she'd never grown it long again.

I became aware of my breathing, which was harsh, bullish, scary. I was trembling, an unforeseen rage somehow intensifying even as it became dwarfed by a miserable all-encompassing feeling with no name. This was a betrayal I had never seen coming.

A tear fell from my eye and landed on Emma's beautiful, traitorous twenty-four-year-old face, smearing it into an unrecognizable blot. I swiped my thumb across the teardrop, melting Nick's face as well, and handed the photo back to him. "Here you go," I said.

"Zadie, wait," he said.

"No, no, no," I yelled, stumbling away from them. I kicked off my high heels and bent to retrieve them. "You two deserve each other. Why would you show me this? Why did you even bring it here? Did you plan this?"

To his credit, he looked chastened. "I didn't plan to show it to you," he said. "I always carry it."

This stopped me. I straightened up. "Why?"

He shifted his eyes slightly in Emma's direction. She stood in exactly the same position she'd been in when Nick first handed me the picture, an unblinking statue.

"To remind myself," he said, so quietly I had to strain to hear him, "of the photographer."

"Who was the photographer?" I asked, but even before he spoke, I knew the answer.

Graham.

Chapter Thirty-five

STOP HITTING ON
MY MED STUDENT

Late Autumn, 1999: Louisville, Kentucky
Zadie

I returned from my call with Emma preoccupied but still eager to see more patients. Up next: a soft-spoken biology teacher in his early forties who said he'd coughed up some blood. "You get his chest X-ray back?" Dr. Tamara asked, rocking back and forth on her heels a little.

"It's up on the board," I said, gesturing toward the radiology reading area.

"And?"

"It's normal?"

"Hmmm. Okay. Order a scan. What's up next?"

"A kid with a bean in his nose. I've got the nasal speculum, forceps, lidocaine ointment, and a teeny bendable retractor. Oh, and some cautery sticks, in case of bleeding. I took a peek, but it's hard to see and this kid is hysterical. I'm concerned we may have to sedate him."

"Well, aren't you the little Boy Scout? Giddyap."

We entered. The child, who was blond and about three, caught sight of me and pointed a pudgy accusatory finger. "No more her!"

The mother eyed us. She was young, with fluorescent bleached hair and a tattoo of what appeared to be a crack pipe on her forearm. "Quit that hollerin'," she mumbled to Nose Bean.

"Right. Here you go, Mom. Let's have you hold him on your lap. Yep, good. Can you hold his arms too? Great," barked Dr. Tamara. I stood at the ready, armed with the nasal speculum, curious to see the extraction technique. As lowly a procedure as this was, it was still something I wanted to do competently, and I'd been baffled by how to accomplish it. That sucker was way up there.

"Okay, Zadie, wave your equipment around in the air. No, bigger," instructed Dr. Tamara. Baffled, I did as instructed and began pinwheeling my arms, dragging the forceps through the air like a demented little airplane.

Dr. Tamara eyed me with what looked suspiciously like amusement. "Great. Now maybe add in some zoomy noises," she said.

"Whoosh," I said, feeling ridiculous.

Nose Bean stared at me, so captivated he forgot to yell. Quick as a wink, Dr. Tamara leaned in and kissed him hard on the mouth. The bean shot out of his left nostril and hit the floor with a tiny *clack*. Dr. Tamara picked it up and handed it with a flourish to the mom, who immediately let it drop back to the floor.

"Wha— How did you do that?" I asked as soon as we'd left the room.

"You forcefully exhale into their mouth while occluding the other nostril," said Dr. Tamara. "Normally you have the mom do it, but did you see the size of the canker sore on that ho's lip? Kid was better off with me. I'm celibate."

Well, any reply to this statement would be fraught with potential missteps, no? Agreeing a herpes-infested crack ho wasn't fit for kissing seemed easy enough, but wasn't it kind of judgmental to assume Nose Bean's mom was actually that degenerate? And there was no good way to touch the celibacy declaration. Maybe honesty was the best policy.

"I really cannot think of what to say here," I confessed.

"Yeah, sometimes I overshare," said Dr. Tamara. "Anyway. Moving on. We've got a call from radiology." She gestured with a thumb toward the radiology outpost in the center of the ER work area. "They've got something for us," she said.

Inside the dark little cave, there was an ambient glow from the ghostly reading screens. This gave the radiology guys a slightly vampirish appearance, like they might shriek and fall over clutching their chests if exposed to the harsh brilliance of the ER proper or, even worse, the outdoors. Our summoner stood up from his chair when we entered, continuing to murmur into a black dictation device as he motioned us over to the gleaming wall. It was covered in rectangular black films, each of them subdivided into smaller images of blacks and whites and grays. This must be the scan of the gentleman who'd been coughing blood.

"George Chang," said the radiology resident, setting down his microphone and extending his hand to me. He was a trim Asian guy in a button-down, with little owl-eye glasses perched neatly on his nose. "And who might you be?"

"I'm Zadie," I answered. "I'm a third-year student. This is my ER rotation."

"And they turned Dr. Tamara loose on you? How are you holding up?" he inquired, his gaze mischievous.

"Well, I—"

"Georgie, you perv, stop hitting on my med student."

"You can't blame a man for trying." He smiled, shrugging. "Seriously, Zadie. Are you free for dinner?"

Dr. Tamara was firm. "I mean it, George. We are busy saving lives here. Move on."

George lost the smile, turning toward the films on the board. "It's really bad for this patient, Alanna."

I looked at the incomprehensible films while Dr. Chang was talking. ". . . soft tissue attenuation, with these scattered well-circumscribed lesions in the lung periphery. And you can see, there are extensive liver mets too. Guy is all eaten up." He pushed his glasses back up absentmindedly.

"Shit," said Dr. Tamara. "This sucks."

"Yes. And, actually, the primary could be colorectal. He'll need a workup, of course, but that's my guess."

"How the hell did we miss this on the plain film?"

"Oh, we didn't," said Dr. Chang, sounding surprised. "That's his X-ray hanging next to the CT. You can plainly see the outline of these larger nodules. Don't you ever look at my reports, Sensei?"

"I thought I'd rely on the third-year med student's reading, Georgie. You hedge too much."

"Oh no," I said, feeling my face betray me with a hot blush. "Oh, I am so sorry. I don't know what I did. I must've looked at the wrong X-ray."

"You wouldn't be the first to do that," said Dr. Chang kindly. "It's a good lesson to learn early. Always double-check the names. You don't want to send this guy home with an 'all clear' and tell the guy in the next room he's got metastatic cancer and a few months to live."

"No, I don't," I agreed fervently. "But, oh my God. Does he have months to live? He's forty."

"Well, let's not jump the gun here, George," Dr. Tamara interjected. "We'll get him admitted and biopsied and let the onc guys get started with all their toxic potions and shit. Zadie, we need to talk with him."

"What are we going to— I mean, how do you tell him something like that?"

"I'm going to let you tell him." Dr. Tamara studied the films as she spoke. "But I'm a strong believer in just coming out with it. Don't use a lot of euphemisms or half the people you're talking to will be clueless from the get-go. Same thing for telling folks someone croaked. You really need to say 'died.' No one will hear a thing you say after that either, so if you have other information to give, you gotta get that in first." She rocked up and down on her heels. "Okay, I'm done with the pearls. Let's roll."

Dr. Chang seized the moment. He handed me a small piece of paper. "Here's my number, gorgeous," he said. "Let's try for dinner, yes?" Clearly, audacity had worked for him in the past, or possibly he was a perpetual optimist. His round owly face was beaming with hope. I had to smile.

"Thank you," I said.

There was a rustle from the other side of the viewing board, and someone stepped into our half of the room.

"Well, looks like you can hang it up right now, Georgie," said Dr. Tamara. "Casanova is here."

It was Nick, and without a word, he moved in, sweeping me backward in a low-dipping embrace, kissing my throat. After a few seconds, he released me, gallantly heaving me upright to face Dr. Tamara and Dr. Chang, who were both agape at this alpha-dog display of prowess.

For once Dr. Tamara appeared speechless. It was George who finally spoke, fixing X with a stare of unabashed admiration.

"I'm going to try that next time," he said.

———

"So," I said, "months of insisting we keep it secret"—I had discovered it was important to avoid the word "relationship," because that shut Nick down like a kill switch—"and you choose to tell the world we're dating with a public attack in the radiology department?"

"I didn't tell anyone anything. I am a man of mystery," Nick said calmly, turning the page of a surgery journal he was reading. He did the sexy-reading-in-bed thing perfectly, clad only in boxers, even managing to look hot in glasses.

Clues to Nick's personal life were sparse. The only photograph in the room was an old black-and-white of a rescue dog afflicted with a terrible underbite, which gave him a lovable but maximally stupid look. This worked out better on a dog than on a human, however: it was one of those he's-so-ugly-he's-cute situations. He was facing away from the camera but was looking excitedly back over his shoulder, with one floppy ear half covering his eye and the underbite giving him a lemon-sucking *Doh!* of a smile. At least this was one thing about Nick's past I did know: the dog in the picture was his favorite childhood pet, who had been named Pedro.

"Well," I said to the man of mystery. "Whether you used words or just relied on the, ah, stunning visual, it was pretty obvious after that display that we're together." I allowed myself a small yawn, in the interest of seeming nonchalant.

"Nonsense," said Nick. "All those dorks know is that the ladies can't keep their hands off me." He smirked at me over his glasses, smugly cocking an eyebrow before returning his attention to the journal.

"You know that was degrading, right?"

"Zadie," he said, setting down his journal and looking straight at me, "you liked it."

I strongly wished to deny this.

He regarded me with a trace of amusement. "Go ahead," he said. "Tell me you didn't."

"I didn't!"

"Oh. Well, my bad. I misunderstood." He idly laid a finger below my waist, right on the prominence of my iliac crest, and began tracing the outline of my hip bone.

"Right, okay," I mumbled, making a heroic effort not to start melting, which could have been construed as a tad hypocritical during one's delivery of a lecture against sexual objectification. "I am hereby declaring I'm off-limits until you acknowledge to God and Dr. Markham and everybody that we are dating."

"I am not at all concerned about your nooky moratorium, my little biscuit." Nick eyed me with amusement. "I know you're not about to start turning it down just to prove a point. You're the sexiest girl I've ever met." He returned to his journal, peering over his glasses to check my reaction.

Well, this was true. I was pretty much a sex fiend. I smiled to myself, then hastily tried to figure out how to redirect the course of events. Somehow, Nick could get the better of me in our conversations without ever seeming to address anything head-on. How did he do that?

I needed to stick to my guns here. "You are the most exasperating human being," I grumped. "Are you going to continue to defy any attempt at discussing the rela—this?"

"Yup," said Nick. Then, reconsidering: "Well, there is something we could discuss."

"What?" I asked.

"This," said Nick, lunging across the bed and tackling me.

"Get off me, you insatiable bull!" I howled. "I'm conversing!"

"Later," he growled, pinning me under him and licking my face with giant disgusting laps until I was helpless with laughter.

———

Later, of course, there was no conversation about it, since we both fell into an exhausted sleep. Although he wouldn't admit it, Nick loved cuddling in bed. It was the one time his face relaxed into unguarded sweetness; he liked caressing my hair, smoothing it over and over with his large hands while he murmured little compliments about my beauty, my accomplishments, my wit. The fact that he clearly appreciated my intelligence as well as my body reassured me.

My sleep was restless. I kept partially waking and thinking of the day, with a hollow half realization that Emma hadn't paged me yet. I sat up and shot a glance at Nick's bedside clock: eleven forty-three. Oh, hell. I'd been completely lobotomized by sex. I should have just shown up at the ER and dragged her out for a minute.

I looked at Nick. He was lying stark naked, flat on his back, mouth open, arms and legs flung wide, managing to look simultaneously ridiculous and dear. All his ferocity was transformed to dopey sweetness. I felt a sudden swelling of love for him; despite his gruff manly exterior, he was a loving person, in his way. In a sudden flash of the future, I saw myself marrying him, kissing him goodbye each morning, tending to a slew of tiny Nicks and Zadies before coasting off to my own surgery job.

I touched his arm and he made a small snorty sound, as if he were a very tiny pig. I leaned in and kissed him lightly on the lips, then rose and gathered up my things. Time to slink out and apologize to my bereaved roommate. I nudged open Nick's creaky bedroom door with my hip.

"Wha'? Zadie?" croaked Nick. "Whereygoing?"

"I gotta go," I whispered. "Emma wants to talk to me."

Slightly less groggy: "She does?"

"Yes. She's going to tell me about what happened with Graham, I think. Anyway, I'll call you tomorrow and tell you about it."

"She's at work; why not wait? Besides"—now he sounded alert—"I have tomorrow morning free. We can stay together tonight, and I'll bring you cappuccino and croissants in bed in the morning before you go into the ER. How often does that happen?"

"What? Never!" I said, excited. He was probably right. How much could we discuss between Emma's patients? Whatever had happened with Graham, it would be better to talk about it privately tomorrow night, when we were both off. I almost never spent the night with Nick; our brutal schedules rarely permitted it.

"It's settled, then," said Nick, smiling at me. He took my pager from my hand and tucked it in his bedside drawer. "Come here, sex biscuit, and cuddle up to me."

"Coming!" I sang. I'd page Emma first thing in the morning; she must be busy now. "But do you mind if I borrow some boxers or something to sleep in? We're facing an enormous hygiene emergency if I don't change clothes soon." I started to pull open the drawer where he kept his underwear, and yelped in fright as Nick lunged out of bed and caught me by the shoulder.

"Those are dirty," he said, shutting the drawer. His bare chest gleamed in the room's dimmed ambient light.

"That's not right," I said, suspicious. "Who keeps dirty underwear in a drawer? What's in there?"

"Nothing," he said firmly, spinning me around toward the bed. "That's where I keep my private items."

I was immediately intrigued. "What private items?"

"Stop being so nosy." He flashed a feral grin at me. "Or I'll tie you to the bed."

"Rawrrr," I purred, casting a longing glance in the direction of the mysterious drawer, resolving to peek in it at the first opportunity. Nick took no chances, however: he tucked me into the crook of his shoulder and flung a muscled leg over my hip, his fingers drifting lazily through my hair. "Say it," I instructed happily.

"I love you," he whispered. "I do." I could feel his heartbeat against my back. I nestled against him, soothed into a happy state of well-being, and fell fast into a dreamless sleep.

Chapter Thirty-six

SURGICAL SECRETS

Late Autumn, 1999: Louisville, Kentucky

Incoming Code Blue. Today I was being supervised by the chief resident of the ER, a beautiful brown-haired doctor named Rachel McMann, who was probably five feet one in heels but nonetheless intimidated everyone with her brusque manner and horrifying New Jersey accent. I caught sight of her now, striding machinelike toward one of the big resuscitation rooms in front.

She saw me too. "Medical student!" she bellowed. "Got a good one coming in. Full cardiac arrest, fifteen minutes downtime."

"Thanks for paging me," I said, trying to keep up without breaking into a full-on sprint. How did such a short person move so quickly?

As always in a code, the room was crowded. Rachel assumed the place at the head of the stretcher and I wedged in at her elbow. Our timing was good; right after we positioned ourselves, the EMTs barreled in. One was bagging while the other did CPR, both of them pausing long enough for the nurses to pull the sheet with the patient on it over to the ER stretcher.

"Forty-nine-year-old male, collapsed during a meeting. Initial rhythm was V-fib, defibrillated times three, total of two milligrams epi. No time to tube him," one of the EMTs reported breathlessly.

The usual flurry of activity ensued. I was hoping Dr. McMann would let me intubate the patient, but instead she did it herself while simultaneously pimping me on the management of various arrhythmias. This was disconcerting to everyone in the code because she kept shouting "Congratulations! You just killed the patient!" every time I fumbled an answer. Meanwhile, one of the second-year ER residents had shown up uninvited and poached the remaining good procedure: insertion of a central line into the internal jugular vein.

The code was not going well. The patient kept getting resuscitated and then immediately dying again. To make it even more confusing, he'd had so much epinephrine it was impossible for him to flatline; the residual drug in his system showed up on the monitor as a little oscillation of activity even though no one could detect a pulse. But nobody wanted to quit. He was too young to die. We were all sweaty and exhausted when Dr. McMann finally called it.

"Time of death, nine eighteen a.m.," she said, her voice flat.

She showed me how to ascertain he was really dead: we checked his gag reflex, checked for pupillary constriction, breath sounds, a pulse; nothing. Then Dr. McMann closed his eyelids and said to the nurse, "Where's the family?"

The family consisted of a wife named Ellen Anne Dubois, the nurse reported, and she was in the family room. We went in, the nurse and I trailing silently behind Dr. McMann. Mrs. Dubois was attractive: mid-forties, smooth ebony skin, thick hair in a ponytail, a slender form encased in exercise clothes. She glanced up with equal parts relief and anxiety when we introduced ourselves, repeating our names with a tenuous smile.

"What has Richie gone and done to himself?" she asked, hugging her arms around herself.

"Mrs. Dubois," said Dr. McMann in a considerably quieter voice than her norm. "Has your husband been feeling unwell lately?"

"No, no, he's been fine," Mrs. Dubois answered.

"Does he have any medical problems? Who is his primary care doctor?"

It was dawning on Mrs. Dubois that these were questions to which Mr. Dubois should have already provided the answers.

"He . . . he has high cholesterol," she ventured nervously. "Is he okay?"

There was a little pause. Dr. McMann spoke: "His colleagues called EMS because he collapsed at work. When the medics got there, they found he was not breathing. They pumped oxygen into him and began measures—CPR and medications—to try to restart his heart. When he got here, we inserted a breathing tube and gave him more medications." She paused again. "Mrs. Dubois, I am so very sorry to tell you we were unsuccessful, despite trying for a very long time, and your husband died a little after nine o'clock."

"What?" said Mrs. Dubois in a tiny voice.

I had a sudden mental image of Mrs. Dubois as a very old woman, sitting alone, hunched in the same posture she inhabited now, her little arms wrapped around herself, mourning and bewildered.

"I am so sorry." Dr. McMann spoke gently. "We tried everything to save him."

Very slowly, Mrs. Dubois lowered her head to her knees. She rocked back and forth a little.

"We have a hospital chaplain," said Dr. McMann. "She'll call someone to be here with you."

"Oh," said Mrs. Dubois.

"That should be her," said Dr. McMann, as a quiet knock on the door sounded. She stood. "You may want to talk to me later, or you might have questions. Just ask for me; I'll come back. We are all here for whatever you need. And Megan will stay with you." Megan, the nurse, nodded.

We swung open the door, but stopped as Mrs. Dubois raised her bewildered face toward us.

"I'm grateful you tried," she said, and her face broke as she tried to smile.

———

"Okay," said Dr. McMann, as soon as we were clear of the room. She had resumed her motorized gait and was churning through the ER like a rocket-propelled grenade. "What killed him?"

"Uh. Heart attack?" I offered, wondering what it was about Dr. McMann that so unnerved me.

"We call it a myocardial infarction, yes. MIs are one cause of sudden death. What else makes you suddenly keel over?"

"Strok— Cerebrovascular accident?"

"Okay. Yep. CVAs, subarachnoid hemorrhages, brain stuff; good. Let's have one more."

Oh hell. Something about Dr. McMann always wiped my hard drive. How long was it academically acceptable to stand openmouthed in a desperate search for data retrieval? Let's see, let's see. A malfunction in the heart or brain could kill you instantly . . . What else? Lungs!

"Pulmonary embolism!" I said triumphantly. Then I deflated. "What do you think happened to him?" I asked.

"He'll be a coroner's case for sure," said Dr. McMann. "You should follow up to find out. Okay. I know we're behind now, but why don't you take ten minutes to grab us a couple good coffees?"

"I will," I agreed gratefully. I headed briskly for the elevator, turning when Dr. McMann called out.

"Medical student?" she hollered.

"Yes?" I answered.

"What did we talk about during the code?" She cocked her finger into a gun shape and fired at me. "Don't forget arrhythmias."

———

The elevator was crowded when I got on. I wedged into the corner, next to two chatting girls in pink scrubs, still thinking about Mr. Dubois. He was clean-shaven, handsome; he looked tall and fit. He'd been wearing a business suit. How could someone like that die without warning? What would his wife do now?

". . . Nick Xenokostas, you know, the fifth-year surgery guy?" said an unfamiliar man's voice somewhere behind me.

I immediately forgot about Mr. Dubois. I arched my neck and slowly half turned, trying to look as if I were not paying attention. The speaker was enormous; he and his companion were both extremely tall, extremely strong-looking men in their late twenties, wearing long white coats and scrubs. Probably orthopedic surgery residents.

". . . told a nurse he'd forgotten his wife's birthday. He said he needed to send her flowers." The ortho guy laughed.

"More like he forgot he has a wife," said the other guy. "Isn't he always banging a nurse?"

"Yeah, but I think his wife lives in another state or something. Maybe she's a resident somewhere else?" The elevator *ping*ed: we arrived at the basement. The ortho residents and the candy stripers and the patients all got off. I stood still, feeling my breath stuck somewhere in the middle of my chest. A new crowd of people got on the elevator and pushed buttons; the elevator went back up.

After a few minutes of riding aimlessly, I found my feet propelling me off, back to the ER. Wordlessly, I picked up a chart and began reading. The words were a hopeless blur. I set the chart back down.

". . . Student . . . ? Hey, medical student!"

It was Dr. McMann. She was waving a hand in front of my face. "Where's the coffee?"

"Uh. I'm sorry," I mumbled.

"Sorry? What?" snapped Dr. M. "You didn't go?"

"No. No, I'm sorry. I can go now."

"Forget it," said Dr. McMann crossly. She was a blazing five-foot tower of irritation. She tossed a lock of glossy dark hair over her shoulder and stalked off. I slumped to the desk in relief, but it was short-lived; Dr. McMann spun back around and issued a pissed-off order for me to go see patients. I nodded dumbly.

Dr. M studied me. "What's the matter?" she asked finally. "Are you upset over the code?"

I had forgotten about the code, but now I glanced over at the room where Mr. Dubois lay. The curtain was pulled, but I could see a set of smallish feet in gym shoes next to the gurney: Mrs. Dubois. She must have been in there with the body of her dead husband, trying to accept the seismic shift in her reality. I nodded again.

Dr. McMann's gaze softened. *Maybe she will let me go home,* I thought, with something approaching relief. Or maybe I'd be given a break to collect myself. I looked up.

"Well, buck up!" barked Dr. M, charging over. "We can't go around falling to pieces when we lose someone or we'd never get through the day. Back on the horse, medical student." She clapped me on the back, causing me to expel my breath in an undignified *oof.* I lumbered up and headed for the next patient's room.

———

Somehow, the day passed.

Later, looking back, I could not remember a single patient I saw or anything I did for the rest of the shift. By late afternoon, Dr. McMann gave up on me and sent me home. Arriving at my door, I lifted my hand, which was as weighty as Jupiter, and pushed open the door. But something stopped me before I entered.

I wheeled around and ran to the street, flinging open the door to the Colt like I was about to be skinned alive if I didn't peel out in under five seconds. The engine caught and I screeched down the street, skidded around the corner, and headed for the Highlands, my breath coming in distraught bursts.

I was going to confront Nick.

Or more likely, I was going to confront his empty apartment, which was fixing to suffer a disaster akin to the wrath of God if he wasn't home. I'd plow through his personal items—starting with the mysterious drawer of boxers—confirming he was a vile, traitorous, contemptible *married* bastard, and then I'd unleash the full fury of a woman scorned, and . . . and . . . Well, I wasn't exactly sure what I'd do at that point. Suddenly I burst into tears, thinking I'd never be with him again, ever.

Arriving at his apartment, I thundered up the stairs to his door and retrieved his spare key from its inexplicably stupid location under the only flowerpot on his porch. Bursting through the door, I started toward his bedroom, but a shuffling sound from the living room gave me pause. I stepped inside and flipped on the light.

Nick sat on the couch.

"Ah," I said softly. Uncertainty gripped me at the sight of his face. In a strangely detached way, I waited to see which of my emotions would triumph. Was I most sad? Hurt? Disappointed? Was I going to cry? No, in fact, it seemed I did have a dominant emotion, after all: rage. "You son of a bitch!" I screamed, picking up a thousand-page study guide from the side table by the couch—*Surgical Secrets,* appropriately enough—and launching it at Nick's head. It missed, so I grabbed another book.

I threw that one, but I got distracted and my aim was off. Someone else was in the apartment too: I froze as I heard a door shut in the bedroom and the faint sound of someone moving around. No. I looked at Nick again.

"Is that . . . ? Is that your wife?"

Nick shifted guiltily on the couch. I noticed he was shirtless, his smooth blond hair ruffled in the back.

"Zadie," he began, looking miserable.

"Don't say 'Zadie' to me!" I shrieked irrationally. "I said, 'Is that your wife?'"

He stared at the floor.

"How could you let me love you if you are married?" I wailed. "How could you?"

"Zadie, I'm sor—"

I felt my face crumple up. "I am brokenhearted," I said in a tiny voice.

A stricken look I'd never seen before crossed his face. He jumped up, starting toward me. "I don't want this," he said. "Please. I love—"

I put my hands over my ears. Then I started running; I ran out of the room, and out of his apartment, and down the street to my car, where I doubled over, the noisy sound of my crying echoing down the empty street.

Chapter Thirty-seven

THE IRONY OF TRAUMA

Zadie, Present Day

I regarded the small penis in front of me. Its owner had been restrained in a supine frog-legged position on a board, his torso and arms tightly wrapped in a blanket, with Velcro straps tying him down. My friend Mary Sarah seized the opportunity to inject lidocaine around the circumference of his penis—three o'clock, six o'clock, nine o'clock—which understandably pissed him off. Quick as a flash, her assistant placed a sip of sugar water in his mouth, and he brightened, greedy sips replacing his outraged yowls. His little eyes squeezed shut, cheeks working hard, as the rest of him relaxed.

"Here we go," Mary Sarah remarked, yanking his foreskin up, clamping it, and slicing it off. "Okay, little dude, you are circumcised." As she began to remove her instruments, I cupped his tiny thigh under the sterile drape, unable to resist a surreptitious squeeze of his baby fat.

Mary Sarah snatched the drape away, exposing my hand. "Getting your fix?"

I grinned. "Squeezing baby fat releases endorphins," I said. "It's science."

"Okay." She gently squeezed his other thigh. "Oh, you're right. That's fantastic. I think I can skip my run today."

I was smug.

She whacked me on the bottom. "There's some more endorphins for you. Now quit molesting my patients and get your echo done."

The nurse wheeled the circumcision baby away, replacing him on the procedure table with another tiny, pink-faced bundle, this one for me. Involuntarily, we both glanced in the direction of the doors just beyond the newborn nursery, which led to the NICU. This baby had no recognizable abnormalities on the prenatal ultrasound, but his twin brother had not fared so well: he'd been diagnosed with tricuspid atresia, a condition incompatible with life without a series of major surgeries.

The ultrasound tech appeared and set up her machine with silent efficiency. The infant, who'd been sleeping, wakened with a squall of outrage as the tech placed the ultrasound probe on his chest. His cries started somewhere in the piercing range and progressed almost immediately to an earsplitting wail.

Mary Sarah tried a pacifier. Quickly rejected.

The ultrasound tech grimly soldiered on but stopped after a moment. "This," she said, "is a really pissed-off baby."

Mary Sarah concurred, hands over her ears. "I can pretty much guarantee the echo is going to be normal. That's quite a workout he's getting."

"I hear babies cry all day," said the tech, "but this is intolerable. How is he so loud?"

"We may need to sedate him."

The baby's face was now a lurid shade of purple. "No worries. I got this," I said. I picked him up and cuddled him to me, forgetting about the ultrasound goo, which immediately melded my shirt to my chest.

He cried louder.

I began the universal side-to-side rocking motion adopted by all life-forms confronted with a screeching baby, to no avail. I turned him around, so his back pressed against my now-slimy chest, and nodded at the tech. "Go ahead."

"You know I need him flat, Dr. Anson."

I laid him down again, lowering my head next to his. He screamed. *"Let's go, le-eh-et's go,"* I sang. *"Don't take it back anymo-or-ore."*

The crying got fractionally quieter.

I increased my own volume. I twirled in place.

The baby stared in my direction, a perplexed expression on his face. The crying dwindled.

"And HERE I am, and HERE I go . . ."

Next to me, Mary Sarah and the tech were convulsed in silent laughter.

I flung my head back and my arms out. *"Da da da NOW . . . I . . . SAY . . . the snow never gets to me anywaaaaay!"*

In the background, other people had joined their voices to mine, a swelling chorus filling the newborn nursery, most of them undeterred by my mangled lyrics. We finished with a spectacular crescendo, pro-claiming our unified resistance to the cold, the last note echoing with a theatrical flourish. The baby hiccupped one last little protest and then peacefully closed his eyes, snorting a little as he drifted back to sleep.

After bowing to a round of sustained applause, I read his echo—normal—and found his battered parents to give them the good news. This was the last of my Monday morning newborn echos, so I decided to head to the physicians' lounge to grab a quick latte before walking down the street to my office. The second I set foot in the room, I wanted to pivot and go back out, but it was too late: she'd seen me.

Emma wore scrubs and a green surgical cap, her sculpted cheekbones thrown into high relief without strands of hair to soften her face. I pretended to study the bulletin board next to the coffee machine, half reading a bossy notice instructing us not to consult a local urology group that had somehow incurred the wrath of the hospital administration. I sensed Emma looking at me and felt my cheeks flame up. This was silly; I hadn't done anything wrong.

I marched toward the door, clutching my hot cup. Emma intercepted me just as I reached it; she placed a cool, long-fingered hand on my arm. I wrenched away.

"I have to go."

"Please," she said. "Five minutes."

I wavered. Emma realized this and pounced, drawing me outside the lounge and into the empty hall. "I'll walk you to the garage."

We trudged along, mute, until finally she broke the silence. "Please let me tell you I'm sorry."

This seemed insufficient for the depth of her betrayal.

"I don't want to talk about it here," I said, abstractly noting some scene playing out in the hospital lobby, with a big family group wailing and gnashing their teeth and rending their garments, metaphorically speaking. We moved past them, silent again.

"You're right," Emma said, once we'd cleared the drama in the lobby. "Meet me for dinner tonight. Let me tell you the truth." She looked me directly in the eyes. "Please."

"Oh," I said, softening.

She continued: "I don't know if I can do anything to save my job, but I know this: if I had to pick between saving my job and saving my friendship with you, it wouldn't even be close. I'd pick you."

I stopped walking. Emma had never wanted to be anything other than a surgeon.

"Did something else happen with the Packards?" I asked. I'd deliberately avoided the thought of the meeting scheduled with them this weekend.

"Not directly," said Emma. "But I just met with Nestor Connolly and the hospital's attorneys. They're advising me to take a leave of absence. Starting tomorrow."

I looked at her: usually ramrod-straight, her spine slumped, and her clear skin held the grayish cast of fatigue. Against my will, I felt some sympathy. It was ridiculous for the hospital to side against Emma; this was not a clear-cut case of medical malpractice. "Look," I said slowly, "I'll meet you tonight. But you agree right now: you're going to tell me the entire story. Everything."

"I will," said Emma, her voice low.

The implications had dawned on me slowly, despite Nick's admission of why he carried the photo. Human nature being what it is, my first reaction was shamefully self-centered: a sharp knife thrust puncturing my core when I recognized their faces. I ached for myself. They did this to me, to me, to *me*.

But they hurt someone else, too.

"You have to tell me what happened with Graham," I said. We'd reached the physicians' parking lot, and I stopped, leaning against my dust-speckled car.

A whispered response: "I know."

"And how it started with Nick and how it ended. All of it."

I could hear her breathing: measured, slow inhalations, a little jagged at the end. "I will."

"Okay, then." I took a belated sip of my coffee. "I'll see y—"

"I used to see him for years," she said hoarsely.

A small dart in my chest. After all these years, how could Nick still have the power to wound me?

"For years?" I managed.

"I'd look up in the grocery, or at the gym, and he'd be standing there

like a dumbstruck giant, with his hair ruffled, in his flannel shirt, looking right into my eyes. I'd blink and look again, and it would be someone else, of course, but for one heart-stopping second, I'd think . . ." She
trailed off. When she spoke again, I could barely hear her. "I wanted it
to be him so badly."

Graham. She meant Graham. "Oh, Em—"

"When you think back on our trauma rotation," she said, her voice
stronger, "it was the hardest part of medical school, right? Working
hundred-ten-hour weeks, staying awake for forty hours at a time?"

I agreed. "Agonizing hours of standing still. Withering barrages of
questioning, daily public humiliation. Foul odors."

Now Emma's voice became clearer. "Right. And people dying. But
the irony of trauma was, I emerged from that rotation unscathed. Every
day on that service dealt some stranger a life-altering—or life-ending—
blow, but I was too dumb to let it touch me. People's lives were disinte-
grating all around me, but the trauma that finally unglued me was all
self-generated. I watched people break apart and I was fine. I watched
people die and I was fine. I gave you a sanctimonious little speech on
understanding the consequences of our actions when your pregnant
trauma patient died, and I was fine. Then I broke me, and I broke our
friendship, and I broke Graham. And *finally* I understood what it means.
Trauma."

A gaggle of young nurses passed us on their way in: tailored pastel
scrubs, ponytails, boisterous bright lips and cheeks. "Emma," I said. I
thought back to the person I'd been as a young adult, and it was like she
had been someone else: a drifting, formless human shape, missing some
elemental piece, until finally enough experience stuck to her to fill in the
gaps. Could I not forgive Emma for something that had happened so
long ago? "I'll see you tonight."

Chapter Thirty-eight

YOU MEAN THERE'S MORE?

Zadie, Present Day

A lighter mood gripped me that evening as I waved goodbye to Drew. Driving through uptown, I felt zippy, lighthearted, relieved of a burden. Anger was such a debilitating emotion; why couldn't people see that? Over the course of the day, I'd resolved to forgive Emma, and it felt good. I tend to follow the same pattern when somebody wrongs me: I stew over it obsessively, my mind churning through all the variables as I replay the incident, thinking of what I should say. I catalog their offenses. I verbally dissect them. Zingy rejoinders fly from my lips until my enemy folds into supplicating apology, humbled by her absolute wrongness. After I've done this several hundred times in my own head, there's seldom a need to confront anyone in real life. I'm over my anger.

Of course, this generally applied to minor dustups, not earth-shattering betrayals. But at the same time, there was so much more at stake here. I didn't want to lose my best friend. I still loved her. And if you looked at this rationally, she'd surely canceled some of her debt with years of steady friendship: soldiering together through our careers, through raising our babies, through various social disasters, and all the other things for which you rely on your friends. Every time I needed her, she'd been there. I knew from the guilt emblazoned on her face that she felt as culpable as Nick—this wasn't a case of unreciprocated pursuit on his part—but I hadn't heard her side of things yet. Maybe she had an explanation.

I hummed as I drove into the garage, moving quickly toward the elevators. I liked these elevators because they came equipped with a pleasant but bossy computerized female voice. "Don't even think about getting on if there are more than ten riders," cooed my elevator when the doors opened to admit me. "There're only eight of us," somebody hollered as I hesitated. Hurriedly, I tried to decide if a weight-challenged person near the back counted as one or two people.

I rolled the dice. We made it up to the lobby, where I waved Drew's work lanyard at a card reader. All the buildings in Charlotte's uptown district connected via pedways, skybridges, and tunnels, making it easy to park for free in Drew's building and hoof it over to the glitzy sky-scraper housing the restaurant without ever setting foot outdoors.

Just before leaving the house, I'd finally fessed up to Drew that tonight's dinner qualified as more than a mundane social engagement. Somewhat surprisingly, he'd made it home in time for me to leave, although he wasn't overwhelmed with excitement at me bailing on the freewheeling mayhem that passed for bedtime in our house.

"You're going where?" he said, his eyes drifting past me to our bed, where all four children had apparently decided to practice gymnastics.

"Dinner with Emma," I repeated, trying to look beguiling.

Drew's consternation grew. "Now?"

"Yes. If that's okay. It's an emergency, actually."

"You have an emergency dinner at a swanky uptown restaurant with your best friend?"

I grabbed Drew's arm and dragged him into the master bathroom, shutting the door on the kids' ruckus. Both of us relaxed. I met his eyes. "Emma and I had kind of a . . . falling-out," I said. Drew started to say something, but I butted in. "More than just a fight."

"About what?"

"About a guy."

Assuming there'd be more, Drew merely raised an eyebrow.

"Right, then." I took the plunge. "Do you remember me talking to a surgeon at the Arts Ball? I dated him once. His name's Nick Xenokostas, but everyone called him X. He was not one of my better decisions."

"Why not?"

Quick assessment: Drew's countenance was peaceful. Forge ahead.

"He was a monumental jackass, actually. It was against all the ethical admonitions of the medical school for us to date, at least while we were on the same rotation, since I was a student. He knew that, of course, and was constantly warning me not to tell anyone. But it wasn't a deal breaker to me; I thought, why should the school control who I see romantically? It was a little bit exciting, even."

"Zadie the rogue."

I checked again. Instead of jealousy, Drew's expression now reflected vague amusement.

"Well. As it turned out, he was less concerned with people finding out about me because I was a student and more concerned with me finding out that he was also hooking up with another student at the same time. And also: he was married."

"Whoa." Drew's face finally relinquished its complacency and took on a more appropriate, repulsed look.

"Wait. There's more," I said. "The other student was Emma."

Now he was truly shocked; his mouth opened in confusion. Eventually he sputtered, "I bet Emma kicked his ass when she found out."

"Not exactly. She knew the whole time. At least, she knew about me; neither of us knew he was married."

Drew processed this. "Holy shit," he said slowly. "I'm sorry, honey."

"It was sordid and disturbing on many levels," I admitted. "Lots of bad decisions on everyone's part."

"You found out about Emma back then?"

"No," I said. "I found out about her at the Arts Ball."

As we say in the South, Drew hadn't just fallen off the turnip truck yesterday. It didn't take an emotional genius to deduce from my tear-stained face and hysterical hiccupping on the ride home from the Arts Ball that something had gone awry. Both of us had had enough to drink that we Ubered home; the presence of the driver rendered me mute until we reached our house, where I'd fled to the bathtub. Drew asked me through the door if I wanted to talk, and I yelled that I didn't.

He nodded his head as he put it together, then folded me up in his arms.

"I'm okay," I said. "I mean, I'm pissed, but it happened a long time ago, and Emma is a genuinely good person. It was totally out of character for her to do what she did. I'm going to let her grovel for a while, and then I'm going to forget about it."

Drew let me go and looked at me.

"I don't think I'd be able to do that," he said.

———

I saw Emma before she saw me; she was already at our table, motioning to the sommelier for a glass of wine. Around her, the city twinkled through the glass walls of the restaurant. She sat with the pinched face and stooped shoulders of a much older woman, as if the ceaseless stress of the last few months had caused her body to turn in on itself.

She stood when she caught sight of me, and she held out her hand in an oddly formal welcome. "You came," she said.

"Of course I came," I said, wincing as I sat. Posset had embraced the farm-to-table craze a little too enthusiastically, settling on incongruous—and massively uncomfortable—rough-hewn log benches for seating.

A waiter materialized and filled our water glasses; another set down a little amuse-bouche of savory phyllo and took our orders. Emma swirled her wine. Her expression changed from weariness into something carefully neutral. "I have to tell you something," she said, her voice modulated.

In the entire history of humanity, no good has ever come of the phrase "I have to tell you something." Alarmed, I stabbed phyllo with too much force, causing it to violently hurl a little spray of cheese across the table. "Well, yeah. That's why I'm here."

The murdered appetizer escaped Emma's notice; she appeared to be pondering her approach. I waited.

"There's more than you know," she said, adding, "About what happened with Nick."

Cautiously: "Okay."

"Zadie." She set down her wineglass. "First, let me say, I'll understand if you can't forgive me. But I finally realized how selfish it is to keep hiding things from you. I want us to stay friends so badly it physically hurts, but I'll never lie to you again."

"Ah."

"And I know you must wonder why I never confessed to you. It was an awful betrayal, but maybe you'd have forgiven me if I'd told you on my own. You're so happy. You have the perfect all-American life: a doctor married to a banker; two beautiful girls, two handsome boys, and even a golden retriever. You're so wholesome it's nauseating."

"Thank you?"

Emma cast her gaze to the heavens like she was looking for backup. Her eyes fluttered back down. "I'm jealous of you. I have always been jealous of you. It's no excuse for what I did, but it is an explanation, or part of one."

I focused on my plate, then looked up. I couldn't process what Emma was trying to say. "This is getting kind of concerning," I said. "I feel like you're about to lunge across the table and spear me with your appetizer fork."

"If anyone gets speared with an appetizer fork, I promise it will be me."

"Whoa. Emma."

"No, no." Emma, granite-faced, ignored my attempt at levity, but she did set down her fork. "You know, Zadie, you've always represented everything I wanted."

I considered this. "What do you want that you don't have?"

"It's not that I'm not grateful for what I have. It's hard to explain. It's—" She looked away, taking in something I could not see. I waited.

"I wanted to be normal," she said finally. "I wanted people to like me without my having to try so hard."

"I don't know what you m—"

"You grew up in a regular home," she said, so intently I startled. "You don't know what it's like to be different."

"Emma, my parents were liberal hippies in an area where a significant proportion of people still refer to the Civil War as the 'War of Northern Aggression.' I had to sew my own clothes! We ate hummus before that was a thing! I wouldn't call my childhood exactly *normal*—"

She held up a hand, stopping me. "My parents couldn't read," she said. "Until a library truck came to our county when I was eight, I barely knew there was an outside world." The embarrassment in her eyes stilled me. "Everything you take for granted was foreign to me."

I'd been to Emma's childhood home once, on a weekend road trip during college. We'd left Louisville and headed southeast on the back roads, passing acres of the black-fenced rolling hills of the grand horse farms outside Lexington. This was the land of the Bourbon Trail, of Keeneland, of artisanal pottery and bluegrass music, of prancing Thoroughbreds with velvety coats and impossibly delicate ankles, everything lush and beautiful and tidy.

In the late morning, we got a flat tire. Apparently there was no pressing criminal action going down in Woodford County, because our breakdown was heralded by the arrival of no fewer than three police cars.

The cops rolled up in sequence and swaggered out. Two of them changed our tire, oozing sweat and gallantry. The others lounged, chatting us up.

We'd rolled to a clackety stop in front of an enormous wrought-iron gate, behind which an imposing structure was just visible. I don't remember Emma talking much until a lull in the conversation, when she glanced behind her and said, "The people who live there must be very rich."

"Ay, yeah," said a cop. He mentioned the name of the owner.

"What a beautiful house," said Emma, nodding toward the building behind us, with its spires and turrets and meticulously painted trim.

The gun belts of the cops rattled, they laughed so hard.

"That's a barn, honey," one said, not unkindly, but I saw Emma's eyes gloss. After that she stayed quiet.

We were headed to my house, an hour farther south in the foothills of the Appalachians, but our trip took a detour when we stopped for lunch. "Let's go to your house," I said impulsively. "You've been to mine a bunch."

"No," she said flatly.

"Why?" I said. "I want to meet your mom. And then we'll head over to Falls Cove"—that was my family's land—"in time for dinner."

Emma declined again, but I persisted. It was a gorgeous day. I wanted to go somewhere new and unknown and different; despite growing up in the country, I'd never been that far east into the wilderness of the state's mountain ranges. And I wanted to see Emma's house and meet her mother; it seemed weird that she knew my family so well but I'd never met hers.

Emma's mother was in her forties, but her face was the weathered crevasse of a much older woman. A pink space yawned in her mouth where her front teeth should have been. I tried to make my eyes look somewhere else when she welcomed us into the peeling pile of boards behind her.

The floor, composed of some kind of rough-hewn knotholed gray wood, had nothing beneath it. No concrete, no insulation. Between gaps in the wood, I could see the ground a couple feet below, which was littered with stuff: tin cans, a shovel, something that looked like a rusty lawn mower engine. I was so fixated on the floor it was some moments before I noticed the interior surroundings. We stood in one of three rooms, all open to one another: a kitchen with a metal table; a tiny living area, dominated by an old boxy television; and a sleeping area with one double bed. I looked around again, but that was it. I could not imagine where Emma had slept growing up.

I couldn't remember much from the rest of the visit. Emma's mother seldom spoke, but she was hospitable; she made us some corn bread in a skillet and insisted we take the last sodas from the short, round-edged refrigerator when we left. If she was baffled by the changes in her only child's fortune, she didn't show it. She hugged Emma fiercely, warmly, when we left, reaching up with a veiny, knobby hand to clasp the top of her much taller daughter's head.

I could not interpret Emma's expression.

———

Now I flushed, seared by the memory. "I—I know how you grew up," I said, uncertain how to reference the extreme poverty in which she'd been raised. "But look at you."

Emma cast her eyes down and started to say something. I could see right through her: a blast of confusion, a wave of self-loathing.

"Don't think that," I blurted, momentarily forgetting the difficult circumstances between us. "I love you."

Suddenly I was very aware of the restaurant noises: tinkling glassware, murmured conversations, the swish of a swinging door between the diners and the kitchen. Emma's eyes shone. "You did love me," she said. "I should have given you more credit."

"Of course I did."

"Anyway," she said, too brightly, "here we go. I'm confessing. And it's okay; I am going to revel in the indescribable lightness of honesty, even if you decide you're done with our friendship. I'll accept whatever you decide, Zadie. I deserve it. When I saw your reaction to the picture of me and Nick, which was . . . not understated . . . it reminded me of what a monumental shithead I am."

"Well, I am a person who feels things keenly," I said, relieved at her switch to a more conversational tone. "It's possible I could even be described as a tad overdramatic."

Emma allowed herself a tight-lipped smile. "I'm aware of your tendency toward keen feelings and drama, since I've been your friend more than half my life. But you were entitled to that reaction. What I did to you was loathsome."

"Right, then." I took the plunge. "Go ahead and lay it on me. What could possibly be worse than you having an affair with my boyfriend? My *married* boyfriend."

Emma shook her head. "He wasn't married."

"I heard—"

"I know what you heard. But that was actually just a rumor Nick started himself, to get some nurses off his back. He wasn't married."

"When I went to his apartment the last time, his wife was there. I heard her."

Emma waited for it to dawn on me.

"Wait. It was *you*? You were the one in his apartment when I went to confront him? He *said* it was his wife!"

She shook her head again, a small, regretful gesture. "He didn't say that. But he let you believe it because he thought it would hurt you less to think he was married than to know the truth. He was desperate that you not know."

She stopped and waited again, a patient kind of pain on her face. I mulled it over; then I gasped.

"He was married to you?"

Emma gasped back. "No!" she said. "Okay, so there *was* one calamity I managed to avoid. No."

"What, then?" I thought about it some more. I'd barged into Nick's apartment one night after an ER shift; that rotation had been in the early winter. All of a sudden, it struck me.

"Emma, that was way after Graham died. Why would y—"

A torrent of epicurean babble interrupted me. "*Who* is the lucky recipient of the *Capon Pistou with Ghee, Aubergine Confit, Wheat Berries, Dusting of Dulse, and Chervil*, and who will be partaking of the *Atlantic Croaker with Gambon, White Maripoix, Patato Saphron Rouille and Persillade?*" Our server was a slender, energetic man with a robust mustache, who deflated slightly at our unenthusiastic response.

"I have the fish?" Emma ventured.

"Tremendous!" The waiter recovered, beaming, and handed her a cutting board with some unidentifiable food heaped on top. "And you, ma'am, must be having the capon."

"Yes," I agreed, adding, "What exactly is a capon?"

"Well, ma'am," the waiter said pleasantly, "I believe it is a castrated rooster."

"Oh, excellent," I said, nodding knowledgeably.

I stared at the plate as the server pranced away. The capon *was* excellent, actually, and also provided a nice respite from the grim tale of yore; we were both quiet for a moment as we ate.

"How's the castrated rooster?" Emma finally asked.

"Delicious," I answered, "although I'll confess to a moment of doubt." The silence returned.

"I know what you're trying to tell me," I eventually mumbled through a mouthful of neutered fowl. "You kept seeing Nick, even after Graham died. You didn't stop, even when you knew it had killed him."

Emma's eyes were far away. "That's true," she said.

"How could you?"

She hung her head, pushing her still-full plate away too. "I tried to quit," she said softly. "I did, for a while. But something rotten inside me kept pulling me back. It would build and build until I couldn't stand it anymore. There was nothing pleasurable or happy about seeing him; it was more like the urge to rip off a scab, or that perverse impulse you get to jump when you're standing near a cliff. I would lock myself in the bathroom when you weren't home and scream until I lost my voice trying to stop myself from doing it. And then I'd do it anyway."

She stopped, one hand drifting toward her mouth as if to stifle her words.

"There's no explanation, other than some horridness at the core of me. I tried to rationalize it by telling myself he'd tire of you eventually, and you deserved a better man than him anyway. You could have had anyone you wanted; and in his heart, he's rotten. I thought he and I were meant for each other because we both seemed to be missing some elemental human piece. Our souls are broken."

I stared at her. "What about Graham?"

Her face twisted.

"Did you give Nick the picture?" I asked, remembering guiltily I'd seen the back of it when I'd snooped through Emma's room.

She shook her head. "Graham sent him a copy too. Nick got it the same day he tried to resuscitate him."

Now I pushed my plate away. "That's sickening," I said. "You both continued . . ."

Emma met my eyes. "It's worse than you think, actually," she said. "First, I don't believe Graham actually intended to kill himself. I think there was even a small bit of cruelty—or insanity—in what he planned: maybe he wanted to hurt himself so his girlfriend's lover would have to try to save him, knowing all the while he was the one who drove him to it. Graham brooded about things. He obsessed about them—in that way, he was something like me. I think he didn't plan to shoot himself in the heart until the very last moment.

"Nick was devastated when he couldn't save Graham. He could never bear to talk about it, and he was telling the truth when he said he carried that picture everywhere."

She paused.

"He hated me. He didn't want anything to do with me after that."

Confused, I said, "But you just said it was you in the apartment with Nick when I came over that day."

She laughed, a sharp, bitter sound. "I was there, yes. I'd show up from time to time." She looked at me. "I tried to stop, but I didn't succeed."

"But he let you in."

"I told him I'd tell you everything if he didn't. By then he was sick of me. He only wanted you."

I jumped up, scraping my leg on the stupid log bench and nearly colliding with the effervescent waiter before I managed to stumble away. I glanced back in time to see Emma thrust a handful of bills at him. She followed me, her stride unhurried but determined.

The bathroom—where was the bathroom? I concentrated on not howling. The woman at the hostess booth took one look at my intense expression and pointed wordlessly toward the hall outside the restaurant, probably figuring she had a couple of homicidal lesbians on her hands as Emma pounded by her too.

She caught up to me at the door.

"You have to hear the rest," she said.

I blanched. "You mean there's more?"

"Yes," she said, resolute. "I'm afraid there is."

Chapter Thirty-nine

THE LUNACY WARRANT

Zadie, Present Day

I leaned against the tiled wall of the bathroom, inert, listening to Emma without looking at her. I decided to disengage; I would hear and comprehend the words, but divorce them from their emotional content. Maybe if this worked well, I could create an alternate personality to handle all distressing future events. The idea had possibility.

". . . never stopped trying to contact you," she was saying. "It was easy if he called and you weren't there. If you were home, I just had to get to it first. I unplugged the phone in your room, and you never noticed, and when I was out, I unplugged the one in the living room too."

The white walls of the bathroom gleamed with antiseptic brilliance, like an OR. I shut my eyes.

"Eventually he stopped calling. But by then we had e-mail accounts through the university, so I had to monitor that too. At home that wasn't difficult, but what if you checked at the med school? It puzzled me for a while, but finally I hit on a solution: I created a new account in your name, and wrote him a short note instructing him not to try again. He ignored it, of course, and began sending e-mails to that account, sometimes multiple ones a day."

This jolted me. "What did they say?"

"At first they were straightforward: he wanted to see you. He needed to talk to you. They were factual, to the point." She leaned forward a little, concentrating on getting it right. "But then they began to change, becoming a little more . . . yearning, I guess. He wrote about loving you."

I made a small strangled noise.

"Those were the hardest to read, initially, so I . . . I pretended they were written to me," she said. "I began to . . . disintegrate a little, replacing every broken piece of me that splintered off with a new, manufactured piece, so I could function. I built a new Emma. And I convinced myself I was saving you from him—I knew he didn't deserve you.

"After a while I began to enjoy reading the e-mails, because even though Nick didn't know it was me in the correspondence, we developed this virtual relationship that was infinitely better than the real thing had been." She'd stopped looking at me, her eyes pinpointed on some unfathomable wrinkle in time. "We never really talked before, but now he was sharing a part of himself with me I'd never seen—that he said no one had ever seen."

I held up a hand. "You were writing him back," I said.

"Yes."

"And he thought this was me."

"Yes," she said again. "He did."

"Why didn't he look for me in person?"

"Because I told him I'd cut him off altogether if he ever contacted me—you—in any other way besides the e-mails," she said. "He agreed, because what choice did he have? By then, the fact that we weren't seeing each other in person gave us this feeling of freedom, the sense we could say anything, no matter how embarrassing, and there would be acceptance from the other person. Or maybe not acceptance exactly—I had to maintain some believable outrage, so he wouldn't press to meet in person—but we reached a point where the e-mails took on a life of their own."

The detached part of me kicked back in. "But you—I—must have known by that point he wasn't really married. Why was I still mad?"

"Because he continued to let you believe he was married."

"Why would he do that?"

"To spare you, I think," she said. "He didn't want you to endure the additional trauma of knowing we'd both betrayed you. Either way, he couldn't win. And then I finally— you finally—told him never to contact you again."

Emma's face held the singular pull of some entirely new human emotion, her features curdled in a molecular rearrangement born of stress. The constant beatdown of her role in Eleanor's death. Years of guilt from this monstrous deception.

"Why?" I squeaked finally. "Why go to those lengths?"

She directed a level gaze at me. "To me, you epitomized the thing I wanted most for myself: social acceptance. And I wanted Nick, or at least I wanted him to want me. But Nick wanted you. It devastated me."

"I still can't believe—"

"And," she went on, as if I hadn't spoken, "I guess I was resentful. Or at least uneasy. You knew about me. You'd seen where I grew up."

"So?" I asked, indignant. "Are you suggesting I thought less of you because of where I was born? Because that's crap. I'd never care about that. Are you saying you hated me?"

Emma gave me a strange look, almost resigned. She shook her head. "I don't think I can explain it."

"Try."

"No," she said. "I could never hate you. It's more like . . ." She trailed off. I waited, focusing on the blue of her irises: so pale and clear they inevitably summoned to mind a host of metaphors related to glaciers and ice and fathomless depths. She blinked, releasing me from the deep, and acknowledged what we were both thinking.

"I wanted to be like you."

For a moment I marveled at the capacity of the human brain—the capacity of my brain, in particular—to register a bunch of conflicting emotions at once. A sting of remorse, accompanied by a surge of insight. The shock of the revelations Emma was laying on me. And even a geyser of irritation bubbling up alongside my hurt: how had I become mired in this sea of melodrama? Normally, if anybody found themselves embroiled in a fit of emotional dysfunction, it was me. Emma was supposed to be the stable one. Instead, she'd carried on a tawdry affair with my boyfriend and impersonated me in the process. What kind of psychopathology was required to bring all this about, and how had I failed to notice it?

"Please say something," Emma said.

I said nothing.

"Zadie," she said, so plaintively I was almost disarmed. "I want you to know how ashamed I am. I am so sorry."

"Why didn't you ever tell me? How did you keep this secret all these years?"

She shifted her teary gaze upward, as if the answer were written on the ceiling. "I did try to tell you."

"When?"

"Do you remember our psychiatry rotation?"

Immediately I knew what she was referencing: a bizarre morning in schizophrenic group, a month or two after Nick and I had broken up.

I had found Emma hunched over a sink in the hideous schizophrenic ward bathroom, the olive-tiled walls echoing with her attempts to control her breathing. Without knowing I was going to do it, I flung my arms around her. "It's okay, it's okay, it's okay," I murmured, holding my friend's shaking thin shoulders. And then, bewildered by the intensity of her grief: "Is it Graham?"

She looked at me and shook her head. "It's you," she said.

By then I was even more confused, but I rallied enough to point out the obvious. "I'm not dead, Emma."

"I'm lost," she said, her body racked by a fresh wave of sobs as she twisted away from me.

"You're not lost. You're right here," I said idiotically, adding, "Do you want me to get Dr. Young?"

Emma stopped crying long enough to manage a side-eyed "No."

"Well, uh . . ." I fluttered my hands until I couldn't take it anymore. I'd never seen her cry, not even when Graham died. "Emma, please tell me what's wrong. This has to be about Graham."

Emma seized my words, gobbling them greedily from the air. "Graham," she said. "He died because of me. We were breaking up. We—" She began pacing around, her eyes alight with a weird, quick intensity. "We . . . I mean, I . . . I—"

A flash of insight struck me. "Emma," I interrupted, "I am *not* just saying this because we're on a psychiatry rotation surrounded by a bunch of bipolar people. But is it possible you're having some kind of manic-depressive episode?"

She stared at me and then began to laugh, a sound that could only be described as a humorless cackle. "Yes, I probably am. But what does that change?"

"It changes a lot," I shouted, energized and relieved to have an explanation of sorts. "We're surrounded by mental health professionals. We're standing in a psychiatric hospital. This is the ideal place to lose your mind!"

Her wild breathing calmed, and this time her laugh had a tinge of the genuine. She unbuttoned the top button of her shirt, fanning air toward her face and throat. When distressed, Emma was unable to thermoregulate: her tomato-hued skin always gave her away. She undid another button. "Ah, Zadie," she said. "If only—" She stopped, sucking her words back into her throat at the look on my face. "What is it?"

"Where did you get that shirt?" I asked, moving closer to inspect it. I could see the upper edge of its design beneath her button-down: the arcing curve of a hostile cartoon bird. The Baltimore Ravens.

She looked down, her lower lip falling open almost comically.

"It was in the laundry," she said. "I'm sorry. I shouldn't have grabbed it."

I blinked, embarrassed at my reaction to a stupid T-shirt. Nick loved that shirt and wore it often. I didn't remember him leaving it at my house—we usually met at his place—but he must have.

"Keep it," I said.

She buttoned her shirt back up, the flames at her throat extending to her face. "There's something I should tell you about Nick," she said. "And me."

"I don't want to hear anything else about Nick," I said. "He sucks, and I shouldn't think about him."

"Are you sure? Because he—"

"I'm sure!" If Nick had hit on Emma, too, I didn't want to hear about it.

"Okay," she said quickly—too quickly—adding: "But if you ever do want to hear about it, just tell me."

"I won't," I said. "I'm never thinking about him again."

———

"That doesn't count!" I said now. "I didn't know what you were going to tell me."

"You're right," she said. "But that was my lame excuse to myself—you didn't want to know, and I didn't want to hurt you more than I already had."

"You took stuff of his," I said. "From his house."

Emma nodded: a terse, efficient jerk of her chin. "A few things he wore," she said. "I left things of mine at his house too, usually in his drawers, under other clothes, so he wouldn't find them right away. I guess I hoped you'd see them."

I groaned.

"He had a drawer . . . where he stashed Zadie stuff," Emma said. "Notes you'd written him. A couple candles. The page from the residency directory with your picture on it."

I yelped and waved my hands to shut her up. Despite the circumstances, I was beset by a brief flash of wonder. It's one thing to contemplate the infinite possibilities you didn't choose, but quite another to have had the choice wrested away without your knowledge. Nick and I had never had a chance. For a moment I drifted in an alternate universe: another husband; different children; shadowy cities and homes and friends I'd never experience. It was too mind-boggling to take in. I stared at Emma.

"Who are you?" I said. I slid down the wall to the floor, landing on my bottom with a little *clunk*. "Who are you?"

Chapter Forty

SOME THINGS ARE
UNAVOIDABLE

Emma, Present Day

I see them in my sleep: a parade of ghostly accusers. Graham, dark-eyed and prescient, fixed in some posture of eternal yearning; the little girl, Eleanor, her bright baby face and her rosebud mouth, all her shiny new-ness crumbling into dust. I see the realization of betrayal cross my best friend's face in a swift, irreparable flash.

There is no more debilitating emotion than shame. Even grief has a redeeming clarity and purity to it: you know there is a terrible beauty in loving something so much that its loss nearly ends you. But there is no redeeming quality to shame. It's ugly.

I think of myself as a good person. But maybe everyone does? Re-gardless of what I think of myself, the undeniable truth is that I've done some very shameful things.

———

Saturday evening, the day of my meeting with the Packards, closed with lingering stickiness, the crackly leaves blowing off the oaks in my front yard on a gust of humid wind. Thanksgiving still lurked two weeks in the future, but already my next-door neighbors had erected a giant blow-up Santa Claus, leering like a deranged Peeping Tom at the level of my second-story windows.

I stepped briskly into my detached garage, practicing the correct facial expressions: empathy and concern and honesty. Contrition, but not at a level suggesting culpability. Human warmth, as my lawyer would say: *You want them to like you. People are much less likely to sue if they have a relationship with you.*

The problem was my face: it doesn't reflect my feelings. My face was as enigmatic and inscrutable as the moon, even when inside all I could hear was whimpering. Somehow I'd have to cast off my outer awkwardness and connect with these people.

It was a task made infinitely harder by Zadie's absence. Not only would she have been a buffer between me and the child's parents, able to leap into the fray without any of my hesitation, but she'd also have served as my emotional proxy. In her case, I'd say it's largely unthinking, but people respond to all her wild emotions as if she's got a control button lodged in their prefrontal cortexes. They love her.

I would have to rely on my own strengths. Zadie and I hadn't spoken in the days since the restaurant when I'd confessed. I missed her even more than if she'd died. At least the dead cannot hate you.

———

Before I could back out of the garage, the door opened and a pajama-clad Wyatt hustled through. If we weren't going out, Wyatt conducted a cherished Saturday night routine of ordering takeout, cracking a giant bottle of wine, and watching movies under a blanket on our most comfortable sofa once we'd put Henry down for the night, generally providing an unsought stream of commentary on the movie's plot as it unfolded. I'd never been able to break him of the habit of talking back to the actors, but I'd acclimated to his interruptions. Now it would seem sterile to view a film without Wyatt's murmured commendations and belches of outrage.

The sight of his bare feet poking out of the rolled-up gray pajamas I'd bought for him in London nearly undid me. He held up a decorative carrier bag, the fancy kind you'd use for liquor or a bottle of wine, and thrust it through my car window. I tried to wave him off.

"I'm not taking the Packards a bottle of bourbon," I said. "This isn't a hostess-gift situation."

"Not for the Packards," puffed Wyatt. "For Zadie."

"Zadie?" I said, surprised. I hadn't been able to bring myself to tell Wyatt about what had happened with Zadie, although until the other day, he alone, of all the people on earth, had known the truth about what I'd done to her in medical school. The day after the Arts Ball I'd spent the day in bed, not speaking, but the next day I'd done what I always did: I soldiered on. I went to work. I came home.

"This can be your night to mend fences," said Wyatt. Optimism shone from behind his smudgy reading glasses.

"I— How did you know something happened with Zadie?"

Wyatt raised his eyebrows. "I'm smarter than I look," he said. "Do you even need to ask?"

"But—"

"Muffin, you have to fix it." He waved his hands in front of him for emphasis. "You don't have to tell me how it went down—I can guess— but you can't let it go. You need your friend."

"I don't think she's coming," I said, feeling a familiar weight level me. "I can't control how she feels at this point." If there's anything I've learned, it's this: the past is never really gone. It's one long chain linking the present and also the future, and sometimes it doubles back on itself, exposing the things you thought were buried. "I told her the truth, and I haven't heard from her once."

Wyatt trotted around to the passenger side of the car and let himself in. "I can't be late, Wy," I said, beginning to fret about the time even though I'd allotted myself thirty minutes for a five-block drive. "Let's talk about it when I get home."

"This will only take a second," he said, leaning across the seat. "Look at me."

I complied, taking in the warmth of him: his round cheeks and round brown eyes, the exuberant gleam of his grin. He smiled at me until I smiled back.

"There," he said. "I wanted to see your face look happy."

The smile felt good; I hadn't remembered it could feel so good. Wyatt reached for me, tracing my cheekbones in his hands, gracing my nose with a kiss. "Your past is set, but your future is wide open," he said. "Go get 'em, pumpkin."

———

I pulled up to the Packards' driveway, and after briefly considering parking on the street, I turned in. The driveway, intricately patterned with some kind of reddish pavers, led to a roundabout parking area where a Tesla slouched at an arrogant angle. I tried to suppress my disappointment. Some irrepressible part of me had clung to the hope that I'd see Zadie's car waiting as I arrived.

To my surprise, Boyd Packard answered the door himself, wearing a blue golf shirt tucked into dark brown pants. "Dr. Colley," he said. "Come in." As best I could tell, there was no overt malice in his expression, but neither was there anything particularly encouraging. I followed him through a foyer dominated by a massive curving staircase and a chandelier the size of a cow, and then down a long hall constructed of wainscoting inlaid with antiqued mirrors. We arrived at a wood-paneled room at the back of the house, the ceiling soaring to the second story, brass-accented ladders on rails reaching to the upper shelves. A library.

"Fetch you a drink?" offered Boyd. He gestured in the direction of a bar: crystal glasses, decanters on trays, every imaginable liquor. The idea of a drink was abhorrent. I shook my head.

"Suit yourself," said Boyd, refreshing the glass in his hand with an amber liquid from one of the decanters. "Betsy?"

I started a little; I had not seen Betsy, her legs crossed at the ankles, perched with balletic grace on the edge of a sofa. She rose and extended a hand to me. "Thank you for coming."

I started to accept her hand but stopped, as for the first time, I saw the rest of the room. It was enormous, wrapping around a corner of the house, with a second seating area tucked into a bay of windows facing the rapidly darkening yard. I caught my breath as the person sitting near the windows rose and turned toward me. A clamorous hummingbird let loose in my chest. It wasn't Zadie.

It was Nick.

———

I looked at him, uncomprehending, and then realized Betsy Packard's hand hung in midair, waiting for me to shake it. I swerved my head back to her, three beats too late, and grasped her hand. "Thank you for having me," I managed.

I drifted along behind Boyd and Betsy, stunned. What did it mean that Nick was here? I could not envision a scenario where this made sense.

We sat: Betsy and Boyd facing Nick, me alone in a straight-backed wing chair. I'd plotted my speech in a meticulous outline, but now I could remember none of it. We sat in awkward silence, no one sure how to proceed.

Boyd finally spoke. "Good of you to come, Nick." He looked at me, and the bewilderment on my face must have spurred him to throw me a bone. He gestured to Nick. "We're friends from the club."

Nick cleared his throat. When he spoke, his voice was smooth. "Given that I'm a hepatobiliary surgeon, Boyd thought it might make sense to have me help interpret things."

"Oh," I said.

So that was it. He was going to hang me.

Nick leaned forward. "Let me start," he said. "Boyd passed on the medical records so I could assess them. And I know"—he leveled his gaze on Betsy—"some of this is going to be very difficult to hear, and you may want to take a break from time to time."

She gave him a tiny nod.

"Okay." He paused. "As you've heard, your daughter likely died from a combination of two things: first, a condition known as abdominal compartment syndrome, which is an increased amount of pressure within the abdominal cavity. In her case, this was a result of the initial crush injury requiring a massive blood transfusion. She also had an unrecognized injury to one of the ducts in the pancreas, which leaked enzymes into her belly."

No one looked at me. It was so quiet I could hear my own pulse.

Nick went on, his voice steady and reassuring, despite what he was saying. "The injury to the pancreas probably occurred during surgery, when the duct was inadvertently clamped. If she'd lived longer, it would have ultimately made her septic."

Boyd spoke up. "Would Eleanor have lived if this duct hadn't been cut? And if she'd not had the abdominal pressure problem?"

Now Nick looked at me.

"Yes," I said.

The poison of the word settled over the room.

Boyd picked up the ball again. "Could she have been saved if this had been recognized earlier?"

I closed my eyes. "Yes," I said again. "It's very possible. Or if I had not closed her incision."

Boyd directed his cold fury back to Nick. "Give me one reason," he said, "that I shouldn't sue her."

Nick nodded, recognizing the question, but kept silent. We all watched him: the alert intelligence embedded in his handsome face, the answer to Boyd's question whirring behind his blue eyes. He stood up.

"Boyd," he said quietly. "I don't believe you should sue her."

I felt my breath freeze in my lungs.

Nick began to pace. "It's hard to explain," he said, "but this would have been a very difficult thing to recognize. Pancreatic anatomy is notoriously difficult, and in these circumstances, with a tremendous amount of bleeding from the spleen, it would have been nearly impossible to discern. It's an error any of us could have made under the circumstances. Hell, it *has* happened to me before. I've done exactly the same thing. Some things are unavoidable.

"And, let me also add, when Emma says she believes your child would have lived otherwise, she's not telling you *why* she would have lived." He looked directly at me, and I had the impression he was searching my face for something, or trying to tell me something. He sat back down, his elbows on his knees, leaning toward the Packards. "It's miraculous that Emma kept her alive at all," he said softly. "That initial surgery was heroic, considering the injuries, and very few people could have pulled it off." Tears began running down Betsy Packard's face, but Nick kept going. "She's an immensely talented, immensely thoughtful surgeon. This—this tragedy—is in every way a disaster, but I believe it was unavoidable. I've looked over all the records, and I cannot see anything I would have done differently. Closing Eleanor's abdomen after the surgery was a judgment call, and it could have gone either way. There were some miscues in recognizing what was happening after the surgery, but I don't believe Emma bears any of the direct responsibility for that.

Sometimes things go badly in medicine, and even the most competent people have losses. It makes our jobs unbearable at times."

He was still speaking, but I no longer heard him. On the wall behind Boyd, a large painting hung under the warm glow of an art lamp: a black-haired, violet-eyed child. Unlike most expensive oil portraits, Eleanor was not seated, or even standing still: the artist had chosen to paint her in motion, charging toward the viewer, her mouth open, her hair streaming behind her. Had they known she would not live to see the end of the year, perhaps her family would have requested her to be painted in a more solemn manner, but as it was, the artist had portrayed her with an expression she must have often worn in life: impish, determined, and joyful, clearly caught in the instant before a burbling, delighted laugh erupted from her.

I cannot imagine my own expression as I looked at the painting, but something of it must have caught Betsy Packard's attention because suddenly her arms were around me. A memory crossed my mind: comforting Zadie many years ago after she told me about screwing up an intubation. We'd clung to each other, my face wet with her tears, and this was what Betsy did for me now. I buried my face in her shoulder, reeling with a thousand wild emotions, still not having spoken a single word in my defense.

"This is over." Betsy kept my hand in one of hers and walked to her husband, picking up his hand too. She brought my hand and Boyd's hand together. "It's over. Not once have you blamed me, honey. You've protected me by blaming her, but you don't have to do that anymore. It's over, Boyd. Please. Let something good come out of this."

Boyd Packard nodded. He looked at me, and something in the mirrored pain on our faces connected, passing a wordless communication between us. He nodded again, releasing me. As he began to cry, his shoulders hitching like a little girl's, Nick and I looked at each other, and then, silently, we headed for the door.

———

We stood outside, in the cooling night air, in front of Nick's car. I had no idea how to interpret the evening's turn of events, so I settled on painful honesty. "I don't know what to say."

"How about 'thank you'?" Nick offered. He flipped his car keys into the air and caught them with a deft hand.

"It's inadequate for what you just did for me. But yes: thank you." I paused, then thought of something. "The duct of Wirsung. You cut it in a patient too?"

Nick grinned, lightness restored to his manner. "Nope," he said. "You stand alone there, Dr. Colley. I'd never do something so asinine."

I wanted to protest: it's bad, but it's hardly an unheard-of complication. I thought of the whole chain of missed chances surrounding the Packard girl's death, and a larger question loomed. "But then why would you say—"

"I know what it's like to lose a patient, Emma." He met my eyes, serious again. "I haven't inadvertently cut that particular duct, but I've made equally unfortunate errors. Bad shit happens sometimes, despite our best efforts; what's the point in punishing you when you did what you thought was right? This wasn't negligence; this was a case of everything going wrong that could go wrong." He paused. "But I think you know me well enough to realize I didn't help you because I was overcome by some infection of altruism, especially for someone who hates my guts." He glanced down. "Zadie asked me to do it."

His voice: so wounded and unguarded. He still loved her. Embarrassed, I closed my eyes, but my brain still burned with the afterimage of his face, so different from the way I usually saw it.

"I'm sorry, Nick."

A blink, and his face recovered its usual self-assurance. "Don't worry about it."

"I owe you. I owe both of you." I had no right to ask, but I couldn't stop myself. "Do you think she'll forgive us?"

It was a tricky question, because I exposed how needy I was by asking it, but also because I had no way of knowing if Zadie had told Nick the full extent of my behavior. But it was a reasonable gamble. She must have protected me this one last time.

He considered this. "I think she's forgiven me," he said. "Especially now. But that's mainly because she doesn't care much about me anymore. For what it's worth, I did ask her to come here with me tonight."

I waited, dread descending on me again.

"She said no."

"That's understandable," I croaked.

He regarded me intently, searching my face for something. Finally, he reached into his pocket and flipped something in my direction: a letter.

"From Zadie," he said. He watched as I unfolded it: a single line of print on stationery from the Ritz. With a start, I remembered this was the weekend Drew had planned a downtown minibreak for her, with a night at the Ritz, followed by the Panthers game. I folded the note and put it in my bag.

"Okay," said Nick. His voice—full of studied nonchalance—was at odds with the disquiet in his eyes. "That wraps up a decade of weirdness, then. Are we good?"

"Yes," I said, meaning it.

He turned toward his car and then abruptly turned back. "I know why I fucked things up with Zadie. But I've never understood why you did it. She genuinely loved you."

"I know."

"And your boyfriend. I always wondered: did you know that he knew?"

I thought of the week Graham had discovered my betrayal.

"No," I lied. "I had no idea."

Chapter Forty-one

THE COSMIC CALENDAR

Emma, Present Day

I don't believe in fate. When people say, "Everything happens for a reason," they are correct: technically, things happen because some series of events happened in precisely the order necessary to produce that occurrence. But that, of course, is not what the saying means. People want to believe that everything happens for some greater good. But if a child dies, it's not because she's needed in heaven, or because there was some cosmic plan for her to die so another child could be born. It's because her mother was distracted when backing up the car, and her surgeon made a series of judgment calls that turned out to be wrong.

I thought about Eleanor constantly, and even now, walking away from Nick, I knew I'd never be free of that. I'd felt it before in my profession, the guilt that comes from the tie of your actions to someone's death. A sense of inescapable doom hovered over me and around me and in me, so pervasive I could see how it could become a self-fulfilling prophecy: a person might do anything to make it stop.

Like Graham did. If I hadn't understood at the time how some miseries were too much to be borne, I did now. I'd never act on these urges—I hoped—because Henry and Wyatt were my buffer against self-harm.

But Graham had not had anyone else to protect him.

———

When I was little, I had a lengthy fascination with metaphysics. While the other girls longed for Cabbage Patch dolls and Jordache jeans, I became obsessed with cosmology after an accidental viewing of the *Cosmos* series on PBS—one of three channels we got—one night when my mother had fallen asleep with the TV on. Right away I liked watching Carl Sagan, whose brilliance was evident even to an eight-year-old girl. It was a revelation to me that there were empirical studies of the physical world, that there were people—scientists—who had such novel and keen ways of thinking it was almost as if they were another race compared to the people I knew. Each new discovery about the universe and its origins led to another, more startling direction of wonder.

Take the conceptualization of time. Essentially what you had to do was imagine the entire history of the universe—more than thirteen billion years—squashed into one action-packed calendar year. You started with the Big Bang on January first. A whole lot of things, like the shaping of the universe, took place in that first magical second. Spring was consumed with the formation of the Milky Way; appropriately, the Sun was born sometime in late summer. The formation of our solar system didn't occur until September 9, and the Earth sprang up around September 14.

In December, things really started smoking. The first interesting multicelled organisms, like worms, flopped into the picture in mid-month. The great geologic periods on Earth began: Cambrian period,

Permian period, Jurassic period. Then, in the waning days of December, primates appeared. They developed bigger frontal lobes and got smarter as, around them, the giant mammals flourished: dim-witted giant sloths, which could reach twenty feet in length; armadillos the size of Volkswagen Beetles; hippopotamus-sized rats; terrifying, voracious short-faced bears, more than twice as tall as a human.

But it was the last day of the Cosmic Calendar that really grabbed my attention. December 31 started out kind of slow, just more primates lurching out of trees and ambling around the savannas. Their brains grew, and their pelvises shrank. (The significance of this last fact would not fully dawn on me until I experienced Henry's birth some three decades later.) The sun set and night fell, and still the earth spun about on its axis, innocent of humanity. Finally, finally, sometime around ten thirty p.m. on the last day of the last month, premodern humans joined the party.

At first they spent quite a long time doing things the hard way. Stone tools: eleven p.m. Domestication of fire: eleven forty-six p.m. Anatomically modern humans rolled in with eight minutes to go, but they kicked around until twenty-eight seconds before midnight before figuring out how to grow food. Once they acquired agriculture, however, the ball began rolling fast: all of recorded history, Sagan said, occupied the last ten seconds of December 31. The kingdom of Israel, the first Olympics: seven seconds until midnight. The life of Christ: five seconds. The fall of Rome: three seconds to go. The American Revolution, the first two World Wars, the Apollo moon landing—in geologic time, they all occur at one second before midnight.

The upshot of all this, to me, was to emphasize how indescribably short and irrelevant the average human life is. But Sagan had managed to describe it; after reading his Cosmic Calendar, I realized I was living in the first fraction of the first second of the new New Year's Day. Then my life would whiff out after an infinitesimally tiny blip on the timeline.

And if my life was barely perceptible, what of Graham's? I would at least pass on my genes to the future, but Graham, the only son of an only son, would not. Even before Nick's reappearance in my life, I still thought of Graham nearly every day and still experienced the physical sensation of shock when he crept unexpectedly into my mind after a lull: that feeling of being kicked in the stomach when memory assaults you anew with loss. And, in my case, guilt.

He had known, somehow, that I'd been unfaithful to him. The week before he died, I'd blown him off for a clandestine hookup with Nick. Graham had planned a picnic in Cherokee Park; we were supposed to meet at noon on Dog Hill so Baxter, Graham's hyperenthusiastic golden retriever, could run joyously free.

That whole week was the loveliest of the fall. It was still warm enough for shorts, but the air had lost its humidity and everything was sharp, crisp, intensely focused. By the time I finally got to the park, the late-afternoon sun was pouring over the deep hills like liquid gold from a goblet, back-lighting the slopes and lawns and forests of the park and turning everything a shade of rosy champagne. I saw them before they saw me: Baxter was racing around in frenetic circles, and Graham was sitting on his old Notre Dame blanket, next to an unpacked basket, his head turned to the side and resting on his knees, which were encircled by his arms. He was very still.

Baxter saw me first. He was overcome with emotion—another human he knew! Here! In paradise!—and he charged toward me but overshot, so he had to skid to a stop and double back. I scratched his ears, which sent him into paroxysms of seizurelike joy.

His owner was calm. Graham wordlessly shifted over on the blanket so I could sit. "I'm sorry I'm so late," I began, but I stopped when Graham put his head back down on his knees. He still didn't speak. "Graham?" I said. "What is it?"

He turned to face me. The dying sun caught him full in the face, suffusing his skin with glowing pinks and golds and transforming his hair into a soft halo. Even though his eyes were brown, they were very clear in the sunlight; I thought I could see right through them. The background noise of dogs yelping and trees rustling and the rhythmic feet of the joggers faded into stillness around us. We sat, hushed, in our pool of dimming molten light. *He knows,* I thought.

"Emma?" he asked.

"Yes?" I turned away, unable to face him.

"Will you keep Baxter for me next week?"

"Of course," I said, relieved, not thinking to ask why.

"Thanks," he said, and reached his arm around me. I settled into him, feeling the familiar comfort of his solidity, the softness and scent of his ancient T-shirt as soothing as a baby blanket. He stared ahead, as if at some unfathomable mirage, and then absently kissed the top of my head, his lips granting me a little jewel of absolution. Relief washed over me, even though I knew he knew. And even though I knew I'd probably do it again. *I must be crazy,* I thought.

It had been inexcusable madness. When I tried to reconstruct, later, what had possessed me to betray the two people I loved the most, it all sounded so diseased and feeble. I'd always been a good girl. I did what people—adults—expected of me, but I was never wholly comfortable in the world of my peers. I was awkward; I never laughed at the right things or said anything funny or enjoyed the easy camaraderie that seemed to come effortlessly to other girls. One-on-one, especially with Zadie, I felt fine, even comfortable and witty sometimes; but with a group, I often floundered. Boys had not flocked to me; they seemed to find something in me off-putting. When Zadie and I walked into a party, within five minutes there would be a swarm of boys around both of us, offering drinks and goofy charm and hopeful energy, but within five minutes more, all of it would subtly shift to Zadie's direction, so all the eye contact and comments and laughter would exclude me. When Zadie spoke, it was to roars of approval; when I spoke, there was puzzled silence. So I stood alone in the crowd, an ice queen, always reacting a beat too late.

Graham had loved me, but Graham had been a little bit of a misfit too. He'd been a part of our circle, accepted, but he was quiet; he had a thoughtfulness and intensity marking him as different. And his devotion to me had made me uneasy. It seemed unearned. Why would anyone feel that way about me?

Nick, on the other hand, had been the epitome of cool. Everyone knew who he was and accorded him celebrity status. He could render you helpless with laughter and then just as easily turn around and cut you dead with the power of his scorn. People wanted his approval.

I harbored an unspoken fixation on him long before our fateful rotation on the trauma service. I'd first noticed him when I'd been a first-year med student, back in the days when first years were given about as much patient contact as the average janitor. Mostly, we were kept sequestered in a lecture hall where we were bombarded with clinically useless information about sodium ion channels and the histological characteristics of squamous cells. Every now and then, though, somebody would slip and bring in an actual doctor to lecture us on something interesting, and one Monday in January, this had been an associate professor in the general surgery department. I remembered one thing very clearly: he'd had a resident with him who had assisted in the slide presentation. This had been Nick, and he'd noticed me sitting in the front row. He'd caught me in an unguarded moment when I'd been staring at him, probably with an openmouthed longing expression. He'd grinned and cocked his first two fingers at me in a smug salute. I'd dropped my eyes and flushed with embarrassment.

Even though that encounter was minimal and slightly humiliating, it had led to a small obsession for me; I recognized from a wordless ten-second interaction that Nick had all the charisma I lacked. I didn't know his name or nickname then, and thought of him only as the Hot Surgery Guy, but his face was the stand-in for my fantasies of a real boyfriend for the next two years. When my class progressed to more hospital interaction, it had been dismaying to realize everyone, male and female alike, had some form of crush on the guy called Dr. X. I had come to think of him as mine.

And then: trauma.

"Which team are you on?" Zadie had squealed, delighted to find we had the same rotation—trauma surgery—first. I had told her: B Team; the chief was Ken Linker. Then I asked about Zadie's team.

"Mine says 'A Team.' Nick Xenokostas. Who's that?"

It was completely irrational to feel hatred for your best friend for something she hadn't even done yet. I'd looked at Zadie. She was wearing a long-sleeved button-down flannel shirt and jeans that tightly encased her slender figure; she also managed to be voluptuous, with curvy hips and a tiny waist. Her face was pleasingly symmetrical and somewhat mischievous, framed by her abundance of pale hair, and her round nose was wrinkled adorably. "Oh, hot damn!" she had bellowed. "Is that the dude everyone calls 'Dr. X'?"

Like some ghastly self-fulfilling prophecy, it all unfolded exactly as my overactive worst-case imagination had envisioned. Nick had wanted Zadie, like I'd feared. I'd watched suspiciously during every joint meeting between our teams, but at first there was nothing to see; Zadie was her usual perky self, collecting covetous glances from males as disparate as Ethan—the pale and bookish fourth-year on the A Team—all the way to Clyde Bevins, the scarlet-faced, lecherous respiratory tech in the TICU. But she said nothing about any particular interaction with Nick, and I relaxed my guard a little. I feigned interest in a vapid but attractive future orthopedist so Zadie would not suspect me of having an obsession with Dr. X. I started dating Graham again.

And then. Out of the blue, one night Zadie had come dragging home from the hospital and moped around our apartment, bothered by some unexplained event in the TICU that day, which I'd later learn had been a botched intubation. But of course, all I could remember of that night was the sickening revelation that Zadie was dating Nick.

I was sure Zadie must have picked up on my distress, since I was flushed and could control my breathing only with great difficulty. But she didn't notice, distracted at first by her worries about the day she'd had and then by the pleasurable phone attention from Nick. She'd even joked about the impending evaluation Nick had to give her: *Oh sure, he'll say I'm the best student he's ever had.* Wink, wink.

Zadie might have been oblivious, but Graham was not. Known for his perspicacity, he must have immediately grasped the significance of my un- usually heated reaction to the news my best friend was carrying on with her chief resident. "You don't like that guy?" he'd asked after Zadie had gone.

"I like him fine," I had answered uncomfortably, still conscious of my pink cheeks. "I just don't want to see Zadie get hurt."

Graham had given me a searching look. "You like him fine," he re- peated. Then, in a milder tone: "He's not a good guy, though, huh?"

In spite of myself, I was interested. "I really don't know much about him," I said. "Do you?"

"Not really," said Graham. "Bad vibe." He'd settled on the sofa, turned the TV back on, and let the subject drop after one last lingering look at me.

So, warning signs abounded and harbingers of doom were every- where, but I careened lemminglike toward the cliff's edge anyway. I made eye contact with Nick during trauma rounds and tried to convey simultaneous desirability and aloofness, correctly sensing the thing Nick might most respond to in a female would be unattainability. The aloof part wasn't much of a stretch. And I was unattainable—or seemed to be—by virtue of being the best friend of Nick's current conquest. Of course, he would assume a true friend would never . . .

It worked.

Maybe I wasn't consciously planning it. Maybe it began as an at- tempt to assuage my wounded pride—just seeking reassurance that it could have been me thrilling to the touch of the man I had mytholo- gized. Certainly I had never carried the thought to its logical conclusion, that to obtain one relationship I wanted, I'd have to give up another. Two others, actually. I would never have made the decision, point-blank, to harm my friend. Or my loyal boyfriend.

Or would I? Looking back on it now, with the terrible gift of hindsight, I had to admit my justifications for my behavior were the most tremendous bullshit. At some point, the theoretical becomes the inevitable. You either cross the river or you don't. I'd known what I was doing, even if I'd buried the knowledge under a toxic mountain of denial. Only the truly psychopathic among us lack the voice of conscience perched on our shoulders, whispering into our ears the words we don't want to hear as we do what we shouldn't. The rest of us simply swat the voice away and convince ourselves it was never there.

Things drifted, as they so often do, a little bit at a time, so on the day I found myself alone with Nick for the first time, it no longer seemed so shocking he would proposition me. The voice in my ear tried to stop me, but I stepped into the river and let it drown. It seemed to me that for once in my life I was throwing caution to the wind, seizing a chance to live dangerously, to really feel. As rationalizations go, these were lacking originality. I wanted him. He wanted me. No one would ever have to know.

If intensity could kill, I would not have survived our first kiss.

———

On the night Graham took our picture, I had no inkling what was coming. I'd gone to Nick's call room, thinking I'd break it off, unable to stomach the deception anymore after the day in the park with Graham. By that point, I hated myself: my weakness, my unceasing self-destruction, the ease with which I'd learned to lie. Nick listened to me with absorption, one eyebrow half-cocked, until I'd finished a long-winded and unnecessary denunciation of our behavior, and then he simply said, "Okay, if that's what you want, Emma."

I nodded curtly, my words exhausted.

He caught me just before I opened the door. "Are you going to say anything to Zadie?"

I wouldn't have thought it possible I could sink any lower into the muck, but it turns out there's a lot of room at the bottom of the moral sewer. My first instinct was not to protect Zadie—or Graham, who was somehow always secondary on my list of people needing protection—but instead a flash of pain for myself. He liked her more; he'd always liked her more. He'd let me go without a second thought, but he cared about losing her.

I'd have taken great vindictive pleasure in outing him, but the problem was, I didn't want to lose her either.

"I don't know," I answered.

His face changed. Something ugly rippled under his skin, distorting it, so for one brief moment I didn't recognize him. Then he pulled me back.

I let him kiss me. Self-loathing thudded through me, but I didn't stop him. "Do not tell her," he said, kissing my forehead, undoing my shirt. *I will never have this again,* I told myself. I closed my eyes and shut off my brain, mindless and thoughtless and numb.

Until the flash of a camera brought me back. I'll never know how Graham got a master key to the call rooms, or how he knew where to find me, or what made him decide to take our picture. I opened my eyes and saw him, his gentle face twisted in pain.

And that's the last time I saw him alive.

———

After Graham died, I steeled myself for the worst self-flagellation I could envision, and I went to my bookshelf and opened *The Screwtape Letters.* Insightful even at the end of his life, Graham had selected that volume as our place to hide letters to each other. This time, there were two pieces of paper inside: a folded poem to which was affixed a photograph, which

I could not bear to open, and a very short note, probably the last words Graham ever committed to paper.

Anything that's truly real can stand up to scrutiny.

They were Carl Sagan's words, spoken as he attempted to explain the nature of death to his young daughter. For a moment I stared at them until my tears blurred them into meaningless black marks on a sea of blinding white paper.

If remorse could kill, I would have died.

Chapter Forty-two

INHALING FIRE

Emma, Present Day

A lush darkness enveloped the city as I drove away from the Packards' house, but you would never know it from the blazing streets of uptown Charlotte. I parked and got out, sidestepping happy drunks and couples on dates and late-working young bankers and the entourage of a world-famous former basketball player. Ahead of me I could see the Epicentre, a multistory conglomerate of outdoor patios, rooftop terraces, and restaurants nestled at the base of the skyscrapers like a toddler at the feet of giants. This was a late-night kind of place; under crisscrossing strings of lights, it thrummed with a stew of polyglot voices and thumping bass. I walked up the stairs, scanning the crowd.

I saw her when I reached the top floor. She sat on a boxy woven chaise, holding a small mason jar sloshing with ice and pale amber liquid. She'd found a relatively quiet corner of the courtyard, her chair tucked in among a bevy of potted flowering trees, a few seats away from the only other patrons, a trio of young guys in suits. A floaty cashmere sweater extended past her wrists in soft flares; her hair flowed around her giant hoop earrings in a frenetic burst of waves.

She looked up from her drink and saw me. I braced myself for reproach, or anger, or worse, indifference; but her face held no clue to her thoughts.

"Hi, Emma," she said as I sat beside her.

I handed over her note as if it were an admission ticket. "Thank you for inviting me here."

Anticipating my next question, she rolled her eyes. "Don't worry. Drew doesn't mind. He's in our romantic hotel suite on a conference call with some guys in Japan." She waved at a passing waiter and held up her mason jar, which smelled gingery. "Another one?" she called. To me, she said, "It's too summery of a drink, but I can't get through this without bourbon. An homage to our homeland, right? But I know you won't drink it neat."

Her voice was slippery. I wondered how long she'd been sitting here, waiting for me to arrive.

"Zadie," I said. "Thank you. I can't believe you got Nick to help me."

Curiosity lit her features. "Tell me. How did it go?"

She listened as I recounted the visit with the Packards, her face growing more animated as I talked. "That's amazing! That's so beautiful, Emma. I love it. And I'm so proud of Nick for helping you."

I was fairly sure I knew the answer, but—"Did you tell him what I did?"

"You mean the little matter of impersonating me?" She was definitely tipsy.

"Yes," I said.

She sighed. "No. I didn't see the point in telling him that. Obviously, he'd have never agreed to help you. And it's totally possible that he'd have burst into the OR and hacked you to pieces with a 10-blade."

"So," I said softly. "You protected me, after all I did to you."

"Yes," she said. "And Nick protected you too, for years, you know, letting me think he was married. If you hadn't made him so angry at the Arts Ball, I might never have found out about any of this."

"Was it weird, talking to him?"

"Uh, yes," she said, and laughed. "He lives uptown, in the First Ward, not too far from here. I made up my mind to do it, and I ran to his apartment after I checked into the Ritz this morning. At first he thought— Well, I felt awful. But he agreed immediately to help you, and I could tell he thought the medical decisions you made were reasonable."

I felt a surge of relief course through me: despite everything, I guess I still craved Nick's professional approval.

Zadie kept going: "Also, I knew he'd been in a golfing foursome with Boyd, Dirk Wynne, and Buzzy Cooper—Buzzy put in a word for you too, by the way—and I figured Nick would have more pull with Boyd than I would."

I faced her. "Why did you do it? Get Nick to help me, after what I did to you both?"

"I don't know," she said. "I really don't. I'm not built for holding on to anger, for one thing. It seemed like it was destroying me. I was so miserable. Then, the other day, I was falling asleep, and I prayed to know what to do, and all of a sudden there was this easing-up sensation in my chest. I felt like I'd been inhaling fire for days, and then, out of nowhere, the soot and the smoke and the pain were gone, and I was breathing clean air again. I felt an overwhelming forgiveness. A real forgiveness this time."

She paused, apparently collecting her thoughts. Or maybe she wanted to cushion the blow I felt certain was coming, because she graced me with a gentle smile and added, "In a way, I'm glad I didn't know all this before. I can't imagine what my life would have been like without you in it over the past ten years. I love my other friends, but they all fit into a unidimensional slot in my life. They're my mom friends or my doctor friends or my friends from school. You're the only person who connects all the dots."

I nodded, trying not to wince at the term "my other friends."

Zadie continued. "It's like—everyone needs one person who gets all their quirks and their history." She cocked her head and a shimmering tear appeared at the corner of her eye. "I want to punch you in the face for messing this up."

"You will never know how sorry I am."

"Well, you obviously lost your mind. Everyone involved lost their mind. Graham loved you. You loved Nick. Nick loved me. If I'd only fallen for Graham, we'd have had a perfect love quadrangle."

I didn't know how to phrase it, what I was thinking. But Zadie and I had always had a kind of sisterly telepathy. "It worked out the way it was supposed to," she said, suddenly fierce.

"You don't wish—"

She held up a hand. "I can't let myself think that way." I risked a quick look at her: she was staring straight ahead. "I love Drew. I love my children. I'm exactly where I'm supposed to be."

"Zadie," I said. "What happens now?"

"Oh, Boyd will call off Macon Bradford. And Nestor Connolly never wanted to fire you in the first place. You'll be—"

"I meant, what happens with us? Can we go back to the way we were?"

She didn't answer. Behind her, lolling test notes from a saxophone floated out from a band setting up by the stairs. The young bankers near us exploded in a raucous bout of head-thrown-back hilarity, and I shivered. Graham and Nick and Zadie and even Eleanor tangled up in my brain in a huge knot of remorse.

This was it: of all the pivotal moments in my life, this was the one I cared about the most.

A cheerful tattooed guy deposited my drink and departed. I ignored it. "Zadie?" I prompted gently.

She sucked in her breath with a whistling sound, then puffed out her cheeks and blew it out. "Oh hell," she said. Sadness curdled the characteristic lilt in her voice, dampening it down into something almost unrecognizable. I waited, counting the upstrokes of my pulse in my neck, focusing on the swishy sound of my blood in my ears so I would not have to think.

"I'm sorry, Em," she said. "I truly forgive you. But I don't know if I can like you anymore."

"I understand," I whispered.

"I don't know how to go forward after this."

So, yes, that was it.

Or maybe this was the first step: after all, she would need time to adjust to the revelation that the Emma of the past was a stranger. How disconcerting, to find your memories—your reality—infiltrated by a cipher. I understood. I got it. I'd give anything to go back in time and alter my decisions, to change direction on those seemingly inconsequential little paths leading to my road of ruin. I'd be such a better person if I could do it again.

I stared down into the swirly depths of my drink and then half rose in my seat, overcome by my inability to give voice to my remorse. "So I'll go."

The irony dawned on me: I was walking away from the catastrophe of Eleanor Packard's death with my professional reputation intact, even as I began to realize what a hollow victory I'd won. For so many years, my identity was inextricably bound to the idea that I was a surgeon. Surely, it was understandable if, over the years, I'd romanticized my accomplishments. Yes, I'd kept a monstrous secret for years, but I'd battled the mighty forces of death! That had to balance out, right?

Now, too late, I saw that somewhere inside me, the power of that secret had metastasized into something I couldn't control. I thought I was changing it, chipping away at it by doing good things, but all the while, it was changing me.

———

Zadie didn't stop me as I walked away. The bankers still laughed, their open mouths morphing into ravenous, dark-throated maws as I passed them, everything in my sight turning sinister. I fumbled my way down the open-air staircase, concentrating on not colliding with anyone.

Footsteps on the metal treads banged above and below me, one set echoing faster than the others. Moments later, a cold hand clutched my forearm, dragging me backward.

Zadie's eyes met mine. She grabbed my waist and hugged me, hard, almost knocking me off-balance. I couldn't see her face, but I didn't need to; she clutched my hand and pulled me after her, one step at a time, past the jazz band, past the drunk bankers, back to our chairs under the brightly lit night sky.

She faced me. "I love you," she said. "Maybe we can't go back to the way we were, but we can find a way to go on from here."

I smiled, feeling something indescribably light break free in my chest.

Zadie shifted so we were once again seated side by side, our hands still clasped. Her hand felt warm in mine, the fragile bones of her fingers imbued with unlikely strength. We sat, still and quiet, our heads tilted together in wordless relief.

I'll always wonder: if our positions had been reversed, would I have forgiven her? My own heart is a mystery to me at times, pulsing in an odd, contradictory landscape of fire and ice. But it's easy for me to understand Zadie's heart: it's warm and sweet and full of grace.

Author's Note

People have been fascinated with medical dramas since the dawn of written language. I can say with absolute certainty that every physician, at one time or another, has thought of writing a book; after all, the story of the weird thing we extracted from somebody's southernmost orifice never fails to delight people at dinner parties. (That's where your mind goes when you ask your ER friend if anything interesting happened at work today. Admit it.)

Medicine is a consuming field. We spend years of our lives training—forgoing meals and bathroom breaks and desirable ski trips and the wedding of our childhood best friend and every other thing you might reasonably want to do. But it is also a career without equal in its reward. We are there when you come into the world and we are there when you leave it. We try our damnedest to ease your pain, to fix your brokenness, to diminish your sorrow. As one of my colleagues says, we have the immeasurable blessing of seeing life in all its anguish and glory.

This remarkable privilege—of witnessing life from its first breath to its last—leaves its mark on every doctor. More times than I'd like to admit, I've slipped into my car after a shift and cried. I've stayed late, making calls for people who've lost their jobs, begging for free specialty help. I've given my lunch to a woman who obviously hadn't eaten in days. I've revived private school kids with bags of heroin in their mouths.

I've demonstrated to teenage couples how to swaddle and rock crying babies, and I've explained to irate housewives what chlamydia is. Once I held the hand of a dying old man from a nursing home who cried out for his boy over and over during his last minutes until I bundled up my hair and pretended to be his son. Every physician could tell these stories; we keep thousands of them in our heads.

I don't have the skill to write the sweeping epic all this raging humanity deserves. But a few years ago, I got it into my head that I could at least write an entertaining story. Following the ubiquitous advice hurled at all novice writers—*write what you know*—I plunged into a manuscript about a group of med school friends. Eventually I figured the story would be better if we could see the lives of the characters after their training, and then I decided there should be some romantic shenanigans, and then I was advised that someone needed to die. And of course, in addition to the anguish and the glory of life, I wanted to reflect some of the hilarity. I'm a member of a giant Facebook group of women doctors who are also mothers (Hi, PMG!), and not a day goes by that I'm not cracking up at the photo of the penis-shaped sculpture someone's preschooler proudly presented, or the tale of how the entire first grade at someone's daughter's school can now describe a hysterectomy in detail. So naturally I had to work some children into the book too. After I'd written approximately two hundred thousand words—half of which would later be cut—this book emerged.

To put this in context, I am a huge book nerd: I read in the bathtub, in bed, while eating, and instead of cleaning the house. (If you're looking for a great read, check out kimmerymartin.com, which is chock-full of book recommendations). Sometimes I read instead of remembering meetings and carpools, which means I'm constantly yelping in dismay as I rush out the door with my clothes on inside out. A lifelong information junkie, I read all genres, from women's fiction to thrillers to biographies to dense science texts. But I'd never written anything, aside from the occasional medical research paper. It turns out that authoring a book is just as consuming as medicine. Sometimes I'd have to screech over to the side of the road to write something down before I forgot it, or I'd solve (or create) problems for Zadie and Emma in my dreams. They never left me alone. And as my characters became more real and more compelling to me, I began to realize how incredibly lucky I am to have stumbled into the two fields—literature and medicine—that perhaps more than any others bear witness to life in all its anguish and glory.

Kimmery

Acknowledgments

To address the most urgent question of my early readers: nobody in this book is real. Well, maybe one character was a tiny bit inspired by a real person but, as of today, this person is a forty-pound illiterate, so any fallout should be in the distant future. Along the same lines, if you are one of those people who insist all fiction is autobiographical, please skip chapters nine, fourteen, and eighteen. Also skip these chapters if you are my mother.

The publication of this book is a testament to many supportive friends, especially Jodi Frazier, Sameena Evers, and Nicole Carrig; thanks also to Billy Cohen, who is a living confirmation of the powers of CPR. My earliest beta readers displayed grace beyond all reason in making it through to the end, especially Katherine Vest, Melanie Piasecki, Rawles Kelly, Ainslie Wall, RaeAnn Doran, and Beverly Edens. The same goes for Jennifer Freno and Heather Burkhart—my beloveds—upon whom the burden of listening to me babble about my book fell most heavily. And no acknowledgment in a book about med school friends would be complete without loving on these people: Jill Howell Berg, Christina Terrell, Whitney Arnette Jamie, Kelli Miller, Kristin Rager, and Casey Dutton-Triplett. I will cherish you for all eternity.

To the trauma surgeons and cardiologists of the world, especially Jamie Coleman, Jennifer Co-Vu, Cindy Wright, Amanda Cook, and the incomparable Will Miles: the rest of us owe you our fervent gratitude. I took some creative license with medical facts here and there; beyond that, any mistakes are my own. Also, of course, physicians in real life are not quite as dramatic and amorous as I've portrayed them, but that would have made for a boring book. Apologies to all my doctor friends.

I'm indebted to many literary people: the Charlotte Mecklenburg Library Foundation, WFWA, PMG Writers, Kim Wright, Marybeth Whalen, my dazzling online writer group (Lisa Duffy, Lisa Roe, Kristin Contino, and Leah Collum), and my equally dazzling in-person writer group (Lisa Kline, Emily Pearce, and Betsy Thorpe), and all my marvelous author friends. A million thanks to Betsy for being the finest independent editor ever. And as for my third writing group—Trish Rohr, Bess Kercher, Tracy Curtis—words can't express what you mean to me.

Thanks so much to Miriam Goderich for fishing me out of the slush pile, and to my fascinating, feisty, brilliant agent, Jane Dystel. And to Kerry Donovan, my editor at Berkley, who is both excellent and endearing. Thank you to the entire team at Berkley, especially Colleen Reinhart for her stunning cover art and Lauren Burnstein and Tara O'Connor in publicity and Fareeda Bullert in marketing.

I enjoyed the immeasurable blessing of a childhood home infused with love, integrity, and a staggering number of books, and for this, I thank my mom and dad. To my sister, Shannan Rome, I'm grateful for your sharp but delightfully uncritical eye. To my children, Katie, Alex, and Annie: you motivate me daily with your irrepressible *joie de vivre*. Both my book and my life would be bleak without you.

And finally, I should amend the disclaimer I made earlier to acknowledge my real-life chief resident—my husband—who might have been the inspiration for the desirable features of a certain character. Jim, I love you.